A KINGDOM LOST

What Reviewers Say About
Barbara Ann Wright's Pyramid Series

"…a healthy dose of a very creative, yet believable, world into which the reader will step to find enjoyment and heart-thumping action. It's a fiendishly delightful tale."—*Lamda Literary*

"Barbara Ann Wright is a master when it comes to crafting a solid and entertaining fantasy novel. …The world of lesbian literature has a small handful of high-quality fantasy authors, and Barbara Ann Wright is well on her way to joining the likes of Jane Fletcher, Cate Culpepper, and Andi Marquette. …Lovers of the fantasy and futuristic genre will likely adore this novel, and adventurous romance fans should find plenty to sink their teeth into."—*The Rainbow Reader*

"*The Pyramid Waltz* has had me smiling for three days. …I also haven't actually read…a world that is entirely unfazed by homosexuality or female power before. I think I love it. I'm just delighted this book exists. …If you enjoyed *The Pyramid Waltz*, *For Want of a Fiend* is the perfect next step…you'd be embarking on a joyous, funny, sweet and madcap ride around very dark things lovingly told, with characters who will stay with you for months after."—*The Lesbrary*

"This book will keep you turning the page to find out the answers. …Fans of the fantasy genre will really enjoy this installment of the story. We can't wait for the next book."—*Curve Magazine*

Visit us at www.boldstrokesbooks.com

By the Author

The Pyramid Waltz

For Want of a Fiend

A Kingdom Lost

A KINGDOM LOST

by

Barbara Ann Wright

2014

ISBN 13: 978-1-62639-053-9

This Trade Paperback Original Is Published By
Bold Strokes Books, Inc.
P.O. Box 249
Valley Falls, NY 12185

First Edition: April 2014

CREDITS
Editor: Cindy Cresap
Production Design: Susan Ramundo
Cover Design By Sheri (graphicartist2020@hotmail.com)

Acknowledgments

Ross and Mom, all books are secretly dedicated to you. Thanks to Writer's Ink for giving me a great writing start. Matt Borgard, Jim Reader, and Deb de Freitas, thanks for being my staunch readers. Also, Pattie Lawler, there will always be feelings at you.

Thanks to Radclyffe and Bold Strokes for their faith, thanks to Cindy Cresap and Stacia Seaman for their wonderful editing work, and thanks to Sheri for her covers. Also, to the person who does my interior layout, you are wondrous. I don't mean to brag, but my books look FANTASTIC.

A last thank you again to my very soft pets. I snuggle you, and I am calm.

Dedication

For George

Chapter One

Katya

The deck swayed under Katya's feet, and she fought not to void everything she'd ever eaten. Captain Penner had assured her that she'd get her sea legs any day now. While she hung over the railing, Katya declared Captain Penner a cheat and a liar, unworthy of even charitable thoughts.

Up in the crow's nest, someone called, "Sails!"

Katya squinted into the sun. The crow's nest was one part of the ship she could put a name to; the rest was a jumble of decks and sails and rigging.

"What colors?" the first mate cried.

"None, sir!"

"Combat stations, Mister Black." Captain Penner raised a spyglass to her eye as the first mate roared her orders to all hands. She never had to do the shouting.

Katya wiped her mouth. They'd had days of clear sailing with only passing merchant ships to mark their way down the coast. Fah and Fay had cursed them with bad luck at last: pirates.

Brutal leaned against the rail at Katya's side. "Wouldn't it be cleverer to fly merchant colors and surprise their quarry at the last minute?"

Katya didn't answer, both because she feared dry heaving again and because his red robe made her queasier. And she knew it was petty, but she still hadn't forgiven him for choosing her rather than staying behind to protect Starbride in Marienne.

Katya's chest ached, and for a moment, she could smell the rosewater Starbride had added to their last bath together. She blinked away threatening tears and took a deep breath of the briny ocean air.

"They fly no colors in order to strike fear in the hearts of their prey, Brother Brutal," Castelle said from behind them. Katya and Castelle hadn't been lovers in nearly three years, but her voice could still pluck Katya's spine. "They hope to drive the pursued into doing something stupid." Her light touch grazed Katya's shoulder. "Are you all right… Highness?"

Katya groaned for her heaving stomach and the title. Since she'd made the decision to accompany her parents into exile, Katya and Castelle had engaged in several fights strong enough to blow the hatches off the ship. Castelle had yelled at Katya to stop torturing herself, that Starbride would be fine without her.

Katya had told her to piss off. When Castelle wouldn't let it go, Katya had pulled rank, turning her shouts into orders. No more nicknames, then; she had gone from Katya to Princess Katyarianna, or just Highness if Castelle wasn't feeling particularly prickly. Maybe Katya's nausea tweaked her sympathy.

Castelle's long curly black hair fluttered in the wind, and she brushed it behind her with delicate fingers. Her athletic frame bobbed with the motion of the ship. Her turquoise eyes fixed on Katya. The tattoo of a rose vine curling around her right eye wrinkled as she frowned. "Are you going to be all right, or should I worry about my boots?"

Any good feelings Katya had about her blew away. "I'm fine." She stalked past. Brutal's large, well-muscled body shielded her from the sun as he followed.

Katya crossed to the foredeck, glad she'd convinced Captain Penner *not* to fly the royal colors of Farraday. Even though the *Spirits Endeavor* carried Farraday's royalty, they didn't want to announce it.

Well, the ship carried all the royalty except the one who'd run off in a jealous fit and those driven mad by Fiends. If the pirates managed to take a few royal prisoners, Katya wondered if Roland would pay to get them back. Maybe he'd even paid the pirates to look for them. More Fiends at his fingertips would mean more power. Unless he got hold of Katya. Without her Fiend, she was useless to him, just an obstacle to be rid of.

Katya thought she might welcome death then, as long as it happened on dry land. "Can we outrun them, Captain Penner?"

The captain shut her spyglass with a snap and shoved it in the pocket of her heavy black coat. She tossed her gray braid over one shoulder and turned her hard, wrinkled face to Katya. "Doubtful, Highness. See how she skims over the water? She's going light."

"Turn and fight, then?"

Captain Penner frowned as if she'd just eaten all the sour fruit in the hold. If they turned, the *Spirits Endeavor* could fire the ballista mounted at her bow. The ship had smaller weapons at the sides and the back, but the giant spear on the front could do the most damage, especially with the long length of chain that ran from it. Trying to flee from the faster pirates would leave them at the mercy of the pirates' forward weapon.

"They'll want to close," Captain Penner said, "and fight hand to hand."

Brutal cracked his knuckles. "Good."

Captain Penner glanced at Katya. "I'm thinking of our... passengers."

Katya slid her rapier out of the scabbard. "Those that need to stay below will stay below."

"Begging your pardon, Highness," Captain Penner said, "but these won't be arming dummies we're fighting."

Katya resisted the urge to push her overboard. "I'd better go get my sharp sword, then." She turned away as the ship began to slow and angle toward the enemy.

"Let's stay away from the railing," Brutal said, "and hang on to something until our ship closes with theirs." He drew his large mace.

"I'll warn those below." Castelle hurried down to tell Katya's family and the cadre of nobles and servants that had fled Marienne with them.

Katya wasn't surprised when Lord Vincent returned with Castelle, both with weapons drawn. As the champion of Farraday, Vincent wouldn't be left out of a fight that might involve his young charges. The pirates wouldn't know what hit them.

"Highness," Vincent said. He bowed as he always did when he saw her, even though they'd been cooped up together for weeks. And unlike most of them, his coat was immaculate, immune to dirt somehow. Katya bet he kept the buttons done up to his chin even in high summer.

He gripped his slender longsword and watched the closing pirates calmly. When the wind ruffled his silver hair, he didn't bother to smooth it, and not a worry line crossed his young face. Katya noted his tightened shoulders, though, and the slight bend in his knees. He was a coiled serpent waiting to strike.

The pirate ship pulled close enough for Katya to see the faces of those swarming her decks. They howled like bloodthirsty beasts as they waved swords and axes.

"Amateurs," Brutal said.

Katya smiled. After fighting Fiends, they weren't that impressive.

The pirates fired their ballista, ripping a hole in one of the *Spirits Endeavor's* sails. Katya ducked as bits of falling rope pelted her.

"Fire!" Captain Penner called, and her ballista bolt thudded into the pirates' hull with its long chain clanking behind it. Katya staggered as the two ships dragged toward each other, each listing sharply, wood groaning and shrieking. The pirates sent grappling hooks whistling through the air to crack into Penner's ship.

"Repel boarders!" the first mate cried

The sailors of the *Spirits Endeavor* drew axes, boathooks, and cutlasses. This wasn't the average merchant ship, but one that worked specifically for the crown, and Katya's father hated having his cargo stolen.

The ships banged together in a deafening crack. Katya rushed forward, eyes on a pirate with a thick black mustache. Her seasickness had fled. Combat seemed just the remedy she was looking for. Now all she had to do was find people to fight all the way to their destination. The mustachioed man swung as if hacking a tree. Katya leaned away from the blow, dipped, and stabbed him in the heart.

None of the pirates proved challenging. Only one gave her pause, clumsily blocking her first few blows, but she tricked him with a feint to the side before she stabbed him. She'd been fighting traitors to the crown since she was sixteen, nearly four years in the past, and they tended to fight a lot harder than thieves.

Castelle and Brutal had the same luck; Brutal sported a disappointed frown. Through a break in the fighting, Katya had to stop and watch Vincent work.

No movement wasted, no stutter of indecision; he fought like the wind in human shape. He slashed a pirate across the midsection, sidestepped the falling body, spun, slashed another across the throat, dropped to one knee to dodge another attack, stabbed his attacker in the belly, rolled, took another in the groin, and then stood again. He never stopped to watch his opponents fall but killed with the surety that his strikes were true.

Katya blocked a pirate who caught her with her feet oddly placed, parried a few strikes, and waited for an opening. Before she could thrust, the pirate fell backward, the back of his neck spraying blood. Vincent had sliced him open, tugged at him so he wouldn't fall on Katya, and then moved on, all before she could get her feet back under her.

"Spirits above!" Brutal said. "Maybe we should have stayed below with the kids!"

As she rushed to help the sailors, Katya called, "I want to see if he kept his coat clean through that!"

The pirates surrendered within moments. Katya wondered how many had seen Vincent fight and just thrown down their swords. The sailors made them kneel at Captain Penner's feet. As Katya's father had said before, this was Penner's command. Unless she did something that put them all in danger, they would let her do as she would on her own ship. Da trusted her, so Katya supposed she'd have to do the same.

Captain Penner gave the pirates a stony glance. "Kill them." She turned her back on the pirates' cries of protest.

Katya nodded even as she grimaced. They couldn't hold prisoners. The ship was full, and they couldn't risk bringing the pirates to shore for trial and have them blabbing to everyone about the royal family aboard the *Spirits Endeavor*.

Katya walked with Captain Penner as the sailors put the pirates to the sword. "What will you do with their ship?" Katya asked.

"Strip it and sink it. I'm not leaving it for some other damned pirate to find." She gave Katya an appraising glance. "You did well. Better than I thought." She stared at Vincent as if he was something otherworldly. "Especially you."

He nodded, all the consideration she'd get as a ship's captain speaking to a lord. She shrugged and went about her business. Vincent barely had any blood on him, the bastard.

Katya went down the ladder and to the captain's old quarters, her family's quarters now. "It's me, Da," she said as she knocked.

The tumblers of the lock clicked, and Ma opened the door. The neck of her coat was open, the same as Da's. Even though it was a grim sight, Katya had to smile. If the pirates had made it into the ship, they would have broken down this door to find that Katya's parents had removed their pyramid necklaces. Add to that a bit of rage, and their Fiends would have slaughtered everyone on board.

Better that than capture. Katya's young niece and nephew crawled out from under the bed and cuddled close to their grandparents.

Katya leaned against the wall. "They're all dead." She didn't bother to check her language in front of the children. Though only three and four, they'd seen enough that a mere word wouldn't faze them. "Lord Vincent…" She shook her head. "I haven't seen him fight since the champion tournament. He's like a winter storm."

Da smiled wearily. As impressive as Vincent was, none of them could get excited about much. It had been a hard couple of weeks. Katya realized with a start that her seasickness hadn't returned. Captain Penner had been right.

As if a dam had broken, thoughts of Starbride rushed to fill the void in Katya's mind that had been preoccupied by her roiling stomach. Left somewhere in Marienne when Katya and her family fled, she could have died, or worse, been captured by Roland. Spirits only knew what he would do to someone with her burgeoning pyradisté power. He couldn't take over her mind—her ability prevented that—but he could find some way to use her.

No, she wouldn't let herself be used. She'd prove too big a liability, and he'd kill her.

Worse still, a voice inside her said, he'd convince her that he held Katya prisoner. If Starbride didn't do as he wished, he'd promise untold tortures. And Starbride would do anything to keep her alive, Katya was sure of it. Starbride would become something she hated just so a madman wouldn't tear her lover limb from limb.

Da patted Katya's shoulder, and she jumped. His smile was soft, sad, and had a twinge of guilt Katya wasn't used to. "It's all right, my girl."

She nodded, but she wanted to scream, "No, it isn't!" But he had to know that. He'd asked her to leave Starbride behind, to help him raise an army and take the throne back from his murderous brother.

"Get some rest," Ma said as Katya left them.

But what rest was there for her when Starbride haunted her dreams?

CHAPTER TWO

STARBRIDE

Pennynail waved Starbride forward. Even in the meager light from the streetlamps, she could make out the white of his laughing Jack mask. She followed him to the end of the alley and glanced into the street beyond. No one traveled the city night with them, no corpses that Roland had imbued with Fiends, and no slaves he'd subjugated with a pyramid.

Starbride gestured to Lord Hugo. He hurried forward on the balls of his feet, his plain brown coat and cap blending with the shadows. When he reached her side, he waved the last of their party forward: Master Bernard, one of the few pyradistés to escape after Roland had sacked the Pyradisté Academy. His left arm, broken some months ago, was bound close to his body, and he'd shaved his trademark red beard. They all had to be more careful. Starbride and Dawnmother always wore their long hair braided, and they dressed in hoods and cloaks to hide their Allusian features. Lucky for them, the cold wind of fall made it easy to wear bulky disguises. Even luckier, Starbride had convinced her maid to stay behind in their underground sanctuary that night. They needed stealth, and fewer people was the only way to make that happen.

Pennynail worked his way down the street, keeping to the shadows. Starbride waited. The balls of her feet ached, and she realized she was standing on tiptoe. She forced herself to relax. They'd heard of a group of pyradistés hiding near one of the warehouses, and Starbride couldn't bring them into her fold if she got a cramp and had to be left behind.

Still, she wished for more speed. If she'd heard about a few hiding pyradistés, Roland certainly would have too. So far, he'd left no pyradistés alive but himself, not trusting loyalty that had to be bought instead of forced. Rumor had it that he never believed anyone who claimed to be on his side unless they had a personal stake in helping him succeed, like his odious henchman Darren. Roland preferred to guarantee loyalty by bending minds to his will with his considerable power.

Pennynail waved them forward, and they repeated the same pattern, stop and go, stop and go. When they neared the warehouse district, Pennynail froze ahead of them. Starbride waited for whatever it was that had spooked him to move on. When she felt a wave of cold harsher than any wind, she knew he hadn't been scared by anyone or anything ordinary.

She squeezed Hugo's arm, knowing he would squeeze Master Bernard's in turn. A pair of corpse Fiends stalked under a streetlamp ahead of them. Starbride bit back a curse and wished them to pass by, but as their damnable kind had done before, these lifted their heads and sniffed the air.

Starbride pressed so tightly to the wall she was surprised she didn't melt into it. Crowe had told her that the wretched Fiends came from the mountains to the north, where the Farradains had originally discovered pyramid magic. Maybe, he'd said, magic was part of their very natures.

All she knew was that there were only two ways to find a pyradisté: with another pyradisté or with a Fiend.

As one, the corpse Fiends turned in Starbride's direction. She dipped into her satchel and hurled a fire pyramid. When it struck them, they hesitated, but not from the flames; it always took them a moment to decide what to do. Corpse Fiends were clever, but they weren't smart, and their hesitation gave Pennynail time to strike.

A knife streaked from the dark and shattered the pyramid implanted in one of their foreheads. The Fiend dropped without another move. Before Pennynail could throw again, the other corpse Fiend fell to the ground and rolled, putting its flames out. Maybe this one wasn't as stupid as the rest.

Just their luck.

The creature howled, a deep, hollow sound that reverberated in Starbride's ears and brought the tang of blood to her mouth.

"Horsestrong preserve us," she whispered. "Go!" Hugo streaked past her and stabbed the downed Fiend in the forehead, shattering its pyramid, but the damage was done.

All through the city, other inhuman throats took up the cry like a pack of hunting dogs. Starbride and the others turned and ran. They had seconds to get away, to try to confuse the pack. At a low-hanging awning, Hugo and Pennynail gave Starbride and Master Bernard a boost to climb to the roof. It wouldn't work forever, but it had slowed other packs before.

Pennynail led them, more familiar with the ways of the rooftops. They dodged chimneys and rooftop hatches, keeping to buildings and houses that sat side-to-side. Starbride had some confidence in her new climbing skills, but Master Bernard would never make the jump across an alley or a street.

They angled away from the warehouse district. If the corpse Fiends followed them, at least they'd be traveling away from the rumored pyradistés. Starbride flagged, her steps growing unsure as even terror gave way to a stitch in her side. They all slowed and crouched together against a chimney. Master Bernard leaned on his knees and wheezed.

"Listen," Hugo said.

Starbride tried to hold her breath as she gripped another pyramid, ready to throw at any sounds of pursuit. The air left her in a rush as she heard the howl of the pack. "Oh no."

The corpse Fiends wailed together from far away, deep in the warehouse district. They'd searched for Starbride and found the hidden pyradistés instead.

And she'd led them there. Starbride clamped her lips together. Tears wouldn't help. Her mother had always said there was no use crying when it couldn't be turned to an advantage. Starbride had changed that lesson. Tears were useless while someone else was depending on her. Katya wouldn't be huddling on a roof, crying her eyes out. Starbride calmed her breathing and imagined Katya's strong hands lifting her up.

"Darkstrong take those monsters," she whispered.

Hugo squeezed her shoulder. "Don't blame yourself."

"Yes," Master Bernard said, "we have to remember who the enemy is."

"The Fiend king," Starbride said, what the people of Marienne called Roland. But at the moment, knowing who the enemy was didn't do much to assuage her guilt. If they hadn't gone looking for their pyradistés, if they hadn't chosen that route, if, if, if...

If Dawnmother were there, she would have said, "Every 'if' is a hole in the road." Horsestrong's wisdom led them still, even hundreds of miles from home.

Pennynail clapped his gloved hands softly and waved them on. There was no use dwelling; they had to get back to their hiding place before dawn.

Their hideout had been a favorite den of Pennynail's, back when Crowe was alive. He and his father had often waited there before meeting with contacts; sometimes, they'd interrogated prisoners there before bringing them to the dungeon beneath the palace.

Starbride had expected any hideout of Pennynail's to be in one of the seedier parts of Marienne, but he surprised her with a cellar under a high-end clothing store. With no homes or apartments crowding it, there was no one to notice their comings and goings, and it was two streets away from any taverns or bars. The owner had been a friend of Crowe's, someone he'd done a favor for, one large enough that he now helped his friend's son, even though helping enemies of the Fiend king would mean his death.

To keep the owner safe, Starbride and her allies never entered the shop. A secret door in the delivery yard led down into the large cellar. Starbride took a deep breath of the cool night air before she descended.

The heat from too many people occupying too small of a space washed over her. The non-pyradistés among them had collected food and water recently, so no one went hungry, but there wasn't enough room.

They'd divided the space with hanging blankets, and low-burning lanterns revealed lumps of sleeping bodies on the floor. Starbride wound past the hangings and stepped over sleepers until she reached the far end. A small room stood separate from the rest by a stone wall with a stout door, a place where she and her friends could discuss the future without alarming the others.

"I'll check on the wounded," Master Bernard whispered as he left them.

Starbride nodded and entered the small room at the back. She cast a longing look at the worktable, anxious for any work that would distract her from their failure that night. She and the other pyradistés were attempting a new kind of pyramid, something that would hide them from the corpse Fiends, and they needed it soon.

Crowe had taught her how to make pyramids that would suppress a Fiend, a technique handed down from kings' pyradistés through the ages. With the Fiends that the royals carried, it was a necessary evil. Starbride taught it to those who now hid with her. There was no use in hiding Fiend magic anymore. Still, she didn't share the fact that the

Umbriels had always been part Fiend. The populace of Marienne knew of Yanchasa the Mighty, the great Fiend. They knew the Umbriels kept him asleep in some fashion, but they didn't know that the royals could only accomplish this by bearing Yanchasa's Fiendish Aspect.

The people thought Roland was the only one living who was part Fiend, that he'd consorted with Yanchasa in order to gain its power. They had the right road, but the wrong end, as Horsestrong had said. Roland was only evil because he'd merged with his Fiend when he'd been near death. The ugly truth was that any of the Umbriels could have been in his place if they'd suffered the same fate. Starbride shivered to think of it.

The suppression pyramids Crowe had taught her could repel a Fiend, but Starbride hoped for something that would let her detect the corpse Fiends from a distance, hide her nature from them, and repel them, too. Fiends were attracted to pyramid magic, but they were also highly susceptible to it. It was a trade she hoped to take full advantage of.

At the moment, it would have to wait. Pennynail followed her into the small room, and Hugo waited outside. He stood on tiptoe as she closed the door, as if hoping to catch a glimpse of Pennynail's naked face.

"We need to move soon," Starbride said.

Pennynail pulled off his mask and became Freddie Ballantine again, one of the most infamous criminals in Marienne's history. Everyone else thought him long dead, and he preferred it that way. At the moment, Starbride did, too; she didn't need her allies abandoning her for the company she kept.

Freddie scrubbed through his short red hair, reminding Starbride so much of his father, Crowe, that she couldn't contain a sad smile as he loosened his collar. She glanced at the wide rope scar around his neck, the wound that left him with a rasp of a voice.

"If you want to move," he said, "there's one good option."

"I'm not leaving Marienne without Katya."

He sighed, and she could tell he was as tired of having this conversation as she was. That didn't matter. He could urge her to leave Marienne until he turned blue. The memory of Katya's hands lifted Starbride out of her depression, but she couldn't continue her fight without the hope of one day feeling Katya's arms around her again.

Shortly after the city had fallen, Freddie had sneaked out to the forest, to a regular rendezvous spot for the Order of Vestra, but no one had been there. Freddie had suggested Starbride and their friends head for the countryside anyway, but if Roland was holding Katya and her family, Starbride would not abandon them.

"If anyone else wants to go," Starbride said, "I'm not going to stop them."

"Patrols have increased. I think it'd be easier to sneak into Marienne than out of it, and Roland's got those corpse Fiends scouring the countryside. If he doesn't have Katya or her family, he's damn sure looking for them." He nudged Starbride with one booted foot. "Or he's looking for you."

"He'd be quite happy to kill you, too, you know."

"If we pushed hard, we could all make it past the patrols together."

She put on a beatific smile. "I'm not leaving without Katya."

"What was it that Dawnmother always called my da? Donkey something?"

Dawnmother opened the door, sliding through to join them. "Mulestubborn," she said. "A name I will gladly pass to you if you insist on badgering my Star." She handed them both a cup of tea. Starbride was tempted to stick her tongue out at Freddie, but she held the impulse in.

"I should have known whose side you'd take," Freddie said.

Dawnmother patted him on the shoulder. With her ever-present cups of tea, Dawnmother's quiet presence soothed Starbride's nerves. Even with everything that had happened, she didn't have a black hair out of place from her simple braid, and her loose-fitting shirt and trousers were as neat as ever.

There was a slight commotion outside, a loud conversation. Starbride opened the door enough to peek out, and Hugo blundered in. His eyes fell on Freddie's face, and Freddie cursed. Dawnmother stepped deftly between them, but Hugo only blinked. Before he could begin to process what he'd seen, Starbride pushed him out the door.

"What's going on?" she asked.

"Captain Ursula and Sergeant Rhys are here."

Starbride glanced behind her. Freddie had his mask on again. "Bring them in, please, Hugo," she said, hoping to deal with what he'd seen by ignoring it.

Roland had kept the city Watch and the king's Guard mostly intact. He'd just replaced the Guard with corpse Fiends. Rumor had it that he would do the same with the Watch, but he clearly didn't consider them as great a threat as the Guard, commoners as they were. She found it predictable that the very people he'd used to bring the Umbriels down now hardly rated his notice.

Still, people seemed wary but content enough not to try to stand up to their new king. Even those that were fearful of Roland recognized that crime had become almost non-existent since he'd made even the pettiest infractions punishable by death. She'd heard some of them say that only miscreants and lawbreakers had to fear the Fiend king. She wondered if they'd be singing the same tune once Roland decided that even speaking one's own mind was a crime.

Captain Ursula took a seat on one of the cots in the small room. Rhys leaned against the wall, languid as ever. With Pennynail's long legs stuck out in front of him in an equally relaxed pose, the two could have been twins, in spirit if not in looks. Hugo squeezed into a corner near the worktable, making the space seem very small indeed.

"What's happened?" Starbride asked.

"I got a letter commanding all captains of the Watch to report to the palace."

"Time to go into hiding, then?" Starbride asked.

Ursula's lips quirked up. "Not just yet. Soon after I got that letter, I received another missive cancelling it."

"But that's good, right?" Hugo said.

Ursula frowned. "It's behavior contrary to the Fiend king's norm. That means it's bad for us. If we can't predict what he'll do…"

"He can catch us off guard," Starbride finished. "He's got something more important planned."

"Like killing all of you," Ursula said.

Starbride's stomach dropped. "Or he's found Katya."

"If she's hiding in the city," Rhys said, "we'd have found her by now."

"Why?" Hugo asked. "The Fiend king hasn't found us! And Princess Katyarianna is adept at hiding, or so I'm told."

Starbride didn't argue with him. Katya was adept at not being seen, but not as much as Pennynail. *He'd* have found her, or more likely, she would have found them. That meant she was either out in the countryside, imprisoned in the palace, or…dead. "Horsestrong preserve us," she muttered. Her eyes fell on the worktable again. There was a reason for everything Roland did, so if he wasn't going to bother turning the Watch into corpse Fiends…"Maybe he doesn't want to drain his essence."

"What was that?" Ursula asked.

"When he makes a new corpse Fiend, he has to pull the energy, the essence, from somewhere. If he drains his own, he gets weaker." He had Katya's cousin Maia to pull from, or Darren, but perhaps he didn't want to weaken any of them. "He needs to recharge." Her stomach hit her feet again. "He has plans for the capstone."

"The what?" Ursula asked, impatience creeping into her voice.

Starbride took a deep breath. "Do you remember what Katya once told you about the Umbriels being the 'foes of Yanchasa the Mighty'?"

"She said it was a symbolic title," Ursula said, "but that sometimes her family had to defeat the thing's allies."

"Good job they did with that," Rhys muttered.

Starbride ignored him. "They face the great Fiend in a very real sense. It rests, asleep, under the palace in a giant pyramid, and they have to keep it there."

Ursula slowly arched an eyebrow. Behind her, Rhys had a smirk on his face.

"Hmm," Starbride said, looking back and forth between them. "I imagine my expression looked just like yours when Crowe first told me about it. It sounds really stupid out loud. There's a ritual, using Fiend magic, a type of pyramid that only the king's pyradisté and a few others know about. But now the Fiend king has polluted this magic to merge with a Fiend."

It was only partly true. She kept back the history of Farraday, how the first king had loosed Yanchasa, and how it took the might of all his pyradistés to contain the great Fiend. She didn't tell them how the Umbriels carried Yanchasa's essence buried deep within them and how an Aspect of that essence could manifest, and they could become mindless Fiends.

"But," Hugo said, "isn't the ritual performed every five years? That hasn't passed since the last time the ritual was done. So...the Fiend king can't fiddle with the capstone and Yanchasa until the right time, yes?"

"I wouldn't put anything past him," Starbride said. "From what Crowe taught me, no one is supposed to be able to commune with Yanchasa except during the ritual. But a pyradisté can always sense the greater Fiend; I've done it." She shuddered at the memory of the cold, inhuman touch. "He shouldn't be able to draw on it."

"But he's done the impossible time and again," Rhys said.

Ursula stared at her sergeant as if he'd grown another head. "You understand all this, Rhys?"

"Nothing much surprises me anymore, Cap."

"Lucky you." She smoothed her dark blond hair over her shoulders. It had gotten a little longer since Starbride had first met her. If it grew any more, she'd have to put it up somehow to keep it out of her face. The thought reminded her of Katya's tidy blond hair, and she had to close her eyes a moment to keep herself together.

"So if he tries to play around with this capstone thing," Ursula said, "how do we stop him? You're not suggesting we go into the palace?"

They couldn't let Roland become a greater Fiend. Maybe he'd gone mad enough to try to let Yanchasa out. Or maybe he had a new plan altogether. Whatever it was, they couldn't let him complete it.

Starbride sat up straighter, imagining Katya's hands on her shoulders again. "We may have to. It's our turn to strike at him."

Chapter Three

Katya

Katya watched at the rail as Captain Penner put the *Spirits Endeavor* into port at Pomanse. The city lights barely penetrated the layer of mist shrouding the harbor at dusk. They dropped anchor in deeper water and waited for a small boat to transport those bound for shore.

Pulling her coat tighter around her, Katya fought not to shiver. She waited in silence with Brutal, Castelle, Captain Penner, and the purser for the *Spirits Endeavor*. They'd sailed halfway to Allusia and hadn't found a safe haven. Roland's forces hunted them through the countryside. They'd had one narrow escape at a port closer to Marienne when they'd put in for supplies.

Captain Penner kept her crew on the ship, not trusting them to keep their mouths shut, especially after they'd had a few drinks. To quiet the grumbling, Katya had bought extra beer for when the sailors were off duty. So far, it had worked.

Katya still needed to go into the city, though. She needed information the captain couldn't get. She also needed to get off the damned ocean for a while.

Once on dry land, Katya, Brutal, and Castelle left restocking the ship to Captain Penner and the purser. Lord Vincent and Castelle's fellow thief-catchers from Marienne protected the rest of the royal family on the *Spirits Endeavor*, trusting that they'd be safer on the ship. Pirates wouldn't dare come so close to Pomanse with its small navy of patrolling ships and catapults lining the shore.

Katya strode through the darkened streets; the chill in the air allowed her to keep her hood up without arousing suspicion. Brutal had traded his red robe for homespun, not wanting to attract attention as a member of a strength chapterhouse. Random duels were a luxury they couldn't afford.

They found a modestly reputable bar, the seat of all gossip no matter the town. They mingled with the middle class, posing as merchants and keeping away from the wealthier taverns and anywhere low-rent enough to be dangerous. No information would come from any establishment too discreet or too wary for questions.

Talk of what had happened in Marienne had just reached Pomanse. Katya took that as a good sign. News traveled faster than troops. Maybe Roland's reach wouldn't extend this far for quite some time.

Of course, sympathy for the Umbriels might not extend this far either. Most of the people who lived and worked in Pomanse had been born there, and news of Marienne might as well have been news out of Allusia for all it affected them.

"Is he going to increase taxes, this new king?" one merchant asked. He twisted a gold ring on his finger as if afraid Roland might march through the door and snatch it away.

"Depends on who's in charge," one of the laborers answered. She stuffed an olive in her mouth and didn't wait to chew before she spoke again. "Think we'll get a new noble?"

The merchant leaned away, picking olive bits off his coat.

Katya shrugged as if she was as ignorant as they were. "What's wrong with the one you've got?"

The laborer laughed, making the merchant back farther away. "Oh, nothing, except she gallivants off to court instead of sticking around and keeping up her own estate."

"That's what *henchmen* are for," the merchant said.

"Ha!" The laborer poked him in the arm. "Sounds like you want to be nominated, eh, Master High and Mighty? Want to be Count Nose In the Air?"

Katya drifted away as the two fell to bickering. Duchess Skelda owned Pomanse and the land surrounding it, and she hadn't made it out of Marienne with Katya's party. She was likely dead, unless she'd convinced Roland that she stood with him. Katya nearly snorted at the thought. Roland wouldn't settle for words. The more she learned about how he'd wanted to operate the Order, the more she thought he would simply change minds via pyramid rather than believe what anyone said.

Katya started a few rumors, just to make things difficult should Roland try to spread propaganda. She called him a monster and described some things she'd seen in Marienne—as a merchant, of course. She told of how people were slaughtered and brought back to life as Roland's soldiers. Few believed her, but that didn't matter as much as the opportunity to sow doubt.

After Katya and her friends left their second bar, they paused, backs to a closed shop where no one could eavesdrop.

"What do you think?" Katya asked.

"We could put ashore here," Brutal said. "And go inland. Roland hasn't come this far east."

"But where are we going to get an army?" Castelle said. "These people haven't felt Roland's monstrous side. They have no reason to rebel."

Katya stroked her chin. That was the truth. With barely any muscle behind her, she couldn't conscript people. She and her family would have to convince them to leave their families and risk their lives. Even the local Watch would have more loyalty to their own people than to some crown hundreds of miles away, and Da had no local noble to back him up.

"We have to convince them that they can't let Roland get more of a foothold than he already has," Katya said.

"They didn't believe us when we told them what he's capable of," Castelle said. "We'd have to tone him down a bit."

Brutal snickered. "We're the, 'the usurper is not as bad as all that' party?"

"You could probably get the local strength chapterhouses on our side, Brutal."

"Maybe. If we let the local pyradistés pry around in our brains, they could convince people we're telling the truth."

Castelle grimaced. "That can't happen to you or your family, Highness. I guess that leaves Brutal and me."

Katya frowned, both at the "Highness" and at the thought of someone picking through her memories. "No, you and Brutal know things other people can't have access to. And if you can't bring yourself to use my real name, use my cover."

"*Miss Marchesa Gant,* then, begging your pardon."

Katya swallowed her temper. "Let's tell my father what we've found out. The ultimate decision is his." Brutal and Castelle followed her to the docks. As they neared the slip for the pilot ship, they heard Captain Penner's raised voice from the small customs shack near the water.

"What in all the spirits' names is a writ of declaration?" Captain Penner yelled. "I've been sailing these waters for twenty years, and I've never heard of the damn thing!"

Katya crept to the edge of the shack and peeked in a dusty window. Captain Penner had her fists on her hips, staring down the harbormaster. The purser was nowhere to be seen.

The harbormaster wore the badge of office around his neck, but the resemblance to every other harbormaster Katya had met ended there. His coat was far too nice, and he had lace at his cuffs. He wrung his hands and sweated. The harbormaster of Lucienne-by-the-Sea, where Katya and her family had started their journey, had been a huge man who didn't take guff off of anyone, ship's captain or no. And he didn't dress like a dandy on his way to a ball. How could this sweaty, shaking man run an entire port if he couldn't take being yelled at by one captain?

"It's a new policy," he whined. "Just…just came down a few days ago, in fact."

"Came down from whom?"

"The…duchess."

Katya slipped her rapier free and heard Brutal and Castelle draw their weapons. Duchess Skelda couldn't have beaten them back to her home port. And if she'd sent orders after the uprising in Marienne, it wouldn't have been for writs pertaining to docking ships.

Captain Penner narrowed her eyes. She knew all that as well as Katya. She stepped close to the sweaty harbormaster. "And how does one get a writ of declaration?"

"You…you apply."

"And how long does it take?"

"Um…hours, only. Maybe a day, maybe." His eyes darted toward the door.

"Go in, Brutal," Katya said. Whatever or whoever the harbormaster was waiting for, Katya wouldn't give them the chance to arrive.

Brutal smashed the window with his mace. While the harbormaster screamed, Brutal leapt the sill and hoisted the harbormaster into the air.

Katya spoke through the window, waiting outside. "Who are you waiting for?"

He only gibbered. Brutal gave him a shake.

"There is no writ," Katya said after he'd quieted. "You're delaying the captain while you sent for someone. I want to know who."

He shook his head. "Please."

"Tell me, or I'll tell them you aided the captain instead of hindering her."

"Please, please, I was only supposed to tell him if someone came into port from the west. He's got my cousin, the real harbormaster, and I don't know what I'm doing, so please—"

Brutal dropped him. It had to be one of Roland's spies. "Come on," Katya said, waving Brutal and Captain Penner toward the window. "If you go out the front, you might run into him."

"We don't have our supplies!" Captain Penner said. "And Mr. Sumpson is still on the docks."

"We'll grab what we can carry as well as the purser, but we have to move."

The door banged open just as the captain began to climb out the window. Katya's stomach shrank as Darren, Roland's chief thug, stood framed in the doorway.

Dressed in a black coat and trousers, painfully nefarious, he smiled and stepped inside. Two dead-eyed, gray-skinned corpse Fiends followed him, long knives in their bony fingers and the glint of a pyramid just visible under their broad brimmed hats.

"Well, well," Darren said, "so it is you. And to think, I was just about to leave this backwater and set my friends here to watch for you." He grinned wider, his mouth stretching too wide as his features blurred. "I'm so glad I waited." Horns jutted from his brow, just below his dark hair, and his eyes bled to all brown, no pupil or iris. Fangs pressed down from his lips, and the sense of cold rolling off him made gooseflesh ripple up Katya's body.

Captain Penner nearly fell through the window, blocking Katya's path. Brutal rushed Darren, but the two corpse Fiends stepped forward.

Katya pulled Captain Penner out of the way and dumped her on the ground. She hopped through the window and dashed for the harbormaster just as Darren bent to grab him. Katya sliced toward Darren's neck, but he pulled away with the blurred speed of a Fiend. The harbormaster scuttled away.

Darren laughed, the noise grating on Katya's ears over the sounds of Brutal and now Castelle fighting the two corpse Fiends. Maybe Darren would be his usual annoying self and taunt her until Brutal and Castelle could help with him.

No such luck. He slashed with his claws. Katya barely blocked. He wasn't as fast as Roland, but he was much improved. Maybe he'd been chastised for his tendency to talk when he should have been fighting.

A cracking noise came from Katya's left, and one of the corpse Fiends fell to the ground.

Katya kicked a chair at Darren. He smashed it out of the way and leapt at her. She stabbed his arm, but he took the blow and rammed into her, knocking her down. Katya kicked him and winced as her ankle threatened to buckle against his hardened flesh. She rammed her rapier guard into his face as he loomed over her. He winced and pulled back, so she hammered at him, but he got a claw past her punches and gashed her cheek. Katya ignored the flare of pain and tried to back him off enough to stand.

Someone shrieked, and Darren turned as something smacked him in the head. Katya hopped to her feet. The harbormaster wept and screeched like all the Fiends in the world were at his back. Still, he whipped a bucket to and fro, his face purple with effort. Darren snarled and slapped the bucket out of his hands. Katya darted in and stabbed Darren in the chest, though it barely slowed him. She thought on Starbride's words about these created Fiends. They needed a pyramid to help them control the monster within. Lady Hilda's had been buried in the back of her neck.

Katya came at Darren with a series of powerful thrusts, trying to get him to turn, even for a moment. Castelle jumped behind Darren, and he whipped around.

There, a glint at the back of his neck, under his hair. Katya thrust.

Darren's hand snaked up, impossibly fast, and grabbed her rapier. Blood pooled around his fingers as they closed on the blade, and with one jerk of his arm, he snapped the end off.

Castelle chopped at his wrist, but Darren kicked her into the corner. Katya tried to stab with her blunted sword. It could still shatter the pyramid if she hit hard enough.

Darren spun and aimed a punch at her face. Katya dropped down and rolled away. She came up hard against Brutal's legs, stopping him, but he swung at Darren anyway. It was Darren's turn to duck, and he and Katya were briefly eye-to-eye. He winked at her, the bastard, and flung her broken sword tip.

Katya jerked her arm in front of her face and the broken tip punched into the back of her hand like a dagger. Darren shot to his feet just as the harbormaster tried to tackle him.

"Where is my cousin?" the harbormaster screamed. "What did you do to him?"

"Get back!" Brutal said.

Castelle grabbed the harbormaster's coat and tried to jerk him away. Brutal pulled Katya upright just as Darren pitched the harbormaster through the window.

Outside, someone shouted, "City Watch! Throw down your weapons and surrender!"

Katya nearly cursed. Captain Penner had fetched the Watch, but maybe they could turn that to their advantage. Darren sighed as if the whole series of events was one big nuisance, but then he grinned his too-wide smile.

"I have more pets," he said. "Your uncle's creations. Surrender to me, and I won't have this place burned to the ground."

Katya laughed at him. "Or we could kill you now."

Brutal swung his mace, trying to drive Darren into Castelle's waiting blade. He went where they wanted, but he ducked Castelle's thrust, and she barely parried his strike from below. It forced her farther into the corner, giving him room to maneuver. Katya stepped closer to keep him from the door.

"Leave this town," he said, "and you condemn it." He ran into the wall, knocking his way through in a loud crunch. Katya stepped after him, but saw only a Watch officer trying to pick himself up where he'd been knocked over.

Katya stepped back from the hole and called her surrender to the Watch. They trooped out of the shack one by one. Luckily, Captain Penner stood up for them, and the harbormaster confirmed that Katya had been trying to help him. Even with the dead corpse Fiends, the Watch remained skeptical of their story.

Captain Penner leaned close to Katya's ear. "These things know you're here. There's no use in hiding. I think your father should address this."

Katya's mouth set in a firm line as she wrapped a bandage around her bleeding hand. She had no doubt Darren meant what he said. As experienced as the Watch might be, they were no match for Darren and his corpse Fiends. He could raze the town.

Unless they were ready for him. Katya's father could talk them into getting ready; she had every faith. Maybe the revolution would start in Pomanse after all.

CHAPTER FOUR

STARBRIDE

Starbride walked dark stone hallways. Pyramids set in the rock flickered with each step she took. Screams echoed around her from victims she couldn't see, and the smell of damp rock permeated the air.

"Hello?" she whispered.

Footsteps boomed down the corridor behind her, and the walls shook, sending dust swirling through the tunnel. Fear trickled through her like icy water. Roland was searching for her.

She ran, but no twists or turns presented themselves. Roland was inside the secret passages with her, and he knew them so well, better than she.

If she could only get out of the walls, get to Katya, everything would be all right. Down the corridor, just at the edge of her vision, a blond woman ran. Starbride's heart leapt, but she couldn't call out. If she made a sound, Roland would find her. He'd turn her into a monster and set her loose among the people she was trying to save, among the people she'd already condemned. Why wouldn't Katya turn?

"Miss Starbride?"

She turned toward the voice, the only one that wasn't screaming, but she couldn't stop running. The footsteps were getting closer, and Katya was pulling away from her. "Don't leave me!" she screamed.

"Miss Starbride!"

When someone grabbed her shoulder, Starbride shot upright and cried out.

In the small, basement room of their hideout, Hugo backed away. "I'm sorry. I didn't mean to scare you."

"What?" Starbride blinked at him. On the table in front of her, her candle had burned down to almost nothing. Her arms rested on a large book. Pyramid crystal and the little tools she used to work it lay scattered around. A little spot of drool marred the pages of the book where her head had rested, and she shifted her arm to cover it.

"Maybe you should try sleeping in the bed," Hugo said.

Starbride shook her head and tried clear the cobwebs from her brain. "I can sleep later."

He frowned, but when she matched him look for look, he raised his hands in surrender. Maybe he'd already figured out that she'd hear the same from Dawnmother.

"Was there something you needed, Hugo?"

He bit his lip and shuffled his feet, reminding her that only days before he'd turned fourteen. In the low light of the candle, his face seemed even younger. "I had a…book when I was a little younger. It was, well, it was stories of infamous people."

A worrying feeling settled in Starbride's stomach, but she gestured for him to continue.

He sat at the very edge of the bed. "It was a really popular book, probably because it was pretty small. They printed enough of them that we had it even out in the country, where I lived with my mother before…" He cleared his throat. "Well, when we went out today to get supplies, I found one easier than I thought. I guess everyone is still fascinated by blood, even after what the city's been through."

"Hugo, your point, please?"

He pulled a very slim, soft-covered book from inside his coat. "Please don't scream or anything." He reminded her so much of Freddie's similar words that she knew whose face Hugo was about to show her.

"Freddie Ballantine," the caption read, "the Dockland Butcher." The artist had gotten the angle of the jaw right and the set of the eyes. The short hair was right, but the picture had no sideburns. Still, the line of the forehead was exactly Freddie's. The nose was a little off, and for some reason, the artist had sharpened Freddie's teeth to points and given him a snarl so feral he looked like a wild animal. Starbride scanned the accompanying paragraphs: the story of ten murders, of Freddie's arrest after he'd been found with a dead body, and then of his eventual hanging, daring escape, and final death during a fight with the Watch.

"He perished in the same Fiendish fires which bore him," she read. She nearly laughed, both at the error that Fiends were hot instead of cold and at the prose itself. She bet the story *would* bore Freddie were he to read it again. She had no doubt he'd seen the book before.

Tired as she was, she considered telling Hugo the truth. Surely all of Pennynail's acts of heroism would convince Hugo that this "Butcher" story was a lie.

But no, she couldn't do that. It wasn't her secret to tell. "What am I supposed to be afraid of, Hugo? This man is dead."

"This...is the man I saw in here the other day. Whoever he told you he is, he's lying. Pennynail is...this."

Starbride put on her most incredulous expression and hoped all her troubles had taught her to be a better liar. "This looks nothing like him."

"I've studied this drawing a thousand times, spent countless hours scaring myself witless with these stories. The old woman who cared for me when my mother wasn't home told me that the Butcher didn't really die, that he..." Hugo blushed to his ears.

"That he remained alive to punish little boys who wouldn't go to bed?"

"Who wouldn't eat their greens."

"Ah, and now you want me to believe that this Butcher has been aiding Katya for years and is now helping us hide from a Fiend, a creature 'from the same fires which bore him'?" She tapped the picture. "This person would rather eat us than help us."

Hugo frowned. "Then why does he cover his face?"

"Perhaps because people keep confusing him with a nefarious criminal."

"Maybe."

Starbride's stomach began to settle. She didn't want to push any more, hoping that with the nudges she'd given, he could convince himself.

Then his head shot up. "Pennynail has a scar."

Starbride just kept from swearing. How could Hugo have such a good memory when he'd only had a glance? "I don't remember him having a scar."

"I know what I saw. It's unmistakable." He pointed to the paragraph that mentioned the hanging and raised an eyebrow.

Starbride fought the urge to sigh. Hugo was as intelligent as the rest of his family; that was a fact. And he was as nettlesome as her when it came to figuring out secrets. She decided to try another favorite tactic of Katya's: diversion.

"All right," she said. "I'll tell you a secret, but you cannot tell anyone else or let on to Pennynail that you know."

"It *is* him!"

"Close. It's his brother."

"The Dockland Butcher had a brother?"

"Yes, and though they weren't twins, they had a strong resemblance. Pennynail was a petty thief, and the Watch confused the two of them. Just as they were hanging Pennynail, they realized their mistake and let him go. The experience left him with an unfortunate scar, and he went into hiding because people kept confusing them. He fell in with Crowe as an informant."

Hugo looked away, and Starbride could almost see him trying to work it out in his mind. She nearly clenched her hands. What she said was implausible, but much less so than a snaggle-toothed, murdering monster cheating death twice and ending up in service to the royal family.

"Can I talk to him?" Hugo asked.

"Then he would know that I told you. He doesn't want the fact that his brother was a murderer getting out."

"I suppose he would have to hide. I mean, anyone who's read this book is going to see the resemblance."

She nodded. Almost there.

Hugo stood, and Starbride nearly sighed again, but this time in relief. "I won't let you down, Miss Starbride."

The words seemed rather cryptic to her, but she had to nod and let them go.

A little while later, as she tried again to finish her new pyramid, Pennynail burst into her small room, and she knew the matter with Hugo was far from dropped.

He nearly tore the mask from his head. "Young Lord Fool is trying to follow me now."

Starbride told him of her earlier conversation with Hugo. "I'm sorry. I thought I had him."

"No doubt he thinks *I've* duped *you* with my 'brother' story."

"Great," she said. "I love to be thought of as stupid as well as oblivious."

"Only as stupid as you're taking him to be. He's going to get both of us caught if he keeps trying to be stealthy without my help. It's like he's forgotten how good at this stuff I am. I had to scrap my fact-finding mission."

"You'll have to talk with him, Freddie."

"Bend him over my knee, more like."

When he wouldn't look at her, Starbride smiled slightly. "It embarrasses you, doesn't it, your past? Even though you didn't kill those people."

He sighed, long and loud. "I haven't had to deal with it in years. Now you really know why I wear the mask."

She nodded. She would have worn it, too. "He's partly grown up on stories about you. Think you can convince him you're not evil?"

"Shouldn't be that difficult. He's actually *seen* evil. And there's no time like the present." Quick as a thought, Freddie cracked the door open, launched one arm out, and dragged Hugo inside by his coat collar.

Starbride stood so quickly her chair nearly fell over. Freddie was right; they underestimated him. She grabbed Hugo's arm before he could draw his rapier. "We're just talking, Hugo."

He gaped like a fish, as if he wanted to say everything from, "I knew it!" to "Get behind me, Miss Starbride!"

Freddie smirked. Starbride frowned at him. The more he enjoyed Hugo's discomfort, the more Hugo's back would go up.

"Let's sit and talk," Starbride said. Once she'd resumed her seat, Hugo sank onto a corner of the bed. Freddie crossed his arms and leaned against the wall.

"There once was a person," he said, "who did some terrible things. I can't tell you who, nor why, nor even how because I made certain promises long ago—oaths, if you will—and I'm sure you both understand the value of those."

Hugo nodded. After a moment, Starbride did the same. She leaned toward his raspy voice, intrigued in spite of herself.

"I broke into a house one night, right as this person was committing murder, not their first. We fought. The killer escaped and left me wounded, and that's how the Watch found me. All of Dockland was frightened. They wanted someone to blame. They had me."

He rubbed the scar around his throat and stared at the wall. "Cimerion Crowe was my father."

When Hugo gasped, Freddie smiled at him. "He knew I hadn't done the murders. He didn't want me to hang, but he couldn't get involved publicly, so he rescued me instead. I set out to find the killer, to deal with them and get back my name, only…" He chuckled. "Only things weren't as I suspected. When it was done and the killer lay dead, no one could know it *wasn't* me. So I pretended to die along with them."

Hugo sat on the edge of his seat. "Why didn't you lay the blame at this person's feet?"

"Like I said, promises and oaths. To pay my father back for how he helped me, I became Pennynail. And I stayed Pennynail because I care about the people in the Order."

Hugo stared at his knees. "And you have to hide because no one will believe you?"

Freddie cocked his head. "Do you believe me, boy?"

"I'm not a boy."

Freddie chuckled as if Hugo's reaction amused him to no end.

"But do you believe him, Hugo?" Starbride asked.

"I need to think."

As he stood, Freddie and Starbride both stared at him.

"I know," he said, "I'm not going to tell anyone." With that, he walked out.

Freddie sighed. "That's a big risk we've just taken. If word gets out…"

Starbride nodded. Just another thing to worry about.

Chapter Five

Katya

Katya escorted her father ashore. He'd seemed dubious when she'd told him she thought he could sway the citizens of Pomanse into fighting for him. He finally agreed to speak with them, no matter his doubts, unwilling to leave them without a hint of what they faced.

To meet the mayor, Da wore the same clothes as when they'd fled Marienne. The dark blue coat and black trousers had been carefully mended, the blood mostly faded. He donned a heavier coat for the walk to the mayor's house. Katya stayed on his heels as he entered the large house while Brutal remained outside. Castelle and some of her friends lingered in the mayor's halls as Katya and her father went through to the office.

Mayor Crispin frowned as Katya and her father entered, his dark eyes hooded and suspicious even after Captain Penner had vouched for them. His gaze shifted to the portrait of Da, the same representation that hung in every government building in Farraday, and he bowed deeply. It was a clumsy move compared to the well-executed turns at court.

"M…Majesty," he said, still bent over. "I am…I…"

Da waved. "Rise, Mayor Crispin."

Crispin's mouth hung open as if he suspected Da knew his name through some magic, and not because Captain Penner had told them. "Would you…" He cleared his throat. "Please, sit down, Majesty, and accept whatever meager repast my office can put together at this hour. That is…not to say that your visit is in any way…inconvenient, of course. I only meant—"

"Thank you," Da said as he sat. "Tea would be wonderful."

"Tea…yes, tea, right away." He poked his head out the door and had a quick conversation with someone. The sound of footsteps hurrying away was overshadowed by another set of footfalls approaching the door.

Katya stepped to her father's side, reaching for the rapier she'd commandeered from one of the nobles. The mayor's desk faced the door; she could turn it over, blocking access while she led Da out the large window. He could jump from the second story. Brutal would catch him while Castelle and her friends slowed their enemies' progress through the hall.

"Softly." Da's light touch on her arm almost made her jump. "Rampaging Fiends do not have a quick whisper in the hallway."

Katya let out a breath as she realized that Crispin was talking to someone. Of course, it could mean he was sending someone to Darren. She wondered if the Watch had found the real harbormaster yet.

Crispin stepped back inside and smoothed his black hair. "Majesty, please allow me to present the caretaker of Duchess Skelda's estate, Mr. Elton Davance."

"Majesty indeed," Davance mumbled as he stepped inside. He was older than Crispin, graying at the temples, with a salt and pepper beard. Tall and broad-shouldered, he easily carried a long portrait in his arms. When he saw Da, he stopped cold, stared down at the portrait, and then at the one on the wall. Katya suppressed a grin, imagining him prying the portrait from the duchess's hall so he could compare it to Crispin's.

Davance bowed. "Majesty."

"Indeed!" Crispin rubbed his hands together and chuckled. "Where is that fool boy with the tea?"

"If we may talk, gentlemen?" Da said.

They both sat, Crispin forsaking the chair behind his desk in order to sit at Da's side, and Davance perching on the narrow window seat. Both glanced at Katya where she stood behind Da's chair.

"This is the captain of our guard," Da said. "Lady Marchesa Gant."

They made seated bows. Katya nodded, glad Da had decided to keep her identity a secret. Perhaps he worried that another royal would give Davance and Crispin heart attacks.

"Begging your pardon, Majesty," Davance asked, "but did Duchess Skelda travel with you?"

"I'm afraid not. We do not know what became of the duchess when Marienne fell."

"We heard rumors," Crispin said, "but we hear so many out here."

"My guards have told me of the rumors circulating in Pomanse," Da said, "and I hope you believe me when I say that the usurper's reach is long. Lady Marchesa has already encountered one of his envoys in your city."

"Looking for you, Majesty," Crispin added. "That is…not to say…"

Da smiled a little, probably hearing the unspoken words as well as Katya: If the king left, so would the threat. "He is looking for whomever he can reach, Mayor Crispin. Unless you've already decided to side with the usurper?"

"No, no, Majesty, of course not. It's just, well, we aren't prepared for war. We're well defended from the sea, but only against pirate attacks. We haven't had to repel a force overland for nearly a hundred years. And if these Fiends are extraordinarily strong, well, how do we prepare?"

"The envoy got in and out without anyone seeing him," Katya said. "You've got no guards on your wall, and those patrolling the streets are lax."

Davance scowled as if she attacked him personally. "We do our jobs well enough."

"*Elton*," Crispin muttered.

"Speak," Da said.

"Well, Majesty," Davance said, "we've had no troubles besides our own for a long time, as the mayor says. The guards who work the duchess's estate have aided when needed, but they're not often needed."

Katya fixed him with a stern look. "They're needed now."

"The usurper wants all of Farraday," Da said. "Now or later, a fight is coming, and you must be prepared for it."

Both men nodded, but Katya could see skepticism in their eyes. She wouldn't tell them of Darren's ultimatum. The urge to give up their king in order to save their city might be too great. Either way, Roland wouldn't spare this place forever.

Katya could almost see the ideas swirling in Davance's and Crispin's minds. Bowing and portraits and tea were one thing. Da could force civility on them, but he couldn't force them to fight, especially if they didn't believe in the cause. Even the dispatched corpse Fiends wouldn't sway them. Unanimated, they looked just like any other dead men.

Da stood, his face an unemotional mask, but Katya knew he'd reached the same conclusion. It was time for one of his rousing speeches.

"We will take our leave now," he said quietly.

Katya fought the urge to gawk. She stayed close behind as he walked to the door.

Davance and Crispin babbled over each other in their haste to offer hospitality. Da shook his head. "We were not planning on staying, but our absence will not guarantee that the usurper and his forces will leave you alone. The crown needs your help to take this kingdom back. When we call, will you answer?"

Both nodded, but Katya could see their relief. They really did believe that if Da left, the trouble would go with him. Katya nearly sneered at them.

Captain Penner's people collected supplies, and they sailed out of the harbor at dawn. Just before the sun bloomed in the east, Katya imagined she saw a burst of light, as if Pomanse had caught fire. She hoped it wasn't a premonition, but even if the place was ablaze, there was nothing she could do about it. If she stayed to fight, she'd put her family in danger. And who knew how many corpse Fiends Darren had with him? If he'd been leaving them all through the countryside, he could have scores, hundreds. What could a few fighters do about that except die at the townspeople's sides?

Da joined her at the rail. "If Darren sacks Pomanse, the survivors will answer my call to arms."

Katya had to look away. The thought was logical but awful all the same.

Da patted her shoulder. "If I had told them to run, they wouldn't have done it. Some people cannot be rallied, no matter the speeches you give them."

"Is this our fate, Da? To sail from port to port, putting everyone in danger?"

"We need to get ahead of Darren. If we can outrun Roland's vanguard, we can head inland and find a place to dig in."

But if the power of a sailing ship couldn't get them in front of Fiendish strength, she didn't know what could.

"We need to go farther than he's even thought of," Da said. He gave her a look out of the corner of his eye.

Katya turned her head slowly to the east, squinting against the sun. Somewhere in that distance was Allusia, a land Roland probably knew little about with terrain that was largely unmapped by anyone but its inhabitants. But would the Umbriels be welcome there? If the Farradains weren't interested in the conflict in their own kingdom, what hope was there that the Allusians would care at all?

And how her heart would ache seeing hundreds of people with Starbride's reddish-brown skin and black hair! And Starbride's mother had returned to Allusia before Roland's uprising. What would Katya say to her? To Starbride's father? They wouldn't accept that Katya had to choose her family's safety, the safety of the crown, above their daughter's. All they'd see was that Katya had left their only child in reach of a monster.

Katya rubbed her temples, too angry to even think of crying. She heard her father speaking quietly to Captain Penner. They could promise money or titles or power to any Farradains that answered the call to war. What might Allusia want? An Allusian army might even see a weakened Farraday as an opportunity. Katya didn't envy her father that diplomatic tangle. She closed her eyes and prayed to the spirits to let Starbride live. Both for her own sake, and for the cohesion it would bring when the princess of Farraday married a daughter of Allusia.

Katya headed below decks to try to get some sleep, though she didn't think it would come easy. When she spied Castelle's shadowy form waiting in the dim, lantern lit darkness of the ship's halls, she pulled up short.

"What's wrong?" Katya asked.

Castelle chuckled. "Something has to be wrong for me to want a private word with you?"

"Lately, yes."

"I wanted to see how you were feeling."

"Feeling?"

"Yes, you know the sort of thing: happiness, sadness…trouser-melting lust."

Katya chuckled. "I'm feeling the same as always: anxious, sad, and frightened."

"You, frightened?"

Katya rolled her eyes. "We really don't know each other well at all, do we?"

"I thought, well, we could try being friends again. Friends that occasionally shout at each other, anyway."

Katya tried to think of a fast way out of this conversation. Her hammock waited.

Castelle clucked her tongue. "Spirits above, you're not flaying yourself again, are you?"

"Flaying?" Katya blinked. "Oh, you mean the guilt."

"Yes, the guilt."

"I'm too tired to have this conversation again."

Castelle stepped close. "Let me help you."

"Fine. You keep up both sides of this argument so I can go to bed." She tried to step around, but Castelle gripped her shoulders.

"I'm not going to let go until you agree to not feel guilty anymore."

"Wonderful. Will you pick out curtains for this hallway we're going to live in, or shall I?"

Castelle's face turned thunderous, and Katya braced herself for the shouting. No, she decided, if the shouting began, she was going to punch Castelle in the gut and then carry on to bed.

Instead, Castelle swooped forward and kissed her with passionate intensity. Katya's eyes flew open, and it took her a heartbeat to realize what was happening. It had been a long while since anyone had held her, since she'd pressed someone close, and she'd forgotten how skillful these particular lips could be.

Before Katya could respond, Castelle straightened, her face blurrily close. "This always cleared your mind before."

Katya's heart hammered in her ears, and she almost leaned forward, almost claimed those devious lips again, but Castelle's words were too similar to something Starbride had once said, and Katya couldn't hold in a sob. She drew back and tightened her arms around herself.

"Katya?" Castelle said, surprised, it seemed, into dropping the Highness. "Spirits, I didn't…hurt you or anything, did I?"

Katya drew in a great, shuddering breath. "The fact that you don't know how much you hurt me proves that we don't know each other *at all*. I love Starbride, Castelle."

"I know, but—"

"No, you don't know. You couldn't, not when you kissed me like that. I ache for her. She *lives* inside me. She'll do that forever, even if she…" Katya mashed her lips together, desperate to keep from falling apart until she could be alone.

"Katya, I'm sorry. I just wanted—"

"Don't ever touch me again." Katya stepped past, wondering what in all the spirits' names Castelle had been thinking. A quick tumble in the ship's hold and all of Katya's problems would be gone? A betrayal of the woman she loved would *clear* her of guilt? Was that how it worked in Castelle's world? Katya couldn't help but wonder how many women Castelle had kept on the side when they'd been together. Their relationship had meant the world to Katya. Maybe it hadn't meant as much to Castelle because she was incapable of feeling real love for anyone.

"Oh, Star," Katya whispered, hurrying to her bunk so she could fall to pieces. "Please be alive, please, please, please."

CHAPTER SIX

STARBRIDE

Starbride held her new pyramid up to the light. Squinting, she polished it again, trying to huff away the last few smudges.

"If you're going to wear it, it's going to get marks on it," Dawnmother said.

Starbride glared at her, but Dawnmother didn't look up from her pile of mending. "I want it to be perfect, Dawn."

"He who tries for perfection will sooner catch the sun."

"Horsestrong really did have a saying for every occasion." But how many did he actually say, and how many did he just get credit for? Starbride wouldn't have been surprised if he'd really been mute. "The better I can make this, the better I can hide from the corpse Fiends."

"I have faith in you, Star. I do not see how worrying to sickness will help the pyramid work *better*."

"You're right. If it's going to work, it's going to work, and there's only one way to test it."

Town criers had passed through the streets early the day before, calling the populace to the palace steps in the late afternoon. The Fiend king wished to address them. Freddie had wanted to go alone, maybe with Hugo, to see what Roland had planned. Starbride had disagreed. She and Master Bernard had finally finished the pyramid that would let a pyradisté hide from the sharpened senses of the corpse Fiends, and they had to know if it would work.

Dawnmother set her sewing aside and looked up. "If the Fiend king himself is going to address the people, he will have many of those...things with him."

"If these pyramids fail, the corpse Fiends will have a harder time finding us in a crowd." She tried to swallow her nerves, but her belly felt like it was full of flies. "Besides, we can't just wander around the largest city in Farraday looking for a lone corpse Fiend. And we won't be at the front of the crowd, just in case Roland tries any tricks."

"Well," Dawnmother said as she stood, "when do we leave?" Starbride started to protest, but Dawnmother lifted an eyebrow. "We'll be safe, yes? That's what you said."

Starbride swallowed her retort. "Let's go." She slipped a tiny chain through the hole at the top of the pyramid and then lifted it over her head. She'd wear it under her clothes, next to her skin like the Fiend necklace Hugo and the other Umbriels had to wear.

As it settled cold against her breastbone, a memory rushed to the front of her mind: kissing Katya's warm throat, her fingers playing over the gold chain that held Katya's pyramid. Starbride took a deep breath and forced the feelings down before they could overwhelm her.

"Star?" Dawnmother asked.

Starbride lifted the pyramid and pressed it to her lips before she dropped it down her shirt again. She and Dawnmother gathered Pennynail and Hugo as they exited their basement hideout. They left Master Bernard behind. Starbride wanted to test her new pyramid on herself before she asked anyone else to risk his or her life.

"What do you think my...the Fiend king wants?" Hugo asked as they hurried through the streets. Starbride caught the pained expression on his face. He wanted to forget that Roland was his father as much as possible.

"I don't know," Starbride said. Coldness settled in her at the thought that Roland might say something about Katya, about how he'd captured her. She walked a little faster.

A few streets from the hideout, Pennynail surprised her by taking off his mask. He'd darkened his hair and wore a scarf high up on his chin. He put a coat on over his leather, buckled outfit, making it look almost normal. He'd smeared coal lightly on his cheeks, making them gaunter, and he pulled a flat cap far down over his eyes. No one would recognize him unless they took his hat off and peered very closely at his face.

Hugo watched the transformation with hooded eyes.

"The mask is just too obvious to mingle," Freddie said. "And the rooftops are out if I want to stay close to you." When he winked, Hugo turned away.

The large square in front of the palace already teemed with people when they arrived. An empty dais stood at the front, blocking access to the large stairway that led inside the palace proper. The heavy doors were nearly closed, leaving a gap just large enough for people to come and go single file. The scorch marks Starbride remembered from the night Roland had taken over had been washed away, and the torn Umbriel banners were gone. Nothing new hung in their place. Perhaps Roland was still thinking on what his new crest would look like.

"Let's stay near the edge," Freddie said. "Any more than a few people deep and we could get trapped in the press."

Starbride glanced back to see how many more people worked their way down the street. Even with all the turmoil, a few vendors had showed up, calling out their wares.

Freddie guided them farther back in the crowd as more people arrived. "If anyone looks too closely at us," he whispered, "head for those vendors and pretend you're buying something."

Starbride resisted the urge to grab her pyramid necklace and Dawnmother's hand. Like Freddie, they wore caps and scarves to hide their features. Hugo and Freddie tried to stay in front of them, blocking their faces from passersby.

The crowd noise swelled for a moment. Starbride peeked around Freddie's shoulder and saw Roland, the bastard, striding from the palace doors. No guards surrounded him, but then, he didn't need any.

Freddie bent close to Starbride's ear. "He's alone. If I can get close enough…"

"He's fast enough to move out of the way of anything you throw."

"Fast enough to dodge a stab to the neck?"

It could work, she supposed, but just as quickly, she knew it wouldn't. Even if Freddie managed to catch Roland without his Fiendish Aspect upon him, the Fiend was always inside him. "I won't risk losing you."

"Aw, do you have a little crush?"

She poked him in the back. "Keep dreaming."

Hugo leaned close to them and glared. "Perhaps you should pay attention."

"Sensitive and easily antagonized," Freddie said. "Ten years ago you would have been just my type, kiddo."

Starbride saw Hugo's ears go red, but before he could retort, she shushed them both.

At the top of the dais, Roland smiled at the crowd, not a trace of the Fiend on his face. Starbride remembered Katya saying that he looked just the same as he had seven years ago, when he'd supposedly died. He was in his mid-thirties, broad-shouldered and good-looking, with a face so much like Katya's father's except Roland's beard was lighter brown. Starbride could almost see his blue eyes twinkling. He seemed so…normal.

The noise of the crowd dropped, but no one clapped for Roland. He smiled harder, as if he hadn't expected a warm welcome.

"Friends and neighbors," he said, "loyal subjects." Even he laughed at that one, his mask slipping. Starbride had to wonder if he'd gone even more insane. "I've called you together to announce that the king and the crown princess have been found."

Starbride's stomach dropped to her knees, and the world seemed to tilt around her. She grabbed Hugo to keep from falling over.

Roland gestured over his shoulder, and two people walked from the palace. Starbride's heartbeat returned to normal. They were an older man and a young woman, but they were no more Katya and King Einrich than Freddie and Hugo were.

Hugo gasped. "It's…really them. But they're *smiling*. He must have used a pyramid to—"

"It can't be," Freddie said.

Dawnmother grabbed Starbride's arm. "Oh Star…"

"It's not them," Starbride said. "They must be wearing disguise pyramids." No other pyradistés in the crowd would be fooled, but everyone else murmured to themselves.

The fakes linked arms with Roland, smiled, and waved to the crowd. To their credit, the crowd managed a bit of sporadic clapping.

"Thank you, good citizens," the fake Einrich said. "With the help of our new friend and his enormous power, we hope to work together for a better tomorrow."

Starbride fought not to gag. Instead of clapping, the crowd seemed more suspicious, glancing at one another and muttering. On the dais, Roland chuckled as he watched the sea of people. His features seemed to ripple, but when they straightened, they were his own, not the Fiend's.

The hair on the back of Starbride's neck stood up. "Get ready."

Around her, faces slackened, and happy, stupid smiles took over people's mouths. Two men near the back of the dais lifted a large, cloth-wrapped bundle into the air. The wind caught the edge of the cloth and tore it away, revealing a pyramid half as tall as Starbride.

She tugged on Freddie's arm. "Let's—"

He dumbly turned toward her, the same goofy smile on his face as on everyone else's.

"Damn," Starbride whispered.

Hugo and Dawnmother shared the same blissful look. Starbride tried to grab all three of them, ready to lead their idle bodies from the square. But how to do it without arousing suspicion? She supposed the grinning crowd wouldn't notice her, but movement to her right caught her eye.

A host of corpse Fiends eased into the square. They lifted their gaunt, gray faces and sniffed the air as they moved through the crowd. Starbride turned Hugo, Freddie, and Dawnmother toward the dais again. The corpse Fiends had cut off the escape routes, and as Starbride watched from the corner of her eye, one of them turned in her direction.

She let her eyes go half lidded and tried on a satisfied smile, difficult with her teeth clamped together. The square had gone eerily quiet, echoing with the shuffling footsteps of the corpse Fiends. One drifted closer, and Starbride fought not to hold her breath. It paused beside her, and she focused on the feeling of the pyramid against her chest, trying to think as Katya would, hoping to borrow a measure of Katya's courage. The corpse Fiend sniffed against her ear, and the scent of it filled her nostrils, dry and dusty like an old riverbed.

It breathed deep, the air moving several strands of her hair. She fought the urge to tremble or sneeze, fought to remember to blink. Well, she wanted a test for her new pyramid. It didn't get any better than this.

After the corpse Fiend *whuffed* a final time, it loped away through the crowd. Starbride wanted to sag to her knees, but other corpse Fiends might be watching. Roland himself was scanning the crowd as his minions moved through it.

Across the square, one young woman screamed and broke into a run. As one, the corpse Fiends took up their infernal howl and leapt after her. When Roland and his two fakes turned in the fleeing woman's direction, Starbride linked arms with Freddie and Dawnmother, grabbed a fistful of Hugo's shirt, and inched toward a side street. She tried to block the terrified woman's screams from her ears, wishing there was something she could do to help, but she couldn't defeat a pack of corpse Fiends on her own.

When she turned a corner with her three charges, she hurried them along until they began to encounter people who hadn't gone to the palace to hear what Roland had to say.

"Who does he…" Freddie started. He whirled around. "What the hell?"

"Where are we?" Hugo asked.

"Star?" Dawnmother said.

Starbride gave them all a gentle push. "Keep walking," she said through her teeth. "Look normal."

They fell into step with her, and she filled them in as they walked.

"Clever bastard," Freddie said.

Hugo patted her shoulder. "Quick thinking, Miss Starbride."

"And now we know your pyramid works." Dawnmother squeezed Starbride's arm, telling of how afraid she'd been, no matter her words.

"I shudder to think of what he's doing to the people he hypnotized back there, how he's…*retuning* them." Starbride thought of the large pyramid and shook her head. Now they knew Roland was continuing his experiments. They had to find a way into the palace soon. Who knew what he could do with a pyramid so large?

Her mind seemed to click then, as if a puzzle piece fell into place. The capstone under the palace wasn't the only large pyramid in Marienne.

"Horsestrong preserve us," she whispered. "The Pyradisté Academy." It was far larger than the pyramid she'd seen just then. How many people could it hypnotize? As far as Starbride knew it was just a light pyramid, but Roland's power was unbelievable. She told the others her thoughts as they walked.

Hugo whistled. "And it's nearly in the center of town!"

"We need to talk to Master Bernard," Starbride said. "Maybe we can…lock it in some way, I don't know."

"I do," Dawnmother said. "If you can't keep him from using it, destroy it."

Freddie laughed softly. "Blow up the second largest pyramid in Farraday? Sounds like the most fun we'll have since this whole business started."

Master Bernard wouldn't think so. Starbride imagined she'd have to hold him as he wept.

CHAPTER SEVEN

KATYA

When Katya first saw Newhope, she thought it must be on fire. It gleamed so. Rows of buildings started at the harbor and climbed up a steep hill toward the center of the city. All of them shone in the dawn. Katya had to squint through her fingers just to look.

"It's a defensive measure," Captain Penner said. "The buildings are painted bright white and decorated with polished metal on the one side. You have to sail at a very specific angle to decrease the glare." The ship tacked, and the light from the buildings decreased. Still, they had to stop far out in the harbor and wait for a pilot boat to lead them in.

The Allusians were a crafty lot, then. It was a lucky thing the Farradains hadn't tried to come at them a hundred years ago from the sea. Katya tried to put such thoughts away. Reminding the Allusians of all they'd lost to the Farradains wouldn't help her cause.

Da joined her at the rail, and Katya nearly leaned on his shoulder she was so tired. "Ready for some land again, my girl?"

"Where do we go first?"

"Straight to the governor's office to throw ourselves on his mercy."

"Do you really think that's likely?"

"Worth a try. Our noble friends can seek out the Farradain families living here and find a safe haven for themselves and maybe us if the governor tosses us out on our ears."

Whatever they did, they couldn't seem like usurpers of the governor's power. The nobles who sailed with them would probably prefer it if they stormed the town and took what they wanted, but the balance of power in Allusia was tenuous. As Starbride's original mission to Marienne had proven, not everyone was happy with the Farradain traders living in Newhope. Allusia might have adopted Farradain laws, but the Farradains themselves didn't always adhere to those laws. According to Starbride, they'd been using antiquated practices to create a trading monopoly.

Starbride had been determined to stop them. The fierce look in her eyes had made Katya so proud. Now, it made her insides tighten with worry. She tried rolling her head back and forth, but her neck and shoulders felt like rocks. If they got any stiffer, they'd split the skin open.

Maybe she could relieve her tension by telling the Farradain traders in Newhope to behave. Of course, Starbride hadn't wanted her to. She'd pointed out that if Katya solved all of Newhope's problems, the Allusian people would never stand on their own.

And with Roland to worry about, discussing trade law seemed rather pointless.

The pilot ship led them into the harbor. Katya stayed with her father as he disembarked. Brutal walked in front of them, and Castelle followed with a handful of her friends. Ma and the children were probably bursting to be on land, but they couldn't risk that, not just yet. If Katya had to hurry her father back to the ship, she took comfort in the fact that sailing away from the harbor wouldn't be as difficult as sailing into it.

Newhope's bright buildings didn't end with those facing the water. Most were painted bright white, contrasting with the red clay of the streets. Smaller houses jostled with larger shops and warehouses, the configuration with no rhyme or reason Katya could discern. Dark wooden accents adorned most of the buildings, either as porch pillars or overhanging the roofs. Some long poles of wood poked from the sides of the buildings, as if the ceiling beams inside were too long, and the builders had just extended them through the wall and then packed the clay of the walls around them. Brightly colored pots and wall hangings interrupted the flood of white like clouds of colorful butterflies. Maybe the Allusians used them to navigate the city.

Katya braced herself for the sight of Newhope's people, hoping she wouldn't see Starbride in every face. She wondered if Starbride had felt the same when she'd first come to Marienne, if everyone had looked alike. The features and figures were different, though. Still, every time Katya spied a red-clad figure, she half expected to see Starbride waiting for her.

"Stop it," she muttered to herself. She counted to twenty, a self-control technique she hadn't had to use in years.

Many stared at Katya and her father as they started up the hill toward the center of the city. Most seemed curious, a few disapproving. The few pale faces in the crowd smiled openly, though many of the Allusians did the same. One Allusian lady on her porch winked at Da. He sputtered a laugh and gave her a little half-bow.

Katya poked him in the arm. "I'll tell Ma on you."

"It's been a long time since anyone winked at me."

She understood his surprised happiness. When she'd first met Starbride, she'd had the opportunity to be anonymous for a little while. It had been nice to be a face in the crowd instead of royalty. "How will the governor know you?"

"I've met the fellow."

"You've been to Allusia?"

"No, he came to Marienne ages ago, but I dare say we'll still know each other."

"Why did he come to Marienne?"

Da was quiet for a moment. "To ask what I intended toward his people. My father had just died, and I'd taken the throne. We were both young. Dayscout has such presence, Katya. He became exactly what his family wanted to him to be, a guide for his people." Da chuckled softly. "Spirits, but we hated each other at first sight."

"And that's something to smile about?"

"He called me arrogant, and I called him bumptious. He called me a tyrant, and I called him an oily little tick."

"So, you wound up friends, I'm guessing?"

"Oh yes. We were honest with each other after everyone else had been sucking up to us our entire lives. We've written each other through the years. I talked him out of marrying a woman who only wanted him for his power, and he talked me through my first year of fatherhood."

"Then why didn't he talk to you about the trading problems in Newhope?"

Da shrugged. "We agreed not to talk policy, not unless we really needed each other's help. I don't even know which trading problems you're referring to. It's probably something he thought he could handle on his own."

Katya smiled. "Because he had people like Starbride working for him."

"Probably so." He touched her lightly on the shoulder. "We'll find her, my girl."

Katya nodded, all she could do without losing the calm she'd forced on herself.

The governor's house wasn't the largest structure in Newhope, but it sat dead center in the city, at the top of the hill, offset from all the other buildings. The road curved around it so that it didn't touch any other structure. Katya had to wonder if Dayscout ever felt he was operating out of a fishbowl.

Their guards waited while Katya and her father approached the front door. The man who answered their knock was clad in simple trousers and tunic that reminded Katya of Dawnmother. Like her, he also had a braid of long black hair hanging down his back. Before Katya had a chance to speak, he smiled at Da and bowed. "Majesty," he said in Farradain, as easily as if kings came to his door every day. "Please, come in."

Katya followed her father into a sitting room crammed with furniture: bright cushions, divans, and large chairs. "Claytrue," Da said, "how have you been?"

"Well enough, thank you, Majesty. I will fetch my master for you."

"Looks like one of them remembers you, at least," Katya muttered.

"You'll like Dayscout, Katya. He's very…excitable."

After Claytrue had been gone a few moments, a cry of surprise echoed down the stairs, and a short, pot-bellied Allusian man rushed down, his arms thrown wide. "Einrich! What in Horsestrong's name are you doing here? No!" He took a deep breath. "Don't answer that. Refreshment first. Sit, sit, sit, both of you! Claytrue, tea, coffee, cakes, sandwiches! Just bring everything!"

He caught Da by the elbows and guided him to a divan. He looked at Katya expectantly. "Won't you sit, too, Miss…?"

"She's my daughter," Da said. "Katyarianna."

Katya was caught with her mouth open, used to introducing herself as Da's guard. But she supposed if they were going to ask the governor for help, they wouldn't be served well by lying from the start.

"Ah!" Dayscout grabbed her hand and shook it over and over, peppering his shakes with little bows. "So happy to meet you, Katyarianna! Einrich and I have been threatening to introduce our families for a long time! Did you bring your wife, too, Einrich?"

Katya had to frown in amused bewilderment. So much in Marienne stood on protocol. This man acted as if they were all one big family. "It's nice to meet you, too," she managed.

He gave her a kindly smile and then sank down on a divan across from them. Katya glanced at her father, wondering if they should start their pleas for help, but he shook his head slightly, and she followed his lead.

Claytrue brought in refreshment and then retired to the corner, just as Dawnmother might have done. When he dug into a small basket and removed a pile of socks to be mended, she nearly laughed and cried at the same time.

"I'm dying of curiosity," Dayscout said after they'd all had a bite to eat. "It's beyond wonderful to see you, but I have to ask…"

Da told their story. He held back the Umbriel Fiends and the fact that Roland was his brother, but everything else he laid out for Dayscout, who absorbed it while he stared into space over steepled fingers.

"And you want our help?" he asked after Da had finished. "Allusian help to take back your kingdom?"

"We need troops, weapons, and a place to rally the Farradain people."

"And I suppose this Fiendish usurper will turn his eyes on Allusia once he's done with Farraday?"

"He's a pyradisté. He'll be after the crystal in your northern mountains, if nothing else."

Dayscout smiled slyly. "Like any Farradain."

"Fair point."

"Well…I do care about you, Einrich, you know that, and if it were just me helping just you, I would do it immediately, but I can't make this…huge…decision alone. I'll need to speak to our council and my advisors, and we'd be wise to have the opinion of the *adsnazi* as well." His bright smile reappeared. "Come, fetch your wife and grandchildren. You dine with my family tonight."

Lord Vincent wouldn't like it, but Katya supposed they'd have to start trusting someone if they were going to get anywhere with their plans. Da seemed to trust this man already. Katya supposed that if Dayscout decided to take them hostage and sell them to Roland they'd just have to find a way out. Either way, they couldn't keep running. Sooner or later, they had to put their feet back on the soil.

After another round of vigorous hand shaking, they turned to go. Claytrue met them at the door with a large basket. "I notice your servants didn't come in, Majesty," he said, "so I packed a snack for them."

Katya smiled broadly. Even though Brutal and Castelle weren't servants, it warmed her to be reminded of Dawnmother's charity again. "Thank you," she said.

He bowed deeply. She took the basket, and after Da thanked Dayscout again for his hospitality, they were off.

Brutal, Castelle, and her friends appreciated the snacks, though they waited until they were on the *Spirits Endeavor* to dig into them. Katya left them to it and went below with her father to meet with Lord Vincent.

He did have a lot to say about venturing into Newhope, precautions mostly. Katya agreed with him for the most part. Everyone except the children would go armed, even if with just a knife, and the children wouldn't leave Vincent's sight. If Allusian custom required them to eat or play in a different room than the adults, he would accompany them. Katya had a sudden vision of Vincent hunched over the children's table and couldn't contain a laugh.

They dressed as finely as they could with what they had on the ship, Ma and Da in the clothes they'd fled from Marienne in, and Katya in an embroidered coat she borrowed from one of the nobles. It was a little loose in the collar and the hips, but it was better, she supposed, than her leather fighting gear or chainmail. Castelle wore the armor, serving as guard, but Katya still wore her borrowed rapier at her hip.

Little Vierdrin and Bastian beamed as their grandparents dressed them in outfits cobbled together from donated clothing. Katya surveyed her family and thought them the most ragged royalty she'd ever seen. Maybe it was for the best; they'd stand out enough in Newhope as it was.

Once they set foot on the street, the children tugged and pulled on Vincent's hands, keeping up a running commentary on everything they saw or heard or smelled. Vincent held them so tightly Katya saw his knuckles whiten. Little Bastian whined, but Vincent only picked him up and carried him, making him pout until Vincent had a strict word in his ear.

To their credit, Dayscout and his wife greeted everyone with open arms. Bastian and Vierdrin were so happy to see other children that they stopped their protestations. When the two Allusian children invited Vierdrin and Bastian into their playroom, Vincent followed on their heels.

Dayscout lifted an eyebrow. Two of his four children still lived at home, and one of those was ten, old enough for a servant, but still

Vincent went with them. "They'll be well looked after," Dayscout said, "if that's what the lord is worried about."

Da chuckled. "To keep Vincent from his duty, we'd have to kill him."

"Well, I think we can forgo that this once," Dayscout said.

During the meal, they spoke of unimportant things. Katya fought the urge to fidget. Some of the Allusian news was interesting, but none of it interested her as much as whether Dayscout planned to help them. Newhope had its own version of a Watch but no standing army or plans on how to raise one. Since Farraday had helped them put a central government in place, they had adopted the same, we'll-assemble-it-when-we-need-it approach to an army, but they needed the governor to put out a call to arms.

When they'd finished dessert, Dayscout laid his napkin aside. "I've sent a messenger to the adsnazi. They won't be coming tonight."

Katya's stomach dropped, and she couldn't help herself from asking, "Is that a no, then? They won't help us?" Her mother nudged her under the table.

Dayscout smiled. "They don't come into Newhope often, and when they do, they never stay for long, not even for dinner with the governor. But they have invited you to come and stay with them. I won't lie; support for your cause is little to none."

"Because no one believes the trouble will come here," Da said.

Dayscout nodded. "For what it's worth, I believe you, but we Allusians are a headstrong bunch. The council and the adsnazi don't obey me because I'm the governor. They obey me because we agree on what we should do. If you do recover your kingdom, Einrich, it might behoove you to consider this parliament you told me about. Even though the idea was put forth by an enemy, that doesn't mean it was entirely bad."

"I was considering it," Da said, "also for what it's worth. Can I speak to this council?"

"Of course. Though if you had the support of the adsnazi, it would go a long way toward swaying them."

Katya began to form a new plan. The governor couldn't help on his own, so adsnazi first, then the council, and then they could get some momentum going. They could start to sweep back west, gathering Farradains to their banner.

"Just so you know," Dayscout said, "the adsnazi aren't going to be easy to convince. They don't take much of an interest in what happens outside their hills. I'm surprised they want to meet with you at all. Maybe it's the Fiends that intrigue them."

Katya didn't care why, only that they wanted to meet. Starbride had told her that Allusian pyramid users were not as skilled as those in Farraday. They didn't even test their children for the ability. If all they could do was produce colored lights—as Starbride had said—it was likely they'd be of no strategic importance during the war. Unless they could learn. The one pyradisté who'd escaped with Katya, a man who'd worked for Duchess Julietta, could teach them some tricks. That might be enough to sway them to join the Farradain cause.

Dayscout's oldest daughter was visiting relatives in the north, so he offered her house to Katya's family. Da agreed. They would be as safe in the house as on the ship, and Katya feared for their sanity if they had to stay at sea any longer. Dayscout had several Watch officers posted on the grounds, but Katya set up a roster of watches inside. She sat up first with Berg, an ex-thief, one of Castelle's friends.

He was short as well as wide. That, combined with his bald head, reminded Katya of a stump. He leered instead of smiled and laughed at all the wrong times. Katya had taken an instant dislike to him when she'd first met him, but he was loyal to Castelle. She didn't have to like all the people she worked with, she supposed.

Their watch passed quietly, but just as Katya started upstairs to bed, someone knocked softly on the door.

Berg opened it a crack. "What is it?"

Katya heard a mumbled reply.

"Wait a minute." Berg shut the door and turned. "It's a Watchman, Highness. Someone's at the gate asking for you, a lady from a, ahem, *prominent* Newhope family." He chuckled, and Katya fought the urge to smack him.

Prominent Newhope family? Katya closed her eyes and prayed to the spirits, but she knew it would be Brightstriving. Fah and Fay had only bad luck for her this evening.

"I'll talk to her," Katya said. "Leave the door open." She pushed past Berg and tried to make her stride confident across the lawn to the gate, toward four darkened figures waiting next to a Watchman with a lantern.

Brightstriving wore a gown in Farradain style. The petal-like layers of pastel fabric almost made Katya blanch. The fashion Starbride had hated, that her mother had embraced, made all of Katya's tender moments with Starbride rush to mind. She managed to reach the gate without falling into a heap. Brightstriving and a man with her bowed. The other two hovered behind, servants likely, meaning that the man was…

Katya swallowed. Not one parent, but two. She pressed her lips together and returned their bows. "Brightstriving and Sunjoyful."

"I'm very happy to meet you, Highness." Sunjoyful's Allusian accent came through more than his wife's or daughter's, but he managed the words well.

"Where is our daughter?" Brightstriving asked.

"Bright," Sunjoyful said, "you said you wouldn't make a scene."

Brightstriving didn't take her eyes off Katya.

Katya took a deep breath. "I don't know."

"Because you sent her away before the real danger started?" Brightstriving asked. "Made her leave Marienne in a carriage, and we can expect her any time?"

"She was with us when the city fell," Katya said softly.

"Then surely," Sunjoyful said, "she's coming on another ship?"

Acid churned in Katya's stomach. "She was in the city. My family was in the palace. We were to rendezvous and leave together. She was…delayed. I had to get my family to safety." She didn't add that her father had ordered her incapacitated, that she'd intended to go back. She'd chosen to stay with her family before they'd sailed away, and she needed to pay for that.

Brightstriving's eyes narrowed to slits. "You left our daughter with those…things? Those Fiends?"

"I'm trying to hurry back to her as fast as I can."

Sunjoyful sagged. "Horsestrong preserve her, oh my little Star…"

Katya fought the tears that wanted to spring to her eyes. She gripped the gate as hard as she could.

"So…" No sagging for Brightstriving; her spine was like steel.

Katya didn't want to offer excuses about how leaving Starbride was the hardest thing she'd ever done, how her heart ached, how she'd been willing to abandon her family and sneak into a city crawling with Fiends in order to find her beloved.

But she also didn't want to hear Brightstriving accuse her of never having cared for Starbride at all.

"No matter what I have to endure," Katya said, "or who I have to face, I will find her, and nothing this side of life will stop me."

Brightstriving drew herself up taller as if she might retort or accuse, but Sunjoyful gripped her arm. She helped pull him up as he tugged her a little lower.

"What matters now is getting our daughter back," Sunjoyful said. "We're with you."

Katya bit her lip hard. "Thank you."

Sunjoyful tugged his wife's arm; Brightstriving's eyes were still hard and dry. "I will not forget this," she whispered before she let her husband lead her away.

Katya could see what Starbride had gotten from both her parents: her heart and her resolve. After this, she knew she wouldn't sleep. All she could do was walk the house and think of Starbride.

Chapter Eight

Starbride

Master Bernard hunched over the pyramid worktable, his focus so tight that Starbride could see his tongue poking from between his lips. She cleared her throat, and he whipped around as if she'd clanged a pair of cymbals.

"I'm sorry," she said. "I didn't mean to scare you."

"No, it's me. I shouldn't be so…." He laughed breathlessly. "Never mind." He gestured to the half-finished pyramid in front of him. "After your success hiding from the corpse Fiends, I decided to try my hand at making a pyramid to block mind magic. Unfortunately, mind magic was never my greatest skill."

Starbride nodded. It wasn't hers, either, but it certainly was one of Roland's strengths. "How close are you?"

He shrugged. "When I finish, we can test it here and won't have to put any of our own in danger." He gave her a look she was certain he'd leveled at many a naughty student.

She was lucky to have known him as a comrade instead of a teacher. He didn't scare her in the slightest. Still, his reminder of how catastrophic her test could have gone struck a chord within her. It had haunted her dreams. She'd spent most of her time since then indoors, making pyramids and crafting a plan about how to break into the Pyradisté Academy.

"More pyramids mean more crystal," Master Bernard said. "When we go to the academy, we'll look around. I can't think what the Fiend king might be able to do with the capstone. He shouldn't be able to retune it, but he's done so much we never even thought about, all this Fiend magic."

Starbride nodded. Roland was more powerful than even Crowe had remembered. When he'd "died," he'd merged with his Fiend while retaining his pyradisté's mind. Being a Fiend made Roland a more powerful pyradisté, but according to everything Starbride had learned, being a Fiend should also have made him vulnerable to pyramid magic, just like the corpse Fiends.

A soft knock made her turn. "It's dark," Hugo said from the doorway.

"Has Dawnmother gone out?" Starbride asked.

He gave her a reproachful look. "If you wanted her to stay behind, you should have just told her."

"Are you volunteering, Hugo? Order her to stay behind and see how it works."

"She's going to be angry."

"Let me handle her. The fewer people with us that can be hypnotized, the better."

"Until I figure out this pyramid, we'll have to risk it," Master Bernard said. "After all, we need your skill with a blade, Lord Hugo."

Hugo stood a little taller. "The academy should be empty, right? All the pyradistés are either hiding, with us…or they're dead."

Master Bernard closed his eyes, clearly pained by the loss of his students.

Starbride rushed ahead. "An empty building doesn't stay empty for long in Marienne." They were words right out of Freddie's mouth, and she almost laughed. "We should be prepared for townspeople who won't want their new home invaded as well as whatever surprises the Fiend king's left for us."

"And on the lookout for any stray crystal," Master Bernard said.

"Wouldn't he have stripped it out already?" Hugo asked.

"We didn't leave it out for anyone to find. Even former students wouldn't know all the secret caches. They'd have to tear the place apart."

Starbride had her doubts. Corpse Fiends didn't need to rest, and they were strong. Tearing a building down wouldn't be a great chore for them. "The sooner we get this done, the better."

She and Master Bernard already wore pyramids that would hide them from Fiendish senses, so they filled their satchels with whatever else they might need, including pyramids that might repel a Fiend and those that would negate magical traps or alarms. If Roland hadn't found all that the academy had to offer, he might have triggered the rest to explode if any pyradistés came sniffing around.

Pennynail joined them as they crept from their basement hideout. He'd told her earlier that if their group was spotted by a patrol of corpse Fiends or mind-warped townspeople, he would lead them away while Starbride continued the mission. She hated that they might have to split, that Pennynail would have to face such danger alone, but he was well used to it. Katya would have trusted him without fear.

As if she'd opened a door, more doubts reared in Starbride's mind. She didn't have to do all these dangerous tasks. She could sneak out of the city, if such a path even existed anymore, and make her way into the country, maybe all the way to Allusia. If Katya was trapped somewhere in Marienne, Starbride could gather allies and return to rescue her. Roland must have been planning something big if he was trotting out a fake Katya and Einrich for the public. Maybe if the people were more relaxed or confused, they'd be easier to control? She didn't know, but she wished for the hundredth time that it wasn't her problem.

But Katya was worth the danger. Starbride imagined Katya's arms around her again, tried to conjure the smell of Katya's hair as they lay together.

Starbride lengthened her stride, renewed with purpose. Katya was depending on her. She wouldn't fail. She took comfort in the fact that her role and Roland's had been reversed. Now he was the one in charge, snug and secure in the palace, and she was outside trying to put all his careful plans to shambles. He would find holding the palace harder than taking it. Enough mischief would distract him from his goals, whatever they were.

The grounds surrounding the Pyradisté Academy and the Halls of Law were filled with shadows. The great pyramid's slanted sides were dark. The dormitories, however, stood alight with candles and lanterns. Even with the students scattered, the space hadn't gone to waste. Starbride didn't know what had happened to the law students, if they were still in residence. Her friends from Allusia should have arrived to start the winter term, but Starbride had heard nothing of them. Starbride hoped they hadn't begun their journey at all, or that some incident on the road had stopped them long before they reached Marienne. Then word of Marienne's troubles could have overtaken them, and they would have gone home.

One by one, Starbride, Master Bernard, Hugo, and Pennynail sneaked across the square that separated the great pyramid from the buildings around it. A sign hung across the pyramid's door, a neatly printed wooden plank that warned residents to keep out, the letters easy to read even in the meager light from the moon and the streetlamps lining the road.

Starbride pulled a pyramid while the others kept watch. She focused, and the dim landscape faded to black and white. She scanned for the telltale glow of guardian pyramids with magically augmented sight. "Two above the door," she said. She fell out of her trance. "Embedded in the jamb."

"There were two guarding it before," Master Bernard said. "They were tuned to catch anyone with violent intent toward the building or its occupants, but the Fiend king could have replaced them. If you cancel them, you'll get the attention of any pyradistés lurking in the building."

Starbride glanced up at the darkened structure. Anyone hiding within would probably welcome meeting a fellow pyradisté who wasn't trying to kill them. "It's a risk we'll have to take. You lead. I'll keep a detection pyramid active and look for any other surprises."

Master Bernard nodded. "I'll hold a light pyramid. We'll move quickly."

Starbride cancelled the two guardian pyramids, Pennynail picked the lock, and they raced inside. Starbride almost wept when she saw the ground floor. The little garden had been smashed, the limbs of dead plants scattered across the floor. The large light pyramid that had caught the sunlight from above lay in glittering pieces. Furniture sat in sad, splintered hulks around the room.

As Hugo kept a guiding touch on her arm, Starbride disabled another guardian pyramid on the stairs before they ventured upward. In the trance, her steps weren't as sure as they'd normally be. Near the first floor, she recoiled from a horrible stench, nearly jerking out of Hugo's grasp. A body lay at the top of the staircase in a pool of dried blood. When they neared, a cloud of flies billowed upward. Starbride clamped her mouth tight and hurried on, forcing herself to fall back into her pyramid.

Master Bernard rubbed his chin and frowned at the wreckage in his office. He pushed away the remains of his desk until he found a floorboard that had been torn away. "Well, that was the easiest cache to find. This way."

Starbride couldn't shake the feeling that they were being tracked, that the shadows themselves were watching. Silent killers might be rushing toward them. She hadn't spotted another guardian or alarm since the stairs, but if the pyradisté who'd made the three was nearby, he'd know they tampered with his work.

Master Bernard checked seven more crystal caches. Two had been plundered, but the rest were intact. Starbride and the others packed satchels, pockets, and bags with unworked crystal and tools. The great pyramid itself was just stone and glass. There was no way Roland could use it for magic, but the capstone was another story. Master Bernard led them up a hidden staircase to where the stone ended. They would have to open a trapdoor and climb outside to reach the capstone itself. Luckily, the thin metal staircase—invisible from the street—that led upward was intact.

"It's the last act a graduating pyradisté has to make," Master Bernard said as he opened the trapdoor. "He or she has to polish the capstone."

"Then the Fiend king knows about it," Starbride murmured. She took a deep breath and poked her head out into the night, suddenly glad she couldn't see down the steep sides to the ground far below. She checked the staircase for traps but found none. Roland must have assumed the others would be enough.

That or he didn't find this whole endeavor worth the effort. Maybe they'd just wasted their time with her ideas about the capstone. She shook her head and tried to dispel such doubts. She stepped out onto the metal stairs, trying hard not to think about plummeting to her death.

"Hurry," Hugo whispered. Starbride leaned toward the pyramid as the stairs circled it to the top. The wind tugged at her hair, and she couldn't help but imagine the gusts plucking her off the edge and sending her into the abyss.

At the top, she gripped Hugo's arm and fell into her detection pyramid once more.

The capstone wasn't active, but this close, she sensed its potential. She focused harder to detect what it could do. It was a light pyramid, an incredibly complex one, intricately faceted inside and smooth on the surface. Its facets were perfectly symmetrical, and this close, she could see that the corners were edged with gold. It was a masterwork, one that had probably taken several pyradistés working in harmony, but it took only one person to operate, and it could change color, as she'd often seen.

But could Roland retune it? Starbride had to focus on what type of pyramid she wanted when she crafted one. She'd never tried to change the purpose after it was finished.

"It's going to take a lot to destroy it," Hugo said.

Starbride winced.

"Are you insane?" Master Bernard cried. Starbride grabbed his uninjured arm to keep him from flailing around. "It's a masterpiece!"

Starbride wasn't sure they even *could* destroy it, it was so thick, but she didn't want to be the one to tell Master Bernard that they might have to. She touched the capstone and fell into it, delighting in its intricate pathways. It *was* a masterpiece, in more ways than one, and it could be used by any pyradisté; that was the problem.

"Fall into it with me, please, Bernard," she said.

When he joined her, she was tickled by his presence within the pyramid. She'd only encountered such a joining twice before, with Crowe when they'd been using the capstone beneath the palace to keep Yanchasa placated. This capstone didn't have the same foul Fiend energy. Together, she and Master Bernard could make it gleam like a dozen suns.

"Can you feel my mind?" she asked.

"Of course." She could almost feel his amusement. "Never had much of a chance to work a pyramid with another, eh?"

His presence gave her an idea. "Maybe that's it. If we can…leave our imprint on this, somehow, so that it takes both of us to work it… could we lock it?"

He was silent for a moment. She could feel him, reach for him. She couldn't read his mind like she could with a mind pyramid on a non-pyradisté. Maybe this was the only way to touch another pyradisté's thoughts. Even then, she couldn't intrude, could only touch. Starbride pulled her mind toward Master Bernard's, and he in turn pulled toward hers.

"I have an idea." Beside her in the dark, he pressed a pyramid into her hand. "Here, a mind pyramid. I've got one, too. Try and fall into it, but don't leave the capstone behind. Try and focus on both."

Two pyramids at once? She'd never done such a thing, but just falling into a mind pyramid didn't require as much focus as trying to use it on someone. Still, she couldn't help but lose her focus with the capstone. Starbride took a deep breath and tried again, first the capstone, then the mind pyramid, but it wouldn't work.

"Try doing both at once," Master Bernard said once, his soothing voice reminding her of Crowe.

The intricacies of the capstone actually helped her fall into the mind pyramid, and she slipped into both like sliding into warm water.

Master Bernard waited for her there. She felt his arm brush hers, and then the mind pyramids touched. A high-pitched whine built in Starbride's ears, and she could sense Master Bernard stronger than before. She still couldn't read his thoughts, but she could sense his emotions, his elation at discovering something new. "I've played around with mind pyramids before," he said, and she could almost hear a whispering echo from his thoughts. "In my school days, but this… It must be the capstone helping us somehow. It's incredible!"

Starbride felt his embarrassment as well as a lingering memory of youthful lust, and she guessed that "playing around" with mind pyramids must have been to heighten pleasure. She laughed out loud, her affection for him growing. "Thank you for sharing."

"Watch."

He dipped into her mind pyramid to pull himself further into the light capstone, using the two mind pyramids as a slingshot. He wove his thoughts into the capstone, leaving a lingering memory of him wherever he touched it. He was so deft, almost effortless, and she knew he wasn't the master of the Pyradisté Academy just because he was good with paperwork.

"Amazing," she breathed, and she felt his pride.

"Now you."

Starbride's first attempt was a rampage, careening into Master Bernard's mind pyramid and giving herself a headache.

"Softly," Bernard said. "Sneak up on it."

She pictured her mind on tiptoes, creeping up on his pyramid, and she felt a brief fracture in her head, as if she was standing in two places at once. The vertigo almost made her sag.

Master Bernard's mind pathways on the capstone were like tributaries on a map. She followed them, and felt them infused with not only him but her, and where she went, she left part of herself, but it didn't feel as strong as what he'd done.

"Think of a specific memory," he said. "That way, whoever uses this pyramid will have to have our memories while they use it. And since no one can take our memories…"

Starbride smiled. Wanting to thumb her nose at Roland, she thought of Katya standing on the balcony the night of the Courtiers Ball, her brilliant clothes, her shining jewels, and best of all, her smile, her laugh, the tingle in Starbride's belly.

With a sigh, Starbride withdrew, determined more than ever to get Katya back, even if she had to tear the palace down.

When they were both out of the pyramid, Starbride tried to fall into it again but found it slippery, its intricate pathways blocked.

In the dim light from the moon, Master Bernard said, "You won't get in without me, a mind pyramid, and that memory."

Starbride smiled in satisfaction. "Let's see the Fiend king break through that."

CHAPTER NINE

KATYA

Dayscout accompanied Katya and her father into the wilderness. Katya hadn't had to try hard to convince her mother to stay in Newhope with the children and Lord Vincent Brutal, Castelle, and her friends were enough to escort them into the hills to find the adsnazi.

Katya had hoped her father would stay behind, too, but she knew he was tired of hiding.

"If you went alone, my girl," he said, "the adsnazi might send you back to collect who's really in charge."

She supposed she should have thanked him for saving her a trip, but she'd feared how much sarcasm would creep into her voice. Meeting with Starbride's parents had turned her mood blacker than usual.

The adsnazi lived in adobe houses near a wide river that flowed through the hills outside of Newhope. Scrubby green brush and cacti sprouted from sandy patches between large red boulders. A cliff side rose just behind the river, though the bank sloped gently down on the village side. It was a good, defensible position. Enemies could only come at them from the track Katya and her father followed. If anyone tried to leave the trail, they'd trip over piles of scree, barren rocks, and the needle-like thorns of the cacti.

A woman and a man waited on the track before them. More people bustled among the dwellings, but they paid the visitors as much attention as they would a lizard. The waiting pair wore simple brown trousers, though their shirts were a riot of swirling colors, his mostly greens and browns, hers reds and blues. They had shaved heads but for one braided lock in the back. The man smiled, a bit sarcastically to Katya's eye, and the woman scowled.

Dayscout dismounted and clasped their hands. The woman gave him a slight smile, as if she was unused to smiling in general. As Katya dismounted and came close, she saw that the man was maybe Da's age, but the lines near his eyes contrasted with his smooth cheeks. The woman was young and pretty, though her features were sharper than Katya usually cared for. Even with her reddish-brown skin and black hair, she didn't remind Katya of Starbride in the least.

Da nodded as Dayscout said, "This is Einrich Nar Umbriel."

The man's mouth twisted to the side. "Who else would he be? He does stand out."

"Thank you for meeting with us," Da said.

"I am Leafclever, and this is my assistant, Redtrue."

Katya and the others bowed slightly.

"Dayscout tells us a daughter of Newhope is lost in your war," Redtrue said.

Katya glanced at Leafclever, expecting him to censure his assistant for speaking out of turn, but he only watched.

"We're going to get her back," Katya said.

"Words are water," Redtrue said, "only as firm as the container that holds them."

"Horsestrong?" Katya asked.

Leafclever smiled wider. "I'm glad you know his name. You're going to need his wisdom in order to succeed here."

"Succeed?" Da asked.

"In convincing us to help you," Leafclever said. "Or did you think we could heal your hurts with a blink of our magic?"

Da smiled. "Negotiation has always been one of my strong points."

"We don't need healing," Katya added. "We need strength."

"Ah," Leafclever said, "well, we'll see what we can do." He gestured for them to follow him toward the adobe houses.

Redtrue walked at Katya's side, scowling at all of them in turn.

"Problem?" Katya asked.

"We're letting our conquerors walk into our home. What could be the problem?"

"You don't look conquered," Brutal said from Katya's other side.

"You used words instead of whips, so what?"

"For someone with such a chip on her shoulder, you speak Farradain very well," Katya said.

Redtrue frowned. "Chip?"

"A grudge."

"We're required to learn your language in our schools. What does that tell you?"

"That your teachers wanted you to be able to speak to your neighbors," Katya said.

"Ah, so you know Allusian? To talk to your neighbors?" She said a few rapid words.

Katya took another deep breath, glad that Redtrue was only the assistant. "I'm sorry, no."

"I bet you're very good at dancing, though? Or wearing jewels?"

"Am I wearing jewels? I'm certainly not dancing."

Redtrue shook her head. "Maybe it will do you good to cast off luxury."

Katya slowed to a stop, memories of all she'd lost strong in her head: Reinholt, Crowe, her grandmother, Averie. And maybe even Starbride, who was more important to her than breath. "If I were you, I wouldn't remind me of all I've lost. When is the last time someone you loved died?"

Redtrue turned away. Katya sped up to stay behind her father as he entered Leafclever's house.

They spent an hour telling Leafclever about Roland and their troubles. Like Dayscout, he didn't say much, just watched and listened. Halfway through the tale, Redtrue made a disgusted noise and left. Katya nodded at Castelle, and she followed Redtrue out. If anyone was going to raise a force to roust them, they needed to know ahead of time.

Katya turned to find Leafclever watching her. "You need not worry for your safety here," he said. "She simply doesn't like the perversion of the *adsna*."

"The adsna?" Katya asked.

He put his fingers together in a triangle. "The magic which flows through us and into the pyramid."

Brutal frowned. "I thought the pyramid did the work, and you pyradistés were just the users."

"I know that you think so."

Katya wanted to roll her eyes but stopped herself. "I'm sorry, Leafclever, but I don't like enigmatic at the best of times."

"So I guessed." When they continued to blink at him, he shrugged. "I'm sorry if it puzzles you. It's as natural as breathing to me and just as hard to explain to someone who's never done it. Perhaps you should ask Redtrue. She needs to learn patience."

Patience was the last thing Katya had to teach, but Da gave her a look over one shoulder, and she knew her usefulness in the house was done. Two of Castelle's friends went with her, leaving Brutal and the last two to guard Da.

She stopped halfway to Castelle and Redtrue, just close enough to hear what they were saying.

"And what do Farradains know of love?" Redtrue asked.

Castelle's well-practiced leer didn't slip an inch. "I'd be happy to show you."

"You're confident. I'll give you that."

"I never disappoint."

Redtrue lifted her chin, and Katya expected her to attempt to tear Castelle down, but she said, "Fine. That small house over there is mine. One hour after moonrise. Be prompt."

Castelle blinked before she bowed. "Happy to be of service."

Redtrue only snorted before turning toward Katya. "Did Leafclever send you?"

"Um, yes. He said that if I wanted to know more about perversion of the adsna, I should ask you." Before Redtrue could trot out her disdain again, Katya added, "He also said you need to learn patience."

She shut her mouth with an audible snap. "Fine." She crossed to a log near a small fire pit and sat. Katya sat across from her, glad of the heat in the afternoon chill. Castelle took a seat a little farther away, where she could watch the rest of the village.

"Tell me what you know of pyramid magic," Redtrue said.

Katya repressed a smile. That was how Crowe started lessons as well. Trouble was, what she knew and what the Allusians knew might not be the same. "I admit total ignorance."

"That's a good place to start. Only a few contain the ability to perceive the adsna, the life force of the world, and we few can make this force manifest through the *fana-zi*, the…world children, I suppose is how you would say it. We adsnazi shape the *fana-zi* into pyramid shapes because that is the best shape for channeling the adsna.

"The early peoples used the adsna to destroy, to covet, to warp one another." She glared at Katya again. "Your people use it for this purpose still, but the adsna is not a weapon. The reason your people were so easily overthrown is because they perverted the adsna to these purposes."

Katya flushed. "The Fiend—"

"I heard your father speak of him. Where do you think Fiends come from? They were made by the early peoples, from their perversion of the adsna. Fiends are the twisted offspring of the *fana-zi* and the minds of the early peoples."

Katya frowned harder. She'd never heard of such a thing. She'd always thought the Fiends were as natural as humans or animals, just another sort of creature. "How do you know this?"

"I read books."

The statement was so reminiscent of Starbride that Katya laughed out loud. "I'm sorry. You just reminded me… Never mind. Go on."

"Twisted adsna in the grip of a twisted creature? I'm sure they're like hand in glove. It's amazing this didn't happen to your people before." Her eyes narrowed. "Unless it already has. I sensed the necklace your father wears. What does it do?"

Katya's insides went cold. "Now why would you want to know that?"

"The easiest way to keep the Fiends from ruining the kingdom they helped you, their creators, make would be to take them to your bosom. Is your family already corrupted, and this usurper more corrupted than most?" She waved the words away. "Don't tell me. I'd rather not know. But mark my words, these events will happen again as long as the perversion of the adsna continues."

"Starbride told me about the adsnazi light shows." But Katya was beginning to think they knew much more.

"A reflection of the world's natural light. The adsna flows with the world's power; we don't subject it to our will."

Katya wasn't going to accept that explanation on one person's say-so. But there was no Crowe to verify what Redtrue said. She tried to blame the Farradains for evil, pyradistés and others alike. Katya's forebears had absorbed Yanchasa's essence for the kingdom's well-being, and Crowe had never acted with evil intentions.

"You doubt me." Redtrue leaned back and heaved a huge sigh. "I work with the adsna. I feel it in a way you never can, and yet you doubt me."

"Well, I don't know you from anyone else in Allusia. And Starbride was learning how to be a pyradisté when I…left. There's never been a person as far from evil deeds as Starbride."

Redtrue's mouth twisted. "One of our own training to be a pyradisté, something Allusia never hoped to hear. We are only adsnazi, and we do not force it upon ourselves. Only those who come to us, seeking the adsna, join our ranks. When you find her, if you find her, you should encourage her to come here."

"She'll do as she wishes."

Redtrue shrugged. "I cringe at the idea of her learning perverted ways."

Katya couldn't contain a smirk. Out of the corner of her eye, she caught Castelle doing the same, though Redtrue didn't seem to notice.

"So," Castelle said, "can you do anything with your fabled powers besides making pretty lights?"

Redtrue sneered. "Your skepticism does you no credit."

"Nor does yours," Katya said.

"Mine is permitted, is it not? Speaking to my conquerors as I am?"

"If you were conquered," Katya said, "then we wouldn't be asking for your help. We'd already have it."

"As I've said before, you conquered us with money and trade instead of weapons. What does that mean?"

"It means most of you aren't dead," Katya said.

For a moment, Redtrue held Katya's eyes, one of her fists clenching and unclenching as if she desired to draw one of her pyramids and use some of that perverted power. "We are not powerless."

"I know that." Katya leaned forward. "That's why we're here, to ask for your help. Maybe you're right; maybe we brought this on ourselves. If our people work together—"

"You seek us as your teachers? Don't make me laugh. You'd no sooner learn from savages like us than you would sprout wings and fly. You want only the strength of our arms and backs."

"Well, if money and trade are your problems, we can always arrange something in that arena. If your people want more fortuitous trading laws or monetary compensation, you can negotiate with my father."

Redtrue crossed her arms. "If we want you gone from our lands, we have only to refuse you now."

"Oh no," Katya said, feeling an evil smile cross her face. "You could chase us out, sure, but *he'll* come for you eventually, with all the perverted magic in his arsenal. The power he finds in Farraday won't be enough for him. He'll want more, and he'll need the crystal in your mountains to get it. Your only hope is our only hope, to strike before his feet are firm upon the ground."

Redtrue held Katya's eyes for a moment before she looked away, but her face had gone from haughty skepticism to angry thoughtfulness. It was a step in the right direction.

CHAPTER TEN

STARBRIDE

After Roland's minions had found the pyradistés in the warehouse district, they'd done a sweep of the area. When Freddie told Starbride about it, she had to clamp her teeth together to fight off nausea. "How many did he get?" she asked in her small room beneath the shop.

"I don't know," Freddie said. "Some good can come of this, though. We're bursting at the seams here. And if Roland thinks he's cleared the warehouses, we have a good place to move to."

It was getting harder and harder to keep their large group quiet. Many of the people hiding with them weren't pyradistés or refugees from the palace. Some simply feared Roland so much they wanted to hide, especially if their friends or family had contracted Fiend king fever, a nickname for anyone who'd had their minds warped.

"You have a particular spot in mind?" Starbride asked.

"A few, one with a very large basement. My father and I knew them well." His gaze went far away before he blinked whatever he was thinking away.

Starbride wished she had some comforting words for him; they were all in need of comforting words. "You think you could convince the owner of this very large basement to help us?"

"I'll appeal to his sense of community generosity. If that doesn't work, I'll threaten to tell his daughters they have two half-siblings. He needs their cash to stay afloat."

Starbride had to laugh. "I don't know who to feel sorry for."

❖

The warehouse's owner agreed to help them if some of their party would work for him during the day, loading crates. Many agreed, if only for something to do while they waited. Waited for what, Starbride didn't know, maybe for her to make Roland disappear. If only she could. At least the coin they earned would help feed everyone.

They moved their headquarters slowly, working day and night to move everyone and everything without arousing suspicion. The enormous basement below the warehouse had already been divided into rooms for storage so they didn't have to live on top of one another.

"I just got word that Roland visited the Pyradisté Academy," Freddie said as Starbride was setting up her crafting table. "Maybe he finally got around to checking his alarms."

"Did he look angry?"

Freddie smirked. "I'd like to think so, but my contact didn't get that close. He did report that the Fiend king left very quickly after arrival."

Starbride leaned back in her chair, glad they were able to foil Roland a little bit. Katya would have been happy to hear it. And Freddie finally seemed resolved to stay in Marienne. He hadn't fought with her to leave in at least a week. "Why are you staying, Freddie?"

"In the city?" He sank down on his haunches instead of on Starbride's narrow cot. "I owe Katya and her family a lot. After everything that happened in Dockland, my life was over. At first, I worked just with my da. I didn't have much to do with Roland, but after Katya took over, she made me…a part of something bigger than…me." He chuckled and stood again. "It sounds so awfully old-fashioned, but once I had a taste of it, I couldn't go back."

Starbride grinned. "So it's not because you're in love with her or anything?"

He burst out laughing and then rubbed his throat as if it hurt him. "She's great-looking, don't get me wrong, and I'll admit to a hero crush, but she'd never look at me twice. That puts a bit of a damper on romance. I do have a weakness for blonds, though. I guess we share that, eh?"

Starbride blushed as she chuckled. "She's my whole world." She felt tears come to her eyes and dashed them away.

Freddie patted her shoulder. "We'll find her, Starbride. I stay for you, too, you know. You're my friend, and I'll fight at your side until I can't fight any longer."

She patted his hand and nodded. "Thank you."

"Until I can't fight any longer just means until I get really tired."

She prodded him with one foot. "Hugo isn't blond. Didn't you say he caught your eye?"

"Like I said, ten years ago, maybe. That was when I was into young, naive, and trusting."

"And now you want wise, hardened, and skeptical? Captain Ursula is blond."

"The woman who hanged me. Nice."

"You told me once that she knew you weren't the Butcher."

He tilted his head back and forth. "She helped me find out who it was before I...died."

Starbride sat forward. "And you got close?"

"Can't you leave any secrets alone?"

"No! You left the door open."

Freddie leaned against the wall. "Well, if I'm going to leave the door open, I guess I can't blame you for barging in and taking everything that isn't nailed down. You'd have made a good thief. I don't think Ursula would appreciate me telling the story. She thinks I'm dead, remember? Everyone does. And if you happen to drop a hint to her that you know something about the murders..."

"I'm in the habit of collecting secrets, not dispensing them. The only person I might tell is Dawnmother, and I tell her everything anyway."

Before he could respond, a knock sounded on Starbride's door. Freddie pulled his mask back on quickly, even before Starbride could say, "Who is it?"

"Hugo, Miss Starbride."

After she'd called him in, Freddie slipped the mask on top of his head. Hugo scowled at him.

"Are you all right, Miss Starbride?" Hugo asked.

"Of course I am, Hugo. Freddie wouldn't hurt me."

Hugo continued to scowl, unable, it seemed, to get the picture of the Dockland Butcher out of his mind.

Freddie stepped close to him. "Even if I wanted to hurt her, what could you do about it, boy?"

Hugo snarled and put one hand on his rapier. Starbride sighed loudly. If Dawnmother were there, she'd have told them to measure their manhoods and get it over with. She picked up a pyramid again, determined to get back to work if they insisted on acting foolish.

As if summoned by the thought, Dawnmother stepped into the room. When Hugo turned to look at her, Freddie pinched him on the rump. He jumped as if bitten by a snake.

"You…" Hugo took a deep breath, shoulders shaking, face red. "Keep your hands to yourself." He managed to snarl and look affronted at the same time.

"How can I?" Freddie asked. "When you make it so tempting?"

Dawnmother pushed past them. "Star, do you want me to shoo them away?"

"Not just yet. Was there something you wanted, Hugo?"

With another frown, he stepped around Freddie while keeping his back to Starbride. "I was going to the market with some of the others and wanted to know if you needed anything."

"You shouldn't be going to the market," Dawnmother said before Starbride had a chance. "You're too valuable."

Hugo smiled shyly. "Thank you, Dawnmother."

She waved the thanks away. "Your Fiend would be too valuable to Roland."

"Oh," he said, looking at the floor.

"I'll go," Dawnmother said.

"Wouldn't you stand out, too?" Hugo asked.

"A servant's footsteps are made of shadows. I know how to get around without being noticed."

Starbride laughed. "Oh, yes, we four are made to go unnoticed: two Allusians, one lord bearing a Fiend, and an infamous criminal. Maybe we should recruit more average Farradains?"

"That would look fabulous on a poster," Freddie said. "Wanted: completely average people with nothing special about them whatsoever. No pay! Long hours!"

"Dangerous conditions!" Dawnmother said. "Must not be afraid of Fiends!"

"We'd have a line going out the door," Starbride said.

Hugo sighed loudly, as if he found their mirth inappropriate. "My…the Fiend king himself would have to be at the market to sense my necklace, and the corpse Fiends don't seem to notice my buried Aspect. I shall be perfectly fine."

"No one's doubting your abilities, Hugo," Starbride said.

He beamed at her. Behind him, Freddie rolled his eyes.

Starbride gave him a warning look. She wouldn't let teasing turn to bullying. "Both you and Dawnmother should go. She can help you sneak, and you can fight if things turn ugly." She dug in her table's one drawer, turned over the few coins she found to Dawnmother, and wished she had another way *she* could supplement their income. No one was hiring pyradistés.

"You know," Dawnmother said, "there's money to be found in the palace. I could sneak inside and fetch some."

"You couldn't go without a pyradisté, Dawn. If Roland's retuned the pyramids in the royal wing to only recognize him, you'd be incinerated."

"He's had a lot to deal with," Dawnmother said. "He may not have gotten to that."

Starbride only frowned. Only a fool would leave sections of the palace tuned to his enemies.

Freddie rubbed his chin. "We need a plan, like in the old days. We need to get Roland out of the palace so we can go in."

Starbride had a sudden flash of the fake Katya and Einrich. A smile started over her lips, and she felt some of the hunger for adventure she thought she'd left behind. "Like a fake king and princess?"

They stared at her.

"If he can fool the populace," she said, "why can't we? The more people who believe him, the easier it is to get into their minds and hold them. He showed the people Katya and Einrich arm in arm with him. What if we show the same people screeching for rebellion in the market square?"

"He might come running," Freddie said. "But what suicidal duo are we going to get to play the fake king and princess? You'll need everyone in this room to help you sneak into the palace."

"Oh, I'm sure we can find some willing recruits. They might have to be *convinced* into willingness, but Captain Ursula and Sergeant Rhys have been itching for more to do."

In Starbride's small room under the warehouse, Ursula stared at the wall as Starbride outlined her plan. "And what would we get out of you getting into the palace, Princess Consort?"

"Depends on how long we have inside," Starbride said. She still had Hugo and Dawnmother with her, but Freddie had become Pennynail again. She wondered if it was hard for him to be so near to someone he'd been close to, maybe even intimate with.

"If the royal quarters haven't been ransacked," Starbride said, "we can take money and jewelry. If Crowe's office is still intact, we can take his pyramids and books, though that's probably the first place the Fiend king cleared out. He wouldn't want the rabble exploring the royal quarters, so he's probably closed them, either by leaving the defense pyramids up or making his own. He might have retuned some of the outer ones and then left the inner as they are."

"He probably doesn't care about jewelry and such." Rhys leaned against the wall near Pennynail, looking as bored as always. "He doesn't need to sell it, and he wouldn't care about wearing it, except the king's crown, maybe."

"Which leaves the rest of it untouched. Maybe." Ursula dragged her fingers through her hair. "Maybe, maybe, maybe." She glanced at Starbride. "I'm glad you were used to playing the part of the sneak before this all started. It's not something I'm used to."

"The sooner we succeed," Starbride said, "the sooner you can stop."

"If we can't get the jewels," Dawnmother said, "there's always the silver and plate lying around."

"Now you sound like a common criminal," Ursula said.

Dawnmother grinned. "That's what we hope to look like. The more common we appear, the less the Fiend king will know what has happened until it's too late."

"Even if we don't find any money," Starbride said, "we might be able to do something about the capstone under the palace, like we planned in the beginning. We could lock it like we did the one on top of the academy."

"This trip sounds longer and longer," Ursula said.

"We'll do what we have time for," Starbride said.

"And you want me and Rhys to be these fake royals that the Fiend king will come after?"

"If not you, perhaps you'd know some volunteers…"

Ursula shook her head. "I wouldn't let any of my officers volunteer for this bat-shit operation if I wasn't willing to take it on myself. Besides, if it's me and Rhys wearing the disguises, then we can take them off before we're caught and act like we're joining the hunt."

Starbride grinned. "I can make you a couple of surprises, just in case the Fiend king does catch you."

Rhys lifted an eyebrow. "Wouldn't that make us easier to detect? The Fiend king can sense pyramids, yes?"

"If he gets close enough to sense it, he'll be close enough to take its full effects right in the face."

"Sounds peachy," Ursula said. "When do we put this whole thing together?"

They agreed to meet in two days' time; that would give Starbride and the other pyradistés time to make pyramids. Starbride didn't mention to anyone the other task she hoped to accomplish while in the palace: searching for Katya and the rest of the royals. She was certain her closest companions knew it. Maybe Ursula even suspected it. It didn't change the fact that the dungeons were going to be her first stop.

CHAPTER ELEVEN

KATYA

Leafclever had a lot to discuss with Einrich, leaving Katya in Redtrue's company. They both had questions for each other, about Allusia and about Farraday. As contemptuous as Redtrue was about her neighbors to the west, she was equally curious, if only to mock.

Katya was more amused by the interaction between Redtrue and Castelle. It seemed they'd kept their rendezvous the first night in the adsnazi camp, but the next morning, when Castelle tried to sidle close and give Redtrue a kiss, Redtrue sidestepped. Katya had watched them out of the corner of her eye.

"What's wrong?" Castelle had asked.

"It was only a tumble," Redtrue had said. "Don't make it into a grand romance."

Castelle had blinked and stammered. Katya had resisted the urge to smirk, wondering how many times Castelle had gotten out of romantic entanglements in a similar fashion, if with a jot more panache.

Redtrue grilled Katya on what Farradain pyradistés could do, and Katya outlined everything she'd seen, though she'd had to remind Redtrue that she had no idea how pyramid magic worked.

Redtrue waved this away. "I don't expect you to. But all this *playing* around in a person's head? Lighting someone on fire? The Fiends were born of such things."

Brutal joined them while they were having breakfast and caught her last words. "Wouldn't the Fiends be born of cold instead of fire?"

Redtrue gave him a withering look. "The medium doesn't matter. It's this mind-tampering evil you should blame."

"The usurper is very good at that," Katya said.

"I'm not surprised. An adsnazi will only touch another's mind during the dream walk."

Katya glanced at Brutal. "I've never heard of the dream walk," Katya said.

"Your pyradistés riffle in the minds of others and never visit their dreams?" Redtrue stared at them as if they'd gone insane. "You expect me to believe that?"

"I've seen a pyradisté go through another's memories and hypnotize someone, but dream stuff is new to me," Brutal said. "You use a pyramid on someone while they're asleep?"

"We do not *use* a pyramid on anyone, whether they are asleep or not!"

Brutal lifted his hands. "My apologies, sister. For once, I'm not trying to start a fight."

Her mouth twisted in wry amusement. Some of the adsnazi were very amused by Brutal, someone who used combat to try to understand the universe. Some found the idea of good-natured brawling appealing. Brutal had been happy to demonstrate.

"We use dreams to communicate between great distances," Redtrue said.

The hairs on Katya's neck stood up. "For the days that we've been here, you could have spoken with Starbride, and you didn't tell me?"

Redtrue blinked a few times before she scowled. "I...well, if what you say about pyradistés is true, your Starbride does not know how to dream walk."

Katya let out a slow breath. "Is there even a chance?"

"If she learned from someone, certainly. Would you like me to ride to Marienne and teach her?"

Katya felt her anger growing. Brutal touched her shoulder. "If you possess any compassion, sister," he said to Redtrue, "please put this particular sarcasm away."

"I don't mean to mock your pain, but you have no reason to be angry with me. I suspected your Starbride didn't know dream magic because of how much of a novice she was when you left Marienne. I didn't know your people don't practice it at all."

"We have a pyradisté with us, in Newhope."

"We know. We just didn't want him here. It is a him, no?"

"Yes," Katya said, "though I suppose from your way of thinking, he's as perverted as the rest of us."

Redtrue cracked a tiny smile. "That is so."

"That doesn't mean you couldn't teach him to be less of a pervert," Brutal said.

That time, Redtrue even laughed. "That would be up to Leafclever. We never send for anyone. Those who desire to practice our ways seek us out. Who knows, maybe your friend will be drawn to us."

"Have you ever tried to touch the dreams of a pyradisté?" Katya asked. "Or do you only touch the dreams of other adsnazi?"

"I wouldn't know how to touch a pyradisté's dreams."

"What about contacting an adsnazi who hasn't learned the dream walk yet?" Castelle asked. She stared at Redtrue with hard eyes, but it seemed her curiosity had overcome her anger. "Is that possible?"

"I…I don't know. We usually start someone on the path of dream walking by having them touch the dreams of an adsnazi with experience, and then they learn to receive dreams the same way, by someone more experienced."

Hope bloomed in Katya's chest. "It would probably take someone with great experience, but he or she could reach out to a novice."

"That would be forcing the adsna on another, and we won't do that."

Katya clenched a fist. "It wouldn't be unwelcome! She would want to hear from me!"

"Even so, it's the beginning of a path we won't tread."

Katya forced herself to take several deep breaths. It was a path the adsnazi wouldn't tread, but Rene, their pyradisté, might. All they needed was for him to "find" his way to the adsnazi camp and be open to learning what they had to teach. But how to get him to come without sending for him? Katya suddenly wished for Pennynail. He could get away without anyone noticing he was gone.

Katya nodded as if acquiescing, but her mind was racing. She'd have to talk with Brutal and Castelle later, when they were on their own. Contacting Marienne from afar was too great a tool to waste. She continued answering Redtrue's questions and asking hers in turn, but she slipped into court mode, letting her body act as she needed while her mind focused on the task ahead.

Brutal touched her wrist, and she knew he sensed her need to slip away. He'd seen the court face too many times. He shifted on their log as if pained.

"What's wrong?" Redtrue asked.

"An old back injury. Acts up during a cold morning." He stood and stretched. "I think I'm going to take a walk, loosen it up a bit."

"Want some company?" Katya asked.

"Well, I didn't want to ask, but if it gives out like it did last winter…"

Katya snorted as she stood, playing along. "I had to drag him back to town through three feet of snow."

Redtrue grimaced. "Perhaps more of us should—"

"I don't want to disturb the whole camp," he said.

"Trust me," Katya said, "if he collapses, I'll shout."

"And I have more questions for you, Redtrue," Castelle said, and whether she was trying to help Katya or plead her own case, it didn't matter. Katya walked away with Brutal before Redtrue could respond.

"Thanks, Brutal."

"My pleasure. Now let's hear the plan you have spinning in your head."

"We need to find a way to bring Rene here."

"Ah, and when we do, he learns dream magic in order to reach Starbride? Do you really think trying to pull something on these people is the right way to go?"

"Brutal…" She searched for words for a moment, unable to believe he couldn't see her desperate need. "We could find out if she's…" She couldn't say it. "We could guide her to us…share info…"

"Ride off to rescue her?"

She gave him a black look. "We're going to do that anyway."

"Exactly my point. It's not worth pissing these people off."

"Not *worth* it?"

"You know what I mean. I'm sorry, Katya, truly I am, especially after I…left her, but guilt won't stop me from speaking sense. If you want to communicate with Starbride through dream magic, you'll have to find a way to get the adsnazi to do it. Remember, if they don't agree to help us, the other Allusians might leave us in the cold, too."

Before she could launch into a tirade against Redtrue, he said, "I know. Redtrue's pretty unreasonable, but the others might not see it her way. I'd try a heartfelt plea to Leafclever. He might not have such a grudge."

"Or such a big stick up his ass."

"Well, Farradains, especially the traders, haven't been good to Redtrue's people. I can see her point of view at times."

Katya rubbed her temples. "Stop making sense and just agree with me."

"Ah, you miss the courtiers already, huh?"

She shook her head, but she was too tired and heartsick to laugh.

Katya caught up with Leafclever that evening, when all the adsnazi gathered for the evening meal. She touched his shoulder before they joined the others. "I'd like to speak with you a moment."

"I've spoken to Redtrue already."

"Please don't ask me to save my breath. I have to speak my mind, or I'm going to explode."

He smiled, and it had a tint of affection that reminded her of Crowe. "Your people have a reputation, if not for lying, then for double-speak. I would be intrigued to hear an honest, impassioned plea."

Her first tendency was to be angry. Everyone she'd met in Allusia had a mocking quality, as if they regarded everything with half a smile. But then she thought of Starbride, who always found something to laugh at in every situation. Katya breathed a chuckle and wasn't surprised to hear a few unshed tears in it. "Well, then..."

She took a deep breath. "I...protect my family before anything else, before my own happiness, my own life, and the lives of everyone around me. When the usurper took Marienne, I got my family out, a task that should have been as second nature as breathing. But it was the hardest thing I've ever done.

"Starbride...turned me upside down." Katya looked hard into his eyes as if she could drill the truth into him. "I've never shirked my duty, but I was willing to throw it away to find her. I've lived in luxury all my life, and I'd keep a cave for her. I'd be her slave, and I love her even more because she'd never want me to. Her fate...weighs on me, Leafclever; it sits in my every thought, my every action, and though we need your help desperately, I was willing to betray your hospitality today in exchange for the *chance* of finding out if she lives."

Leafclever hadn't lost his enigmatic little smile, even when she'd admitted her attempted treachery. When she didn't speak for several seconds, he patted her shoulder. "I hear your words, and I believe them. I've also been in love, and I thought no one had ever loved like I did. If I may ask, what convinced you not to pursue this betrayal today?"

"My friend reminded me that even if I care about Starbride more than I care about my kingdom, I shouldn't work against my family toward getting that kingdom back."

"Wise." He stroked his chin. "Redtrue said it, but I'll repeat it: We don't force our power on anyone, no matter the good intentions."

Katya took a deep breath. "I don't want you to sacrifice your values, but there has to be some way to reach out to her, not to force your presence into her mind, but to…knock."

"Someone familiar with the dream walk might 'knock' upon the dreams of another, but the recipient must be familiar with the magic in order to answer."

"Couldn't she, I don't know, learn as you knock?"

"She wouldn't even know what's going on. Likely, she'd experience a vague presence within a dream. Unless the person sending the message actually invaded her dream, she wouldn't even know there was someone on the other end."

"Would invading her dream harm her?"

"That's not really the point, is it?"

Katya nodded, but her mind was already working. "You say you don't see how she could answer, but you don't actually know. What's the harm in trying? Someone very experienced in the dream walk might be able to make Starbride see the truth."

"Persistent," Leafclever said, his smile widening.

"I hunt traitors. I'm as tenacious as a hound when I get a scent in my nostrils."

"So I see. Well, as you say, there's no harm in trying. I'm curious to know if we can even contact someone as far away as Marienne. It will be hard to find one mind among so many on whose dreams we can knock. Wouldn't it be something if the only mind we could find in such a jumble is this usurper of yours?"

Katya shuddered. "If that happens, I suggest you walk away. Are you the best dream walker?"

"Rarely is someone a leader because he's best at anything but being a leader, as Horsestrong said. No, I'm afraid you need look no further than Redtrue."

"Fabulous," Katya said before she could stop herself.

He chuckled. "She can be hard to get along with, but I believe you'll be good for each other. After dinner, we'll discuss it."

When Katya and Leafclever approached Redtrue later, she was arguing softly with Castelle. Castelle put one finger under Redtrue's chin and tilted her face up. Katya was about to turn away, but Leafclever cleared his throat.

Redtrue jerked her head free. "What can I do for you, Leaf?"

"I need to speak with you a moment." He led her away a few steps.

Katya stepped closer to Castelle. "Trying to get her into your bed again?"

"Some have been known to find comfort there."

"Apparently not everyone."

"She'll come around."

Katya didn't think so, but she didn't mention it. Redtrue was getting heated during her quiet discussion with Leafclever, but since they spoke Allusian, Katya couldn't understand them. By the end of their conversation, she seemed resigned if still unhappy. Katya could live with unhappy; whatever got the job done.

"This is a waste of time," Redtrue said as they all joined one another.

Katya shook her head, for once not angry at all. "Love is never a waste of time."

"Horsestrong could not have said it better," Leafclever said.

Redtrue frowned, but she seemed too smart to argue.

"If you say you'll help me, I know you will," Katya said. "I sense that about you, and I'm rarely wrong about people."

Redtrue eyed Katya as if she didn't know what to say. Maybe she was revising her less than stellar opinion yet again. "We'll have to wait until it's been dark long enough for the denizens of Marienne to be asleep."

"Denizens? You make them all sound like Fiends," Castelle said.

Redtrue just gave her a haughty look.

"Do you need to be asleep as well?" Katya asked. "Is that a stupid question?"

"As Horsestrong said, we could not seek the truth if we did not question all that surrounds us," Leafclever said.

"No, I must be awake." Redtrue's gaze flicked toward Castelle. "And so I must find a way to stay awake until then."

Castelle's lips quirked up, and she studied the desert night.

"Can I be there?" Katya asked. When both Castelle and Redtrue gave her wide-eyed looks, Katya nearly laughed out loud. "When you try and reach Starbride?"

"You will see nothing besides me sitting there. Why would you want—"

Leafclever patted her shoulder. "You may be present." Redtrue stared at him in confusion. "Ah, my young friend, you've never been in love. Trust me. She's needs to be there."

Redtrue sighed but nodded. Katya was tempted to throw her arms around Leafclever and slap him on the back. "Thank you both." She walked away, her spirits lifting for the first time in days. It would work. It *had* to work. Maybe not the first time; there was no use in getting her hopes as high as they could go, but Redtrue would reach out and find someone. Every pyradisté in Marienne would be Roland's enemy. Redtrue would find someone who could then find Starbride and tell her about the dream magic and then...

Katya nearly held her breath. It felt so good to hope at last, to hope that even through a surrogate she would hear Starbride's voice again.

CHAPTER TWELVE

STARBRIDE

Starbride studied Captain Ursula and Lieutenant Rhys with their disguise pyramids active. She saw through the illusions, of course, but if she concentrated, she could almost see Katya and King Elnrich standing before her. She cupped her chin. "Not exactly perfect."

"Good enough, I'd say," Hugo said. "Uncanny, really."

"I wouldn't be fooled," Starbride said.

Ursula snorted. "I won't be taking my trousers off, so I won't have to fool you. These are good enough. We'll wear our cloaks to the marketplace, reveal ourselves, and stir up the crowd."

Starbride looked back and forth between them. "You'll both have to talk."

Rhys shrugged, his eyes more half-lidded than Einrich's ever were. "I can speak well when I want to, and if not, I'll let Cap do most of the talking." He stood up very straight, going for haughty, but he looked as sleepy as ever, and he was still a few inches too short.

Starbride sighed. Maybe the crowd would think Einrich was just a little slouchy…and drunk. "Here, this is a fire pyramid. It won't kill the corpse Fiends, but it should slow them down long enough for you to attack if you need to."

"And the Fiend king?"

"It might catch him off guard, but I recommend you stay out of his path. As soon as he's close, take the disguise pyramids off and throw them somewhere."

Ursula nodded. "Are you ready?"

"Almost," Starbride said. Pennynail waited for her outside. They'd thought about taking Master Bernard, but his injured arm made him slower and less agile than the rest of them. Instead, Starbride loaded her satchel with Fiend suppression pyramids, detection pyramids that could cancel anything Roland had left for them, plus so many destruction pyramids she was afraid her satchel might blow up. She and Hugo collected Dawnmother on their way. Dawnmother wasn't a fighter, but she knew the servant's corridors of the palace better than any of them.

They hurried through the streets as night fell, headed in the opposite direction of Ursula and Rhys. Though only the four of them were going into the palace, they had watchers stationed around it to tell them when Roland left. Other watchers would rendezvous with Ursula and tell her that Roland was on the way.

Luckily, they didn't have to wait on anyone. Shortly after Starbride and her party settled in, Roland rode out of the royal stables, his human face on, but in the torchlight, his brow was pinched and angry. Two corpse Fiends loped behind him, and Starbride clutched the necklace that masked her pyradisté abilities. The corpse Fiends didn't even sniff the air. She had to be careful and make sure her creation never fell into Roland's hands or he'd surely find a way to counter it.

Pennynail led them to his old secret entrance. He helped them scale the false wall, and they ran down the narrow hallway to the actual side of the palace. Starbride focused on her detection pyramid. The pyramid embedded in the door shone like a beacon to her enhanced eyes. As far as she could tell, the door hadn't been retuned, but according to Pennynail, when Roland had been part of the Order, he and Crowe hadn't found this little door yet. Pennynail had explored every inch of the secret passageways and had discovered more secret doors and tunnels than even Crowe had dreamed of.

When Starbride tapped Pennynail's arm, he slipped his glove off and pressed it to the pyramid guarding the door. It swung silently open, and they hurried inside. They moved slower than Starbride liked as she searched for traps or alarms. The others held candles to light the way. It wasn't until they approached the dungeon that Starbride found a pyramid that would have alarmed its creator of her presence.

Of course, if she disabled it, Roland might sense that, too. All she could hope was that he was far enough away to miss it. She disabled the pyramid as quickly as she could, and they hurried through to another lightless, stone-covered passageway. Starbride had to disable two more pyramids before they reached the dungeons, and her hopes began to soar. Why would Roland want the dungeon so secure unless he had important prisoners to protect?

The door to the dungeons was still tuned to only accept Fiends. Hugo opened it, and they all listened, waiting to see if anyone waited in the dungeon halls.

When they heard no one, Hugo and Pennynail moved through, candles held high and weapons out. Starbride waited with Dawnmother and fought not to hold her breath. She heard the clatter of doors opening and then feet on stone. She clenched her fists, praying to Horsestrong to let Katya come through those doors. At that moment, she didn't care about the rest of the Umbriels, as long as Katya made it out alive.

Four people stumbled out of the doorway, led by Hugo and Pennynail, two women and two men. Starbride's shoulders slumped as she recognized two of them as heads of the Pyradisté Academy. They'd been her teachers. Bruises decorated their hollow cheeks, and she could see their ribs and collarbones through their torn clothing. The second man she didn't recognize, but when the second woman lifted a dirty face, Starbride almost fell to her knees.

"Averie!" Starbride hurried forward and helped her to stand. She hadn't known Katya's maid well, but Averie was as loyal to the Order and to Katya as anyone could be.

Averie sagged in Starbride's arms, so light Starbride nearly lifted her. "Is that…Starbride?" Her bloodshot eyes blinked sleepily in their bruised sockets.

"Yes, Averie, you're safe now. We're going to get you out of here."

"Forgive me…Princess Consort."

Starbride blinked away tears. "It's all right, I—"

"We have to move," Dawnmother said. She held up the unknown man who introduced himself as Claudius, the head of a blended discipline at the academy, alarms and traps.

The others were Effie, the head of utility magic, and Ansic, the head of destruction. As they ventured into the secret passageways again, the captives told of how Roland had imprisoned them and tried to get them to tell him all they knew about their respective areas of expertise.

Starbride wondered if Roland trusted the information he'd gotten through torture, or what they could have told him that he didn't already know. But what did he hope to learn from Averie?

"I think," Averie said when asked, "he hoped to use me as a lure… somehow…for Katya."

Starbride breathed a sigh. Katya wasn't in the palace. But if not the palace, then where? In the city? The country?

In a ditch somewhere?

She shook off that thought. Starbride wanted to ask Averie's opinion but feared she'd lose consciousness. The others, even for all their injuries, seemed in better shape. Maybe Roland had simply dropped Averie in a cell and forgotten about her. It was a wonder she hadn't starved to death.

In their favor, Roland hadn't bothered to trap most of the secret passageways. Perhaps he'd only done the hallways and didn't think anyone who knew the secret passages would be crazy enough to sneak into the palace.

Still, it was slowgoing. Pennynail finally touched Starbride's arm, then pointed up as if at the moon. They were taking too long. She eyed the freed captives. "We split up, cover more ground." She gave detection pyramids to the other three pyradistés, and then sent one each with Hugo and Pennynail, keeping one for herself, Dawnmother, and Averie.

Effie came with Starbride, and they made quick work of the pyramids they discovered. She bet Claudius and Pennynail did even better.

Starbride's old apartment looked much as she'd remembered it, just as tidy as when Dawnmother had left. The looters hadn't been able to get past the pyramids that guarded the royal hallways. Effie and Averie sat while Starbride and Dawnmother ransacked the room. Dawnmother took their hidden money and Starbride's jewelry box and stuffed it all in a bag. Starbride collected any pyramids she'd been working on, and then they took anything valuable they could sell. The dishes and linens were decorated with the royal seal, and they couldn't have Roland tracking them that way. Luckily, the silver wasn't so marked. They stuffed candlesticks and trays in their bags

"It has to have been an hour by now," Dawnmother said.

They wouldn't have much more time than that. They met Hugo and Ansic in the passageways again. "We looted Katya's and Reinholt's rooms," Hugo whispered.

"We're headed to Crowe's office," Starbride said.

Dawnmother tapped Hugo's arm. "Come with me. We'll see if we can get anything from the servant's cupboards."

He left with her and Ansic. Starbride kept going with Effie, who managed to walk on her own. She even helped support Averie a little. As they tried to get close to Crowe's office, they encountered alarm after alarm, and time started to slip away. Soon enough Pennynail caught up with them.

"We couldn't get near the king and queen's quarters," Claudius said. "There were too many pyramids. I'm ashamed to say that some of the things I told the Fiend king probably helped him make them better."

"Same here," Starbride said. "I think Crowe's office is a lost cause. Damn, and I was hoping to take some of his books."

"Maybe there are still some in my house in the city," Claudius said.

"Or mine," Effie added. "We didn't keep everything of importance at the academy."

Dawnmother, Hugo, and Ansic caught up to them as they spoke. "We took everything we dared," Dawnmother said. "We didn't want to venture far from the passages."

Starbride nodded. "That just leaves the capstone."

Claudius blinked at her in the wan light from her pyramid. "What are you talking about?"

"Do we have time?" Hugo asked.

"The capstone on top of the academy?" Effie asked.

"What's that got to do with anything?" Ansic echoed.

Starbride chewed her lip. The fewer people who knew about the capstone under the palace, the better; telling Ursula had been enough of a risk. Some secrets still had to be protected, even with everything. Yanchasa's prison couldn't be widely known. "Pennynail, you and Hugo take everyone else out. Dawnmother and I will catch up to you."

Hugo protested just as Pennynail shook his head. "Please don't argue with me," Starbride said. "I don't know the passages as well as you, Pennynail, but I'm certain I can find my way."

Probably.

"That's not our worry," Hugo said. "How will you handle a pack of enemies on your own? What if the Fiend king comes back?"

Starbride bit off a curse and wished they'd stop worrying about her and just get on with it. Before she could lash out at them, Dawnmother took Averie from Starbride's arms. "I know the way out. I'll guide the pyradistés and Averie." She brushed Averie's matted brown hair away from her forehead, and Starbride recalled that they'd been in the process of becoming friends when the world had gone to Darkstrong.

"Thank you, Dawn," Starbride said.

"Hurry." Dawnmother waited until Starbride had given the heads a few pyramids, and then they were off through the dark, the light pyramid with Effie as she led the way.

Starbride jogged down the passageway with Pennynail and Hugo beside her. They had to really hurry now. Who knew if Roland had figured out their ruse yet, or whether he was headed back to the palace. Starbride thought of all the times she and Katya had been on the other side of this fight, chasing ghosts while Roland ran circles around them. It felt good to be the ones striking out for a change, but it was just as nerve-wracking waiting to be caught. She wondered if Roland ever worried about it.

Most likely not. There was something to say for the confidence of the Fiend, the surety that came with the emergence of the Aspect.

The door to the capstone's cavern was more guarded and alarmed than any of the doors they'd yet encountered. Starbride cursed. She should have brought Claudius with her. They couldn't get through to the king and queen's quarters or Crowe's office, but they had to try harder here. The capstone was too important.

Freddie shoved the mask on top of his head. "Starbride..."

"I know." She worked faster. From down the dark hallway, they heard the scrape of feet on dusty stone.

Starbride tried to put the sound out of her head. She disabled another trap, then another alarm, working as fast as she could, but these were powerful. She saw them in her head as golden bubbles to be popped, but they seemed stronger, more opaque than anything she'd ever encountered.

A wave of cold brushed against Starbride's back. Keeping her mind on her task, she heard Hugo grunt and then the ring of steel on steel. She risked a look over her shoulder. Hugo and Freddie stood shoulder to shoulder, facing off against three corpse Fiends. Luckily, the Fiends got in each other's way as they tried to stand together in a hallway that was too narrow for them.

Starbride went back to her task, not knowing if these creatures had been alerted by her tampering or if this was some sort of random patrol. If it was the former, Roland could be on their heels. If it was the latter, more might come around the corner any moment.

She popped another alarm bubble, then a trap, then an alarm so tiny she almost missed it. The fighting behind her continued, but neither Freddie nor Hugo called out in pain. Starbride faced the last trap, a huge, roiling gold bubble that protected the door itself. Sweat rolled down her forehead as she concentrated. The pyramid on the door was ancient; it had guarded its secret for generations, and it wasn't tuned to her anymore or she was a horse's uncle. She couldn't disable it. She'd have to retune it.

Starbride rested her hand against the lock and focused. With a final mental shove that made pain reverberate through her head, Starbride imprinted herself upon the pyramid, sharing that honor with Roland himself. Starbride pushed the pyramid, and the door swung open.

Inside, bathed in the soft glow of the capstone, corpse Fiends packed the cavern. They perched atop the stalagmites or roamed the rocky floor. There had to be at least fifty. As one, they turned and opened their mouths, letting loose their ghastly howl.

Starbride whipped out her Fiend suppression pyramid and held it aloft. Those closest to her shrank back. Freddie stepped to her side. "We need to run," he said.

"Those behind us?" she asked.

"Dead," Hugo said as he stared into the cavern. "Spirits above."

Starbride launched destruction pyramids into the cavern, one after another. Fire blossomed and detonation pyramids cracked and boomed, shaking dust from the ceiling. If any of the Fiends came too close, Starbride focused harder on her suppression pyramid, and those that didn't leap back fast enough caught one of Freddie's daggers in its forehead.

"Shut the damned door!" Freddie cried.

Starbride tried to look past the Fiends, to see the capstone, but they were as thick as a swarm; there was no way she could reach it. Hugo helped her throw pyramids, but they didn't have enough, and more Fiends could be coming. She grabbed the door; they'd have to flee, but the locking pyramid grazed her palm, and she was seized by a sudden thought: there was only a lock on the *outside* of the door. She edged into the room.

"No!" Freddie said. "Starbride, leave it!"

She turned her back on the snarling Fiendish mob, their waves of cold surging toward her like a winter storm. "Keep throwing, Hugo!" She reached above the door to wedge one of her pyramids into a crack in the stone while Hugo continued to lob destruction pyramids into the corpse Fiends' midst. No alarm or trap would stop Roland any longer than they'd stopped her. She'd brought every pyramid she thought she might find useful, and one of those was tunable, a lock like the one she'd just retuned, but it had protected the door from anyone seeking to get in. No one ever thought to protect a door on the way out.

This lock was already tuned to her; all she had to do was put into it the idea of the door opening and closing. She felt a billow of heat amidst the cold. The nearest corpse Fiends were on fire and writhing on the ground. Hopefully, they'd set their fellows alight, but as Starbride felt the coldness coming closer, she knew it wasn't so.

She finished her pyramid and the door began to swing closed. Hugo grabbed her arm and dragged her into the hall. A few corpse Fiends lunged at them, and Starbride focused on her suppression pyramid again, sending them stumbling back. One Fiend reached an arm through the door, and Freddie stabbed it, driving his dagger into the rock wall.

When the door eased closed, they all collapsed in a heap. Starbride tried to slow her breathing and the rapid tempo of her heart.

Freddie took his dagger back, dropping the arm to the floor. "What did you do to the door?"

"I put a lock on the inside." She drew her own knife and slammed the pommel into the ancient lock, crunching it into lifeless shards. "This door isn't like the counter-weighted ones in the secret passages. It needs a pyramid to open. Roland can't retune my new lock because he can't touch it. Cancelling a lock you can't see is tricky because they aren't active until used, but I don't suppose that will stop Roland for long. But then he'll have this chunk of stone to break through. That should take a pretty piece of time."

"Smart," Freddie sad.

Hugo sniffed. "From Miss Starbride, you should expect nothing less."

"Easy, there," Freddie said. "Let's everyone keep his trousers on."

Hugo opened his mouth, but Starbride said, "Enough. Now is when we run." She took off without waiting, and they caught up to the others on their way to the exit. They'd managed to hit one storeroom before they ran out of time, and their bags bulged around them.

"How did it go?" Dawnmother asked. "Did you lock it?"

"Lock what?" Claudius asked. "What is going on?"

Starbride gave Dawnmother a warning look as they hurried. "Let's hurry and leave the questions for later."

"Best idea I've heard all day," Effie said. She was breathing hard, they all were, all but Averie who seemed half dead. Starbride helped Dawnmother drag her along. The prospect of finally being free of their prison seemed to have given the rest of the former captives a second wind.

As they hurried, Starbride heard a boom behind them. Someone else had entered the passageways, and it couldn't be anyone good.

"Go," Starbride said. Pennynail swung Averie over his shoulders. Everyone else grabbed a pyradisté as they ran.

Was it Starbride's imagination, or did a wave of cold filter down the hallway? When they reached the hallway that led to the secret door, Starbride put out her light pyramid, not wanting the glow to give them away.

Effie gasped, but Starbride whispered, "Keep straight." When they reached the door, they all smacked into one another. Starbride and Effie stumbled back, and then the complete blackness was interrupted as the door swung open. They hurried through and shut the door behind them. If it was Darren or Maia following, they'd be stopped by the pyramid. If it was Roland, he'd retune or destroy the pyramid in a moment. Starbride cursed the fact that she'd only brought one lock with her. Now that she knew a clever way to use them, she promised herself she'd take them everywhere.

The captives were too weak to climb the wall, but they were light enough to be hauled up, pushed from below, and pulled from above to be dropped over the side. Starbride hoped they wouldn't break anything. She heard scratching behind them, as if someone was trying to claw his way through the wall. Not Roland then. Starbride could have shouted in glee.

When they were up and over, Starbride heard a howl from the palace, the booming, grating sound that could only come from a Fiendish throat. Their thievery had been discovered. She helped to pick up the captives and tug them along, sending the watcher who'd been waiting for their return to collect the others and take a roundabout way back to their hideout. The warehouse district had never seemed so far away, and Starbride knew that whoever had howled in rage wouldn't be far behind them.

CHAPTER THIRTEEN

KATYA

Katya kept herself from fidgeting, just. She studied the furniture crammed into Redtrue's little adobe house. A couple chairs and a table stood off to the side, all of it made from very pale wood. In the sitting room, two chairs with wide seats and padded cushions faced each other. Redtrue perched, cross-legged, on one, and Katya sat across from her. Paintings covered the wall, color-splashed canvas stretched in frames made from that same pale wood.

Most of the paintings were vague shapes Katya couldn't make out, but if she squinted at the one behind Redtrue, it looked like a rolling valley leading to a river. A large, intricate pot sat in one corner and held what looked like a tree, very bizarre. A stand in another corner held a wash basin and pitcher. Maybe Redtrue preferred to wash in her sitting room instead of in her bedroom.

Katya leaned back in her chair, trying to look through the half-closed door to her right. In the flickering candlelight, she saw the edge of a thick pad on the floor. She didn't know if most Allusians outside of Newhope slept on the ground, if it was an adsnazi adoption, or if Redtrue was afraid of falling out of bed.

Redtrue sat still, eyes closed, face serene, with a pyramid sitting in her lap. The pyramid seemed delicate, almost fragile, much thinner than Katya had ever seen. Some of Crowe's and Starbride's pyramids were beautiful, but they had a sturdiness to them. Redtrue's seemed to be made of air.

Katya had promised to be quiet, but meditation had never been her strong suit. She squinted at the river picture again. Would Redtrue notice if she got up and wandered around? Her left leg gave a warning twinge, as if it might cramp. Katya lifted up on her arms, wincing as the chair creaked, and then lowered her feet to the floor. The chair was too deep for her to sit up without slouching, so she scooted to the front, trying not to make a sound. Redtrue wasn't exactly asleep, but she'd insisted that dream magic took intense concentration.

Katya chastised herself for fidgeting. Starbride was worth a little sitting still. She should have stayed outside like Redtrue suggested. Out there, she could have paced and complained to Brutal. What she wouldn't give to pace at that moment…

When Redtrue opened her eyes, it took Katya a moment to process the fact that something had changed. Redtrue didn't blink or speak, and Katya thought she might still be in a trance. Katya didn't move, afraid to wake her before it was time.

"Yah!" Redtrue cried, thrusting her arms forward.

Katya leapt up, knocking her chair backward, and reached for her rapier. Redtrue laughed long and loud.

Katya's heart hammered in her ears. "What…what are you…"

"I'm sorry. You were so intense. I couldn't help it."

Katya rammed her half-drawn rapier back into its sheath. "Very funny."

"It was, yes."

Katya picked her chair up and thumped it upright. "Tell me what you found before I strangle you."

"I'd die happy. I stretched further than I ever have before, and I sensed many minds that can touch the adsna. It has to be your Marienne. Though"—she tossed her long braid over her shoulder—"there weren't as many as I thought there might be."

Katya's stomach dropped. "Roland's killing the pyradistés."

"Or they fled."

"Were you able to…"

"Knock at any mind doors?" Redtrue smiled. "I approached a few minds, but none had the strength to know me from a dream."

Katya's shoulders slumped, and she was more tired than she'd ever been.

"Oh, don't sulk," Redtrue said. "One try and you're ready to give up? All we have to do is find a very strong mind, someone used to lucid dreams, perhaps, who knows how to take control of his or her mind while asleep."

"You're rude, but you're right."

"No one here will indulge your self-pity. Well, some of those in Newhope might, some who like to pretend they're Farradain." Before Katya could respond, Redtrue stood and stretched. "Are you going to your tent now, or do you intend to try to sleep in my house, like your friend?"

"Oh no, that's between you and her. Good night, Redtrue, and thank you." She hurried out, not missing the shadow that approached the house as she left, no doubt Castelle trying to get back in that bed. She'd never met someone she couldn't charm before. Maybe she thought of Redtrue as an interesting challenge.

"Good luck, Cass," Katya whispered. She climbed inside the tent she shared with her father and Brutal. It was dark and quiet as she sat inside the flap and took off her boots before crawling into her own nest of blankets beside Da.

"Any luck?" he asked.

"I thought you'd be asleep by now."

"How could I when you were close to finding Starbride?"

Katya smiled, oddly touched by the fact that he was anxious for her.

"Besides," he added, "who can sleep well on these rocks? I'm too old for camping."

"Thanks anyway. No luck, but Redtrue was hopeful enough to want to try again tomorrow."

"Good news."

"And Leafclever? Any luck there?"

"Your impassioned speech swayed him quite a bit, but he's a tough old bird. I think he's been getting some coaching from Dayscout. The Allusians want a say in how they're governed, and frankly, I don't blame them."

"You'll grant them noble titles?"

He clucked his tongue. "Fancy titles aren't going to sway Dayscout and Leafclever. They want their people to be able to have a say. As misled as Magistrate Anthony was, it looks like his parliament idea might come to be."

"It would be harder for someone like Roland to stir the people up if they were part of the very thing they were trying to overturn."

"My thoughts exactly."

A parliament...the idea was intriguing, though her father, with assistance from her mother, usually took care of the politics. She'd always expected her brother to one day take charge in Marienne, aided by his steadfast wife.

Now Reinholt's treacherous wife was dead, Reinholt himself was missing, and Katya would inherit the throne upon her father's death, at least until her niece was old enough to be queen. Even then, little Vierdrin would have to lean on whatever family she had left. And Katya fully planned to be alive for Vierdrin to lean on. Hopefully, Da would still be in charge until Vierdrin was old enough to learn from the master.

Of course, all that was dependent on getting the kingdom back. In the face of that, a parliament seemed a small thing, never mind that it would change the face of politics in Farraday forever. The nobles might have a harder time fighting for the kingdom if they knew they'd have to share it with the common people, but the commoners might fight harder.

But how would any of them react when they found Allusians among their army? The commoners might resent them, but the nobles would be happy to use them. When everyone discovered that the Allusians had helped shape a new parliament, the tables would turn: the nobles would loathe it, and the commoners might laud it if it helped get them the government they wanted.

Katya rubbed her temples before she felt her father's touch on her shoulder. "Easy, my girl. You're grinding your teeth. Remember what I once told you? Never worry about politics unless you have to, and right now, you don't have to."

"But *you* have to, Da. As the heir—"

He chuckled. "You can't take the whole kingdom on your shoulders. Even if I should blow away as dust tomorrow, you won't have to worry about the parliament problem for a long time, even if you have to promise the Allusians a seat to get them to help you."

"Blow away as dust?"

"Something I picked up from our hosts. I rather like this Horsestrong fellow."

Katya smiled softly. If her father promised the Allusians a role in the government, he'd keep his word. If they regained Marienne, he'd give them a place even if he had to make one up. She hoped Leafclever realized that about him. She hoped everyone did. As much as they might not like Farradains, they had to see that her father was the most fair-minded one they'd ever come across.

Katya turned on her side and tried to make her mind go quiet. There was so much to worry about, but missing sleep wouldn't do her any good. She tried not to think of Starbride, either, but that thought wasn't as easy to put aside as politics.

❖

The next day, Dayscout came to visit them and sequestered himself, Da, and Leafclever away. Katya hoped that was a good sign. The more they spoke with her father, the more they'd see how much he deserved to be king, no matter what pyradistés might do.

Castelle wasn't as hopeful. When Katya had gotten up for her watch shift, she'd seen Castelle's feet sticking out of the tent next door. If Redtrue had let her in, she hadn't stayed the whole night. When they were all up in the morning, Castelle was moody, barely eating her porridge.

"Did you have a good night?" Katya asked.

Castelle gave her a gloomy look as she chewed.

"She got in late," Brutal said as he sat.

Katya smiled slowly. "But she didn't let you stay."

"Before I forget who you are and tell you to shut up," Castelle said, "I'd appreciate it if you dropped it, Highness."

"You can tell me to shut up all you want," Brutal said.

"I'd rather spar," Castelle said.

"You shouldn't fight angry," he said. "If you're only fighting to escape yourself, you will never reach enlightenment. To begin to understand existence, we must first understand ourselves."

"Pass," Castelle said.

Katya snorted a laugh. "I'll spar with you, Castelle. Strikes with the flat of the blade only. If you accidentally wound me, Brutal will kill you."

"True," he said. "If you wound her, make sure you mean to."

Castelle smiled slightly. "Then you won't kill me?"

"Oh, I'll still kill you, but at least you'll die because you meant to."

She laughed then; Castelle wouldn't be kept down forever. After they'd eaten, Katya took her coat off despite the biting breeze that morning. She'd be sweating through her shirt soon enough. She stretched to loosen up, and then she and Castelle squared off, both of them armed with rapiers.

Castelle was as quick as Katya remembered, but she played it safe. Katya could tell by the way she stood that she was holding something in reserve. Katya tried a fake stumble, but Castelle backed off instead of pressing her advantage.

Katya tried a series of lunges, hoping to put Castelle off balance, but she wouldn't engage, smoothly giving ground. Katya snarled. "I thought you wanted a fight, not a dance!"

"I thought you were supposed to be teaching patience, not the one who needs to learn it."

Katya leaned back, waiting for Castelle to come to her. Castelle tried a series of feints and lunges, clearly trying to get her measure. Katya went fully defensive, giving her nothing.

"Boring, isn't it?" Katya asked.

Castelle came on hard and fast. That was more like it. Katya parried one strike after another, and then threw one wide, coming in hard after it while Castelle was open. Katya whacked her on the thigh.

"Touch!" Castelle said. They broke apart slightly, and Castelle put the "injured" leg forward as if she might with a real wound. She needed to keep her strong leg behind her in order to push off. Katya pressed her advantage, but Castelle could defend well with only one strong leg. She feigned a stumble, snaked in from the side, and whacked Katya's arm.

"Touch!" Katya called. Luckily, it was her left arm, so she could keep it behind her. She didn't need to pretend to feel the sting. She'd have a quite a bruise, maybe a welt. So, someone was smarting from her rejection and needed to inflict a little pain.

Katya knocked Castelle's next strike wide and stepped inside her reach. Castelle leaned back, but she wasn't fast enough. Katya rammed her rapier guard toward Castelle's face, stopping just short of her nose.

Castelle staggered back, eyes wide.

"That's the match," Brutal said. "That punch would have broken your nose, Cass. Might not have killed you, but it would have staggered you enough for her to finish you."

Castelle frowned as if she wasn't convinced.

Katya grinned. "I could break your nose, and we could see."

With a huge sigh, Castelle rammed her rapier home. "It's not you I want to fight. She let me in, we got close, and then she said, 'Thank you.' Like I'd just…polished her silver! She didn't ask me to leave then, but she ignored me until I did."

"Maybe she doesn't like chitchat," Brutal said, "or cuddling."

"She said I could come back whenever I wanted, come back and polish her silver and then she'll show me the door!"

Katya crossed her arms. "Have you ever had someone *not* fall in love with you?"

"No!" Castelle said, and then, "Well, not when I'm really trying."

"Why are you really trying?" Brutal asked.

"You're trying to win just because you've never lost?" Katya said. "Even though you don't really care about her?"

"Well, it's not that I don't care about her. I'm not in love with her, but…"

Katya stuck her tongue in her cheek, wondering if she should say anymore, but she couldn't help herself. "You're upset not because she's using you but because you can't use her."

Castelle's mouth worked for a few moments before she stalked away, her back as stiff as a board.

"Was that necessary?" Brutal asked.

Remembering Redtrue's words, Katya shrugged. "Let her feel sorry for herself on her own time." She left to find her father, catching up to him just as he broke from his conversation with Dayscout and Leafclever.

"We're headed into Newhope tomorrow, my girl," he told her as they walked a small distance from Dayscout's house. "Dayscout's gotten us a meeting with the Allusian council."

"And Leafclever? Did he say for sure that he's going to back you?"

"He's nearly there. The deuce of it is, he's not ready to commit until he hears me speak to the council."

"You give them a speech, they look to him, and what if he says no? Are we sunk?"

"The council will want to make up its own mind. If they just went with whatever the adsnazi wanted, Allusia wouldn't need a council at all, and they damn sure wouldn't need Dayscout. If I can rally them, Leafclever will probably go over to our side, to say nothing of Dayscout, who I believe is already with us based on what we've discussed."

"A parliament."

"Just so. Now all I've got to do is promise them the moon and hope that when the time comes, it's low enough in the sky to grab. Whether the Allusians commit to us or not, we need to move soon. Take most of our people and whatever scouts the Allusians will part with and ride into Farraday to see what support you can drum up from those closest to the borders."

Katya frowned. "Like Pomanse?"

"Walls make cities feel secure. Start with the villages and the country nobles who don't come to court. There are a few littering the wilderness out here. We should be able to convince them."

Katya wished she had someone like Countess Nadia to *help* her convince them. "Right."

"If Roland's creations have been rampaging about the countryside, they might do your arguing for you. It's a dammed shame, but the sooner people can see what they're up against..."

"The sooner they'll see the need to fight. I wonder if Horsestrong had a saying about that."

Chapter Fourteen

Starbride

Master Bernard began the long process of nursing Claudius, Effie, and Ansic back to health. Starbride put Averie in a small space near the back of their hideout, leaving her in Dawnmother's care. Both seemed to take pleasure in looking after their new charges. Even though Master Bernard hadn't been present when Roland sacked the academy, Starbride knew he felt guilty. He'd had to assume the heads were dead along with everyone else, but the survival of these three gave him hope that more had escaped.

It was late afternoon before Captain Ursula and Sergeant Rhys made it back to the warehouse. They'd eluded Roland for as long as they could and then thrown the disguise pyramids away. Ursula kept the fire pyramid, claiming that she didn't know when it might come in handy.

"He passed within a few feet of me," Ursula said. "Bastard is cold as ice."

"You should see him with his Fiend face on," Starbride said. They sat in her small room, taking turns drinking from a wine bottle. After the night they'd had, they deserved it.

"After we'd chucked the disguise pyramids, he looked straight at me, and I could have sworn by Ellias's balls he knew who I was."

Starbride sputtered a laugh. "And?"

"And nothing. He said, 'Keep the people back,' while he looked around." She took a long pull from the bottle. "I heard from outside the city this morning."

Starbride nearly dropped the bottle as Ursula passed it. "Katya?"

"Oh, I'm sorry, no."

Starbride's heart stopped pounding. No news could mean good news, as Horsestrong said. "What is it?"

"A few of my men who were caught outside the city when the trouble started have been watching the countryside for me. They caught word of a group of Allusians traveling to Marienne and managed to stop them before they ran into the Fiend king's patrols."

Starbride held her breath for a moment. "The students!"

"What students?"

"They were coming to the Halls of Law for the winter term. Katya offered them her patronage. I'd hoped they'd heard of the troubles and turned around, but I wouldn't have recommended them to the school if they'd been short of courage."

"I was hoping for a group of Allusian pyradistés."

"Adsnazi, and I doubt they could help unless you need some pretty lights." Starbride winced, wondering when she'd developed such a low opinion of her own people, but after seeing the wonder of Farradain pyradistés, she couldn't help herself. She'd gone undetected by the adsnazi, after all. Who else had they missed?

"Turn the students back," Starbride said as she took a long pull of wine. "I don't see how they could help."

"It's a miracle they weren't picked up."

"Yes, miracles make me…suspicious." She hated to say that, too. She sounded more and more like a Farradain every day.

Ursula gave a sideway smile. "You think the Fiend king found them in the country, left the city without anyone noticing him, warped their minds, and then snuck back in?"

"Is anything you just said beyond his power?"

"No…well, if they can't be returned overland, maybe my contacts could take them to the coast and put them on a boat."

"Anything that gets them home."

"They might not leave without you, Princess Consort."

Starbride smiled slightly. "And I can't leave here." Katya wasn't in the palace, but she might still be in the city. And even if she wasn't, Starbride had no idea where to start looking.

"Never said you should." Ursula smiled softly, and Starbride wondered if she was thinking of her own lost loves, lost opportunities, maybe even of Freddie. Starbride couldn't bring that up, though she longed to. Freddie would never forgive her.

As if summoned by her thoughts, Pennynail stepped into the doorway and knocked on the jamb. Starbride waved him in. Ursula gave him a suspicious look before she stood. "I'll get word to our people and send the students away." She left without saying good-bye, as Starbride had come to expect.

Pennynail shut the door before he stripped his mask off. "It's so… odd to see her from in here."

"She doesn't trust Pennynail."

He gazed into the laughing Jack mask's manic grin. "Not many people do until they need my help."

"So bitter. Did something happen?"

"I'm just a little sick of not being able to show my face. I mean, a spirits bedamned Fiend is walking around freer than I am. Maybe he isn't showing his true face, but his minions are out in broad daylight."

"You saw how Hugo reacted to you, Freddie."

"Maybe I could make a better disguise, something smaller than this mask that still conceals my identity."

Starbride wondered how long it would be until any disguise was too much, but she couldn't say it. Having his friends distrust him seemed to cut him as deeply as it had his father. As much as Crowe had always spoken of suspecting everyone, he wanted to be trustworthy. His mother had been servant class, after all. Trustworthiness was part of who they were.

"Is there something you can try on a select group first, some who won't lose their wits at the sight of the Dockland Butcher?"

He winced, but she had to drive home what he was asking for. An infamous murderer in their midst could drive their little group apart. Freddie was silent for a moment before he nodded.

"You could try it on Ursula," Starbride asked. "If you can fool her…"

"She might refuse to work with us."

"She knows you didn't do the crimes you were accused of."

He shrugged.

"I suppose finding out you're alive would make her feel betrayed, especially if you two were close," Starbride said.

"Quit digging."

"If you're committed to this, I won't have to dig. It'll all come out on its own."

"I'm going to give it some thought."

"Is that all you wanted to tell me? Or did you just want to get the mask off for a while?"

"Both," he said, "though it's getting colder and colder outside. I picked a fine time to want to go bare-faced."

"We're going to need more blankets soon." That wasn't all they needed. Their luck couldn't keep holding out, especially not since they'd robbed the palace. "Did you sell the silver?"

"Yep, though my fence is touchier than usual these days. There's one person at least who wouldn't care who I am even if I walked in there stark naked. He couldn't take all the silver, though, and the other fences I know are in Dockland. It might be worth sneaking over there and having a look around. I doubt Roland's bothered except for securing the docks."

She wondered if she'd have to sell the jewelry as well; it pained her to think so. When they'd first gotten back, she'd looked through all the boxes and touched every piece, the enameled necklace her father had made for her as a child, with "Bride" and "Lucky" spelled out in gold wire in between yellow starbursts; the diamond necklace that seemed to depict both snowflakes and dancers; her rubies and sapphires, all lovingly made by her father. She'd stared at the emerald consort's cuff for a very long time. She'd also recognized many of Katya's pieces, too: the sapphires from the Courtiers Ball; her silver diadem; and nestled in the corner of the box, in its own velvet bag, the butterfly hairpin that Katya had turned into a brooch.

With shaky hands, Starbride had pinned the brooch to her own pyramid necklace, determined that it wouldn't be sold. It wouldn't fetch them much money anyway. She'd almost curled up and wept then, but her mother had been right about tears in one way: they didn't do any good, not only when no one was around to see them, but at all.

Freddie's slight touch on her arm brought her back to herself. "We'll save as much of it as we can," he said softly.

Starbride smiled into his warm eyes. "I'm trying not to be silly. We can't eat jewelry, after all."

"Well, anything with Allusian writing on it would attract too much attention. With the others, we can pry the stones out and sell them separately, but we can start with Katya's."

Before Starbride could protest, Freddie said, "She's not as attached to them as you are." When her mouth fell open, he laughed. "It's no secret. You spent hours last night fondling your jewelry box."

"I wasn't fondling anything. Why were you spying on me?"

"No spying. I came to the door, saw the fondling, and left."

She rolled her eyes. "How much do you think we could get if we sold you?"

"No one has that much money."

"Are you going to Dockland, or are you going to crack jokes all day?"

He smiled and shrugged. "It might be tricky. Don't expect me for a couple of days."

Worry gnawed at her then. "Do you want some company?"

"You're the leader of our little resistance. You can't leave these people alone that long."

"What? I'm…I'm just staying around for Katya. I'm no one's leader."

He gave her a sour look. "You're the highest ranking person here, as well as one of the most powerful, and you just robbed the Fiend king, the monster who overthrew the kingdom and who's making life very difficult for the populace. You're standing up to him, Starbride, albeit sneakily, which is the best way to stand up, in my opinion. You're the leader."

"I care about people, that's all."

"A good quality in any leader."

"Look…do you want anyone to come with you or not? We have some capable pyradistés. A few of the younger ones could keep up with you, and if you need someone more combat capable, there's always Hugo."

"Hugo would sooner clean my boots with his tongue than he would leave you in order to watch my back."

"He'd go if I asked him."

Freddie tilted his chin up. "I'm sorry, Miss Starbride," he said in a raspy falsetto, "the very idea is unthinkable. I cannot leave you in the arms of unknowns while I accompany some ruffian!" He grabbed her hand and laid kisses all over her knuckles.

Laughing, Starbride tried to reclaim her hand, but he cuddled it to his chest. "Freddie, stop!"

Starbride's door flew open. Hugo raced into the room, rammed into Freddie, and knocked him over.

Starbride staggered back from where they rolled on the floor. She closed the door again before they could attract more attention. "Stop this!"

Freddie flipped Hugo over and sat on top of him. "Someone's frisky!"

"I saw you pawing her, you honorless blackguard! She told you to stop!"

Freddie knocked Hugo's arms out from under him as Hugo tried to rise. "So you thought you'd rough me up a bit, eh, junior?"

"Leave it, Freddie." Starbride knelt until she could look into Hugo's face. "Do you think I can't take care of myself?"

That made both of them stop and look at her.

"I know you think you're defending me, Hugo, but you're not giving Freddie or me any credit. He wouldn't hurt me, and I am not helpless." She stood and put her fists on her hips. If she was the leader, by Horsestrong's name, they'd treat her like one. "Freddie, let him up. Hugo, stop acting foolish."

Freddie stood with one smooth motion. He didn't bother to offer help to Hugo, who stood on his own. He frowned, but his face had gone scarlet. "I'm sorry, Miss Starbride, I thought—"

"If you can't trust him, trust *me*, Hugo."

Hugo took a deep breath. Freddie wisely kept silent. Hugo offered both of them a shallow bow. "I apologize."

"Accepted," Freddie said.

Hugo cut his eyes at Freddie. "I wasn't apologizing to you."

Starbride sighed, tempted to demand they work together to hurry the trust issues along. "It's all right, Hugo. You'll learn."

He shuffled from foot to foot. "I just wanted to see if you needed anything, and then I heard you say stop."

"I don't need anything, thank you."

Freddie pulled his mask over his head. "I'd better be on my way."

"Good luck," Starbride said. "Be safe." He strode out the door.

Hugo hung his head. "I'm sorry I angered you."

Starbride pulled her hair behind her in a ponytail before letting it fall. She rarely wore it up these days because it gave her a headache, or maybe she had a perpetual headache.

"I do think you're capable," Hugo said, "and I believe in your abilities, I just…"

Starbride prayed to Horsestrong to keep Hugo's tongue in check. The last thing she needed was for him to admit his crush. "I know you care about me, Hugo," she said, hoping he'd leave it at that. "And I hope you'll care about Freddie, too, eventually. It took me a while to get used to him without the mask. Despite his colorful past, I know you can do the same."

"I'll try."

"If he teases you too much, let me know."

He smiled softly before bowing and leaving the room. Starbride sat again, asking Horsestrong to save her from uncooperative people: one man who couldn't help himself from being her protector and another who couldn't resist teasing a young man already out of his depth. If he were there, Brutal could have made them behave.

Now there was a thought. Many of the city's chapterhouses had closed their doors when the trouble started, taking in their closest parishioners and their brothers and sisters, but otherwise keeping mute. They still tolled their bells at sunset every day, so each had someone inside.

Starbride tapped her chin. If Brutal had managed to find shelter in a chapterhouse, he would have come looking for them by now. Starbride had always assumed he'd be with Katya. Still, his brothers and sisters were no friends of the Fiends. At Lady Hilda's trial, the head of the strength chapterhouse had helped defend Katya. If Freddie was right, if they were the resistance instead of just a group of people trying to stay alive, they'd need more allies. She'd have to speak to her fellows about making contact.

CHAPTER FIFTEEN

KATYA

Once it had been dark a few hours, Redtrue again attempted to contact Starbride. Katya decided to pace outside, more comfortable walking her boots off as the temperature dropped than sitting in the warm comfort of Redtrue's small house.

She saw no waiting Castelle this time. Brutal watched over her father, leaving Katya alone with the starry night. It was clear as well as cold, and the stars coated the sky like sugar on a cake.

Katya's stomach rumbled, though not from hunger. It had been a long time since she'd had sweet cake. The Allusians didn't make many sweets, though she had tasted bread made with honey and hard, brittle candy. When she thought of the chocolate mousse from home, she had to swallow several times, though that was nothing compared to when she thought of meringues. Katya grinned. If they regained Marienne, never again would she take her life for granted.

But how could she even think about dessert when the people of Marienne were probably suffering and dying, when Starbride might be—? She dashed the thought away and resumed her pacing, willing Redtrue to hurry. She didn't know if Redtrue would accompany them to Newhope. With Katya gone, she might stop trying to contact Marienne. Katya couldn't wait around to find out. They didn't have long before the snow began to fall. That wasn't much time to raise an army and march all the way home.

Redtrue's door creaked open. Katya spun around. "Well?"

"I found someone. Not your lover," she added before Katya could ask. "But a strong mind who may have believed me to be more than a dream. I gave him instructions on how to make a dream-walking pyramid, but I don't know how much he'll remember. I urged him to wake and write everything down. And now that I know where he is…"

"You can find him again." The world seemed lighter on her shoulders. Surprising herself, she clasped Redtrue's hands. "Thank you. I know you didn't want to do this. It means so much to me."

Redtrue smiled, genuinely, it seemed and gave Katya one squeeze. "This doesn't mean I'm going to quit berating your people and their practices."

"Does Horsestrong have a saying about keeping people on their toes, ready for anything?"

She thought for a moment. "Surround yourself with friends who surprise you, and the enemy will never catch you off guard."

"There must be a book of these sayings that Allusian children memorize."

"The servant caste is required to learn more than anyone else."

"Are you servant caste?"

Redtrue blinked at her. "You didn't know? Well, I suppose *you* wouldn't. It's such a part of everything here…I just thought…"

Katya didn't let herself react, but she put the pieces together. Perhaps Farradains weren't the only people who made Redtrue so touchy. Perhaps she didn't like being constantly looked on as a servant. Katya hadn't seen her interact with all the adsnazi; maybe some of them fell into old patterns even out in the wilderness.

"Well, whatever you were born as, you're a fantastic adsnazi," Katya said.

Redtrue grinned crookedly. "Since you haven't seen many of us work, that seems a hollow compliment."

"I gathered enough from Leafclever to know that what you've just done is unprecedented. If it wasn't difficult, someone would have tried it before."

"You have a keen mind."

"A compliment? From you?" Katya grabbed her chest and stepped back. "I think my ego just exploded. Stand back! I wouldn't want to get any on you."

"Enough, charmer, away with you." She gazed at Katya through her lashes. The meager light glinted in her brown eyes.

Starbride, naked and waiting on Katya's bed amidst a host of candles, flitted through Katya's mind. A familiar heat bloomed through her insides, making her flush.

"Thanks again," Katya said lamely. She nearly jogged toward her tent. Her pulse roared in her ears, so much so that she didn't hear any footsteps before someone grabbed her arm from the shadows.

Katya twisted out of the grasp and leapt backward, drawing her rapier as she went.

"It's me!" Castelle said.

Katya squinted at the shadow, barely making out Castelle's features in the meager light. "What in the spirits' names are you doing?"

"I might ask you the same thing!"

"Going to my tent?"

"I saw you! Holding hands with her, flirting. The way you two looked at each other, I'm surprised you're not over there mauling each other on the ground."

"What?" Katya slid her rapier back into its scabbard. "Are you... jealous?"

"Oh, you with your high and mighty values. 'I love Starbride,'" she mocked, "'I ache for her. She lives inside me.' What a bunch of shit. If you were just saving yourself for the next Allusian, you should have told me."

Katya's fist lashed out and caught Castelle in the mouth. Castelle staggered back. Katya waited, her knuckles throbbing. She was suddenly grateful she no longer had her Fiend, or everyone in the camp might have died that night.

"Why did you pick the *one* person I had my eye on?" Castelle said, her voice labored as if she had to drag the words through her anger. "Are you still trying to punish me, or did you decide it's time for the student to surpass the master?"

Katya sneered. "Pathetic. Get out of my way, or I'll go through you."

Castelle drew herself up, and Katya thought she might attack. Good. They both needed to drain off the adrenaline. But Castelle bowed and stepped aside. "As you will, Highness."

Katya strode past her. Castelle wouldn't strike her in the back. If she had that in her, she would have done so from the start instead of calling Katya out, the arrogant fool. The spiteful part of Katya wished she *had* kissed Redtrue then, a full kiss that would have made Castelle scream. She didn't want Redtrue; she was only missing Starbride, but she had to admit that Castelle's jealousy felt good. She'd inspired it in Katya many times during their relationship. It felt nice to have the shoe on the other foot.

As Katya crawled into her blankets, she put Castelle out of her mind, focusing on the good news: they'd contacted a pyradisté. If Redtrue would keep trying, and her words suggested she would, all they had to do was convince *him* to find Starbride.

In the morning, Katya had breakfast with Brutal as usual, but Castelle was nowhere in sight. "I heard you two fighting last night," he said. "Did you hit her?"

Katya nodded. "Did you think you'd have to jump in?"

"If she'd pulled a weapon."

"She's lost her mind."

"Maybe she expected this to be just another adventure," he said. "Now that it's life or death, she's trying to turn it into a conflict she knows."

"Fumbling her way into women's beds and then getting pissed about it?"

"Something like that. Want me to have a word?"

"Let her have a word with herself. We're going into Newhope today, and if she can't keep herself in check, she can stay here."

When they finished eating, they packed their meager gear. Castelle sported a bruise on the corner of her mouth. Katya wished she could make it permanent. Maybe that's why she'd gotten the tattoo near her eye.

Leafclever and Redtrue accompanied them toward Newhope. Katya was glad to see it, glad of the opportunity to keep an eye on Redtrue's progress. Whether Castelle was happy about it, Katya couldn't tell. Castelle didn't look at Redtrue either.

Katya rode close to her father. "Did Leafclever drop any hints about what he'll say to the council?"

"No, though he does understand that I'm not the only one making decisions about the government in Farraday. Dayscout told me that some of the nomads in the north will be coming down. They're hearty fighters, and we could use their strength." He leaned close. "Other than lending their voice, have you seen any way the adsnazi can help us? Their nature-conscious approach is all very well-intentioned, I'm sure, but what the deuce can they do in a fight?"

"They hate pyradisté pyramids. Maybe they can cancel them like Crowe could. Roland won't be able to get a leg under him if the adsnazi keep darkening his weapons."

"Hmm, yes, could be quite handy." He sighed. "I'm not looking forward to speaking with our tagalong nobles again. Every one of them is going to want to be a general."

"That's not a problem. There's the general in charge of latrines and General Horse Picketer."

"Yes, and no doubt they'll create some new posts like general in charge of shouting and time wasting."

"Make one of them in charge of uniforms or horse barding; that ought to keep them busy."

After they shared a quick laugh, Da rode toward Leafclever, leaving Katya alone with her thoughts. It lightened her heart that events were finally in motion. Up until then, it had seemed like every step she'd taken had been *away* from Marienne, but now she could finally go toward it.

❖

Katya and her father traveled straight to their borrowed house. The children were ecstatic to see their aunt and grandfather, more agitated than Katya had seen in a long time. Days of safety had apparently brought back memories of home. Lord Vincent reported that they'd been crying often, asking not only about their mother but their father as well. He'd comforted them as best he could, but Katya could tell he was troubled by the fact that they were so disturbed.

Katya didn't think she'd be any better at comforting them than he was, but she gave them a cuddle and promised they'd be all right, all she could offer at the moment. When little Bastian cried that he wanted Starbride, Katya held him close and said, "Me, too."

All through the day, the Allusian council had been gathering. Katya and her father joined them after a quick change of clothes. They met in Newhope's largest community building, a structure that had seen every kind of crowd: courts, funerals, any gathering with at least a hundred people, even weddings if it was raining outside.

Members of the council filed in and took chairs in no order Katya could discern from where she stood beside the wall with her father, Castelle, and Brutal. Dayscout sat near the rear, talking with people as they entered. Katya spotted Allusians dressed in Farradain style and some that wore flowing, multicolored garments like the adsnazi. Some were sparklingly bejeweled; others wore aprons spattered with mud.

All of them mingled together, though, even Brightstriving and Sunjoyful when they arrived. They seemed too preoccupied greeting the others to notice Katya. When her father started to speak, she was certain their eyes would be locked on her.

Just before Dayscout moved to the front of the room, other Allusians trickled in. These wore leather and sported blades at their hips. Most had pulled their hair behind them in horse's tails or braids. Some kept it very short, but the one in front—a tall, powerfully built woman—had hardly any hair except for a short stripe running from her forehead to her nape. Katya recalled Starbride once telling her that women who'd taken up the sword in Allusia often shaved their heads.

"Must be the nomads," Da muttered.

The shaved woman met Katya's eye and regarded her with a hard, black gaze. She and her people sat far from everyone else. The room had gone quiet at their entrance, and Dayscout's clap in the sudden silence made many people jump.

He said a few words in Allusian before he switched to Farradain. "Thank you all for coming," he said. "We meet today to discuss the situation in Farraday. Our neighbors need our help, and we must decide what sort of help to offer them. I will let Farraday's own king make its case."

The room stayed quiet as Da walked to the front. He was dressed in what Katya called medium-regal, the best they had: embroidered black coat of good quality, a pin with the hawk of Farraday and a slim circlet that Ma had commissioned from a jeweler in Newhope, maybe even Sunjoyful himself. She'd traded some of her own meager jewelry to have it done.

Da held his arms out as if inviting the company in and spoke a few words in Allusian. The members of the council glanced at one another. Near the front of the room, Leafclever smiled.

"You might think I learned that this morning," Da said, "a clever ploy by a crafty neighbor trying to buy your regard. In truth, I learned it long ago, when Dayscout and I became friends. From the beginning of my reign, I knew Allusia and Farraday would remain linked.

"We have a history," he said above a brief murmur. "And like all families, it's not an altogether *happy* history." That got a few laughing snorts. "The kings and queens of old saw Allusian crystal and nothing else, and they were willing to go through your people to get it.

"I knew differently. My father knew differently. During our reigns, our people have grown closer, linked by trade, by marriage in some of our border towns…and by love within my own family."

He gestured at Katya. She met the room's regard with steady eyes, though she didn't look toward Brightstriving and Sunjoyful.

"Before our troubles began," Da said, "I saw our two lands moving closer. I thought we would mingle slowly, harsh feelings softened by time, but the murderous usurper has made that impossible. He is a pyradisté, and he hungers for the crystal in your mountains. He will not be sated with how our miners have sought to leave your people in peace. He will challenge your people like the Farradain kings of old, but he will do it with Fiends, creatures made from nightmares, as the adsnazi can attest.

"Fight alongside us," Da boomed, once again shouting down mumbling. "Help me reclaim a kingdom that will be forged by all of us, Farradain and Allusian, governed by a council such as this. Help me protect your lives, your families' lives. Together, we can defeat the usurper and then…we will thank him."

Da paused, giving the council time to glance at one another. Katya noticed that the nomads watched Da with little smiles on their faces as someone translated for them.

"We will thank him for ushering in an era which would have been many years in the making had he not shown his face, an era of peace and prosperity between our peoples and the birth of our new, joined kingdom."

Dayscout began the applause, and the others followed suit. It wasn't the cheers Katya hoped for, but no one was booing either. When Leafclever stood, the council fell silent again. He crossed to where Da stood and placed a hand over Da's heart. "This man believes what he says," Leafclever said, and then spoke in Allusian.

He smiled at Da and dropped his arm. The council erupted in mumbles, each of the occupants turning to speak with one another. It was certainly the most subdued council Katya had ever seen. No one was on his or her feet screaming at anyone else.

She heard snatches of debate from those closest to her. Leafclever had apparently given his support, at least partly, and now the council discussed. She edged a little closer to one group speaking Farradain and heard them weighing the notion that they'd continue to have a say in how their own land was run *as well as* a say in how Farraday worked. Some spoke of the money to be made. Others worried about Fiends invading their land.

One of the nomads stood, the woman with the mostly-shaven head. The hall fell silent as they noticed her. She spoke in Allusian, and a shorter woman next to her translated.

"Hawkblade say, why you never come before?"

Da shook his head. "I'm afraid I don't understand."

After another quick exchange, the small woman said, "Now you speak of riding together, now that trouble come. Without us, you ride alone, *neh*? You like that enough before."

Katya held her breath.

"You speak the truth," Da said. "If not for our current troubles, I would not be here talking of joined governments. But I believe such an arrangement was always in our future. In my own city, politicians had put forth the notion of a parliament, where the common people have a say in how they are governed. If it were not for the usurper, the idea would be long in forming."

If Reinholt hadn't ordered a member of the populace murdered, the idea of a parliament might have been even longer in coming. Da didn't add that, however.

Hawkblade laughed and said something else. "Everybody here think money, maybe, but it not buy wind or ground or sky. You say Fiends come for us. Maybe we wait, and they pass on like you."

"The usurper will not die on his own," Da said. His calm features went sad for a moment. "No one knows how long a Fiend can live. Maybe they are eternal, never aging, never dying. He does not value the wind or ground or sky. He does not value coin. He values crystal and power and the dead. He will not stop until he has all the land under his sway and a host of corpses to experiment on. Do not fight for me or for Farraday or Allusia. Fight for your very lives, for whatever you hold dear. Come with us into the countryside, if you do not believe. Come with us into Farraday and see for yourselves. I'm sure the usurper will oblige you."

When this was translated, Hawkblade sat down. Her movements were fluid and sure. If her parents had wished for her to be a weapon, it seemed she'd succeeded. Katya wondered why she didn't have a better translator. Maybe she didn't trust anyone else.

The rest of the council looked to Leafclever, who nodded. Katya frowned at that. Was he reading her father with a pyramid somehow? She thought they'd forbidden that sort of thing. And she hadn't seen him with a pyramid yet.

Dayscout spoke next, in support of committing troops and resources to reclaiming Marienne. He spoke of not only what it could give their people, but what he felt was right as far as one human being helping another.

Then the council discussed again, individuals standing now and again to ask questions. In the end, for a myriad of reasons, they agreed. Katya overheard one group saying it was too great an opportunity to pass up. After all, if they retook Marienne, Da would have to give them what they wanted or risk his own army turning against him. Katya had to pretend she hadn't heard, but it was a good concern to keep in mind. She just had to hope that when the Allusians saw the Fiends for the first time, they'd fight for what was right instead of what they wanted. At the very least, they'd fight for their lives.

CHAPTER SIXTEEN

STARBRIDE

Starbride sent several messages to the strength chapterhouses and got a quick response. A few monks from one would meet with her. She didn't like going without Pennynail, but she had Dawnmother, Hugo, and Master Bernard. As strong as the brothers and sisters of strength were, they couldn't match a pyramid.

She set a meeting near the grand marketplace, still not telling them who she really was. As far as they were concerned, she was just someone interested in finding out what the chapterhouses thought of the Fiend king.

The marketplace was as noisy as Starbride remembered. Even with all the troubles, people still needed to shop. Rows of stalls occupied the huge square and spilled down several streets, making the space seem small. Striped awnings fought with blankets upon the cobblestones.

Starbride kept her hood up and pretended to browse a wagon covered with silk ribbons. Hugo stood in the middle of an aisle behind her, looking back and forth. He would approach the monks first while the others watched from the crowd. Starbride wouldn't show her face until she was sure it wasn't a trap. She couldn't confirm for Roland that she was still in the city.

Three red-robed figures glanced over an assortment of knives down the lane. Starbride peered at each face. None of them was the supreme head of the strength chapterhouses. Maybe she was hiding and waiting, too, though that didn't seem her style.

Hugo strolled down the lane, bumped into one of the strength brothers and said something. When the man replied, Hugo led all three into a short alleyway. Starbride and Dawnmother headed closer so they would have a good view. Master Bernard leaned against the wall just outside the alley entrance and watched Starbride and Dawnmother, waiting for a signal.

In the alley, the monks crowded close to Hugo. Two men and a woman, none of whom looked younger than Brutal, but they didn't seem old enough to have been on the path for long. The crowding could be eagerness on their part, she supposed, or fright.

The man doing the talking, the largest, gestured at the alley mouth, as if insisting on something. Hugo shrugged and shook his head. Did they want him to call Starbride? Surely they understood why they couldn't immediately be trusted. Or maybe they were anxious to get on with the meeting and get away.

The female monk edged close to Hugo, enough to either kiss him or head-butt him. She grabbed the collar of his coat. He jerked away, and several of his buttons popped off, the coat gaping open to reveal his shirt underneath. Hugo struck at her, but all three monks leaned in. The smaller one caught one of Hugo's arms, and the leader reached for his shirt.

"His necklace," Starbride whispered. "They're trying to get his pyramid necklace." She signaled Master Bernard. He stepped into the alley mouth, shouted to get the monks' attention, and threw a flash bomb.

Starbride shielded her eyes, hoping Hugo remembered to do the same. She heard two distinct yells and then started for the alley. If anyone heard the cries, hopefully, the clamor from the market would prevent them from determining the source.

Dawnmother paused at the alley entrance to discourage anyone from wandering close while Starbride went inside. Hugo faced the one monk still standing, the leader. The others writhed on the ground, holding their eyes. Hugo had drawn his rapier. The monk was unarmed, but he took a wary stance, both hands in front of him as if to bat any strikes away.

Master Bernard raced for the smaller man and placed a pyramid against his head. With a few quick jabs, Hugo backed the leader away. Master Bernard crossed to the fallen woman and put his pyramid to her head as well; it would keep them unconscious. The leader feinted and jabbed two fingers into Hugo's wrist. Hugo grunted and sprang back, nearly dropping his sword, his arm wobbling.

Starbride lifted a mind pyramid and whistled. The leader glanced at her, and their eyes met. He fought against her as she drew his thoughts in, but Starbride let the pyramid do the work instead of making it a battle of wills. Within seconds, he was hers, lost in the pyramid's sparkling facets. "I have him."

Master Bernard pressed his mind pyramid to the leader's forehead, and he crumpled.

"Let's do this quickly." Starbride hated that they had to do it all. She'd hoped that the chapterhouses hadn't been infiltrated, but these monks were either working for Roland willingly, or they'd been coerced. And there was only one way that Roland coerced.

Starbride pressed a pyramid to the female monk's forehead and looked deep inside. It would have been easier with the monk conscious. Sleeping minds tended to take unwanted paths. Starbride let the mind envelop her until she knew the monk as Scarra. She'd been born Clara Aubet, but the strength monks took on rougher names once they'd set their feet on the path.

No, they didn't take them, Starbride saw as a memory rose to the surface. The names were given in a special ceremony attended only by other monks. Starbride left that ceremony alone, not wanting to pry more than she had to. She settled the memories into their respective strands, calling up thoughts of Roland's coup.

Scarra had been in the chapterhouse when it happened. Only weeks from being fully initiated, everyone and their pet cat had challenged her to a fight, one after another. It was…exhilarating. She learned so much, about herself, the fight, and those she fought. At the rate she'd been going, she thought she might attain total enlightenment that afternoon.

She'd just walked into the dining hall when Blade had charged in, the supreme head of all strength chapterhouses, here in her house, large as life! She'd been so sure, so strong. Scarra had gawped at her in awe. Blade called for Ruin, the head of Scarra's chapterhouse and said they were going out. The fight of a lifetime was in the making. Monsters had taken the throne, and the strength chapterhouses were going to defend the king.

What a fight! What a chance to prove herself, to learn more lessons of the universe! Scarra had leapt to her feet, ready to join the charge, but Ruin stopped her and told her to hold the chapterhouse. Hold the spirits bedamned chapterhouse when the city was burning!

Starbride pulled back from the memory, fighting not to get caught in Scarra's rage. As angry as she was, Scarra had obeyed the order to stay behind. She'd had plenty to do, helping the higher-ranking monks, taking in refugees or wounded monks from other houses. She didn't see Blade or Ruin for weeks and wondered what had happened to them. When Ruin returned, he seemed different, more arrogant. Scarra assumed by his swagger that he had won the fight, but swagger had never been in his nature. When the others asked him about Blade, he said she was still at the palace, that they'd made a mistake, that the Fiend king was stronger than King Einrich had ever been.

Scarra was confused. Pure physical strength wasn't what they strived for or respected. What one did with his or her strength was just as important as the strength itself. Still, when Ruin told her and some of the others to go to the palace, to see the king for themselves, she'd gone. If Ruin believed in him, he had to be worth a listen.

She'd met with this new king and heard him speak. Ruin had been right. This stronger king was much more capable than the other had been. Scarra was completely convinced after meeting him *once*.

Starbride backed up to when Scarra had met Roland. The memory shift was subtle, barely a wrinkle in the flow, but if Roland had known Scarra at all, if he'd bothered to pry, he would have known that it took more than words to convince her. Deeds were Scarra's measure of a person, and Roland had shown her nothing.

Starbride dug into the memory and pulled the thread slowly apart. Roland hadn't erased Scarra's memories. He would have had to rebuild all her memories from the coup onward in order to make new ones. No, he did what Starbride suspected he'd once done to Hugo: placed new memories over the old.

Underneath, Starbride found the real memory. Scarra had walked into the throne room with some of her fellows, and Roland had pulled the cover from a large pyramid. Scarra had foolishly stared into it. Roland had simply changed her from a skeptic to a true believer in a blink. With a disgusted sigh, Starbride unwound the new memory. Unfortunately, she had to take everything from there on, the entire thread. Scarra wouldn't even remember that she'd inadvertently turned traitor.

Starbride saw that Roland had commanded the strength monks to capture certain people at all costs, some of whom would be known by their pyramid necklaces. Scarra wouldn't remember that order either, wouldn't have any idea how she'd wound up in an alley at the market.

When Starbride surfaced, Scarra remained unconscious. Master Bernard had finished the leader, and told them his name was Rage.

Starbride helped him with the last, Fury. All three had been brainwashed at the same time. With Hugo and Dawnmother's help, they sat the monks against the wall and settled in to wait.

"Should we bind them?" Hugo asked as he held his coat closed.

"Their confusion upon waking should work in our favor," Master Bernard said. "Though we should be ready in case their first instinct is to attack, I don't think we can risk binding them."

Starbride picked up Hugo's buttons and slipped them in her pocket. Dawnmother could help him fix the coat later. "If a stranger makes it past Dawnmother, we can tell them our friends are ill, and we're waiting for them to recover. Not so easily sold if they're bound." She kept a mind pyramid out in case she needed to hypnotize them again but cupped it in her palm, out of sight from anyone on the street.

The monks came to at the same time, their drooping heads lifting haltingly as they tried to overcome the lethargy that accompanied a mind pyramid. They blinked at Starbride, at each other, and at their surroundings.

"Gently," Starbride said. "My name is Starbride. This is Master Bernard from the Pyradisté Academy, and Lord Hugo Sandy. You're in an alley near the grand marketplace."

"How did we get here?" Rage asked. He was nearly as tall as Brutal, though a little less bulky. His eyes darted between all of them.

"Did you kidnap us?" Scarra kept her eyes on Starbride alone, and through the fatigue, Starbride saw anger brewing. Fury didn't speak but stared at Master Bernard curiously, as if they'd met before.

Starbride laid out their tale as best she could. They all remembered the pyramid in Roland's throne room but nothing after that.

"I'm no one's lackey," Rage said.

Scarra touched his arm. "And the Fiend king was going to use us to capture you?"

"How do you know?" Fury asked at last. "You were the head of the Pyradisté Academy. And you..." His bright blue eyes fixed on Starbride. "You're the princess consort."

Scarra's eyes went wide, and she tried to bow from a seated position. "Oh, um, hello, Highness."

Starbride bit her lip to keep from laughing. "You don't have to bow."

"I wasn't planning on it," Rage said.

Scarra nudged him. "She's the princess consort, idiot."

"So?" Rage asked.

"So? Do some...courtly shit." She clapped a hand over her mouth.

Starbride did laugh then. "Let's get somewhere safe, and I can tell you more."

Scarra stood immediately. After a shrug as if he wanted to see what would happen, Fury followed. Rage stood, but he didn't lose his scowl. "I think we should check on our fellow brothers and sisters first. If what you say is true—"

"You'll go right back into the Fiend king's clutches when your hypnotized fellows get hold of you," Hugo said.

"If he bothered to mind-hump three scrubs like us, this infection goes deep," Scarra said. "Everyone in our house could be f—" She glanced at Starbride, blushed, and made another clumsy bow. "Excuse my speaking, Princess Consort. Ma always did say I have a mouth like a penny whore."

Fury snorted a laugh, his intense expression replaced by a boyish look that made him seem about fifteen.

"Since you haven't reported back," Starbride said, "the Fiend king might already know we've broken his hold on you." As she stared at them, she wondered if having her break his spell had been Roland's plan all along, the reason why he'd only sent three people to capture or kill her. Now he'd expect Starbride to try to free all of them. Now he'd set a bigger trap.

"I suppose if you wanted to kill us," Rage said, "you would have done so while we were down, but how do we know you didn't do this to us? That we were shopping, and then you used a pyramid on us?"

"Does that change how you feel about the Fiend king?"

Rage looked down as if doubting everything he'd ever seen or heard.

"Let's hear them out," Fury said. "Seems like we're in it up to our ears anyway."

When Rage agreed, Starbride led them to their old hideout. Down in the dark space, she and Master Bernard lit pyramids and set them on the small table that remained.

Starbride cleared her throat, still thinking of traps. "The Fiend king has been known to…implant pyramids in those he captures. It happened to me once, and since you probably would have been unconscious, it wouldn't be in your memories. He could have developed a pyramid that could track you. Do you mind if Master Bernard and I examine you?"

The three monks glanced at one another.

"You can stay together if you like," Starbride added hurriedly. "Or we could examine you one by one, in private."

Scarra chuckled. "It's not modesty we're worried about. It's close in the chapterhouse. But a pyramid stuck up one of our...um." She shrugged out of her robe and stood only in her well-muscled body and meager undergarments. "Well? How do you test?"

Like her name suggested, her skin was a map of scars. Even though most of her fights were probably barehanded, she'd certainly had others in her time, even if she looked only twenty or so. "Well... let's look for new scars, red or pink. How many of those do you have?"

Scarra shrugged as if she couldn't be bothered to remember them all. Fury helped her look, joking as he did. Even Rage seemed to relax as they laughed. Starbride didn't think she'd feel the same being so scrutinized. She turned away.

Scarra hooted at her. "Nothing you haven't seen before, Princess *Consort.*"

Starbride felt the heat rush to her face. When she tried to stammer a response, they only laughed harder until Scarra shushed them.

"Only joking, Princess Consort."

"I think you should call me Starbride if we're going to be poking around in each other's underwear."

"Oh, so you're joining us now?" Fury asked.

Starbride shook her head. Hugo began what was probably an affronted response, but Starbride stopped him. They continued to search each other, Starbride not daring to look when Fury took his undergarments off, and the others cried for him to spare their eyes.

"Put your lad away in front of the nobles or it'll be off with your head," Scarra said. "Both of them!"

Starbride had to laugh, and she noted that Dawnmother continued to watch the monks with appraising, unashamed eyes. Master Bernard simply chuckled and leaned against the table, waiting for them to finish.

Neither Scarra nor Fury had new scars, but on Rage, they found what Starbride expected: a new scar, pink, still a little red around the edges. Starbride bent close to look. Luckily, Rage had kept his undergarments on, but the scar was on his thigh, very close to his... Starbride shook the thought away.

"This could be what we're looking for," Starbride said. "If there's a pyramid in there, we have to get it out."

"Careful," Scarra said. "Cut him wrong there and he could bleed to death, not to mention the fact that a clumsy knife could rob him of his...pride."

"We'll need a surgeon and some way to put you to sleep," Starbride said. "I can use a pyramid on you."

Rage shook his head. "Pain helps me focus. I'll meditate."

"A detection pyramid first," Master Bernard said. "To make sure it's in there, and to see what we're dealing with. If it's a destruction pyramid, we might need to break it as soon as we have it out."

Starbride brought her detection pyramid near the scar and focused. There, just beneath the skin…

As soon as her mind touched it, it leapt to life. She barely had time to cry out before it exploded, blowing a gaping hole in Rage's leg, nearly taking it off. He collapsed, and the rest of them staggered back before rushing forward again.

"Rage!" Scarra cried. He stared into her face as he coughed his last breath, blood streaming from his leg. "What in the name of Best and Berth was that?"

Blood soaked the floor around Scarra's bare legs where she knelt. Starbride could feel the wetness on her face and neck. She had to be covered in red. One moment he'd been laughing and joking, years ahead of him, and now dead within seconds.

She felt her lips pull up in a snarl. "Track you?" she spat. "Why did I worry that he'd track you when he could kill you?"

"What are you—" Scarra asked.

Starbride surged to her feet. "The Darkstrong-cursed Fiend *king*. I was worried he'd track, but why would he bother? I'm trapped in the city. He'll find me sooner or later; time is on his side. Why would he spend energy trying to chase me when he can just *kill his puppets before I free them*?" She shouted the last words, and angry tears started in her eyes. She swallowed them down.

Scarra looked down at her mostly-naked body. "Is it in us too?"

Starbride took several deep breaths, trying to quiet her rage so she could comfort the little child she heard in Scarra's voice. "You don't have any new scars." Even so, she wasn't going to check. "He wouldn't need to trap all of you. One in three is probably good odds in his book."

"Just enough to make us frightened of taking any action," Hugo said softly. He stared at Rage's body with tears standing in his eyes, and Starbride knew what he was thinking. His father had done this. He'd only been six when Roland had first died, but that was old enough to remember how much he'd loved his father.

Starbride took his hand as she tried to think. Dimly, she became aware of Dawnmother washing the blood from her face and directing the monks to get dressed. Starbride could free the monks mentally, but some would be left with a trap inside them. As soon as she touched it with her detection pyramid, it had activated, leaving her no time to focus or shut it down. Roland probably had the means to detonate the pyramids from a distance, just like he'd once done to the fire pyramid he'd put in her. It might be kinder to leave the monks hypnotized. Then Roland wouldn't have a reason to blow them apart.

Starbride let go of Hugo. It wasn't her decision to make alone. "Many of your brothers and sisters probably have these pyramids now. If we're going to get them out, we'll have to do it without using detection pyramids."

Master Bernard cleared his throat. "That might cause them to detonate, too."

"We could leave them as they are," Starbride said.

Scarra bit her lip. "They wouldn't want to be slaves."

Fury nodded. "They won't care what the risk is. They'd rather go down fighting."

"I'm...very sorry about Rage," Starbride said.

"He died free," Scarra said. Her voice had hardened to the woman Starbride recalled from her memory, though she leaned down and closed Rage's eyes. "If we can give the others the same, let's do it."

"I'll help any way I can," Master Bernard said.

Still staring at the body, Hugo nodded. Dawnmother gripped Starbride's shoulder and gave her a look that said she'd never have to ask for help.

"We need to get to Ruin or Blade," Scarra said, "and free their minds. They'd know the best way to get everyone else."

"No one's seen Blade, though," Fury said.

"I think I can get Ruin alone, and then you can hypnotize him like you did us, Princess Consort. Tonight, near the chapterhouse."

"If...the Fiend king sent you to find us," Hugo said, "and you haven't come back, he'll know something happened."

"So I'll go back," Scarra said, "tell Ruin there were too many of you, that you got Rage and Fury."

"He won't just follow you out of the chapterhouse," Fury said. "He'll want a full report, and you're shit at lying."

Before they could get in an argument, Starbride said, "Then we go in after him. The Fiend king can't be everywhere at once. He might not expect us to go breaking into a strength chapterhouse. Not tonight, though," she added before they could begin to plan. "The person we need the most for this job is currently skulking around Dockland."

"I hate waiting," Scarra muttered.

"His skills will be helpful," Hugo said quietly. Starbride could have hugged him. Besides waiting for Pennynail, they had a body to bury, something else they'd have to do in secret.

CHAPTER SEVENTEEN

KATYA

K atya watched the Allusians setting up tents and gathering equipment and provisions outside the walls of Newhope. A number of adsnazi came down from the hills to join them. Seemed many people were taking Da up on his offer to come and see a Fiend for themselves.

Hawkblade and her fellow nomads camped beside them, mobile towns with families, tents, and horses, all of it able to be packed and traveling within a few hours. Katya cringed at the thought of taking children to war, but she supposed the nomads knew what they were doing. After all, she wasn't leaving her niece and nephew behind in Allusia.

Leafclever and Redtrue organized the adsnazi and those who camped near them as well. Katya suggested separating everyone into groups, pairing those with combat experience with those who had none. The nomads taught anyone who had the will.

Brightstriving arrived at the camp mid-morning. Katya groaned, certain they were in for another confrontation, but Brightstriving only said, "Good morning," and stuck to Katya's side. Speaking Allusian and Farradain fluently, she offered advice, echoed Katya's suggestions, and when she had to, spoke in a quiet, almost deadly voice to those who resisted.

Sunjoyful helped manage the provisions, sorting food and making lists. He was as much a natural organizer as his wife, only a lot softer about it. At the moment, Katya was glad to have Brightstriving's volume. "I can't tell you how grateful I am for your help," Katya said.

"I do it for my daughter's sake, but I accept your thanks. I'm glad you are wise enough to take help when it is offered."

"Let's thank both the spirits of wisdom and Horsestrong for that one."

In the afternoon, Katya caught Brutal as he made his own rounds among their slowly growing army. "How are they looking?" she asked.

He glanced over to where people were training. "Most look like sheep trying to use a pitchfork, but they'll come around. And, uh, I know you told me to leave it alone, but I couldn't stand Castelle's moping any longer."

"Did you hit her, too?"

"I just reminded her that when she inherited her noble title, she swore an oath to protect the crown at all costs."

Katya had to laugh. "They all have to say that, but look how many took it seriously."

"Seemed to wake her up a little. And I spoke to Redtrue for you. After a lot of sighing and eye rolling, I got her to promise she won't give up on contacting Starbride just because we're on the move."

She could have hugged him. "Thank you, Brutal."

"Thank me by beating Roland into paste."

"As you command."

With a lighter heart, Katya returned to her parents' tent to look over local maps. So far, Ma had taken over the duties of writing flowery letters to the nearest nobles, making the borders ornate, and drawing a crown with the hawk crest of the Umbriels at the top. They'd already gotten a response from Count Mathias of Baelfest, just inside Farraday's border. Ma sent out invitations to other nobles to meet the royal party there.

Ma used sparkling pins near her temples and the back of her hair, giving the illusion of a crown where there wasn't one. She wore fine clothes from Allusia: tight fitting trousers with a loose shirt held under a bodice. Instead of Starbride's jewel tones, Ma stuck to a pale blue that complimented her fair hair and light blue eyes. They were quite a pair, the king in his Farradain finery and the queen complimenting Allusia. Katya wondered if she should commission an outfit that was half and half.

"If we were lost in the desert," Katya said, "you'd make a suit fit for a ball out of mud, Ma."

Ma's mouth turned down. "I suppose that's a compliment."

"On your ingenuity."

"To the nobles, power has markers. We have to put on a show, even with everything that's happening."

Katya nodded. She knew the importance of show. She used it all the time. The Allusians loaned them some of their best horses, all with polished tack and saddles. Katya thought they cut a fine figure, maybe not quite as fine as in Marienne, but better than they had in a long time. Even Dayscout seemed impressed as he rode with them.

Count Mathias met them at the gate to his estate. Together with Brutal, Castelle, her friends, and a band of Newhope's guard, the royal party was large, but Count Mathias regarded them calmly.

He wore a dark green coat of fine make, but it wasn't that or his leather breeches that caught Katya's eye. An enormous bearskin cloak cascaded down the back of his black horse. The cowl, the bear's head, was down, revealing dark stubble on Mathias's nearly bald head.

He made an awkward bow from his saddle, his dark eyes never leaving Katya's father. His full black beard was neatly combed, and he didn't have a spot of mud on him. From the wilderness he might have been, but he knew how to dress for visitors.

"Majesties, Governor," Count Mathias said, "welcome to Baelfest."

"Thank you for greeting us personally," Da said with a smile.

"And for opening your home to other nobles," Ma said.

Count Mathias' eyes shifted to her, and he smiled a trifle nervously. "I have no courtly spouse, Majesty, so I'm afraid my hospitality might be a little rougher than you're used to."

Ma gestured at the forest that had begun shortly after they'd left Allusia. "In nature, one finds all the beauty one desires, Count Mathias, and a welcoming home is never a rough one."

"Well said." Dayscout beamed. "It's nice to see you again, Count Mathias."

"Governor. Shall we ride to the house?"

He fell in beside Katya's father. Katya stayed on Da's right. The other guards fanned out as much as the road would allow. Several of the count's men walked with them, leading hunting dogs.

"Do you do a lot of hunting, Count Mathias?" Katya asked.

"It's a way of life out here, Highness. We keep very few animals, so hunting provides for my household, the farmers that live on my estate, and many in the village beyond. I have heard that you enjoyed a spot of hunting yourself."

Katya didn't miss the past tense. Count Mathias knew what had happened, and he wasn't entirely ignorant of court if he'd heard of her persona. He might even think her as silly as the character she'd so carefully crafted.

"My days of idle hunting are over," Katya said. "I've seen what can be lost and what must be regained."

He only nodded.

Count Mathias' house was made from logs instead of stone but still had two floors, and judging by the windows, at least five rooms on each floor. A butler answered the door, but he threw it open as if he wasn't used to providing that service for his lord. Katya wondered if he'd only been given the job that afternoon. Or maybe he was much better versed in helping Count Mathias during the hunt than at the house. He took everyone's cloaks and hung them up. Count Mathias led them through a foyer to a study. One of the walls was lined with bookshelves, but the others sported weapons of every variety as well as a multitude of animal trophies.

A fire roared in the huge stone fireplace, and several well-worn but comfortable looking sofas dotted the room. "Please, sit where you like," Count Mathias said.

Ma, Da, and Dayscout sat on a sofa near the center of the room, Count Mathias opposite them. Katya sat near a window. Brutal lingered near the corner, and Castelle took a sofa not far from Katya. The rest remained out in the hall.

Count Mathias glanced at everyone. "There's no need to have your guard present, I assure you."

Da gestured over his shoulder. "Brother Brutal is a childhood friend of my daughter's and accompanies her everywhere. And Baroness Castelle Burenne deserves to be here according to her rank."

Count Mathias nodded slowly. "Well, then welcome, Baroness, Brother Brutal. Shall we come to it? I'd prefer not to wait for the others. And it might do me good to hear it twice."

"You know of the troubles facing our kingdom," Da said.

Count Mathias chewed his mustache before he called over his shoulder, "Bring it in."

Castelle and Katya leapt from their chairs. Da signaled them to wait as two of Count Mathias' men brought in a corpse. Not just any corpse, Katya saw as she stepped closer. This one had the gray look of someone who'd been dead for days, and the divot in its forehead held a sparkling residue of crystal.

Dayscout crept to Katya's side. "Horsestrong preserve us. Is that…"

"Yes," Katya answered.

Once they'd had a good look, Mathias said, "Burn it." He looked back to Da as his men took the corpse out. "Hardest fight of my life. Took two of my men before we killed it, before I figured out *how* to kill it. I trust you know already."

"To kill this one and worse," Katya said.

"Worse?"

"That's only a corpse Fiend, a dead person with a bit of Fiendish essence."

"Dead people up and walking?" Dayscout asked.

"We did warn you, Governor," Katya said. "There are other Fiends who have the essence in them while they still live, and there's no pyramid in their forehead to aim for." There were two of them in the room, though not everyone knew it.

Count Mathias leaned forward. "As I see it, Majesties, you're telling me I have the chance to defend me and mine, all the folks who depend on me, *and* hunt the most ferocious creatures I've encountered in the whole of my life?"

Da tilted his head. "I've never heard the last bit, but yes."

Count Mathias grinned widely. "Tell me where to point my spear."

"And he didn't even need a parliament," Dayscout whispered in Katya's ear.

"I hope the rest of the nobles agree with you, Count Mathias," Ma said.

"I fear they will not, Majesty. Some of the nobles who were in Marienne during the trouble are out here now, staying with kin or demanding space from those they outrank. They won't be eager to reenter the fray or to let you take their guards. If they've run afoul of these corpse Fiends, that will make them all the more reluctant to give you their support. The narrow-minded will argue for digging in here and starting afresh."

"Abandon Marienne and build a new one, simple as that?" Ma asked.

Dayscout sat again. "It might seem that simple to those that think houses are built by magic and that the wind delivers the tea."

"I'll bet they're running low on all the food they were used to," Ma said. "Perhaps your hospitality could find itself even…rougher, Count Mathias."

"That it could, Majesty. I didn't hear of any dukes among the nobles' company. Perhaps if they saw the highest of them living low…"

"Something like that," Ma said.

❖

The first group of nobles arrived in a clump. Their charge was led by a baroness and a viscount who'd infringed upon the hospitality of the first lower ranking noble they'd found out there, Lord Kline. He was a country lord like Count Mathias, with only a large house on the outskirts of a village; he had no property to speak of. Katya was betting the nobles he was sheltering had eaten him out of house and home already. Count Mathias was lucky his rank was too high for them to infringe upon him.

Lord Kline had a wide-eyed, hollow look, as if explosive pyramids were constantly going off around him. The viscount and the baroness staying with him were both from lands on the other side of the Lavine River, so far from where they were now that it might as well have been on the other side of the world. Except for Lord Kline, all the lords and ladies with them had been at court, most of them having escaped together. They complained long of their journey and almost as long about their current accommodations as they clustered in Count Mathias's study.

Those desiring sugar or coffee were put off with an apology. Count Mathias had let his fire burn low, and the room was chilly, even with all its occupants. They drank a local tea that was harshly bitter without something to dilute it. Ma sipped hers with no trace of a grimace on her features, though Katya bet she swore inside.

"You don't actually need us to fight, right, Majesty?" one of the lords asked. "I mean, you just need soldiers. There are plenty of people in the villages." Others nodded, as if the villages were stuffed with disposable people.

Da shook his head gravely. "We must all ride together. The more of us there are seen supporting the common people, the greater the numbers that will join our banner."

"But can't you just…command them to follow you?" the viscount asked.

"As I can command you, you mean." As the viscount blanched, Da looked to the rest of them. "We don't have the manpower to press people into service."

"Besides," Katya drawled, "that only works well on ships, where you have a captive workforce. On land, they could just run away."

"Will you join us," Da asked Lord Kline, "and ask your people to join us as well?"

"I…" He cleared his throat. "I'm a farmer."

The other lords and ladies laughed, and Lord Kline went scarlet to his ears. Da clapped him on the shoulder. "A farmer the people know and respect, Kline. Don't worry about rousing speeches; leave those to me. All you need do is stand with me. We'll leave enough people behind so that those returning from war will have something to eat, but we need as many as can be spared, and those need to be trained. The opponent we face is a fierce one, as Count Mathias can tell you."

"But we can stay behind once you have the recruits you need?" one of the ladies asked.

Katya wanted to shake them and shout, "What if it's your own skins? Would you fight then?"

"The cinnamon shipments will be coming into Marienne soon," Ma said. "And velvet from upriver, just in time for the Winter Ball." Every eye in the room turned to her. "You know, I remember last year's party particularly well. We watched from the balconies of the palace as the candle parade wound through the streets, and the chef made those sumptuous cinnamon twists. We stayed up far too late and drank too much spiced wine." She sighed, a happy smile on her face that was echoed by many in the room. "When we finally fell into our featherbeds that night, we must have slept until noon the next day and had to have more spiced wine for medicinal purposes. Snug by the fire, I can still feel the warmth of a new robe around my shoulders." She took a sip of the revolting tea, her eyes fixed on nothing.

The nobles glanced at their own teacups, at one another, at their surroundings.

"When do we leave?" the viscount said quietly.

Da smiled softly. "First light."

Chapter Eighteen

Starbride

While Starbride waited for Pennynail's return, she decided to speak to Dawnmother about a problem she'd been avoiding too long. "How is Averie?"

"Getting stronger every day. She should be ready for the pyramid."

Starbride grimaced at her matter-of-fact tone. They hadn't found any new scars on Averie's body, but that didn't mean Roland had left her mind alone. They'd needed her to be a little stronger before Starbride could use a mind pyramid on her, and now there was no putting it off. Starbride tried to banish the memory of Rage's body from her mind.

She and Dawnmother entered the small space that housed Averie's cot. Her eyes flicked open as they entered. That was a good sign. When they'd first rescued her, she would hardly wake for anything.

"There you are," Averie said. "I feel so lazy just lying around."

"Get out of that bed, and you'll never hear the end from me," Dawnmother said.

"Best not to argue with her, Averie," Starbride said. "I learned from an early age to avoid being sick around Dawnmother if I ever wanted to stand on my own."

Averie nodded against the pillow. "I know why you're here."

Starbride held her pyramid up. "I'm sorry, but—"

"Don't apologize. I understand." As Starbride came closer, Averie squeezed her fingers. "Katya would be so proud of you."

Starbride's breath caught. "Just relax." She waited for Averie to still before she pressed the pyramid to Averie's forehead. She wouldn't pry, she promised. She would stick to the captivity and leave the rest alone. She separated the memories into their threads and searched for Roland.

The ballroom curtains were on fire, the air thick with smoke. Screams of dying men and women surrounded her, but Averie only had eyes for *him*.

She worked quickly, putting arrow to string, aiming, and firing. One thudded into his arm, another into his chest. He just kept coming. She tried not to see his horns and claws and fangs, but spirits above, those all blue eyes drew her in.

Averie blinked, breaking the spell enough to glance behind him. Katya and King Einrich had reached the exit. Katya called Averie's name and looked back, surely thinking something stupid like rushing to her rescue. "Go, go, go," Averie repeated. She loosed another arrow as she ran backward. Through her terror, she felt sudden gratitude that no one she knew would see her die.

Her right foot skidded, and she glanced down to see sheets of blood and a body under her feet. She felt *his* cold then but couldn't look. She called to the spirits to protect her, to tell Katya she was sorry; she hadn't slowed him down enough.

Starbride tried to pull away from Averie's terror, but it caught her. She felt the blow as Roland's fist slammed into Averie's side. Averie's memories released her then, growing fuzzy and unsure. She'd barely been conscious as she'd crashed into the wall. It had been so hard to breathe…

Starbride let her own emotions surround her, fear and sorrow as Averie lay at the bottom of that wall, below a haze of smoke and face-to-face with a corpse. Averie had only flashes of memory then: being dragged by her ankle from the ballroom. Someone had tossed her on a pile of rags. No, they weren't rags but people, a pile of corpses staring at her sightlessly. She'd tried to struggle, but it felt like she'd been squeezed in a vise. Her head pounded and swam. Her vision wouldn't clear; she could barely stay awake.

"Get clear, get clear," she'd said to herself, the words mostly in her head. She had to free herself from the bodies' clutches and find out what had happened, if Katya had escaped. Through her agony, she wriggled free of the pile, able only to crawl. She froze when she saw him.

Roland bent over a worktable, his Fiendish face put away. He fished around in the corpse pile, a horrid rustling sound, not seeming to notice Averie on the edge. He flopped one woman in green livery onto the table: Cristine, a friend and fellow maid. Her brown hair had come undone and cascaded down her face. Roland brushed it away almost tenderly before he crunched into her skull with a dagger.

Averie fought not to gag at the grisly sounds, at the way Cristine's body jerked after Roland put a pyramid in her. She sat up, her now-gray eyes glassy and unfocused before they grew hard and cruel. Averie tried to be still, but every part of her wanted to cry out, and she couldn't control her shaking. Cristine's dead eyes focused on Averie with lightning quickness, and she let out an ear-splitting howl.

Averie tried to crawl away. She whimpered as Roland's footsteps came closer. When he lifted her, she screamed. He held her under her arms, making her body shriek where it was broken.

Smiling, Roland was very handsome, but Averie could see the Fiend curling beneath his skin. He could never rid himself of the cold of the grave, no matter his face. "Hello, pet," he said.

Averie sobbed as she fumbled for her belt knife. She couldn't get her shaking hands to close over the grip.

Roland cuddled her close. "There now, dearheart, there, there." He rocked her as if she was a little babe; her ribs screamed and screamed. Black and gold spots raced across her vision. "You're a very broken baby, aren't you?"

"Let...let me...go."

"Don't think I don't remember you," he whispered. "I'm so glad you lived, darling. Now we can have a proper conversation."

Starbride yanked out of the memory before the torture could start. She skipped ahead before looking again. Roland had let Averie heal before he'd tortured her anew, asking the same questions: Where was Katya? Einrich? Starbride? Reinholt? He asked her with pyramids and without. Crowe had taught her the mental exercises to resist a mind probe, and she'd used them all. In the end, she'd broken, giving up every Order hiding place she knew of. She'd also told him that Crowe and Pennynail had many more hideouts she didn't know. She'd rejoiced at this knowledge even as he'd bled her for it.

Starbride tried to block out the pain and look for planted memories, changed ones, anything that didn't make sense, small overlays like the one she'd spotted in Scarra, but found nothing. After all the torture, maybe Roland didn't think he'd needed to change Averie, not if she was going to die in the bowels of the palace.

Starbride pulled out of Averie's memories and let her own sobs overtake her. She felt Dawnmother's arms around her.

"I knew it was bad," Dawnmother said. "I've held her many times these past few days."

"I can't stay in here," Starbride said. "It's too small."

Dawnmother hurried her from the room. Averie would remain unconscious for a short time. Starbride didn't know if she could be there when Averie awoke, didn't know if she could face someone who'd been through so much horror. It made the time Starbride had spent in hiding seem like a gentle outing in the country.

The door to the outside loomed ahead, and she changed her mind. Roland was out there. They met Pennynail coming in. Starbride grabbed him and led him to her room. "Take care of Averie," she said over her shoulder to Dawnmother. Too small was far better than too large.

"What happened?" Freddie said as he took off his mask.

"Averie's memories...I can't speak it. Tell me of your journey."

He eyed her for a moment. "I fenced the silver and renewed some of my contacts. They're pretty anxious for news. The corpse Fiends have taken over the docks but left most of Dockland to be its crime-ridden, refuse strewn self."

Starbride hugged her elbows as she paced. "I'm sure we'll find a way to use that. Right now I'm just glad we can feed everyone for a little longer."

She related what had happened in his absence, lingering on the monks and hurrying through Averie's memories. She had to pause at the end, thinking it strange that Rage's death paled to what had happened to Averie. Starbride had only seen him die. She'd lived through Averie's terror.

"Sneaking into a strength chapterhouse?" Freddie said. "Sounds like fun."

"Only you would say that."

"When do we leave?"

"Tonight. I don't think our young monk friends will wait any longer now that you're back."

❖

After dark, Scarra and Fury led Starbride, Hugo, and Pennynail to their chapterhouse. Fury strolled in the front door, one more red robe to blend with the rest. He would discern if Ruin was within as quickly as he could and then give a signal from the back of the building. Scarra led them there to wait.

There were no walls around the large building. A simple garden lay at the back with a short wire enclosure to keep out wandering feet. People didn't often try to rob the strength chapterhouse. Anything they found within wouldn't be worth the beating they'd take.

Within moments, Starbride spotted a candle flicker on the third floor. The window swung open, and a knotted rope fell down. Starbride held in a groan. As good as she was getting at climbing, using a rope to scale a sheer wall was another animal. Scarra climbed up as easily as any other person would slide down. Pennynail leaned close to Starbride's ear. "Just tie it around you, nice and tight, and we'll haul you up."

He scampered up quick as a wink, not as muscled as Scarra, but lean and wiry. Hugo helped Starbride tie the rope under her rump, so she could sort of sit on it. The thought of being lifted three stories, dangling above nothing, made her heart dance in her mouth much more than the time she'd climbed a townhouse with Pennynail. At least then, her fate had been in her own shaky limbs.

"Don't worry," Hugo said. "I'll be right behind you."

"I'm not worried about being up there; it's getting there that's the problem."

"I mean don't worry about being embarrassed. I'm going to have to ride just like you are. I'm built for rapier fighting, not climbing."

She gave him a grateful smile, gave the rope a tug, and she was off. She ascended so quickly she nearly yelped. She had to trail her feet along the building to keep from smacking into it.

Pennynail pulled her over the sill while Scarra and Fury kept the rope taut. After she was loose, she leaned against the wall in the small storeroom while they pulled Hugo up as fast as they'd pulled her. She took out a detection pyramid but hesitated. If she detected one of the traps Roland had put in the monks, it would explode.

No, she'd really had to focus, had to be practically on top of that trap before it exploded. They had to risk checking for what they couldn't see. She half wondered if Roland had modified the exploding trap after she'd sneaked into the palace. Maybe he was tired of people poking around in his things.

"Everything seems normal," Fury whispered. "There was a light under Ruin's door."

Starbride kept her detection pyramid out as well as a Fiend suppression pyramid. Scarra, Fury, and Rage had been missing for a few days. Ruin wouldn't know whether they were alive or dead. He might assume his three protégés were infiltrating the rebels' lair. The thought that she had a lair nearly made Starbride laugh out loud.

She sent the monks out first, each with an excuse as to why they were on the top level where only the highest ranking monks had rooms. If Ruin had been the only senior monk to be mind-warped, the others might not know about her new friends' mission.

After the monks, Starbride, Pennynail, and Hugo moved as a clump, the better to defend one another if they were surprised. Down a short hallway, they heard voices. They paused and waited. A door shut, and Scarra leaned around the corner and waved them on.

Every creak, every quiet cough or snore from within a shuttered room made Starbride's stomach turn over. She tried to conjure some of the excitement she'd felt when breaking into someone's house, but what waited for her at the end of this journey made it too serious to enjoy.

That and Averie's memories kept ricocheting through her head.

She stopped occasionally to use her detection pyramid but kept coming up empty. She met Scarra and Fury just outside the door to Ruin's room. Pennynail and Hugo stood to the sides of the door, out of sight. Fury stood directly in front with Scarra behind him and Starbride hidden behind her. When Ruin opened the door, the two monks would step aside, and Starbride would hypnotize Ruin before he could call out. Then they'd all pile inside the room, and Starbride could get to work.

That was the plan, anyway.

Fury knocked. "Who is it?" came a call from within.

"It's Fury, brother. We're back."

Footsteps neared, but they sounded off to Starbride, as if the walker had more than two legs. She peeked around Scarra's shoulder, hoping to remain hidden in the dim hallway.

"Fury?" A large man opened the door, his hair gone gray, but his blue eyes shining. "Did you report to the quartermaster? He was supposed to tell me when you'd gotten back."

Scarra tensed, but Starbride grabbed her arm as a shadow shifted behind Ruin's back. A woman stepped into the light. "Fury and Scarra," she said. "What are you doing up so late?"

"Uh, hello, Drive," Fury said. "How are you, sister?"

"Well enough. Are you going to tell me what brings you to Ruin's door this late in the evening, or do I have to guess?"

Starbride half expected Fury to ask Drive the same question, but she seemed older than him, more in charge. Starbride's mind raced. What were they going to do?

"Where's Rage?" Ruin asked.

"Well, um, we'd like to have a chat about that, brother," Fury said, "if we may."

He nodded. "Drive, would you mind giving us a few moments?"

No! Drive couldn't come into the hallway without giving the game away. As Drive stood on tiptoe to kiss Ruin's cheek, Starbride whispered, "Go!"

Pennynail leapt around the corner and barreled into the two older monks. Hugo followed, but Drive caught Pennynail's wrists and threw him neatly away. Ruin ducked, tripped Hugo, and while Hugo was falling, stood up underneath him and flipped him onto the floor. Both monks' faces seemed almost serene as they fought. Fury and Scarra burst into the room after that, and Starbride followed.

She slammed the door behind her. When Ruin looked at her, she lifted her pyramid and pounced upon his mind.

Oh, what a disciplined mind it was. He squirmed against her as she tried to fracture him with the facets of the pyramid. He took two shuddering steps forward.

"Whoa!" Drive cried in a happy voice. "You almost had us! Who are these two? New recruits?" She turned in Starbride's direction. "What in the spirits' names are you doing?"

Starbride felt them move, piling on top of Drive to keep her from crying out. They tried to reason with her as they scuffled.

Ruin took another step forward, his fists clenching and unclenching. Starbride swallowed her fear and stood her ground, trying like Darkstrong himself to put Ruin under her will. Finally, he fell to one knee, his mind in too many fragments to keep going. Starbride pressed her pyramid to his forehead. He went limp, and she let him slide from her arms to lie still.

Fury and Scarra had tackled Drive, but she squirmed against them and Hugo as he tried to cover her mouth. Pennynail lay atop her legs, but even under all their weight, she wriggled so; any minute she'd be free.

Starbride knelt next to her. After the way Ruin had dismissed her, Starbride guessed she hadn't been mind-warped by Roland. Still, they couldn't have her shouting.

"Listen to me, and we'll let you go," Starbride said.

Drive's eyes rolled upward, giving Starbride a look that told her where she could stuff her demands.

"Your friend Ruin has been mind-warped by the Fiend king, and my friends and I are here to help him."

"Please listen to her, Drive," Scarra said.

"Just knock her out!" Hugo whispered.

Drive quieted when Starbride showed her the pyramid. "I don't want to use this. I want you to see what we're going to do. We're trying to help him. Hasn't he been different these past few days?"

Drive ceased her struggles and watched Starbride intently.

"Fury, Scarra, and Rage had been acting strangely, too, ever since they visited the palace," Starbride said. "But I helped them." All but one. She shook the thought away.

Someone knocked on Ruin's door. "Everything all right in there? Having a midnight brawl, are you?"

Starbride bent lower. "You'll be awake to watch the whole thing. When I'm finished, he'll be the man he was."

Drive nodded slowly. The knock on the door sounded again. "Ruin?"

"Let her up," Starbride whispered. Everyone backed away as if Drive were a wild animal. She leapt to her feet in one easy motion, and everyone tensed as if they'd have to jump her again, but she only eased the door open a crack.

"What is it? We're busy." She sounded out of breath, and her hair was a mess. The man in the hallway laughed and made some comment. She said, "We will if you go away." Then she shut the door and turned. "If you do anything bad to him…"

"Understood," Starbride said.

Drive straightened Ruin's legs so that he looked more comfortable. "Who the hell are you?"

Hugo grinned. "We're the resistance."

"Against the Fiend king?" She smoothed Ruin's hair. "We were suspicious, didn't know whether to back this new king, and then one day, Ruin just…wasn't suspicious anymore. He's a slow burner. He doesn't make snap judgments, good or bad."

"There's a reason for that," Starbride said. "The Fiend king changed his mind for him, just like he did for Fury, Scarra, and Rage."

Drive looked them over. "Where is Rage?"

Starbride tensed, but Scarra touched her shoulder. "The Fiend king killed him."

Drive's eyes went wide. "With this mind thing?"

"No, afterward. When Ruin is awake, we'll tell you both."

Starbride placed her pyramid on Ruin's forehead and looked for the day he met Roland. He'd been skeptical; most people were. But Roland had won the kingdom by right of arms, and there was something to be said about that. Well, right of arms and pyramid magic, which seemed less honorable, and those walking corpse things gave Ruin the creeps. But Blade said she'd been won over by him, and she was suspicious of Fiends after what had happened at that noblewoman's trial. If this Fiend king could convince her, Ruin supposed he was worth hearing.

Starbride found Ruin's overlay in nearly the same place as Scarra's. Instead of the rousing words he thought he remembered, there was the pyramid, though Ruin had resisted. Ultimately, he succumbed. Everyone succumbed to Roland in the end. Starbride plumbed every memory that came after. Blade and Ruin began visiting chapterhouses all over town, convincing high ranking members to "hear the Fiend king out." Starbride saw the names and faces of everyone he'd taken to see Roland, including Fury, Scarra, and Rage. Drive wasn't among them, but Starbride said the others out loud so they could be written down. After she'd gleaned everything she could, Starbride lifted out the manufactured memory, again having to take the thread, everything after Ruin had gone to see the Fiend king.

Then, they just had to wait for him to wake. They told their story while they waited. When Ruin woke, he stammered and blinked at them. Starbride filled in the gaps as he regained his senses. Just how many times would she have to tell the same story? Like Rage, Ruin couldn't believe that time had passed from when he'd gone to Roland's throne room until now. Drive quietly related what had happened that night, and then Scarra and Fury told him what had happened to them. Then all that was left was for him to stare at Starbride.

"I know you," he said. "The princess consort, yes?"

"That's right."

"Apparently," Drive said, "they're the resistance."

A light started in his eyes. "Tell me about Rage."

Once again, Scarra came to her rescue. "The Fiend king shoved a pyramid in him. We found a recent scar near his...on his thigh. He couldn't remember it. Fury and me don't have one. When the princess consort tried to eyeball it, it blew up."

Starbride wished she was able to discuss death so casually. She couldn't even bring herself to talk about what had happened to Averie.

Ruin's eyes grew wide. "And you think more of my people have these?"

"And probably you," Starbride said.

He stripped with as much compunction as the others had, making Starbride look away from his nude, albeit superior, body. The others helped him search until they found a scar in the same place as Rage, high on his upper thigh where he wasn't likely to notice it.

"No wonder you wouldn't let me into your bed," Drive said. "The Fiend king probably poisoned you against the idea so that no one would find that scar."

Ruin pulled on his trousers and robe again. "You can't get this out, Princess Consort?"

"I can't touch it with a pyramid. We could try and cut it out without disabling it."

"Would that set it off?"

She had to shrug. All of Master Bernard's meetings with the pyradistés they'd rescued had turned up nothing. He'd joked that if they survived Roland, they would have advanced pyramid research a thousand years. Starbride didn't think that was necessarily a good thing. "It's up to you whether you want to risk it."

"We have to know."

"Ruin," Drive said, "you can't."

"We need you," Scarra and Fury said, nearly on top of each other.

"You did well enough without me before now. I have full faith in your abilities should I die."

They protested again, but he waved it away. "First, we have to cleanse everyone's minds. Scarra, Fury, go and fetch Battle. Knock quietly. Tell him there's been a duel death, and I'd like to see him. Once he comes in, the princess consort will take care of the rest, yes?"

Starbride nodded, secretly relieved to be taking orders, at least for a little while.

CHAPTER NINETEEN

KATYA

The nobles spent the morning scrambling, trying to pack whatever meager possessions were left to them, never mind how many times they were told to take only what they needed. Da left the bulk of them in Ma's charge. In the meantime, Katya took her father to the villages nearest Count Mathias's and Lord Kline's homes.

Count Mathias's villagers watched their lord with soft smiles and squared shoulders, respect and even idolization in their eyes. He was impressive, a huge bear of a man *wearing* a bear. Da was no less striking. Chameleon that he was, he took a note from Count Mathias's book and left out any "ladies and gentleman" trappings, speaking to the villagers as a man who knew he was their liege but who also put his trousers on one leg at a time. He presented the war with the Fiends as an obstacle to be overcome and a challenge to be met. He reminded everyone of the old tales, of Farradain ancestors who'd had to defeat Yanchasa the Mighty or forfeit their lives. In the end, he gave the listeners a chance to be heroes.

They cheered him, man and woman, and Da left Castelle to sign up recruits.

Lord Kline's farmers gathered quietly and listened with furrowed brows. They weren't hardy woods-folk; they eked their lives from the soil, patiently and slowly. Da spoke to them of family, not sugarcoating what might happen to their kin if the Fiends weren't stopped. The farmers glanced at each other nervously, but Da didn't let up his onslaught. The hulk of Count Mathias behind him brought home the looming threat, and Lord Kline's quiet presence added weight to his words.

Murmurs instead of cheers ran through the crowd when Da stopped speaking. He lifted his hand for silence. "I know you fear for your crops, for those who will be left behind. Do not take what I ask lightly, for a heavier task has never been undertaken. Foulness is growing within the land, a pestilence whose ally is time itself. Give the usurper room to grow, and he will overwhelm us all, burying you and your families under the bootheel of evil, subjugating you and yours to his cause through any means necessary."

"But why?" someone in the front blurted.

"No one knows," Da said softly, and they all had to lean in. "What used to be a man is now a creature, and all that creature cares for is seeing others suffer."

The farmers glanced at one another as if they couldn't conceive of such a thing. Lord Kline stepped forward. "As our families have always said, we pluck the weeds where we can."

Da patted him on the shoulder. "Lend us your arms so that we might all be safe to pluck the weeds another day."

They had fewer recruits than in the last village, but then, the farmers had fewer people to give. There were no shows of bravado as these signed up. Katya sensed that was how war should have been: without applause.

After Katya saw her father back to camp, she met up with Castelle again and ventured south into the countryside, wanting to visit the next closest village before nightfall and scout around. As they neared the cluster of buildings, she noticed doors flapping open in the wind. No one stirred in the streets.

"Berg, go," Katya said. The former thief rode ahead, staying in sight as he meandered down the main street, peering left and right.

When he returned, he said, "No bodies, no people. Nothing."

The wind shifted, and a horrible stench floated past Katya's nose.

"Something's dead nearby," Brutal said.

When the smell came again, Katya nudged her horse in its direction, a large barn near a farmhouse. The doors banged shut when the wind picked up. When next they blew open, a carrion bird arced through, screeching as it flew over Katya's head.

"Spirits above," she whispered. The air was thick with putrescence and a sharp, coppery tang. Katya pressed her sleeve over her nose and signaled a halt. Blood had trickled down the slope in front of the barn, forming a macabre little stream in the dust.

"I'll go," Brutal said.

"Stay in sight."

He dismounted, pulled his mace, and jogged to the side of the barn before inching close to the doors, just enough to peer inside.

The color drained from his face. Katya's grip tightened on her pommel. Brutal didn't blanch for much. Still, he didn't bolt and run, just leaned back, his pale face the only indication that, whatever he'd seen, it was bad.

He stalked to Katya's side. "It's bodies."

"You've seen—"

"No." He wiped his bloodless lips. "There's *nothing* but bodies. It has to be the whole village."

Katya dismounted.

"Don't," Brutal said, but he stayed by her side.

She had to see. She couldn't shake the sense that she owed someone…something. If the entire village lay dead within the barn, the least she could do was see them, remember them.

Light trickled between the slats of the walls. Katya pressed her hand to her face so hard it hurt. Even then, she could taste them as she breathed through her mouth.

She had expected orderly rows, but the villagers had been heaped in the center, piled on top of one another, eyes wide open, faces stretched in pain and horror, limbs and blood and innards mingling. She couldn't tell where any one ended and the others began in the red and black sludge.

Katya raced around the barn. Her stomach emptied in heave after heave.

Brutal rested one large palm on her back. "Why not leave them where they fell? Why do this?"

Katya spat in the dust. "If they were trying to send a message…"

"In the open, they'd have been easier to find."

"Maybe the corpse Fiends… No, this took thought. Corpse Fiends would have left them to rot in the streets. This was *Darren*."

"Thrice bedamned son of a whore."

"He did it so they wouldn't rot as quickly," Katya said. "So they'd still have…impact when we found them."

Castelle's boots crunched in the dirt as she approached. "Is it as bad in there as it smells?"

Both Katya and Brutal nodded.

"We've found tracks, feet and horses, at least a dozen."

"Corpse Fiends aren't known for their equestrian skills," Katya said. "It's probably other locals, terrified out of their minds. This message wasn't just for us."

Da would say to burn the barn where it sat. It would take too much time to bury everyone. And news of the massacre would spread. All they could hope to do was stay ahead of it and use it if they could to drive home the danger and let people know that their monarchy wouldn't abandon them, even in death.

And what comfort could that bring? Darren was probably on the move, promising people that if they stayed out of the war, they would be spared. How many would listen? How many would be willing to leave their families behind with such a monster on the loose?

"We have to find him," Katya said. "We can't leave him out here to do this. We can't leave what he's done unanswered."

"Agreed," Brutal said, "but where do we look?"

"And what do we do when we find him?" Castelle asked. "He was nearly a match for the three of us on his own. He might have more allies by now."

"We almost had him last time," Brutal said.

"That was then! Who knows what tricks he's amassed?"

"Enough," Katya said. "He's not the only one who's gathered allies."

"You think Redtrue and her adsnazi will help us?" Castelle asked, and Katya couldn't tell whether the idea pleased or repelled her.

"Today all we have time for is to try and warn the nearest village." Katya glanced at the barn. "And to give these people whatever rest we can."

They lit the barn, set two of Castelle's friends to watch it, and rode hard for the next village. When they arrived, they found another small gathering of houses amidst a host of fields, but the streets were just as empty as the last.

Katya feared the worst until she saw movement inside the closest house. "Look there."

"It might be Darren," Castelle said.

"Good." Brutal lifted a hand to his mouth. "Hello! Anyone home?"

The door on the outermost house opened, and a man paused half-in and half-out, as if to ensure he could leap back inside. "Go away!"

"What happened here?" Katya called.

"We don't want none of your fight!" the man yelled. "Just leave, or…we'll attack!" He darted back inside.

"With what? Pitchforks?" Castelle muttered.

"Damn," Katya said. "Either Darren's been here, or they've seen the barn. We can't stand here yelling at closed houses. We'll come back when we have Darren's head on a pike."

"Tell us where he went," Brutal called, "and we'll leave you in peace. We'll kill him, and you and yours will be safe."

Nothing stirred for a moment, but then another door opened slowly, just farther in. A woman stood framed in it, and there was movement around her knees as if children tried to see past her. "He went southeast," she said. "He marched in like the king of shit-eating grins and promised us bloody hell if we sided with anyone who came after. He killed the best two hunters we had like they weren't nothing. And now their kids are in here with me, never to see their ma and da again."

Anger blazed from her eyes and not just at Darren, but at Katya and everything that had happened since war had landed on her doorstep.

"We can't bring anyone back," Katya said. "But we can see to it that he doesn't make any more orphans."

The woman's chin shot up. "You do that, Miss Fancy. I'd *like* to see his head on a pike." She slammed back inside her house.

"Well," Castelle said. "Do we head southeast, Miss Fancy, or report to camp?"

"I'm not an idiot," Katya said. "We wait out the night, get reinforcements, and then find his track." And then Darren would pay for the people he'd killed both before and after he'd become a Fiend. He'd pay for all the trouble he'd caused Katya's family, for siding with Roland, for having Carmen Van Sleeting for a mother, and following in her traitorous footsteps.

Katya nearly slept through the report to her father. He finally ordered her to bed, but she couldn't sleep before she washed the smell of the barn from her skin.

She scrubbed herself as well as she could with a bucket of water colder than a Fiend's heart. She couldn't help but be reminded of the few times she'd bathed with Starbride, and the one time she'd been so tired that Starbride had bathed her. Such thoughts almost made the water seem warm.

When she finished, she fell into her bedroll, but someone cleared their throat outside her tent. Katya rubbed her temples. "Who else has died?" she called. "Because that's the only thing I'm coming out for."

A mostly shaven head appeared in the tent flap. "Then I will come in," Redtrue said.

Katya shot upright. Since she had a tent to herself, she slept only in her shirt. She fought the urge to clutch the blankets higher, glad she hadn't yet put out the lantern.

Redtrue glanced at Katya's clenched fists. Half her mouth quirked up. "Do you fear I've come to seduce you?"

"I...didn't... What can I do for you?"

"What did you do for Starbride?"

Katya's mouth worked for a few moments. What was it about Allusian girls that left her speechless? Redtrue's smile said she was joking, well, mostly. "If I call for Brutal, he'll haul you out of here by what little hair you have left."

Redtrue burst out laughing. "I merely wanted to test the resolve of your affection. I have my answer. I have contacted my pyradisté again."

"What news?"

"I wish I had him here so I could give him a good, hard smack. He insists I am not real. When asked if he wrote down the instructions I gave him, he says yes, but isn't sure he should be listening to a 'dream.' He thinks himself insane."

"Wonderful. And this is progress?"

"Tsk. When I finally do speak to Starbride, I will ask her if you were always so gloomy before you left your home. I convinced him that if he is insane, he loses nothing by doing as I say, as he cannot become *more* insane."

"Hmm, did he say he'd look for Starbride?"

Redtrue shook her head. "He says it is difficult to move about in your Marienne. These corpse Fiends you've spoken of can sense his abilities. I...fear for him."

Katya let the silence linger. She feared for everyone. And if Roland's corpse Fiends could sense Starbride somehow... "I hope you urged him to be cautious."

"The great lover does not wish to give up caution in order to find her dearest lady?"

"The pyradisté can't find her if he's dead."

"Ah, and here I thought you might care for *his* well-being."

"You're one to talk!" Katya said. "I've seen how you treat someone who shares your bed, let alone complete strangers." Spirits, she must have been tired to give her brain leave to speak whatever it wanted.

Redtrue's mouth fell open. "What happens in my bed is none of your business!"

"But the well-being of my guards is. If you're going to treat Castelle like a servant, please do me a favor and just bar her from your bed altogether. She's gotten better at hiding her sulking, but I know she's not completely over you."

Redtrue's spine stiffened so much that Katya expected it to lift her off her rear. "And why do you not simply command her not to sulk?"

"I did. But in case that doesn't work, I thought I'd talk to you as well."

"You...bet on both horses?"

Katya sighed heavily "I'm not asking you to love her. All I'm asking is that you talk to her, tell her what kind of relationship you're looking for—"

"I would think my actions speak for me."

"Some people need to hear it aloud."

"Whenever we talk, we..."

Katya thought back to something Starbride had once said. "End up in a hayloft together?"

Redtrue barked a laugh. "Something else learned from your Starbride?" She got to her feet. "I will think on what you said; that is all I can promise you."

"If this pyradisté does find Starbride," Katya said, "she might not believe him. Tell him to call her Miss Meringue."

Redtrue nodded once and then left.

Katya tied the strings of the tent behind her, blew out her lantern, and collapsed, too tired to even reflect on everything that had happened that day.

CHAPTER TWENTY

STARBRIDE

Starbride stretched her neck and back; it had been a long night. Halfway through freeing the monks, she'd stopped paying attention to names or faces. She'd hypnotized them and then cleansed their minds, one after another, over and over. Whenever one awakened, Starbride was allowed a short reprieve as Ruin handled their initial shock and surprise—Starbride could have recited his speech from memory by the end—and they were hustled away. As dawn peeked over the horizon, Starbride cleansed the last one.

She leaned against the walls after she left Ruin's room. Pain roared through her shoulders. She tried to breathe through it, but deep breaths reminded her of the awful crick in her back.

Hugo patted her shoulder. "Are you all right, Miss Starbride?"

"A few hours of sleep and I'll be fine, Hugo, but we have a little work to do yet."

Scarra escorted Starbride, Hugo, and Pennynail downstairs to where the rest of the monks ate breakfast. At one corner, the newest arrivals were having everything explained by Fury.

Most turned to stare at Starbride, Hugo, and Pennynail. They hung back, waiting for Drive to explain. She told the monks who hadn't had their minds tampered with to keep calm; the strangers' presence would be explained shortly. Then she gave Starbride a tray with so much food even Horsestrong couldn't have eaten it all: eggs, sausage, porridge, toast, an entire bowl full of fruit, plus butter, molasses, and three different kinds of jam.

"There's more if you want it," Drive said.

Starbride laughed, even as tired as she was. She sat a table where everyone received coffee and fruit juice and a jug of water apiece.

Hugo gobbled his food. Freddie declined, but Starbride knew he must be hungry. "Maybe you could take some food and find a quiet corner," she said.

He shrugged and stayed put. The monks clearly didn't like strangers in their inner sanctum. It was best to stick together until their presence could be explained.

Ruin came downstairs at last to stand at the head of the room. "Brothers and sisters, you are free today because of a small fighting force opposed to the Fiend king." He gestured at Starbride's table. "I've decided to join in their fight, and I hope you'll do the same."

That got a murmured assent from everyone. They did love a fight, or they wouldn't be there.

"There is one piece of our story I have yet to reveal," Ruin said, "I ask that you check yourselves for a new scar." He showed his inner thigh. "If not here, check your entire body."

There was a shuffling as they obeyed right then and there. The disrobing struck Starbride as terribly funny, and she had to stare at her plate to avoid any ill-timed laughing.

"If you have the scar, please stand."

Twenty of the fifty people present stood. Too many, by Darkstrong, but now they knew.

"These scars," Ruin said, "are trap pyramids planted by the Fiend king. They are designed to kill us if a pyradisté tries to destroy them."

Starbride let out a sigh, so glad he didn't say, "Explode." The monks, to their credit, only glanced at one another.

"The Fiend king killed Brother Rage with just such a device. We may be able to remove these pyramids, but we're not sure what the outcome of such an attempt would be. Would any volunteers remain standing?"

Not a one of them sat down.

Ruin looked to Starbride as if to say, "So you see?"

Starbride nodded. "Shall we draw lots?"

They agreed that was as good a method as any, discussing a decision that might get them killed as if it was nothing special. Starbride had to admire their bravery even as she wished they had a greater sense of self-perseveration.

When the volunteer was chosen, Starbride left the extraction to the monks. She'd seen enough blood. Scarra escorted her, Hugo, and Pennynail into a side room.

As the wait stretched out, Hugo said, "Maybe we should go home."

Starbride shook her head, too tired to respond aloud. She couldn't go anywhere until she knew for certain. When she heard the bang from the other room, her stomach went cold.

Ruin ducked his head in. "He's dead."

Scarra let out a string of curses, and Starbride wished she had such a vocabulary at her disposal.

"At what point did it…?" Starbride asked. "Once it was removed?"

"After the scar was opened, and the medic reached inside."

Starbride bit her lip, glad for once that she was too tired for grief. "Trap pyramids are partly mind pyramids," she muttered. "Mind pyramids can read intent…"

"What do we do now?" Hugo asked. "What else can we try that the Fiend king hasn't thought of?"

Starbride heard the weariness in his voice and almost snapped at him to stop whining, that they were all tired, and why, in Darkstrong's name, was everyone always looking to her for answers? She took a deep breath. "We need Claudius and Master Bernard. Together, they can tell you far more than me. When we get back to the hideout, we'll send them over."

"Shall I see you home?" Scarra said.

"I have all the protection I need. Besides, I'm not the only one who's had a busy night."

Scarra touched Starbride's arm, and Starbride almost jumped when it turned into a half caress. "Take care of yourself."

"Thank you," Starbride said. First Hugo and now Scarra? Did no one remember she was waiting for Katya? They left by the back door and hurried through the streets that were gaining people by the moment.

"Did she…rub your shoulder?" Hugo asked.

"It was a friendly pat," Starbride said.

He frowned as if unsure. Pennynail gave his arm a little push, pointed to the green lining of his cloak, and then to his face.

"Shut your…finger," Hugo snapped. "You have no idea what you're pointing about."

Starbride wondered how they could joke with everything that had happened, but maybe they were *all* too tired for grief.

Back at the warehouse, Starbride found sleep a long time coming. Tired as she was, the enormity of everything she had yet to accomplish weighed on her. She thought she'd beaten Roland at one of his games. She'd found a way to defeat one of his pyramids, but what of the others?

She'd sent Claudius and Master Bernard to help with the problem, but what if they couldn't find a solution?

And even if they solved the trap, a little voice inside her whispered, what if that was what Roland wanted them to do? What if there was a trap within a trap within a trap? The mind control and pyramids might be just hard enough to throw her off the scent of real danger. If he *wanted* her to find and defeat them…

Starbride sat up in her bed and lit a candle. What would Katya do in her situation? She had many wonderful qualities, but refraining from second-guessing herself wasn't one of them. Still, Katya would push on while keeping her eyes open. To do anything else would be to paralyze herself.

Starbride wrapped her hand around her pyramid necklace and stroked the butterfly pin as she lay back down.

She woke after only a few hours. Her candle hadn't even burned out. She yawned and stretched. Easier to wake up and be tired, she supposed, than sleep through the entire day. She'd go completely nocturnal at this rate. Right then, she needed to make plans. Katya took solace in them, and Starbride needed to speak to the other strength chapterhouses that day. If she couldn't free the monks' bodies, she could at least free their minds.

With Ruin by Starbride's side, it would be easier to gain entry to the second chapterhouse. They could simply walk in the front door. Starbride thought they should cleanse the intelligence and wisdom chapterhouses next. Strength was an asset, but she preferred to put her faith in knowledge.

Even with little sleep, the day seemed brighter. With not only Hugo and a hooded Pennynail but Ruin, Drive, Scarra, and Fury by her side, Starbride thought it would take Roland himself to defeat her.

The second strength chapterhouse looked much like the first from outside. Twin statues of Best and Berth performed feats of strength on the cornices and eaves. People came and went into the public chapel. Senior monks spoke with those interested in finding enlightenment. No one gave Starbride and her friends a second glance with red-robed strength monks surrounding them.

An itch settled between Starbride's shoulder blades. It was too easy. She could almost feel Darkstrong sapping her good feelings.

Perhaps they should cleanse the luck chapterhouses next and get Fah and Fay on their side.

Before they crossed into the restricted areas of the chapterhouse, Starbride caught a glance from one of the trainers in the chapel. Instead of the clear-eyed, almost challenging look she'd come to expect from the fighting monks, this one shifted away.

"Turn around," Starbride whispered.

They looked terribly obvious as they turned together, but that didn't matter as long as they made it out alive. "What's wrong?" Ruin whispered.

Starbride fought to keep from staring at the fighters in the corner. Those farthest from her had ceased their battles. "Keep moving."

The doors to the outside boomed shut.

"It's a trap!" Hugo said for those who weren't paying attention.

Ruin and Drive ran for the lone door that led into the chapterhouse. Starbride's heart sank, thinking herself betrayed, until the two monks pulled the doors shut, and she realized they were keeping any reinforcements from coming through.

Starbride backed toward them, wanting to keep together. The other monks advanced.

"He thought you'd go elsewhere," someone said from the corner, near a rack of padded practice weapons. "He thought you'd be smart enough to stay away from the other houses after what you'd done, but I said no." Maia stepped from the shadows, a smile on her pretty face. "You're a creature of habit."

Starbride slipped a hand into her bag, her heart pounding. "Stay away from her," she said to her comrades. "She's part Fiend."

Maia's smile widened. She'd slicked her baby-fine blond hair back from her face, making her pale features too severe. Her light blue eyes sparkled, though, as if the happy girl she'd been was still in there somewhere, but her black coat and trousers reassured Starbride that any girl was merely a ghost.

"No." Maia's features blurred, and her eyes became all blue as her teeth grew into fangs. Horns sprouted from her brow, one arching over the crown of her head and another on the side starting at her temple and circling back. Her ears lengthened to long points, rising almost past her hair. "I'm all Fiend." Her voice grated in Starbride's ears, filling her mouth with the taste of copper.

Starbride heard a commotion behind her as someone tried to come through the door, but she didn't take her eyes off of Maia. The fighters charged.

Hugo set his feet. Fury and Scarra settled into fighting stances, and Pennynail rushed to the side. He buried a dagger in the knee of one attacker as he ran. The man stumbled, and Maia knocked him out of her way.

Maia came for Starbride, but the others avoided her. Roland wanted her alive. Well, he wasn't above making a few mistakes. Maia leapt, a blur. Before she could close the gap, Starbride lifted her Fiend suppression pyramid and focused.

Without contact, suppressing a Fiend wasn't a switch she could flip. It felt more like an invisible wall. Starbride could feel Maia's Fiend as if she laid fingers on it, oily and sharp and so cold it burned.

Maia hissed, but Starbride kept her focus, paying attention enough to stay out of the other fights. Maia tried to edge around as if faced with a real wall, but Starbride kept her in view.

"Grab the pyradisté," Maia snarled. The enemy monks broke off their attacks and focused on her. Hugo stabbed one in the side, but the other slipped past and lunged for Starbride. She dodged out of the way, fighting to keep her mind on the pyramid. She might have crippled the enemy's greatest weapon, but she'd also crippled herself.

"Shit," she said as she tried to keep on the move. Hugo backed off her attackers. Out of the corner of her eye, she saw Fury and Scarra guarding her flanks, but something knocked into her from behind. Starbride stumbled, and the pyramid skittered from her grasp. She caught herself as she fell, sending shockwaves through her elbows. She pushed up and reached for the pyramid.

A leg slammed into her side. Starbride's breath left her in a rush as pain bloomed first from her side and then from her shoulders as she slid several paces. She fought to breathe and crawl at the same time.

Averie's memories loomed in her head. "No," Starbride hissed. She reached for the pyramid that gleamed in the midst of so many feet.

"Leave her. She's mine," Maia said.

Starbride reached into her bag. Maia hauled her upright. Starbride shut her eyes and slammed a flash-bomb into Maia's face.

Maia shrieked and released her. Starbride stumbled away, but Maia clamped on to her wrist. Starbride dipped into her bag again, but Maia batted her next pyramid away. It burst into flames on the other side of the room, lighting the practice mats on fire.

"Going to burn me again?" Maia asked. "I thought we were friends." She ripped Starbride's satchel from her shoulder, nearly wrenching the arm out of the socket. Starbride punched Maia's elbow, but her arm didn't give. Starbride's knuckles ached as if she'd hit a frozen branch.

Maia's fingers clamped around Starbride's neck. "Are you going to come along like a good girl, or shall I break your neck and give your corpse to my father?"

Over Maia's shoulder, Starbride saw Hugo bash another opponent in the face and then reach inside his coat.

"Katya didn't keep you around for your memory, did she?" Starbride asked.

Maia cocked her head. Hugo's Fiendish form barreled into her from behind.

Starbride dove for her satchel, but Hugo's and Maia's thrashing bodies kicked it across the room. As she scrambled after it, one of the mind-controlled monks reached for her. Starbride dropped, grabbed one of his legs, and yanked. As he fell, she stood again, searching for the satchel.

Pennynail scooped it up and threw it in Starbride's direction. She winced as she ran to catch it. How long could it get thrown around before one of her destruction pyramids broke? Now she knew why Crowe used them so sparingly.

Starbride dove for the satchel, but a monk knocked her to the side. He grabbed the bag out of the air and backed into Scarra. She elbowed him in the back of the head, and he lurched forward.

Starbride grabbed the satchel, but the monk came with it. She tried to copy Scarra's elbow move, only aimed at the monk's face. Pain rolled up her arm as she connected. His nose crumpled, and blood jetted from his face as he collapsed.

Starbride dug in her bag, found a flash bomb, and cried, "Temperance!" as she threw it toward Pennynail's attackers.

The flash bomb exploded in the monks' midst, and they cried out almost as one as they fell to the ground. Pennynail was among them in a moment, bashing the pommel of a dagger against their heads.

Ruin and Drive still held the door, but their faces had turned purple with effort, veins standing out in their temples. Scarra sported a reddened eye that was swelling shut, and Fury's left arm hung crookedly. Maia and Hugo rolled along the ground, leaving a trail of blood in their wake.

Starbride ran for them; Pennynail raced to join her. She scooped up her fallen Fiend repellent and directed it at both of them.

They hissed and pulled away from each other. Starbride threw a flash bomb, closing her eyes at the last second. They both shrieked, and Starbride went for Hugo. "Hold Maia!"

She tried to tackle Hugo, but his claws dug into the scars on her shoulders. She wrapped her arms around him and buried her pyramid in his thigh.

Starbride blocked out his struggles and focused. There it was, the rusty handle that all the Umbriels held inside them, the switch that would turn off their Fiends. As always, it resisted her, but she pushed and struggled, screaming in her haste to beat the Fiend back where it belonged.

Hugo grunted, and she felt the handle turn. As he became himself again, he sagged against the floor, losing consciousness.

Starbride struggled to her feet. Pennynail and Scarra were trying to hold Maia, but she bucked like a wild horse. Scarra had her from behind, and Pennynail tried to grab her legs to knock her over. Maia twisted and kicked him away. Scarra grabbed Maia's wrists, but Maia hurled Scarra up and over her head to slam into the stones.

Starbride focused. Maia took two steps forward, away from the repelling force. Starbride jumped at her and buried the pyramid in her neck.

Maia screeched. Pennynail grabbed her legs again, sending her face first to the ground. He lay across her legs and Scarra pounced on her arms.

Starbride searched for Maia's switch, but there was something in the way. Roland had brought out her Fiend, but she'd never Waltzed, never communed with the progenitor of her Fiendish Aspect. She needed help to unlock her Fiend, unlike the others who needed help keeping it inside.

There, in Maia's neck, Starbride found the pyramid that fought her. It was like Lady Hilda's, but her Fiend had been weaker than Maia's. This one Maia had possessed since birth, and the implanted pyramid let it out but also helped her control it. As Starbride tried to turn Maia back to human, she saw that the control was a lie. The Fiend was threaded throughout Maia, as it probably was with Roland. By merging with it, they had let it corrupt them completely.

Starbride fumbled in her satchel, trying for her cancellation pyramid. Her fingers finally closed around it, but if she fell out of the suppression pyramid, Maia could overpower them.

"Can you knock her out?" Starbride said.

"Not likely," Scarra answered with a breathy grunt. "Cut her fucking head off easier!"

"We have to go!" someone else yelled.

"I'm so close." Starbride sat atop Maia's back and locked her legs around Maia's waist. "Maia, if any of you is left inside, help me fight!"

She withdrew from the suppression pyramid. Maia bucked. Starbride heard even Pennynail's cry beneath his mask as he echoed Scarra. Starbride fell into her cancellation pyramid as quickly as she could.

The pyramid in Maia's neck fought her as hard as Hugo's Fiend had. Maia bucked, pushing Scarra away. Starbride clenched her legs tighter as she would with an unruly horse. Maia bore Starbride's weight as she pushed up on her arms. If she shook Pennynail off, Starbride would be flying right behind him.

"Come on!" Starbride screamed, pitting all she had against the pyramid, forgetting her safety, forgetting everything but getting Maia back.

She set her passion against Fiendish cold, to smother it, melt it, whatever she had to do. As she cried out, she felt it give.

A splintering sound filled the room. "Time to go," Scarra said.

"Almost."

"Now!"

The splintering sound came again. The monks within the chapterhouse were breaking down the door. Scarra wrapped her arms around Starbride's middle, but Starbride kept her focus, pushing, pushing...

"There!" she cried as the pyramid yielded to her at last. She came back to herself and clung on to the now-unconscious Maia, forcing Scarra to lift them both. "We have to take her."

"Fine!" Scarra said. She let Starbride go and hefted Maia over her shoulder like a sack of flour. "Now will you go?"

Ruin and Drive tried to hold the remains of the door while monks reached for them from the other side. "Move!" Starbride cried, lifting a pyramid.

They dove to the sides as the fire pyramid smashed into the door, sending those on the other side scrabbling back. Pennynail had Hugo over his shoulders, and together, they staggered for the doors leading outside.

"What if they're barred?" Fury yelled.

Starbride launched a disintegration pyramid at the door, one of the few she possessed. She couldn't afford to care if anyone outside was caught in its wake. A deep, hollow sound filled the antechamber as a black sphere blossomed. Everyone gasped. Starbride imagined her teeth were vibrating. When the sphere faded, it left a perfect half-circle cut in the wooden door and a bowl-shaped divot in the floor.

Outside, three monks backed away with terror-filled faces. Mind controlled as they might be, no one wanted to stand up to that. Roland should have sent corpse Fiends. Maybe with all the patrols, they had too much to do.

Ruin and Drive knocked the waiting monks down. When they looked back at the chapterhouse, their eyes widened. "Keep running," Ruin said.

Starbride didn't question him; she just made sure no one got left behind. It was very early evening, and they couldn't be seen carrying two unconscious people through the streets. Drive led them into an alley, and they jogged into the back ways of Marienne.

Original

Chapter Twenty-one

Katya

Katya awoke the next day ready to hunt Darren down. The only question was how many allies she could take with her. Many of their fighters were occupied training new recruits. Katya had a thought about trying to entice Lord Vincent away, but she knew he'd rather die than shirk his duty to protect the youngest heirs.

She wasn't surprised when Count Mathias joined her; he brought men, dogs, and an enormous boar spear that might give even Darren pause. He added considerable strength to Katya, Brutal, Castelle, her friends, and several Allusian trackers. Still, Katya breathed a sigh of relief when Redtrue and two other adsnazi joined them as well.

"What did you come up with to fight the Fiends, Redtrue?" Katya asked.

"I won't give in to the destructive ways of your people."

"Yes, pyradistés are bad. We've covered that."

Redtrue grinned wryly and drew a pyramid from the bag at her side. It had no filigree, only a few large facets. When she held it up, it cast little rainbows along her lap. "It will either repel the creatures or attract them."

"You don't know which?"

"You know these Fiends better than I."

"I'm no pyradisté. Spirits know I'm no adsnazi either."

"Maybe you should have brought your pyradisté."

Katya shook her head. "He doesn't know anything about Fiends."

"I thought you had fought them before."

"Us," Katya said, gesturing to Brutal, Castelle and herself. "No one else has much experience with them. Despite what you may think, Marienne wasn't always awash in evil monsters."

Redtrue shrugged as if she didn't quite believe that. Her adsnazi friends were armed with the same pyramids as her, none of them knowing what they would do. Katya had to laugh at the absurdity. At least it would be an adventure.

As they left, Hawkblade and a few of her nomads joined them. She simply nodded to Katya as the nomads guided their horses alongside everyone else. Katya glanced at Redtrue. "I don't suppose you're willing to offer your services as translator as well as adsnazi?"

"A Farradain phrase feels apt here: How much is it worth to you?"

"I'll leave Castelle in charge of payment."

Redtrue only snorted.

They circled the village Darren had visited, and the scouts spread out. Count Mathias's dogs quickly picked up the trail. By the tracks, Darren hadn't come to the village alone, though he remained on foot. Katya guessed the corpse Fiends couldn't ride. No horse would stand them, and he wouldn't want to leave them behind, coward that he was, not if he might be fighting anyone stronger than farmhands. By midmorning, they were fast on his track.

"How can he stay ahead of us?" Count Mathias asked.

"The corpse Fiends are faster than humans, and they don't tire. I don't know what Darren's limits are."

He leaned forward as if willing his horse to go faster. Katya admired his enthusiasm even as she found it a bit unsettling.

One of the nomad scouts rushed toward them over a rise. "What have you found?" Katya called.

He yelled something in Allusian. "He spotted someone," Redtrue said, "but they disappeared into a copse. He says they ran faster than anyone he's seen before."

They broke into a gallop, keeping their outriders just ahead. The dogs began to bay and headed for a break in the forest. As the horses broke through, Katya spied a sleepy little hamlet in a small valley below.

"Oh, spirits," she whispered. Screams floated on the wind. Katya kicked her horse into a run, but it shied, already tired. It barely reached a canter, huffing and puffing.

At the outskirts of the village, they dismounted. Smoke billowed between the houses, and the horses backed away from it.

Katya let hers go. "Stay together." She drew her rapier as she moved. People dressed in homespun dashed past her. When some of them saw her party, they bolted in another direction.

Count Mathias called, "Where are the monsters?"

One or two villagers pointed up the lane, but Katya followed the smoke. In the center of the village was a chapterhouse decorated with carvings of all ten spirits. Flames danced along its roof. Darren popped out of the doorway, his Fiendish features plain upon his face. Injured people writhed on the dirt in front of him. When he saw Katya, he grabbed a weeping man and held him as a shield. The scouts kept their bows up but didn't try for a shot.

Darren laughed, grabbed another villager, and tossed her into the burning building.

"Bastard!" Katya yelled.

He laughed, and the grating sound made Katya's ears ache. "Tell you what. I'll take my leave now, and you can rescue all the poor unfortunate souls trapped behind me."

"You die *here*," Katya said.

"Come and get me. I'll be slaughtering peasants until you do." He jumped inside the building with his hostage, and Katya heard more screams.

She looked to her fellows. They could wait for the building to burn down around Darren's ears, but there was no guarantee that would kill him. It would kill everyone else, though, if Darren didn't do that first.

"Cover the exits," she told the scouts. "If he comes out first, shoot him and call for help."

The rest of them ran into the chapterhouse. Just inside, a corpse Fiend flew at them from the left. Count Mathias blocked its short blade with his boar spear. He pushed it away and braced his legs for another thrust. Katya was ready to leave him with his men, wanting to find Darren, but Redtrue lifted her pyramid. Pure white radiance flowed out, and the room seemed to gray around the edges. When the light touched the pyramid in the corpse Fiend's forehead, it exploded with a bang, taking the Fiend's head with it.

Brutal whooped. Count Mathias's face fell as if disappointed. Katya felt like cheering.

Redtrue shook her head. "I...I didn't know..."

"Better than we hoped!" Katya said.

She turned an appalled look Katya's way. "I can't use this." She looked to her fellows, who nodded, faces pale. "It's...destructive!"

"What in all the spirits' names…" Katya turned her back; she didn't have time to argue about how people's lives were at stake. She moved deeper into the chapterhouse, through another set of doors into a large room filled with benches. Crude portraits of the ten spirits ringed the walls. Another corpse Fiend leapt up from its hiding place. Katya blocked its attack with her rapier, but it jumped to the side and skewered one of Count Mathias's men, too quickly for a human.

Katya aimed for its head, but it ducked under one of the benches and scuttled away like a spider. Hawkblade leapt a bench and stabbed at it. Katya glanced upward at the smoke, not knowing how much longer the roof would hold. Some of the nomads and adsnazi were dragging injured people toward the door. They needed to find Darren.

"Come on, Brutal." Katya raced for the doorway leading deeper into the building. He stayed by her side, Castelle and three friends with them. Count Mathias stayed with Hawkblade, facing off against the corpse Fiend. Redtrue started to come with Katya.

"Get out," Katya snarled over her shoulder. "Tend the wounded."

Redtrue turned away without a word. Up ahead, down a narrow hallway, a man yelled, "No!"

Katya hustled forward, but the hallway was filling with smoke. "Why is it always fire with that bastard?"

"Have to hurry," Brutal said.

Around a corner, Darren still held his captive. He lobbed a pyramid into a nearby doorway, and flames burst from it. Katya put up an arm to shield her face, and when she lowered it, Darren had moved on. They started to hurry forward when Katya heard coughing. The room was full of villagers, their only door now blocked by fire. A window behind them offered escape for some, but the larger ones wouldn't make it. Still, they clawed at it like wounded animals.

Brutal leapt the flames and hurled villagers out of the way until he could reach the window. He slammed at the wall with his huge mace, widening the hole.

Katya hurried after Darren. She couldn't shake the feeling that if they lost him here, they wouldn't catch him again. A hall of closed doors ending in a dead end waited around the corner. The building was built as an un-joined square, leaving Darren no place to go.

He had a supply of pyramids from Roland. They had to be ready for everything. "Take a door, open it, then duck." Castelle and her friends obeyed, but all the rooms stood empty.

"He had to have gone out a window," Castelle said.

"Come on." The windows led to a garden at the heart of the structure. The villagers from the fire room were crawling out from the wall facing Katya and stumbling toward an iron gate that led into the village beyond. Another pyramid sailed their way from a clump of bushes.

"Look out!" Katya called. The pyramid burst across the gate, catching the wood of the building on fire as well as one man stuck in the gap. The others staggered back, faces red and blistered. Smoke from the roof floated down around them.

Katya squeezed through the window just as Brutal did the same through his widened portal across from her. They rushed the bushes, and Darren sprang out. His villager shield was gone, but their archers were on the other side of the fire.

"I knew you'd get my message," Darren said to Katya. "Thanks for giving me all night to plan my little party. Very smart."

"You needed all night to trap yourself with us?" Katya asked. "Who's the smart one?"

He dashed for the clump of villagers and slashed one with his claws. She fell, screaming and trying to keep her intestines where they belonged. Katya moved, but Darren was so damned fast. Two of Castelle's friends rushed him, but he cut down another villager before they could reach him.

"Can't you even save one?" Darren called. Brutal moved to cover the villagers, swinging his mace to drive Darren away. Darren leapt backward; he'd learned to stay out of reach since their last fight. Katya wished she had Maia or Pennynail, anyone with good aim and a throwing weapon.

Breaking glass caught her attention, and a massive spear flew at Darren, nicking his side. He grabbed it and threw it, impaling another villager. Katya heard the sound of hacking wood. Count Mathias was trying to come to their aid, but Darren was slippery as an eel, quite content to kill villagers and let the roof burn. He had a sword on his hip, but he hadn't bothered to draw it.

Katya's throat burned from the smoke. The fire blocking the exit had grown as if Darren had treated the ground. As she watched it, the earth seemed to roll like a wave at sea. It smothered the fire in one gulp.

Redtrue strode through the gap, holding another pyramid. She faced the fire still burning the chapterhouse's sides, and the earth lapped at what it could reach, putting it out. "This way!" she called.

Hawkblade and her nomads climbed into the garden and shepherded villagers toward the exit. Katya darted for Darren. She pressed him over and over, forcing him toward Castelle who stabbed at his back. He leapt to the side, into Brutal, who bashed him so hard it sent him flying.

Count Mathias stumbled through the remains of the wall, pulled his spear from the dead villager, and threw it, pinning Darren's arm to the building.

He screeched, and Katya fought the urge to cover her ears. Instead, she ran for him. One of Castelle's friends threw a knife into Darren's leg now that he'd stilled, but that didn't stop him from trying to work the spear out of his arm. He pulled it out in a jet of blood and hurled it at Katya. She ducked out of the way, willing the others to keep attacking. Behind her, she heard a gurgling scream.

Darren sagged, and Castelle stabbed him. He leapt to his feet, less hurt than they thought, and rammed his claws into her belly.

"Cass!" Katya yelled. Darren let her go and ran from Katya's blade.

Castelle sank to her knees, hands over her wound.

Darren leapt around Brutal and streaked for the exit. "Redtrue!" Katya called. "Use the damned pyramid!"

Count Mathias sprang for Darren, swinging his bearskin cloak. It tangled in Darren's legs and tripped him. Redtrue backed away, her eyes horrified.

"Redtrue!" Katya called again. Redtrue looked to her and then to where Castelle knelt on the ground. Darren had regained his feet. "Use the pyramid!"

Redtrue looked at the one she was holding. Katya raced toward her, about to call, "Not that one!" but before she got a chance, Redtrue focused on Darren, and the earth did that little hiccup again. He pinwheeled in midair a moment, came down on his stomach, and then fought to get to his feet. With a leap, Brutal brought his mace crunching down on Darren's back. Dirt flew up around him, and the snapping sound echoed through the garden like a breaking branch.

Darren howled. Katya slid to a stop and stabbed Darren in the neck, over and over, seeking a pyramid like the one they'd found in Lady Hilda. Even after Count Mathias joined her in stabbing, long after Darren stopped moving, Katya hacked away.

"He's dead," someone behind her said, and the quiet voice broke her concentration. Redtrue stared at her as if she were a monster. Darren lay in a bloody heap at her feet, back flattened and neck and head a ruined mess.

"No trophy, then," Count Mathias said. He leaned on his gore-covered spear. "Shame, but I supposed he looked human when he actually died."

Katya's bile rose at the thought of a human trophy. She turned away and hurried toward where Brutal tended Castelle.

"We can manage these," Brutal said. "He didn't hurt you too badly."

Castelle shook like a leaf, her face stark white. "Could have fooled me."

Count Mathias knelt by her side and offered her a flask. She drank it, spit part of it up in a cough, and took another long pull. Count Mathias offered it to Katya. "Brandy?"

She shook her head, but Brutal said, "I could use it." He lifted Castelle's bandages and poured some over her wounds.

She stuttered out a cry. "Trying to get me drunk from the inside, Brutal?" she asked through her teeth.

"It'll keep infection away. If you're well enough to joke, you're well enough for me to carry you out of here.

"How romantic," she said. "How's Harry?"

Katya looked to Castelle's dead friend. "Not good."

"Dead," Count Mathias said, "just as my man Hull is, as more would have been if not for…her."

He said "her" quietly, as if talking about a spirit. Katya followed his admiring gaze to Hawkblade and her nomads.

"We'll drink a toast to the fallen later," Brutal said.

Katya searched what remained of Darren but found nothing. If he'd been receiving orders from Roland, he'd left them elsewhere or destroyed them. She left the chapterhouse with everyone else.

"Can you do anything about the rest of the fire?" she asked Redtrue.

"Only near the ground."

At least she was good for something. She shook the thought away as she left the garden. Redtrue was a possible link to Starbride, and Katya couldn't risk breaking that link. But Redtrue had a way to kill Fiends instantly and didn't use it. How many people would be alive if she had? Count Mathias's man and Castelle's friend, countless villagers.

Katya headed around the building, lost in thought. Something hit her broadside, biting into her shoulder, and knocking her feet out from under her. She tried to scramble up, but pain rolled up her arm. From the corner of her eye, she saw a corpse Fiend's knife coming for her face. She snarled and kicked, catching the Fiend in the stomach. It gave her a little distance, enough to bring her rapier around.

She tried to call out, but the corpse Fiend lunged again; it used to be a man, now as gray-skinned and nondescript as the rest of them, dressed in rags. It stank like a tomb. She ducked its thrust, still on her knees, and its blade grated off the wall of the chapterhouse. Katya sliced its wrist. She cut deep, but blood didn't flow from the wound. She grabbed its arm and hacked the blade from its grasp.

Its fist slammed into her chin, and she saw only blurs as sounds seemed to slow. She wriggled away, kicking and slashing, anything to keep it off balance. Her free hand found its weapon, and she threw it behind her. She shoved backward, into the wall, using it to get to her feet. She shook her head to clear it just as the corpse Fiend darted inside her reach.

Katya rammed her rapier guard into its forehead. The corpse Fiend's icy fingers closed around her neck, cutting off her air as quickly as a noose. Katya punched again. Cracks spread through the pyramid, but little bursts of light danced across her vision. Katya focused on the pyramid rather than the cold, dead face. She summoned all her strength and tried one more punch. The pyramid shattered, and the corpse Fiend dropped like a puppet with its strings cut.

Katya sank down with it, coughing and sputtering, her throat aching with every breath.

"Katya!" Brutal called. He pulled the corpse Fiend away, knelt in front of her, and put pressure on her bleeding shoulder.

She would have yelped, but she couldn't stop coughing. It felt like she'd been drinking fire.

"Where else are you hurt?" Brutal asked.

Katya waved to her neck.

Brutal gently unbuttoned her coat. He checked her throat all the way around, softly lifting her hair, and she almost laughed at the way someone so large and ferocious in battle could be so tender. Just as quickly, she nearly burst into tears, at the mercy of adrenaline and fatigue and lightheadedness.

"You'll have a hell of a bruise," he said. "I need to get your coat off so I can look at this shoulder." He turned and barked at someone. "Fan out, search for more of these things!"

Brutal helped Katya shrug off her coat. He tugged her shirt over her shoulder until he could look at the wound. "There's no tearing. Still, I don't trust a corpse to keep its blade clean. We need some of the count's brandy." Lacking that, he bound her shoulder with what he had on him and helped her put her coat back on again. "Can you talk yet?"

She nodded, swallowed several times, and said, "Bastard surprised me." The words hurt, and she grimaced, wishing she had one of the water skins they'd left on the horses.

"I should have been with you," Brutal mumbled.

Katya swatted him on the arm.

"I know, I know, save the guilt for when we can relax."

"Katya?" someone called from behind them. Redtrue's brows were drawn in concern. "Did something...?" She trailed away as she looked at the corpse Fiend. "Are you all right?"

"No thanks to you," Brutal said.

Redtrue stepped forward, fists clenched. "I will not become evil to fight evil! It was bad enough I helped you kill that man."

"Save it." Katya rubbed her sore neck. "Come on, Brutal." She glanced at Redtrue. "Stay near the fighters."

Redtrue bared her teeth as if she might argue, but she knelt by the corpse Fiend.

With Brutal, Katya helped search the town. They found one more corpse Fiend lurking around the village, but Count Mathias and Hawkblade hunted it down.

Brutal helped set up a makeshift hospital where he and the village healer could treat the injured. Trackers were sent into the woods to gather the villagers who'd run away, but it would be a long time before they found them all. They pulled down the burning chapterhouse and heaped dirt around it to keep the fire from spreading. Redtrue and her adsnazi were the greatest help there, using their dirt trick to put the fire out where they could.

Katya took a long pull from her retrieved water skin as she watched. When Redtrue wandered near, she couldn't help but say, "Guess killing fire doesn't break your oath."

"I don't wish anyone to be hurt."

Katya snorted.

Redtrue turned slowly. "We fight destruction. Can't you see that?" She gestured behind her where the other adsnazi were still battling the fire. "Twisting the adsna, using it to kill? That's the path that created these Fiends."

"You don't know that for certain. Besides, killing a corpse Fiend isn't the same as killing a person; the people who used to be in those bodies are long gone."

"And you don't know *that* for certain. There could be a way to cleanse the Fiends."

Katya laughed so hard it hurt her throat again. "Have you seen them? They're dead, Redtrue. They don't bleed. They don't feel."

"It looked like a man."

"Dead for a long time, just no longer mobile because I destroyed the pyramid that powered him. The corpse Fiends are one of the usurper's strongest weapons, and you can annihilate them without breaking a sweat."

"I can't. The one that I helped you kill…he was still alive."

"Do *not* shed any tears for Darren. He deserved such a death and much more. If you won't use your pyramid, teach Starbride how when we finally speak to her."

Redtrue's chin lifted. "I won't teach destructive magic. When we do speak with her, I'll teach her how to use the adsna properly."

Katya rubbed her temples. "All I hear is that you're willing to let countless people die, all for your precious high ground."

"You don't understand!"

"Go tell it to the dead." Katya turned away. She found Brutal at the hospital under the canvas that had been strung up as a roof. Katya knelt next to him and offered her water skin.

He took a long pull. "We've done all we can for the critically wounded. Ten won't survive the night." He rubbed his face with bloodstained hands. "Most of the others will be fine: a few stab wounds, lots of burns. They'll have some scars here." He glanced at her and chuckled. "That's an angry face. Been talking to Redtrue?"

"Stubborn ass."

"Seconded."

"Would you use a weapon like that, Brutal? When your chapterhouse places the fight, the struggle, above all else, would you use a battle-ender like that pyramid?"

He cocked his head. "It's the *overall* struggle that's important here, not the individual fights. Human against human, that's the fight that teaches us about the universe. This?" He gestured around them. "This is slaughter; all it teaches me is that Fiends need to be put down. I'd use that pyramid if it meant my soul would be kept from enlightenment until the end of time."

Katya squeezed his shoulder. "Good to know."

"How can we change Redtrue's mind?"

"We let Da, Dayscout, and Leafclever fight it out."

"Or we could go to the other adsnazi. Scenes like this might affect some of them more than Redtrue, or maybe one of them lost a loved one to a murderer or something; they'd be more sympathetic."

"Looking for revenge, no matter the target?" Katya asked.

"It's a thought."

"Before, it was me talking about creating a rift amongst our allies, and you talked me out of it."

"I wasn't this pissed off before."

"If we can convince Leafclever, it won't matter what Redtrue thinks. He can give us other adsnazi, maybe some who'll follow orders."

"Yeah," Brutal said with a snort, "like that won't create any rifts."

"If I anger Redtrue, I'll never be able to speak to Starbride."

Brutal winced. "Couldn't you find another adsnazi?"

"She's the best, and her Farradain is perfect."

"So, lazy, get better at Allusian."

She nodded. "You're right. What else do I have to do, after all?"

As they packed up to leave, many of the villagers approached them, some terrified that the Fiends would come back. Those begged Katya to stay. Others yelled at them to take these troubles and leave, never to return. Still others asked to come with them, wanting revenge on the monsters that had killed their families.

Brutal leaned close to Katya's ear. "Let's take them," he said. "There are enough left to help the wounded recover."

Katya agreed. They needed recruits if they were going to stop the same thing from happening to another village. With the bodies loaded onto the two free horses, the villagers were forced to walk. After they'd gathered their meager belongings, fifteen people followed in Katya's wake. She was more than happy to ride slowly. Her shoulder throbbed, and her neck burned, especially when she had to turn her head. By the time they reached camp, it was past dark; they'd been forced to go even slower in the blackness.

Katya went straight to her parents' tent, not missing that Redtrue and her adsnazi went to their tents without speaking to anyone.

Da had heard most of the news from Katya's messenger, but she filled in the gaps for Dayscout, Leafclever, and Ma. Count Mathias joined her for the retelling. When they came to the part where Redtrue had made one of the corpse Fiends explode, Da's jaw dropped, but Leafclever shut his eyes as if the news pained him.

"After that, she refused to use the pyramid," Katya said.

"What?" Da asked. He glanced at Leafclever. "Why?"

"Is there more to the tale?" Leafclever asked.

Katya went on, trying to swallow her anger and speak only the facts; she couldn't help but linger over the deaths that could have been prevented if Redtrue had used the power she'd created. When she came to her own attack, she could feel her mother's eyes boring into her.

All through her tale, thunder had rumbled in the distance. When she finished, it boomed nearly overhead, and the rain began. The temperature dropped so sharply, Katya shivered. She glanced out the tent flap to see what remained of the campfires gutter and die. Soon, it wouldn't be rain but snow.

"At least we can take comfort in the fact that Darren is dead," Da said. "But we should talk about this new weapon."

"There is no new weapon," Leafclever said. "We cannot turn the adsna against itself. To avoid creating these Fiends or other evil, one must use the adsna as it is meant to be used: in harmony with the world."

"You think the corpse Fiends unnatural," Da said, "against the adsna. Destroying them should be just like putting out a fire that someone started."

He shook his head. "Part of them is human."

"Part of them *was* human," Count Mathias said. "They don't even bleed."

Leafclever shut his eyes as if the horror was too much to contemplate. Katya sympathized a little, remembering when she'd first encountered a corpse Fiend, the disgust she'd felt, but that hadn't stopped her from killing them.

"We cannot use such a pyramid again, not against these corpses or Fiends themselves," Leafclever said with a tone of finality. Dayscout said something in Allusian, his tone pleading. Leafclever shook his head. "I will speak to Redtrue, and we will find another way."

Katya glanced at her father, too tired to fight. He nodded toward the tent flap, dismissing her. Ma squeezed Katya's arm before she left, a little motherly concern that could be expressed in front of non-family.

Katya squelched through the mud back to her tent. She sat inside, stripped out of her wet, muddy gear, wincing both at the pain in her shoulder, the soreness of her muscles, and the dull ache in her throat. For a moment, she just sat in her blankets and thought of nothing. Darren's death brought her no joy, not in the face of all they had yet to accomplish. And with this new conflict in the camp, Starbride seemed very far away.

"May I come in?" Redtrue asked from outside.

Katya blinked at the entrance and didn't know what to say.

"It *is* raining," Redtrue said.

"I know."

Redtrue's sigh carried even through the tent wall. "I have news of Starbride."

"Come on, then. But you better not be using that to come in and make more excuses."

Frowning, Redtrue sat down inside the tent, laying her wet cloak close to the entrance. "I'm sorry you and Castelle were hurt. I'm sorry for all the people who died."

Katya remained silent.

Redtrue rolled her lips under. "I contacted the pyradisté again, and I did not stop berating him until I secured a promise that he would find Starbride tomorrow."

"And you think he'll honor his promise? Or you'll haunt his dreams?"

She slipped her cloak back on. "I shall tell you when I've found her."

Katya barred the way out of the tent. "You helped me before out of pity. Now you do it out of guilt."

"And so?"

"Thank you, but as long as you hold the key to victory, the guilt will stay with you."

"Let me pass. I have other visits to make this night."

Katya scooted out of the way, wondering if Redtrue was going to visit Castelle and then realizing that, at the moment, she couldn't care less.

She laid back and let memories surround her until she could almost feel the warmth of Starbride's body next to hers.

CHAPTER TWENTY-TWO

STARBRIDE

"Here." Drive stopped at a red alley door. She kicked it open with one swift movement and waved everyone inside.

Starbride hurried into a small storeroom lined with shelves, most of them holding ceramic bowls and glass bottles. The overpowering scent of vanilla oil and incense rolled over her, and she covered her mouth with one sleeve. "Where are we? A scent shop?"

Drive shut the door and put a large jar in front of it to keep it closed. "It's a brothel, but it doesn't open until later."

"A...what?" Starbride pulled back from touching one of the shelves.

"The only one who *lives* here is the proprietress," Drive said. "I'll tell her we're here before she comes downstairs with her cudgel."

Starbride swallowed a few times and hoped a cudgel was a weapon. She knelt beside the unconscious Maia and Hugo. "I didn't know they had brothels in Marienne."

"They have brothels everywhere," Ruin said. "We're just lucky Drive knows this one." He nudged Fury. "Remind me to ask her *how* she knows, eh? Now, let me take a look at your injuries." He examined Scarra's swollen eye and Fury's oddly hanging shoulder, and then had Scarra and Pennynail help him pop Fury's shoulder back into place.

Starbride tried to shut her ears against the sickening crunch and examined Maia with a pyramid. The pyramid in her neck remained dark and inactive. Still, they couldn't just leave it in there. "Ruin, can your monks remove a pyramid from Maia's neck?"

"Well, the Fiend king had to get it in there somehow. That means we can get it out, though we might have to seek a surgeon from outside our ranks. Can you keep her unconscious until we return to the chapterhouse?"

"I hope so." In the meantime, Starbride tucked a suppression pyramid into Hugo's coat. He'd dropped his necklace somewhere in the chapterhouse, and unlike Maia, he didn't need a pyramid to keep his Fiend *awake*.

"I'll find Drive," Ruin said.

"Don't get sidetracked," Scarra called.

Starbride pressed a pyramid to Maia's forehead, looking into her thoughts as well as keeping her asleep.

Maia's mind was a jumble, like any sleeping person, but also oily and hard to see, as if the creature inside her had coated her thoughts in slime. She'd been assigned to the strength chapterhouse by her father, with orders to send for him if she discovered Starbride or any important fugitives, orders she'd ignored.

Starbride smiled at that until she realized why Maia had disobeyed. She didn't defy her father for the sake of her conscience; it was the Fiend. Beyond murderous brutality was a need to be solitary. The Fiend that had merged with Maia wasn't happy obeying Roland's orders. Starbride bet the others felt the same. Maia's human side recognized that she had to work with her father in order to win, but the Fiend took any little chance to rebel. Maia thought she could handle Starbride on her own; she'd relished the chance to sink her claws into flesh.

Starbride hurried away from that memory and gleaned everything she could about Roland instead. Katya and the royals weren't inside the palace. Starbride had known that, but it still filled her with relief to have it confirmed. Roland suspected they'd fled the city; he'd sent Darren with a host of corpse Fiends to find them.

And Darren hadn't yet returned. Another wave of relief washed over Starbride. Katya and her family were still on the run, and Starbride bet they were half a step ahead of Darren and building allies in the countryside.

She looked for other clues to Roland's plans, but she didn't know how useful they would prove to be. Roland would soon know that Starbride had captured his daughter. He'd change his plans accordingly. Starbride's stomach turned over as she saw that if she had chosen to go to the largest knowledge chapterhouse that day, she would have met Roland himself.

Starbride pulled away from Maia's memories and brushed a strand of hair away from her face.

Hugo began to stir. He sagged against the wall as if his head was too heavy to hold up. "Is she going to be all right?"

"I'll do what I can," Starbride said. "Listen, Hugo… You can't take your necklace off again. If you had gotten away from us, your Fiend would have hurt innocent people."

He smiled, too tired, it seemed, to manage a blush. "I knew I'd attack her first. Fiends like to fight each other."

"And if you'd killed her?"

"I couldn't let her hurt you."

Starbride glanced at Pennynail, but he shrugged. Hugo knew Starbride would never forsake Katya, but it seemed he would do as he wished whatever the truth was. She couldn't command him not to have a crush on her.

"Would someone like to tell us what the f—" Scarra cleared her throat. "What's going on?"

"Not polite to whisper," Fury added.

"Fiend king, corpse Fiends," Scarra said. "Everyone's got a Fiend coming out of her ass. Now we have ally Fiends? You going to run up and paint them before each fight so we know which ones to beat the shit out of?"

Starbride had to smile at Scarra's selective swearing. "This is Maia Nar Umbriel, King Einrich's niece, and the Fiend king's daughter." She pointed at Hugo. "Hugo is his son and Maia's half-brother."

Hugo waved weakly. Scarra's mouth hung open. Fury studied them in silence.

Scarra finally nudged Pennynail with her foot. "Who are you? The queen?"

He saluted her, and Starbride had to hold in a laugh.

"Well, I'll be dipped in sh—" Scarra glanced at all of them again. "Never mind."

"I thought I recognized her," Fury said. "If she's really Einrich's niece and an Umbriel and the Fiend king is her da, then the Fiend king is Einrich's brother. But he only had one sib that the public knew about, the brother who died."

Scarra glanced at him as if he'd caught fire. "You're in the wrong chapterhouse, brother."

"I'm a dyed-in-the-wool royalty watcher," Fury said. "So, is the Fiend king a bastard or is he a corpse?"

"Both," Starbride said, "but not in the ways you're thinking. He is the dead Prince Roland, come back to life. More and more people are going to be working that out."

"Back to life because of the Fiend, I'm guessing?" Fury asked.

He *was* in the wrong chapterhouse. Starbride nodded.

"So you kill them, but they don't stay dead?" Scarra's brow furrowed so hard it looked painful. "But then… How many are there, and if we can't kill them…"

"It's a long story," Starbride said, "and not all of it is relevant. I can promise you, though, if we stab the Fiend king enough, he will stay dead."

Fury cocked his head. "Is now when you ask us to keep this secret?"

"That would be nice," Starbride said, "if only to keep me from having to repeat myself."

He shut his eyes as if he could no longer be bothered to care.

Scarra hadn't lost her frown. "I'll keep my gob shut, if that's what you want, but Drive and Ruin probably noticed what was going on, too. You might have to repeat yourself at least once more."

Starbride nodded. She couldn't hope for anything better. She'd have to tell Katya that she'd kept the Umbriels' secrets as best she could.

Shortly thereafter, Drive and Ruin returned with the mistress of the house. They introduced her as Lady Beatrice, a title that Starbride doubted.

"My customers will be coming in soon," Lady Beatrice said. "I can't hide you forever." She gave Scarra and Fury an up and down glance. "Unless you're looking for work." They both laughed.

"Not today," Starbride said. "Thank you for letting us take shelter here."

Lady Beatrice shrugged the gratitude away. "The strength house has sent good customers over the years, and my boys and girls can use all the endurance Best and Berth will bestow upon them." She clapped Drive on the shoulder. "Still, time's wasting."

The monks snuck out and headed for their home chapterhouse, promising to bring a horse and wagon. It would be less conspicuous than Pennynail or Starbride hurrying through the streets, especially carrying Maia. As afternoon approached, the monks returned. They disguised Maia in a pile of blankets and loaded her into the wagon.

Starbride and Pennynail crouched beside her and tried to be as invisible as possible.

"We can't take her to the hideout," Hugo said in Starbride's ear.

She looked at him sharply. "I'm not leaving her alone."

"Neither am I," he said, "in case our father finds her again. But we can't remove her pyramid, and the monks can. Besides, until she's herself again..."

"We can't risk her knowing where we're hiding," Starbride finished. She patted his cheek. "When did you get so wise?"

He only smiled. At the chapterhouse, they all decided to stay. Master Bernard and Claudius had returned to the hideout to continue puzzling over the trap-pyramid problem. The monks closed their doors to outsiders and posted guards on the lookout for trouble. They brought in a surgeon for Maia, and then there was nothing to do but wait.

Ruin gave them a small room and two beds to share. Once they were behind closed doors, Pennynail pulled off his mask, becoming Freddie again.

"Finally," he said. "I feel like I've been wearing that thing for weeks. Did you send word to Master Bernard?"

"Scarra volunteered to tell him we're back."

Freddie gave her a lopsided grin. "She does a lot for us."

"Maybe she has a crush on you, Freddie."

"Yeah, right," Hugo said. When they both stared at him, he turned red. "What?"

"Thanks a lot." Freddie sank down in one of the room's two chairs. "Think I'm too old for her? I certainly feel it after the day we've had."

He reminded Starbride so much of Crowe that her breath hitched.

"I was talking about the mask," Hugo said, "not you. Who could love that mask?"

"And without it?" Freddie glanced at Starbride. "He thinks I'm gorgeous."

"I never said that!"

"He didn't *not* say it."

"Enough," Starbride said before they could continue, but she was glad no one was throwing punches. Given enough time, maybe they could even learn to like each other. In, say, a thousand years? She sat on one of the beds. "I'm tired, but I'm...happy."

"I'm glad we got her back," Freddie said.

"What is she like?" Hugo asked. "I mean, what was she like before..."

"Young," Freddie said. "And naive, but that was all right because she was so positive about everything. Even the job, the Order. She got depressed, but she bounced back. She loved life."

"And she loved Brutal," Starbride added. "She blushed at the drop of a hat." She glanced at Hugo, but he wasn't looking at her. "She was eager and better at the job than she gave herself credit for."

"An incredible archer," Freddie said. "I wonder why she never came after us with arrows when she was a Fiend."

"The Fiend likes getting its hands dirty," Hugo mumbled. He still carried a suppression pyramid in his coat pocket, but Starbride needed to make him another necklace.

"Maybe the part of her that was still Maia wouldn't let the Fiend use something so special to her," she said.

He nodded slowly, and she could almost see his mind working. If there had been a part of her that was still Maia, there might be a part of Roland that was still a man, a father. Somehow, Starbride doubted it. Maia had most likely had her Fiend forced upon her. From what Starbride had heard of Roland's near demise, he'd chosen to become a monster.

As night fell, Starbride awoke at a soft knock. It cut Hugo off mid snore, and Starbride heard Pennynail rising from his pallet. He struck a match and lit a candle before he pulled his mask on. When he was covered, Starbride opened the door.

Ruin had dark circles under his eyes, but they seemed as bright and alert as ever. "It's finished." He held out a scrap of cloth with a bloodstained pyramid in the middle.

"She's…?"

"Alive and resting," Ruin said. "They gave her a sleeping draught for the procedure, of course. She mustn't move for a few days in order to keep her stitches closed. Lucky for all of us, this wasn't deep."

Starbride took the cloth and its grisly prize. "When will she wake?"

"Soon."

"Thank you, Ruin, for everything."

"You awakened us, dear lady. What can I give you that will ever cover that debt?"

He left without an answer. Starbride turned back to Hugo and Freddie's relieved faces before they trudged to Maia's room.

She seemed smaller and even paler. Someone had undone her hair, and tendrils of it floated in the draft from the window, just as Starbride remembered from when they'd first met. She laid her fingers on Maia's forehead.

Maia's eyes fluttered open. Starbride braced herself. They'd removed the pyramid that let Maia's Fiend loose, but she half expected Maia to fly at them, tearing for their throats.

"Starbride?" Maia whispered.

Starbride's shoulders relaxed. She used a cloth to dribble some water on Maia's lips. "You're safe."

"What happened?"

Starbride took a breath, not knowing how much to say, how much Maia would remember. She'd hoped Maia would forget her entire time as a Fiend, as the other Umbriels did when they changed. She could have tried to erase the memories, but she didn't know how much she'd be forced to take. The entire thread of the Fiends? Of her father? Of the Order and Katya?

Maia's mouth slipped open, and her forehead drew down in pain. "Oh spirits, I...." She began to sob, a breathless, papery sound.

Starbride sank down at her bedside. "It's all right, Maia. You're safe now."

"I...I..."

"Gently," Starbride said. Pennynail moved to her other side and held her hand. "You'll tear your stitches."

"I want...to..."

"No, it will be painful—"

"I want to...die!"

Starbride leaned over, trying to hold her, awkward as it was. The part of her mind that had learned caution at Marienne's court warned her that she was putting herself in the perfect position for the Fiend to strike, but she couldn't listen to that now, not with the pain raw and real in Maia's voice.

"It's all over, Maia. He can't hurt you now."

"I hurt *you*! I hurt...so many."

"It's all right."

"It's not all right!" Maia wailed. "I let him...I wanted... Oh, spirits, I...with Darren and Hilda!"

Starbride bit her lip. She guessed that meant it was *Maia* who'd passed the Fiend to Darren and Lady Hilda, and there was only one way to do that: She had to have bedded them. It had probably been her first time or near enough, and it was with a man and woman she hated just to satisfy the whims of a monster, her father no less.

Maia tried to curl into a ball. Pennynail held her down, but she started to thrash.

"Someone help!" Hugo called.

Footsteps hurried across the floor, and one of the monks pressed a cloth over Maia's mouth. She quieted against the mattress, her eyelids fluttering until they stayed shut.

"She cannot disturb herself like that," the monk said.

"That's why we called for help," Hugo shot back.

The monk glared at him and then left them alone.

"Regret will tear her to pieces," Hugo said. "I should know."

"You weren't in your right mind when you conspired with Roland, and neither was she," Starbride said. "As soon as you were set loose from his claws, you realized your true self. We just have to help Maia do the same."

"What did she mean about Darren and Hilda?" Hugo asked.

"Never mind that now. We need to get back to Master Bernard, gather some supplies. Dawnmother will tend to Maia better than we ever could. Maybe we can move Averie here, and Dawnmother and the monks can mind them both."

When they returned to the warehouse, Dawnmother heaved a sigh of relief. "There you are, Star."

"Did you get my message?"

"Of course, and Master Bernard forbade me from going to you. He seemed to think it too risky." She crossed her arms, and Starbride imagined that words between them must have been epic indeed. "We found a new pyradisté. Well, he found us, actually, and he needs to see you desperately. I don't understand half of what he says, but perhaps you will."

Starbride frowned. "Has anyone confirmed that he *is* a pyradisté?"

"We're not idiots, Star. He is neither a mind-controlled assassin nor some poor soul fitted with an exploding pyramid."

"I'm sorry, Dawn. I'll be jumping at shadows soon."

"And I'll be snapping at them alongside you. Don't let my bad temper hinder you. Come."

She led the way through the warehouse to an unkempt young man, barely a student by the looks of him, dressed in rags. He leapt from a chair at the sight of her.

"At last!" he cried. "She won't let me sleep!"

Dawnmother half stepped between them.

"What's your name?" Starbride asked.

"Dekken, but that's not important. Since I've found you, she'll let me sleep in peace."

"Who?"

"He says a pyradisté haunts his dreams," Dawnmother said, "demanding he find you."

"Adsnazi," Dekken said. "Redtrue won't let me forget that."

Starbride almost took a step back. She didn't recognize the name, but it was Allusian, and how many Farradains had heard the word adsnazi? "But how—"

He sank into his chair in a miserable heap. "She said since I don't know how to dream walk, it's hard to talk to me. She speaks in my dreams, calls to me, and it's like I go out of my body to reach her. She told me how to make a pyramid so she could more easily speak. I never should have done it. She didn't want to teach me, but she said the princess was extremely persuasive."

Starbride almost stepped forward and grabbed his collar. "The princess?"

Dawnmother touched Dekken's shoulder. "Perhaps you should start from the beginning, the right end of the road as Horse—"

"Please don't quote Horsestrong!" Dekken cried. "If I never hear of him again, it will be—"

Starbride knelt in front of him. "If you tell me your story, and show me what you know, you might never speak to Redtrue again."

His eyes lit up as if he were a drowning man and she a passing ship. For days, he said, he'd had dreams of an Allusian girl. At first, he'd thought them nothing, but she always repeated the same story. Her name was Redtrue, she was an Allusian adsnazi—*not a pyradisté*— and she had a message from Princess Katyarianna to Princess Consort Starbride. The more real she seemed the more he'd been convinced he'd gone insane.

Dekken had been living off scraps in alleys, striving to stay one step ahead of the corpse Fiends, afraid to trust anyone, terrified that the Fiend king seemed determined to kill every pyradisté in the kingdom. What snatches of sleep he'd been able to steal had been interrupted by this persistent woman who demanded she listen to him.

Dekken laughed. "She didn't force herself into my head, but she just called and called, and I couldn't ignore her. All the hallucinations in the world, and I get the bossiest."

"Go on," Starbride said. Clearly, Redtrue hadn't been bossy enough because it had taken Dekken so long to craft a pyramid at her direction.

Even then, when he presented it to Starbride, it was a sloppy piece of craftsmanship. He'd been working from a castoff bit of crystal he'd found near the academy. It was deeply flawed and cloudy, and Dekken said he only heard Redtrue a little better when he used it. Or maybe it was the fact that he focused on her that made her easier to hear. Instead of sleep, he fell into a trance when they spoke and was able to hear her and to somewhat feel her emotions.

"Once," Dekken said, "when she thought I wasn't concentrating enough, I felt her anger, and then…it was like she slapped me." He laughed, and the sound had the edge of hysteria. "I have no idea how she did it."

Starbride's mind raced. She had no idea how Redtrue did any of it. She'd never heard of such a thing; she bet Master Bernard hadn't either. So the adsnazi had more tricks than just pretty lights. She'd always put them far behind the Farradains in ability and power, but she might have to rethink that. "And the princess?"

"With Redtrue near Allusia."

"Did she say anything else?"

"That if you didn't believe me, I was to call you Miss Meringue."

Starbride's stomach lurched. She wanted to weep and cry out with joy at the same time. "Teach me how to use this pyramid, and I promise you a bed to yourself for as long as you want it."

His expression bloomed into hope before he straightened. Using the pyramid sounded easy in theory. Focus on it and fall in like any pyramid, but then the user had to focus outward, putting herself into a deep trance that left her open for contact. Starbride tried again and again. Dekken's chin quivered as if he might weep when she tried a fourth time and still couldn't manage it.

"Please hurry," he said. "She'll come looking for me any time now."

Instead of focusing hard on the pyramid, Starbride thought of Katya, how good it would be to hear her, even through a proxy. Like with the academy pyramid, she seemed to fall through this one, as if opening her mind to a shared experience, offering a spectral hand and waiting to be grabbed. At last, she felt a glimmer.

"You're not that idiot," an Allusian voice said in her mind. "Starbride?"

"Yes," she said, her excitement so palpable, she felt her trance slipping.

"Relax!" the voice said. "Don't fight."

"Are you Redtrue?"

"Yes, and it's nice to work with someone not completely inept. I was afraid Dekken was never going to get it."

"Well, he was exhausted and running for his life."

"We don't have the luxury of pity, I'm afraid. One moment."

Starbride felt Redtrue's attention stray, and for a few moments there was only silence. "Redtrue?"

No one answered. Fear grabbed at Starbride's heart; she was so close. "Redtrue!"

"Hold your reins. Katya is babbling at me."

Starbride stiffened at the mention of Katya's familiar name from this strange woman's mind, but that melted away. "She's there? Katya's there?"

"She sends a thousand proclamations of love and desperate pleas for your safety."

"Tell her I love her, too, and I'm safe." She briefly spoke of the resistance and heard in turn Katya's reports of building an army. "I should stay here, then, and wait for you…her?"

"Like any lovesick fool, she doesn't want to put you in danger."

"Ha! I'm there already. And with me here, we can attack the Fiend king on two fronts."

"She calls him the usurper… Now, she's spouting love at you again."

Starbride laughed through a sob. "Oh, Katya, I love you, too." Starbride put all her feeling behind the words and heard Redtrue's gasp.

"Not…so strong," Redtrue said. "Are you trying to make me fall in love with her, too?"

"Is there no way she and I could talk?"

Redtrue was silent for a moment. "You'd need me for a conduit. I would have to enter her mind just enough for her to speak to you."

Starbride sensed her reluctance. "You don't like using mind pyramids?"

"If I took up this time to admonish you about these so-called mind pyramids and lament the fact that you were trained by Farradains, Katya would kill me."

They spent the rest of the time discussing plans and telling of the past, that and promising to see each other again. By the end, Starbride could tell Redtrue grew tired of the many love messages she was forced to pass on.

"If we're going to get any real sleep tonight, we'd better say good-bye," Redtrue said.

"Wait, I…" Starbride paused on the cusp of telling Katya that they'd rescued Maia and Averie, but she kept remembering Maia's despair and what Averie had been through. There was no telling if either would ever be the same. Starbride hated to give Katya hope if she might have to pull it away.

"Yes?" Redtrue prompted. "More love?"

"Yes. More love."

Redtrue sighed. "And she loves you, as well, as if anyone doubted. Now, I'm saying good-bye for the both of you. Look for me again tomorrow night."

With that, she was gone like early morning mist. Starbride opened her eyes and found gentle fingers wiping her cheeks. She looked into Dawnmother's worried face.

"It must have worked," Dawnmother said. "You've been crying for nearly an hour."

"Was it just an hour?" Starbride asked, feeling her throat tight. "Where is Dekken?"

"Sleeping in the corner, puddled like an old rag. Horsestrong himself could ride into this room, and he wouldn't wake."

Starbride let Dawnmother lead her to their room. She had Dawnmother gather Freddie and Hugo and told them what Katya had said. Shortly, Dawnmother left to tend Averie and Maia while the other two absorbed the information.

Hugo rubbed his face. "War. I mean, I know we've been fighting, but the idea that it's a war…"

"Does it matter what it's called?" Freddie asked.

"You're telling me that just the idea of war doesn't scare you?"

"Sure it does. That's why I prefer to think of it as the fight we've already been fighting for the past few months. The only thing that's changed is we'll have a few more allies."

Starbride didn't know what to think, of war or otherwise. Katya was alive. Call it war, call it springtime, call it the end of all things; none of it mattered. Katya was alive.

Freddie nudged her. "I know what you're thinking."

"Everyone should know. Everyone should feel as I do right now."

"I don't think everyone has had the same experience with our beloved princess."

"It's lovely," Hugo said with a soft smile.

Starbride beamed, happy that his crush extended beyond her, that he loved Katya too. Maybe he was just in love with love.

"Did you tell her about Averie and Maia?" Freddie asked.

"If we end up with something that will cheer Katya, I'll share. If not…well, I don't want to put that on her shoulders."

"End up with something?" Hugo said. "Is Maia a *something* now?"

"Hugo, that's not what I meant."

"Then what?" He seemed angry, but when he looked at her, it was terror in his eyes, not only for his sister, but for what might happen if he fell into Roland's grasp.

Freddie patted Hugo's shoulder, and Hugo didn't shrug it off. "Maia *and* Averie will recover, but it might take years. There's no need to tell Katya now."

Hugo stilled his face and nodded.

"We need to gather allies quicker now," Starbride said. "Roland might lock the other chapterhouses down. We'll need to get as many as we can, step up our efforts to find pyradistés, and see who's with us among the regular populace."

"I know a good place to start," Freddie said. "Dockland's not happy with the Fiend king."

Starbride's mouth turned down at the thought of the odious city and its criminal inhabitants. She still remembered her trip to the mad Warrens and didn't know what help they'd find in such a place.

Freddie laughed at her disgust. "Lest we forget, I spent a great deal of my life there. Thieves and vagabonds they may be, but they know how to fight, and the Fiend king has been cutting into their profits. There are rumors that he wants to wipe them off the map."

"Kill them all?" They weren't her favorites, but she'd never think to simply murder them.

"They may not have much," Freddie said, "but they're ready to fight for it."

"Would they follow us?"

"No, but they'd follow him." Hugo gestured to Freddie. "Dockland's most notorious son."

"You want me to play the Butcher?" Freddie asked. "Why in the hell would the Butcher want to help anyone, especially those who hanged him?"

"He'd want to defend what little he had, that's what you said."

"I can try and persuade them as myself," Freddie said, "but I'm not going to pretend to be something I never was, a figment I have to hide from even now."

"But they all *think* you're the Butcher," Hugo persisted. "I still can't quite believe you're not. They might even believe you came back from the dead."

"It might rally some to our cause," Starbride said. "If they believe the stories about your strength and ferocity—and ability to cheat death—they'll want you in front of them rather than behind."

He frowned. "I can't…"

"Maybe you're right, Freddie," Starbride said, saving him from growing distress. "The legends might scare more people than attract them. And we wouldn't want the families of the Butcher's victims trying to get revenge. But your laughing Jack persona could be a symbol for us. Jack and Jan are the patron spirits of thieves, yes?"

"Among others. I could be a symbol, but I don't have a voice. Even if I spoke from behind the mask, no one would hear me unless he was standing beside me."

"What about you, Miss Starbride?" Hugo asked. "You've done a good job leading here."

"I think the fact that I'm Allusian and a noble would hurt more than help with the Docklanders, unless I played the rogue noble popular in some of the juicier storybooks."

Freddie leered. "Just what kinds of books do you read?"

"Any I can get a hold of. That's how one learns."

"Oh, thank you. Now one understands."

"Katya will know how to play it," Starbride said. "When next we speak…" She couldn't contain a shiver and a happy laugh. "I'll ask her."

"I can feel it all coming together," Hugo said. "I'm off to visit my sister. I'll check in when I get back."

Freddie lingered after Hugo left. "Don't fall back on old habits."

"What?"

"An hour conversation, and you're already waiting to get Katya's advice. You've been making decisions on your own for a while. Don't just pass that off now that you'll have her input. You have a good brain; continue to use it."

She bristled. "I ask advice from everyone whenever I can!"

"Advice, sure, but I get the feeling you're going to wait for Katya to tell you what to do."

"And why shouldn't I?" she snapped. "She's been at this game far longer than I."

"The war-with-a-Fiend-king game? Not hardly." He pointed at her. "You're the more experienced hand here."

Starbride half turned away, feeling a headache pound through her temples. "I am *tired*, Freddie. She's probably tired, too, but I'm…"

He patted her shoulder. "By all means, ask for her advice, ask for mine, hell, ask for Hugo's, but trust yourself to make a good decision. You're doing fine."

"People have died," she said softly.

"And more will die, but Roland has to be stopped."

"And what if Hugo dies? Or Maia?"

He chuckled. "Or the spirits themselves? I'll tell you now: If I die, you'd better fight on unless you want me to haunt you forever."

She sagged, worn out. She was beginning to sympathize with Dekken. It felt like she hadn't slept in years. "I didn't set out to be a leader."

"The Umbriels did, and look where that got them."

She gave him a black look.

"When King Einrich takes back the throne, he'll need you in his circle for all the goodwill you've fostered here. Luckily, you'll be his daughter-in-law, so you won't be hard to find."

The thought of wedding Katya made Starbride curl her toes inside her boots. She wanted it now, yes please: Katya in Marienne, at her side, in her bed. "She gives me strength, Freddie."

"Strength is fine, just don't let her—"

"Message received. I'm the decision maker."

He nodded. "You look like you could use a rest."

"It's early yet."

"I'll wake you if anything noteworthy happens, but I have the feeling that all of us should rest while we can."

"What about you?"

"I'm too awake to sleep. I'll send word to my Dockland contacts now that I've found them again. Maybe they'll have some clues as to how we can rouse that den of thieves." He winked. "I bet they'll come up with something even Katya wouldn't think of."

Before she could hit him, he ducked out the door. Starbride stretched on her bed without putting out the candle. She hadn't realized how happy she'd be to let Katya take over, to let someone else play leader for a while.

But that was it, wasn't it? She felt like a little girl at dress-up. Any moment, someone would discover that she wasn't a leader, that she'd been faking all her supposed knowledge, her paper-thin confidence. They'd demand she relinquish control to the adults.

Or they'd be so disgusted with how many people she'd let die that they'd throw her to Roland.

Starbride shuddered. So far, everyone seemed to think she was doing a good job, but she couldn't get past the idea that she was fooling everyone. She tried to tell herself that was stupid. She'd proven herself, and her allies trusted her. Why would they suddenly stop?

Because people would be dying in droves. The days before her were filled with blood. Thoughts of Katya momentarily forgotten, Starbride curled around her own unease and tried to reach for sleep.

CHAPTER TWENTY-THREE

KATYA

Katya hugged her knees and nearly rolled around Redtrue's tent, torn between singing in joy and weeping from worries finally set at ease. Even her sore shoulder and neck didn't stop her. Surely, any minute now, she would burst open from the pressure of so many emotions and scatter into light.

"Am I forgiven?" Redtrue asked quietly.

Katya wasn't angry now, couldn't be, but she knew the feeling would return. "Thank you for doing this. It was better than I imagined. I love her so much."

"I know."

"I bet you do, after all the times you had to hear it."

"I felt it."

"You what?"

"Not your love, of course, since I was only speaking to you, but she pushed her emotions through the pyramid, and I…" She chuckled. "I hope you never doubt that she means what she says."

Katya felt another great surge: love for Starbride, embarrassment that someone else could see into her and Starbride's hearts, and jealousy that she couldn't feel Starbride's love in the same way. "I'm sorry. I didn't know."

"You might be able to." Her eyes pinned Katya to the spot. "If I were to enter your mind, just a little, and we were to communicate with her again, I might serve as a bridge between you. You could converse and feel each other without my voice to connect you."

Katya's stomach dropped to her feet. "Truly?"

Redtrue cocked an eyebrow, and Katya could nearly read the question there, another plea for forgiveness.

Katya's mouth worked for a moment. "Does my forgiveness mean that much to you that you'd hold Starbride to get it?"

"No, no, I…" She took a deep breath. "Your people still infuriate me, and I will not abandon the path of the adsnazi for you or for anyone. But your passion has…moved me, and I appreciate your sense of humor, and you are one of the few non-adsnazi who has never treated me like a servant—"

"I get it. You want us to be friends, but, Redtrue…"

"I should not have dangled your Starbride like a carrot before a donkey. I'm sorry."

Katya burst out laughing. "I never had many friends, so I appreciate the offer, but I don't understand your position on destructive pyramids; I never will. I've had to abandon my principles in order to do my duty, but I've only ever considered abandoning my duty for her. I can't see letting people suffer for anything less than love."

"But don't you see?" Redtrue asked. "It is for love, love of the adsna, the very world spirit, love for all things! How can I abandon it to evil? Piling evil atop evil will not fix the Fiends. If I used that destructive pyramid, who knows what consequences it would have in the future?"

Redtrue took a deep breath before she continued. "Your ancestors used the adsna however they chose, never thinking that you and your kin would pay the price. What you're asking me to do might destroy the world one day or place the children of another generation in the same peril we face now!"

Her entire body quivered with passion. Katya had thought her eaten up by cynicism. It was nice to see that she was truly a believer. Now Katya saw some of what Castelle must have spied in her.

"I value the living more than those who might someday live," Katya said. When Redtrue opened her mouth, Katya shook her head. "You can't see the future. If we try to prepare for every outcome, we paralyze ourselves." She stood. "We may never see eye-to-eye, and I can't force you to do anything. I appreciate what you've done for me and Starbride, and I will always defend your life because of it. I will try to be your friend. But I can't promise that, even after our struggles are over, I will forgive that you had a weapon that could kill a Fiend and didn't use it."

When she stepped out of Redtrue's tent, Katya spied Castelle nearby, not making any attempt to hide the fact that she was watching.

Katya marched up to her, and Castelle leaned back as if expecting another punch. She held a hand to her abdomen as if the sudden movement pained her wound.

Katya reached for her, favoring her wounded shoulder. "You two make a wonderful, utterly confused couple, and if either of you let your anger or pride come between you, you're fools. Get your ass in there."

Castelle blinked for a moment and then stepped around Katya and headed for Redtrue's tent. Maybe they could love their way through their frustrations and wake up in the morning cleansed.

❖

The army marched very slowly. Just getting everyone organized took all morning. Good to get the fits and starts out of the way, Katya supposed, before they got farther into Farraday. It would be good to have the army closer while Katya rode out scouting. The next villages were too far away to ride back and forth in one day. And if there were more corpse Fiends wandering around, she dreaded the idea of camping with just a small force.

As she rode, Katya noticed a disturbing separation among the people: the Farradains kept close to one another, and the Allusians did the same, keeping the royals and Dayscout almost in the middle.

Katya rode closer to Dayscout's horse. "Do you see what's happening?"

He smiled brightly. "Good morning to you, too. If you mean the gap between our peoples, oh yes, I noticed."

"What should we do about it?"

"Nothing, I should think."

She blinked at him. He chuckled.

"In my experience," he said, "you cannot force people to be friends, Highness."

"You can call me, Katya, Governor."

"You are an affectionate people," he said with a smile. "Better to be Katyarianna and Dayscout, however. The shortening of a name among my people is...delicate."

Katya nearly swore. She knew that, but... "Redtrue calls me Katya."

"Her feelings are her own, but I am a leader and a husband."

"I see your point. Still, do you think we should encourage people to mingle?"

"I think that will happen on its own." He gestured forward, and Katya looked through the marching masses to where a group bearing Count Mathias's banner crossed to Hawkblade's nomads.

Katya recalled the way he'd looked at her with near worship after the fight with Darren. Maybe he was making his own effort to bring their armies closer together. "Some might be tempted to follow in his wake," she said.

"True. It's hard for me to see one so young as you worry so much." He tapped his own temple, then pointed at where her hair had begun to gray.

It still startled her every time she looked in a mirror. "Yes," she drawled, "you'd think there was a war on."

"I'm sure it will have cleared itself up by spring," he drawled back at her.

"You've been hanging around our nobles too long."

"Perhaps this Fiend king was exactly what some of them needed. Horsestrong said, spend too much time in comfortable furs and lose your way out of them."

"Did he also say that people have to die for others to learn that lesson?"

"Alas, in my knowledge, he was silent on that subject, but no doubt you could find someone with a different opinion."

❖

Katya rode close to her parents, niece and nephew, and Lord Vincent. He gladly accepted her into their circle, his face almost relaxing when he could keep an eye on all the Umbriels at once. She wondered if he ever thought about Reinholt, but she knew he'd never offer that information. She'd have to pry to get him to reveal anything.

They were getting close to Oldsport, his homeland, though he didn't own it. His title came from winning the champion tourney. He *was* the son of the noble; he just had the misfortune of being a second child.

Oldsport was owned by Countess Esme Lakewood, Vincent's sister. She'd never come to court, and Katya had only heard of her because of her more famous brother. Still, there was no reason to think her disloyal. Katya had heard that Countess Esme stayed away from court only because of an accident in her youth that had taken her right leg below the knee. After getting to know Vincent a little better, Katya was willing to bet that Esme never came to court because she just didn't care what went on there.

They reached her estate at midday. After a quick scout, Da decided to visit. As with Count Mathias, Countess Esme's approval would go a long way in securing local volunteers. Vincent accompanied them only after Katya's mother ordered him to go. Still, he secured a personal pledge from Count Mathias to watch over them.

Esme met them at the door to her large house. She sported silver hair like her brother, and like his, it contrasted with her youthful features. She wore it tied in a tail over her dark blue coat. Katya noted traces of silver from head to toe, buttons to jewelry to the cane she leaned on and the length of silver that served as the lower half of her right leg.

Vincent presented Katya and her father and then Castelle. The rest, as commoners, he dismissed. Katya resisted the urge to roll her eyes.

"Majesty, Highness, Baroness," Esme said with a bow. She looked at Vincent and raised one slender eyebrow. "Vincent, you look well."

"Thank you, Esme, and you."

It had all the charm of a funeral. "Warms my heart," Brutal murmured.

"Some refreshment?" Esme asked.

They followed her inside, Da making small talk. Esme was polite but cold with her replies, as if she saw no reason to be otherwise. She reminded Katya so much of Vincent that Katya kept glancing at him, just to make sure they really were two different people.

"I'm sorry I'm late," a woman's voice called as they reached a sitting room.

Katya glanced over and had to stop her jaw from dropping.

A petite blond woman in a green riding outfit rushed into the room. She smiled, and the light in the room seemed to brighten. Her green eyes glittered as she paused near Esme and bowed. "I wish I could have met you at the gate, but I just got back from town, Majesty, Highness, and…" She looked at Castelle.

"I'm…um," Castelle said.

"Baroness Castelle," Esme said smoothly. "Majesty, Highness, this is my wife, Yvonne Van Lakewood."

Da put on his most charming grin. "A pleasure, dear lady."

She matched his smile and then graced them all with the same. "Won't you sit down?"

As the others moved to sit, Castelle grabbed Katya's arm. "How in the spirits' names did that cold fish nab that glorious woman?" she whispered.

"Keep your roaming hands to yourself."

"A year ago, I would have bankrupted myself chasing her. I'd have been writing promissory notes all over the kingdom."

Katya elbowed her gently before they both took a seat. Castelle grimaced and touched her stomach where Darren had wounded her. "Maybe you should have stayed behind," Katya said.

"And miss this? Never."

The quiet, cold countess of Oldsport and her beautiful, effervescent wife made a strange pair. Yvonne was happy to chat away, though she seemed neither flippant nor silly. Katya sensed great intelligence in both of them, just of a different variety. It was like seeing light married to darkness, or air to earth.

When the talk turned to war, Yvonne frowned, her eyes sad; Esme's expression didn't change. The two of them pledged whatever help they could offer to the war, promising to speak with the villagers at Da's side. Katya wondered who would move the villagers more, their stoic countess or her expressive lady.

When they were preparing to return to camp, Vincent rose to go with them. "Do you want to stay the night, Vincent?" Katya asked. "Catch up with your family?"

He blinked at her as if he didn't understand the question. "I thank your Highness for your consideration, but no, I would like to stay with the children."

She shrugged, giving up trying to figure him out for the moment. As they rode away, Castelle stared over her shoulder at the house.

"Stop that," Katya said, "or I'll tell Redtrue on you."

"If she keeps tossing me out of her tent, she deserves what she gets."

"I thought you two were making up."

Castelle's sigh spoke volumes, but of what Katya didn't know.

"If you make one flirty move toward the countess's wife, I'll reopen your wound."

Castelle frowned. "Since when are you so intent on protecting everyone's virtue?"

Brutal grunted. "Since the countess and her bride come with several hundred souls to help us fight."

"Not you, too, Brutal," Castelle said. "I thought you believed in love at first sight."

"Best and Berth teach us to pick our battles and not fight for foolish reasons."

"Love is not a foolish reason," Castelle said with a sniff.

"I wouldn't call what's happening in your trousers love, exactly," Katya said.

Castelle gave her a withering look that turned to a smile almost immediately. "Fair point."

When they returned to camp, Katya sought out Vincent again, having had the opportunity to wonder about his family for most of the ride. She watched him check on the children and then return outside to begin a series of forms with his sword. When he noticed Katya watching, he bowed and then resumed his exercises.

"How did your sister and Yvonne meet?" Katya asked.

"I do not know, Highness."

"How could you not know?"

He paused. "Have I offended you, Highness?"

"No, I just... You don't know how your sister met her wife?"

"One day she was not married, the next she was."

"She didn't tell you she'd met the woman she intended to marry?"

He stared at nothing for a moment. "She needed neither my permission nor my assistance."

"Of course," Katya said, but she still tried to puzzle it out. Once Vincent had left Oldsport, he and his sister had forgotten about each other, it seemed, especially after Vincent won the champion tourney and left for Reinholt's keep. But was it dislike or apathy that kept them apart? If Katya asked, she was certain she'd get the same questioning look.

"Vincent." Katya had seen the look on Vincent's and Reinholt's faces after they'd kissed. They were passionate about each other. And there had to be something about Esme to make Yvonne choose her over all the others that had to have been clamoring for her attention.

"Yes, Highness?"

"I know that if I asked you some personal questions, you'd do your best to answer."

She almost saw his body tighten with anxiety. "Yes, Highness."

"Well, I can't seem to help myself, so I'll give you an out. I'll ask five questions, and you get two draws." She held up her hand, thumb touching her index and middle finger. Combatants used it during the champion's tourney to pass on their current opponent and draw another. Each competitor got one draw, and it had to be used before the finals. Some used it to find a more challenging opponent, some to find a weaker one. Katya knew that Vincent had never used it, so he had at least two saved up, she supposed.

He bowed, faced pinched as if wondering what he'd done to deserve this. "As you will."

Katya didn't want to pry, she told herself, except she really did, almost felt that she had to. Maybe Starbride had rubbed off on her. "Do you love my brother?"

He touched his thumb to his fingers and drew an invisible line as if crossing the question out of the air.

Katya nodded, but she wondered which response he thought would offend her more: that he loved someone above his station or that he didn't?

"Have you thought about looking for him? Seriously considered it, I mean?"

"I have," he said softly. "But duty does not permit it."

"I understand."

He offered a tiny smile, so slight most might have missed it.

"Are you angry at him for leaving? And if you are, don't think you have to hide it from me. I'm plenty angry already."

He slid his thumb across his fingers as if considering voiding the question, but that left two more with no way out. "I…was surprised at his highness, saddened."

Katya nodded. If Reinholt returned to them, she had no worry that Vincent would shirk his duties, but she wondered if he'd return to Reinholt's bed. Maybe he'd become as cold to Reinholt as he seemed to everyone else.

"Do you love Bastian and Vierdrin? Even beyond duty? I won't be offended if you say yes."

There was that smile again, only a little bigger this time. "I would never offend your Highness or their Majesties. I hope you understand when I say that I would not exchange my sacred charge for anything upon the earth or among the spirits."

Katya grinned at the most she'd ever heard from him. "Very eloquent. Is that a yes?"

"Yes."

She smiled and wracked her brain for a last question he wouldn't automatically cancel.

"Is that all, Highness?"

"I have one more question."

"Forgive me, Highness. I thought I counted five."

Katya went over their conversation in her head and realized she'd repeated her last question. "Clever thing, you."

He gave her a confused blink. "Highness?"

"Never mind. Thank you for humoring me, Vincent."

"I bow to your Highness's will in all things."

She left him to resume his practice, now knowing he was far more slippery than he appeared.

❖

After the army settled, Katya took a little time to relax and give her wounds a rest. She drank tea with her mother while her father visited with Dayscout and Leafclever in Dayscout's tent. Brutal watched over him, but Katya didn't miss the way Vincent kept casting looks at the door. The children played together in the furs on the floor.

"You are allowed to sit, Vincent," Katya said.

"Highness." He cast a quick glance at the chair, as if deciding whether what she'd said was an order or just a statement of tact. Then he sank fluidly into the seat. One of the nannies poured him a cup before retreating into the background.

A drop of tea rolled down the side of the cup. Vincent's eyes tracked it and then flicked toward the nanny, the barest hint of a frown creasing his mouth.

"I...I'm sorry," the nanny said. "I—"

Vincent held up a finger, and she stopped speaking. "My apologies, Majesty, Highness. Sarah is not as adept at pouring tea as she is at caring for children."

Katya coughed over a laugh. Only Vincent would adhere to strict protocols in the middle of nowhere, at the heart of an army. At the same time, he vouched for Sarah's other abilities, as he had no doubt been the one to choose her as a nanny.

"Quite all right," Katya's mother said. "We've all become adept at maneuvering outside of the circles we were once so comfortable in."

Sarah allowed herself a little smile behind Vincent's back.

"You're not a field medic, Lord Vincent," Ma said, "but only yesterday, you bound Bastian's war wound."

"War wound?" Katya glanced at the children, both of whom were interested now that one had been mentioned.

Little Bastian held up his bandaged thumb. "Nicked it."

"A new word for him," Ma said.

"Big baby." Vierdrin glanced at Katya's lap as if considering climbing into it before she went to Vincent.

"Am not," Bastian said as he followed her. When they'd asked permission, he pulled them up on his knees.

The other nanny poured them two small cups of tea before stepping back to join Sarah. "Thank you, Felicia," Ma said.

Katya leaned back and inhaled the aroma. Slightly different from what they'd had in Marienne, it was worlds better than the bitter concoction she'd been forced to drink at Count Mathias's estate.

They all were silent for a few moments. Even the children seemed to drowse on Vincent's lap. They'd had a long day. Katya had already told her parents about contacting Starbride; she was loath to bring it up again in front of Vincent. He wouldn't have blinked or offered comment, but Starbride didn't like him, and Katya didn't want to share anything between them.

A small noise outside almost passed beneath Katya's notice, but she glanced up to see Vincent staring in that direction. It was a footfall, close to the tent's side. Probably a guard, as no one else was allowed close to the royal tent. Perhaps it was her father retuning.

Why then, did the hair on her neck stand up? It sounded too much like someone trying to be quiet. Her father wouldn't bother, and the guards weren't supposed to be milling around the side of the tent but guarding the front.

Katya and Vincent stood at the same time. He put the children in his chair and shushed them as they protested.

"What is it?" Ma whispered.

Katya waved Sarah and Felicia forward, and they crowded around the table with Ma and the children. Katya didn't want them close to the walls. If a corpse Fiend was lurking outside, who knew where it would come through?

Vincent drew his sword and moved to the flap. Katya drew her rapier and stood close to the others, trying to hear. If an enemy was close, it was likely the guards were already dead. If she shouted, would anyone hear, or would she just give her position away? Vincent ducked low in the doorway. If he could get outside, he could raise the alarm.

A short blade stabbed through the flap where his head would have been. He sprang back, staying low. Katya expected a corpse Fiend to speed in after him, but a normal man stepped inside. He took a defensive stance with a calm, murderous look upon his face.

Bastian and Vierdrin screamed. Ma and the nannies herded them behind Katya as another man followed the first through the flap. Katya heard the rip of fabric and turned to confront a woman who slipped through a new slit in the back of the tent.

"Ma, watch the door!" Katya said. They could be wearing disguise pyramids and be corpse Fiends all the same, but they didn't have an aura of cold. Katya moved to engage the woman's short blade. Someone had outfitted her just like the men, from her blade to the chain shirt she wore.

Katya came on furiously. It was unlikely she could penetrate the mail, so she went for the head. If these were corpse Fiends, that was the place to stab them anyway. The chain-woman blocked, keeping Katya at bay. Behind her, Katya spotted movement. A barrel-chested man followed the chain-woman inside.

"Shout!" Katya commanded those behind her.

Ma and the nannies shouted for help. The children cried along with them. Katya heard the ring of steel behind her.

The barrel-chested man rushed Katya. She ducked and stuck her leg out, tripping him. Brutal would have never depended on his size that way. He staggered, and she heard her shouting family move away. The chain-woman came on hard: short, harsh swings designed to tear Katya's weapon from her grasp. Katya feinted, pretended to stumble, and when the chain-woman came close, Katya stabbed her in the knee. She broke off with a howl. Not corpse Fiends then.

Katya heard a gurgle behind her. Vincent had stabbed the barrel-chested man in the back of the head, and he crumpled. The other two were dead in the entryway. Ma had grabbed her necklace, ready to rip it from her throat.

Katya leapt forward as the chain-woman limped for the slit in the tent. Katya grabbed her elbow. She spun, sword aimed. Katya ducked, and Vincent blocked the blow.

"Take her alive!" Katya called.

The chain-woman didn't have time to strike again before Vincent's fist rammed forward. The sword in his grip added enough weight to the blow to send her flying into the tent wall. She sagged against it, unmoving, the fabric bowing around her. Vincent hauled her closer before leaning through the bottom of the hole and calling for help.

Several yells answered him. Katya knelt next to the chainmail woman as Berg popped his head in the flap.

"What in the spirits' names happened here?" he asked.

"Go and make sure my father is safe," Katya said. "We need guards, the pyradisté Rene, and someone to sew up that hole." As he disappeared, Katya turned to her mother. "Do you have any rope, Ma?"

Felicia hurried to find some while Sarah tried to calm the children. As Katya bound the chain-woman, Katya asked, "Do you want me to do this somewhere else?"

"No," Ma said as she buttoned up her coat. "I want to be here while you question her."

❖

Katya bit her thumb as she watched Rene plumb the mind of the would-be assassin. She hadn't even bothered trying to get the adsnazi to help. They would have objected from the start.

Vincent had moved the children to another tent with Brutal and Castelle's friends watching over them. If they had been the assassins' targets, Katya thought it might be a good idea to keep the royal party moving, never occupying the same space in camp two nights in a row.

Katya's parents watched the interrogation, though they hadn't said much. That was all right. Katya preferred the silence.

Watching Rene at work made her ache for Starbride or Crowe. Rene was rumored to be good at his job. When she'd investigated him as a candidate for the bearded man—before she'd found it was Roland—she'd discovered he was a top graduate in his class. But either he hadn't been practicing or mind magic was never his forte. After what seemed like an eternity, he straightened.

"Well?" Katya barked before he had a chance to wipe his brow. He'd lost a lot of weight since Marienne, but he was still stout, and even this meager work seemed to tire him.

"Your pardon, Highness, but a sleeping mind is hard to sort through."

"Of course." She tried to rein in her tone. "Anything useful?"

"Definitely mind manipulated."

"You're certain?"

"This woman was a baker, who up until a few weeks ago was just trying to live her life. I would imagine the others were the same. Overnight, she developed a passionate hatred for your family, particularly the young children, and decided to make it her life's work to hunt you down."

"They were just ordinary people."

"This one was, certainly. For the dead, I cannot say."

"Corpse Fiends aren't enough, it seems," Da said. "Now he's warping our own citizens to kill us, the very people we're trying to save."

"And he'll make us cut through them in order to get to him," Ma said. She clenched Da's arm.

Katya looked to Rene. "How many people could a pyradisté warp in a day?"

"It would depend on the—"

"Someone very good at mind manipulation."

"I don't know, Highness. As many as he could do without tiring."

But Roland didn't get tired. "Is it possible to warp more than one person at a time?"

"If one had the skill and a large enough pyramid, certainly."

Starbride could suddenly find herself surrounded by enemies, even in her own camp. And if Roland had a large mind pyramid, he was probably keeping it close by in the palace. If Katya could reach it and put it in friendly hands... "We might be able to free them," she muttered.

She turned back to her parents. "When we get close enough to Marienne, I might have to ride in first, sneak in, like I used to."

Before her parents could ask, she said, "Not just for her. If I can cripple the usurper it will help all of us."

Da smiled softly. "But part of it is for her, of course." He touched Ma's chin. "Our family's always been more romantic than is probably good for us."

Chapter Twenty-four

Starbride

Someone shook Starbride awake, but a candle blocked their features. "Who? What?" she mumbled.

The flame shifted, revealing Freddie's face. "I'm sorry to wake you, but it's an emergency. You didn't answer my knock."

Starbride tried to still her hammering heart. "Is it Maia? What time is it?"

"Just after dark. Dawnmother hasn't sent any word about Maia or Averie."

"Are we under attack?" But of course not. He wouldn't be so calm.

"My contacts in Dockland have found someone. You need to come now."

"Found someone?" As she pulled on her boots, Starbride tried to gather her wits. "Another pyradisté?"

Freddie's mouth was grim as he shook his head. "My contact didn't name this person directly, but from his note about the black sheep of a preeminent family, I think we can guess who it is."

Starbride stared at him as she tried to shake the last of the sleep from her mind. "Black sheep?"

"The shameful member of any family. I think you called such a person a rogue noble earlier. And there's only one preeminent family that would rate a hasty note from my contact."

At first Starbride thought it must be Freddie's family for him to be so concerned, but then it hit her so hard, she nearly dropped her boot. "The Umbriels." But they only had one black sheep, and he was currently on the throne.

No, a voice inside her said, Roland was a Fiend, but he wasn't the member of the family who had caused them real shame. "Reinholt?" she whispered.

"It must be."

"In Dockland? Why?"

Freddie gestured impatiently at the door. "That's why we have to go see."

"And you can trust this contact?" Starbride asked as she threw her cloak around her shoulders.

"He's beyond reproach."

"No one who can have their mind altered by pyramid is beyond reproach."

"Roland wouldn't bother to warp someone like my contact. He's beneath notice; that's what makes him so valuable. So let's collect Hugo from his sister's bedside and be off."

Starbride loaded her pyramid satchel with everything she might need, including a mind pyramid for Reinholt, if it came to that. Too much was at stake to let him run loose if he insisted on being a problem.

Pennynail didn't take any routes out of Marienne that his father had known about. If Crowe had known them, so would Roland. Like Katya, Roland had hardly ever sneaked out of the city. He'd ridden out on some faux errand and then operated outside of town. It was likely he didn't know Pennynail's secret way under the walls using the sewer that dumped into a creek outside of Marienne. It was one of the most odious journeys of Starbride's life, and she was glad over and over of the cloth smeared with cologne that Freddie had insisted she tie around her nose and mouth.

It took hours of hurrying through the dark until they reached the outskirts of Dockland. The small city at night was just as awful as she remembered. It stank of wet wood, fish, and burning garbage, the miasma strong enough to choke a mule.

No guards stood at the gates. No one cared who left or entered. Starbride wondered if an invading force would even go into the hive of thieves and murderers. She tried to shake the thought, tried to remember that there were innocent people there, too, people just trying to live, but the prejudices of Marienne had penetrated her brain. Every foray she'd made into Dockland had reinforced those prejudices, though it wasn't the fault of the innocent residents if the Order of Vestra always dealt with the more unlawful of Dockland's citizens.

They met Pennynail's contact in a small shop in one of the more well-to-do areas of town. Of course, the wealthiest street in Dockland would be the poorest in Marienne. The houses were too close together, and all the windows were shuttered since most didn't have glass. The streets were narrow and cramped, and the streetlights far apart or darkened altogether. But unlike most of Dockland, they spotted the occasional Watch officer and had to duck into alleys to avoid being seen.

After Pennynail's soft knock on the shop door, a thick man with a bristly, brown beard ushered them inside. His head brushed the ceiling when he straightened, and he rubbed his long fingers together as if washing them. Starbride spotted tall shelves running the length of the dimly lit shop, dividing it into rows. Every surface was crammed with jars and bins filled with nails and pegs and screws. Pots of glue lined one shelf, and stacks of wood lay near the back. It smelled of cedar, and the floor was coated with sawdust.

To Starbride's surprise, Freddie slipped off his mask. "Starbride, Hugo, this is Owen Bradstreet, one of the truest men you'll ever meet."

Owen bobbed his head as he smiled, as if embarrassed by the compliment. Starbride didn't have time to ask how they knew each other, but she was dying to know. Instead she said, "Thank you for contacting us. Where is he now, the black sheep?"

"Got him in the basement, thank the spirits, before many people had a chance to see him. He's been down there all day. I was selling yesterday, down where they're building a new warehouse, and there he was, sneaking in the shadows. He's lucky it was dark, and I was on my way home. I recognized him at once, even more since I've been keeping an eye out, you know, for any royals on account of what Pennynail told me about them going missing."

Starbride nearly started at the name. She hadn't been able to even think of Freddie as Pennynail without his mask. "How did you convince him to come with you?"

Owen rubbed his palms together harder. "I, um, well…"

Freddie patted his shoulder. "Owen had to give his guest what we in Dockland call the alleyway tickle."

Starbride blinked slowly, hoping her expression said it all. Freddie seemed amused, Owen embarrassed. It had to be that Farradain gallows humor, so that probably meant a much worse kind of contact than tickling.

Hugo leaned close to her ear. "I imagine they hit him over the head, Miss Starbride."

"Thank you, Hugo. I had just come to a similar conclusion."

"This way," Owen said. "He's not happy. Yelled bloody murder after he woke up. Thankfully, the people who owned this shop before me designed the cellar to block out just that."

Starbride grimaced but followed him down a set of stairs. When Owen opened the door at the bottom, revealing a root cellar lit by a single lantern, Starbride paused, but Owen didn't seem inclined to push her in and lock the door behind her.

And Freddie trusted him. She glanced over her shoulder, and he pulled his mask into place before they walked in. "Reinholt?" Starbride called.

He stepped from the shadows at the back of the cellar. His face was splotched with dirt, and his eyes looked sunken, his cheeks gaunt.

"It's you," he said. He wore ragged homespun, but his unkempt beard and hair were the same golden color she remembered. He looked like he'd been walking Darkstrong's road, but he was unmistakably the prince of Farraday. "What in all the spirits names are you doing here? What's happened to my family? Did you order this man to lock me up?" He took one step closer.

"Calm down, and I will tell you all."

"Calm down? Calm *down*? Don't you order me about, you Allusian cur, you—"

He lifted his fist. Before Hugo or Pennynail could make a move, Starbride whipped her hypnotism pyramid from her satchel and fell into it with barely a thought.

Reinholt lurched to a halt, caught in a web of her anger, but his mind was free to work and his senses to perceive.

"I am not defenseless, you arrogant prick. Now, sit!"

He plonked down on the root cellar's dirt floor, eyes locked with hers.

"I'm doing you a courtesy even speaking to you," she said. "You're more trouble than you're worth. With your unlocked Fiend, Roland would love to get his hands on you, and I can't allow that. It would be extremely practical to kill you where you sit."

"Miss Starbride!" Hugo gasped.

Pennynail didn't speak, but Starbride could almost feel his approval. She had Horsestrong behind one shoulder; Darkstrong behind the other. She wasn't going to kill Reinholt, but it would serve her well if he believed she might. He fought her pyramid and lost.

Starbride knelt in front of his face. "You're not in charge anymore, little prince. Even were your family here, you still wouldn't be in control. Now, here's what's going to happen. I'll free you, and you'll sit there with your mouth shut unless you have something useful to say. I will not let your pride get anyone else killed."

She stepped out of reach before she dropped her focus. Reinholt gasped as if he'd been holding his breath. He glared at her, shoulders heaving, and she waited for him to decide what to do.

"What happened to my family?" he asked at last.

Starbride nodded, glad to hear he was concerned about something besides his own skin. She told him about Roland's attack and the Umbriels' fleeing, how they were gathering support while she was making all the mischief for Roland that she could.

He glanced about as if he could see the horrors she spoke of in the shadows of the darkened cellar. Several times, tears hovered in his unblinking eyes, and he seemed almost pitiable.

Starbride had questions: Where had he gone? What had he been doing? But she didn't quite care enough to ask. His next words would determine what she did with him.

"Thank you for helping protect my children," he said softly.

Starbride cocked her head. It was on the tip of her tongue to say, "Unlike you?" but she couldn't quite manage it. She couldn't kick a horse after it had already fallen.

"What are you going to do with me?" he asked.

"That depends."

"On what?"

"On what you want to do."

He blinked up at her. "What?"

"I wasn't kidding when I said that Roland would love to have you, but he wants to catch all of us. For you, however, he'd go out of his way. I can't let you wander around on your own, here, in Marienne, or anywhere else. Roland has patrols all over the countryside. You must have had Horsestrong at your shoulder to have eluded him so long."

Reinholt's chin inched up. "I stayed away from the patrols."

"You seem a good sneak," Hugo said.

Starbride was so surprised she smirked. Reinholt frowned around her. "Still got your pup, I see."

"I wouldn't mock him," Starbride said. "He's done more for this kingdom in the past few months than you probably ever have."

Reinholt's mouth dropped open. Starbride rushed ahead. "If you keep civil, I will do the same. The moment the over-privileged prince comes out, I will remind you that not only did you aid Roland on his journey to the throne, you ran away rather than help your family deal with the consequences of your actions."

His mouth snapped shut.

"Now," Starbride said, "the question remains. What do you want to do? What did you hope to accomplish in Dockland?"

"I…I wanted to see if my family was all right."

"And if they weren't?"

"I wanted to rescue them." He wiped his mouth and drew his legs up to rest his elbows on his knees. "It sounds ludicrous, I know. What could I do against Roland? But I had to try. I heard so many rumors."

She supposed that was a good sign. He'd risked his own miserable hide to find out what had happened to his family. And he'd sneaked into Dockland, seeking a way into Marienne from there rather than just going cold to Marienne's gates. That showed cunning, even if it also showed he had little knowledge of Dockland itself. He was lucky Owen had been the one to give him the alleyway tickle and not a gang of thugs.

"Any ideas you had about saving the day?" Starbride shook her head. "Get rid of them. I know you always wanted to know what was going on with the Order of Vestra, wanted to be part of that world. Your ideas probably came from storybooks." She smiled. "I know mine did."

He glared at her.

"Katya operated from the shadows. We do the same. We don't get any accolades. No one cheers. And if Roland finds you, you'll become more evil than you ever thought you could be."

"That," Hugo said, "or you'll be dead."

Reinholt opened his mouth as if he'd snap at Hugo.

"You're going to need his help," Starbride said, "all the help you can get."

"I don't need help from a boy," Reinholt muttered.

"That's fine," she said. "We can hypnotize you into compliance."

Reinholt sat back as if finally beginning to understand. "You're as bad as Roland."

Starbride shrugged. "You don't know half of what he'll do to you. We're giving you the chance to help your family get Marienne back, the only chance you're going to get."

He lifted his arms out and then dropped them. "Then I suppose I accept!"

Starbride turned to go upstairs. When Reinholt began to follow, Pennynail's arm shot out and stopped him.

"I'm just to wait?" Reinholt called as they shut him in the cellar.

In the shop above, Owen stood close by, wringing his hands. Pennynail took off his mask. "You know he's going to try and escape the first chance he gets?" Freddie asked.

Starbride nodded. "He gave in too easily."

"Use the pyramid," Freddie said.

"Wait," Hugo said. "You can't. It's not right."

Starbride rubbed her forehead. "We might have to, Hugo. We can't risk letting him be captured."

He stood a little taller, and Starbride knew he was going to object, but she glanced at Owen, hoping to signal that they shouldn't have any further discussion in front of a stranger. Hugo's mouth snapped shut.

"Just...keep him close," Starbride said to Freddie. "If he tries to bolt, knock him out the old-fashioned way."

Owen chuckled. "If the poor man keeps getting hit over the head, it's going to scramble his brains. I never imagined that princes would be so hard to handle."

"You don't know this one," Starbride said.

"I don't know any, and I'm very glad of that." Owen clasped Freddie's shoulder. "Take care of yourself, Pennynail. I wouldn't want anything to happen to you; well, anything else."

They led Reinholt out of the cellar and into the streets. Pennynail stuck to him like glue, and if Reinholt had any designs on running into the night, he kept them well hidden. He wasn't stupid; he might be biding his time, at least to see where Starbride ran her operation before he decided to bolt. Maybe he thought they'd get him closer to the palace where he could confront Roland in grand, glorious combat.

When they returned to the hideout, they decided on a rotating guard to watch him. If he felt like a prisoner, tough. Until he'd proved himself, Starbride wasn't willing to treat him any differently. She sat in her room and waited to meet with Katya, focusing on the pyramid Dekken had made. Master Bernard had been intrigued by it and had studied it in Starbride's absence, leaving Claudius to work on the pyramid embedded in the strength monks, but Master Bernard hadn't had any luck decoding its secrets. Maybe only certain people could use the Allusian pyramids, maybe only those with Allusian blood.

The thought almost shook Starbride's concentration. Could pyramid skills be specific to a certain people? As of yet, she hadn't encountered a type of Farradain magic she couldn't do. Maybe Dekken had Allusian in his ancestry, and Master Bernard had none.

Starbride felt a familiar prickle over her scalp that signaled Redtrue calling her.

"Greetings with many effusions of love, Starbride," Redtrue said, the same note of sarcasm tingeing her voice.

"And many outpourings of love to Katya as well, Redtrue. How are you?"

"Finally, someone asks how I am. Very well if a little chilly. If you'll hold on, I'm going to try reaching into Katya's mind, though the thought abhors me."

She seemed to hesitate until Starbride said, "Is something wrong?"

"Adsnazi do not believe in this so-called mind magic that the Farradains use so often."

"Even with the person's permission?" Starbride could almost feel her flinch. "Isn't that what dream-walking is?"

"A dream walk is a connection between two pyramid users, like you and I. A hand is offered and accepted. No one's mind is invaded. As a pyramid user, you can deny me. For you to speak to Katya, I would have to enter her mind, and she could not stop me as you could. Do you see?"

"I think so," Starbride said. "Still, it's not invasion if she wants you to do it."

Redtrue gave another one of those mental flinches. "I will not invade deeply. Just enough to pull you and then you may muck around her mind to your heart's content."

Starbride found that phrasing repugnant. If she were to meet Redtrue in person, she wasn't certain they would be friends. Still, for the chance to feel Katya again, she would stand any language.

After a few moments, Redtrue said, "Katya's mind is stubborn. She'll invade all the other minds she wants, but she seems to think her own is sacrosanct."

Starbride frowned at the tone…and then she realized that her irritation wasn't solely hers. She felt herself drawn forward, the strangest feeling tingling through her temples as if her brain stretched through her skin. She let herself be drawn with it, felt anger give way to confusion, a stubborn unwillingness to hope, and then the timid beginnings of joy.

"Katya?" Starbride breathed.

"Star?" The voice was faint, but emotions surged from it, love and concern, fear and admiration, all of them so passionate they wrapped Starbride like a thick blanket.

"Calmly," Redtrue said, and this time, it was her voice that was faint.

"Oh, Star," Katya said.

Starbride managed a breathless laugh at the love she felt. She'd known that Katya loved her, but to *feel* it was so different, so marvelous.

"I love you," Starbride said, "I love…" And for a while, all they did was exchange emotions with half said words more felt than heard. "I'm so happy… I'm so glad… Are you… Yes, and you… I love… I miss... Remember when..." They were lost in the past, in deeds and emotions felt but unsaid because there just weren't enough *words*.

Starbride recalled stolen moments spent on the settee, in their beds, in the bath. Katya returned the memories, and Starbride felt such heat gathering within her that she moaned. Sweat beaded on her forehead and aches rushed through her body at the remembered touches and caresses and kisses.

"Ah, Katya," Starbride groaned as passion surged within her. She felt Katya reach the same heights nearly at the same time, repeating her name as they became lost in each other.

"Horsestrong preserve us," Redtrue said softly, and she sounded as exhausted as Starbride felt.

Keen embarrassment heated Starbride's cheeks. "Redtrue, I'm so sorry!"

"Yes, um, sorry about that," Katya said.

So softly Starbride almost didn't catch it, Redtrue said, "Don't ever be sorry about *that*."

"Well," Katya said. "I guess we have missed each other after all."

Starbride laughed, feeling giddy and tired, just as if they'd really...

"Please, not again!" Redtrue said.

Starbride pulled back from the thought. "I'm just so happy we can speak." She took a deep breath. She wanted to say, "Tell me what to do," but then she remembered Freddie's words. Still, she had to ask Katya's advice on at least one matter. "I've found Reinholt."

Katya listened, and Starbride felt her shock. "I can't believe he came back," Katya said. "I'm glad you didn't take any of his guff."

"After dancing around Roland and his henchman, Reinholt is about as threatening as a stiff breeze."

Katya laughed, and Starbride felt her pride as well as her fear. "You've risen to the occasion as I always knew you could, Star. I'm just so sorry about all that's happened."

"Did you invite Roland in? No, so don't take the blame. How are my mother and father?"

"I thought your mother formidable on her own. Together they're unstoppable, and they've been a huge help."

Starbride grinned. "I'm glad they're helping instead of pestering."

"Pestering can be helpful, never doubt that. If any noble doesn't fall in line, I send your parents. With Brutal at their backs, they're usually obeyed quickly."

"And how is everyone else?"

"As well as can be expected. Tell Reinholt his children are fine, if a little lost. Lord Vincent's taken very good care of them. Did you know he reads to them?"

Starbride shook her head before she remembered Katya couldn't see her. That didn't matter; Katya would feel her surprise. "I suppose I'll have to change my opinion of him, if only a little."

"Maybe information about the children will make Reinholt more pliable. You're the only way he has to get news. If his guilt is pricking him, and I think we're past due for that, it might make him cling to you. Still, he might also run, given the chance, either to exact vengeance on Roland or to build his own army, not trusting yours."

"His own army…"

"I felt that curious twinge. What are you thinking, Star?"

"Well, he was very good at speaking to people, right? Rallying the crowd?"

"Oh yes, he was always good at getting people to fall in love with him."

"I'm better at running missions, freeing people's minds, the kinds of jobs the Order used to do. We need someone who can sway people with words. Who better than a black sheep? A rebellious prince who's come back to save his people from being overrun by evil, living as they do, fighting as they do."

"Is that from one of your books?"

"If it works…"

"Star, you are perfection."

Starbride curled her toes and remembered kissing Katya, trying to pass that feeling on, a spiritual kiss. She nearly felt Katya's lips brush her own as Katya focused her own memories.

"We dare not go further," Katya thought, her voice a silken whisper. "We'll embarrass Redtrue again."

"I'm too tired to be embarrassed," Redtrue said.

That was their cue to break contact again. Starbride nearly wept as she tried to hold on to the feeling of embracing Katya and being held in turn. She could almost smell Katya's scent of lavender and leather, could almost see a ghost of Katya in her mind's eye.

"Good-bye for now, Star. I love you. Always remember."

"I will. I love you, too, Katya, I love—" The connection dissolved, and Katya was gone. Starbride frowned at Redtrue's rudeness. She'd have to make a pyramid of her own and experiment with it so she could be the one making the connection. Maybe then it would be up to her when it was severed.

CHAPTER TWENTY-FIVE

KATYA

Katya wiped her forehead. It was warmer in Redtrue's tent than outside, but still not warm enough to make her sweat. Then again, it wasn't that kind of heat. Katya glanced across the furs that she or Redtrue had kicked into a wad. Redtrue leaned back in them, more than a little sweaty herself.

She watched Katya with a hungry look that made Katya's stomach swirl. She still had more than a little desire left after her encounter with Starbride, but Redtrue unsettled her rather than brought her embers back to fire.

"I should go," Katya said. She stood, but Redtrue stood with her, blocking her exit.

"I...would very much like to feel such passion," Redtrue said.

"Even if we were to...indulge," Katya said, "I can't make you feel it. Starbride and I let ourselves go with each other. It's nothing special about me. It's something special about us."

Redtrue tilted her head as if not certain that was the case.

"If you want to experiment," Katya said, "there's always Castelle."

"She doesn't know how to let go any more than I."

Katya ducked past Redtrue and out the door. As she expected, Castelle waited there, thunder on her face, no doubt at some of the things she'd heard. Katya didn't try to argue. She was too tired. Instead, she threw her head back and laughed.

"Have you gone mad?" Castelle asked.

"I spoke to Starbride without using Redtrue as a proxy. Anything you heard was Starbride and me, though I'm afraid we might have caught Redtrue in the middle without meaning to. Oh, Cass, I'm so happy."

Castelle smiled crookedly, though she still appeared confused. "I'm…happy for you, Katya, but—"

Katya waved away whatever she'd been about to say. She pointed behind her. "Get in that tent, don't hold back, and tonight, I think you might find something wonderful."

To her credit, Castelle saluted and nearly dove into the tent. Katya strode away, not caring if they fought or fornicated. She felt energized; nothing could stop her. Half of her wanted to run the length of the camp, and the other half wanted to sleep until the world melted down around her.

She settled for sleep, knowing she'd need that more. She wrapped herself in thoughts of Starbride as she lay down, trying to recall every word. Starbride had done well keeping Roland off balance. She'd even thought of a task for Reinholt, but could she convince him to rally the people on his own, or would she need some pyramid help?

Could Starbride even bring herself to do such a thing? It was against Crowe's credo and smacked of Roland. Needs must, Katya supposed. The spirits knew Katya and her father had been making promises hand over fist. Not all of them could be kept, probably not even half. But all of that could be settled when the smoke cleared. They'd have a foot in the door, and everyone could argue it out, nobles and commoners, Farradain and Allusian alike.

First thing in the morning, Katya reported to her parents that Starbride had discovered Reinholt alive and free.

If they'd had cups of tea, she imagined they would have dropped them. "When?" Ma said.

"How?" Da asked.

Katya told them the tale.

Ma stared at nothing for a moment. "He was concerned about what happened to us?"

"Apparently," Katya said. Secretly, she hoped her mother wouldn't forgive all the hell Reinholt had put them through after one bout of *caring*.

Ma caught her look. "I'm not a fool, Katya, but it does count for something."

"What the deuce is she going to do with him?" Da asked.

"Do with him?" Ma asked.

"He's not exactly stable, Cat," Da said. "Is she going to keep him locked up?"

"If he won't comply with her orders, she's going to have to," Katya said.

"Orders," Ma mumbled.

"She's leading the rebellion, Ma," Katya said, fighting the urge to pace. "If not for her efforts, Roland would have Marienne completely under his boot."

Ma arched a brow, and Katya forced herself to breathe. Even though she didn't have to wear a pyramid necklace to keep her Fiend contained, that was no reason to lose her temper.

"No one's doubting Starbride's contributions, my girl," Da said, "and I'm thrilled beyond belief that she's not only alive but willing to help us. And I wouldn't blame her if she chained Reinholt to the floor." When Ma gave him a sharp look, he returned it with a steady one. "Both to keep him out of her hair and for his own safety. His Fiend is unlocked, Cat. Roland could easily turn Reinholt into a copy of himself."

Ma's eyes widened in horror. They were alike, Roland and Reinholt. Both were rebellious, both had a temper, and both wanted things only done his way. If Reinholt merged with his Fiend, Katya had no doubt that he'd turn out exactly like Roland. Of course, they might also destroy one another.

But Reinholt could still be saved.

"Redtrue enables you to speak to Starbride directly?" Da asked.

Katya nodded.

"Maybe she can do the same with me. I want to speak to Reinholt."

❖

That day's ride brought them to Castelle's barony, not as close to Allusia as Katya once thought. But all the nobles in Marienne thought anything even remotely close to Allusia might as well be in its yard.

From the blank stares she received, most of the villagers in Castelle's barony didn't know who she was. Katya held in a smirk. Castelle had spent too much time away from home, having her "adventures." Still, she gathered them together, determined to make a speech.

She spoke of her father, and by their happy smiles, it was apparent they remembered him. He'd spent a great deal of time at court but every winter in his home. By the time Katya's father made his speech, most of the villagers were primed and ready to march.

"Any feelings popping up?" Katya asked as Castelle looked at the land that had been her home when she was young.

"Only a few small ones." Castelle pointed to a large oak near her family's estate, a place she hadn't wanted to go into. "My first kiss was there. Just kid stuff."

Katya didn't press. Castelle had been quiet all day but friendly. However things had gone between her and Redtrue, neither of them was raging around the camp. "How's your wound?" Katya asked.

"Mending. Brutal was right. It wasn't as bad as I thought. It just felt like I'd been stabbed with a thousand red-hot knives. How's the shoulder and neck?"

"Mostly whole. Are you going to switch from thief-catcher to Fiend-catcher when this is all over?"

Castelle barked a laugh. "Not likely."

The new recruits were folded in with the rest, and the army marched on, still slower than Katya would have liked, but gaining speed with each passing step. As they set up camp before sunset, Katya nearly ran to Redtrue's tent. She cleared her throat loudly, not wanting to catch Redtrue in the middle of anything intimate.

"Time already?" Redtrue asked. "You aren't in such a rush with all things, are you?"

Katya barked a laugh. "You'll never know." But Redtrue *would* know every little detail of her relationship through their link within the pyramid. In the afterglow of the night before, it hadn't mattered. Now, sitting in Redtrue's tent, waiting for contact, Katya fidgeted, embarrassed to share so much with someone she knew so little.

When Starbride made contact, Katya held back her emotions, even after Starbride poured hers through the link.

"What's wrong?" Starbride asked.

The ferreter of secrets never missed much. "Nothing, my love." She let a little of her feelings out but kept the rest restrained, using the techniques Crowe had taught her to resist a mind pyramid.

She could feel Starbride's skepticism. Alarmingly, she felt Redtrue's, too.

"Starbride," Redtrue said, "excuse us a moment. A situation needs my attention." Before Starbride could protest, Redtrue cut their connection.

Katya glared at her. "If you keep doing that, she's going to get annoyed."

"Should I fear her?"

"Someday soon, you *will* have to face her in person."

Redtrue threw her braid over her shoulder. "You are holding yourself in check."

"I wasn't—"

"And you were doing it because you feared my reaction."

Katya sighed. "It's not your fault."

She snorted. "Fault is not my concern. Neither of us wants to make the other uncomfortable, but what you two shared with me…I…" She took a deep breath. "I don't want to be the reason you stop."

"Are you and Castelle in love?"

"What does that—"

"Yes or no."

"I…wouldn't know."

Katya smiled. It wasn't a no. "What if she were here, holding you? Then you wouldn't feel so left out."

"Are you suggesting she and I… While you and Starbride…"

"I just meant that she could be here for you. She wouldn't be privy to the conversation, but you could feel her presence, her body next to yours."

Redtrue looked away. "We'll try it." She unfolded and ducked out the tent flap, returning a few moments later with Castelle.

Castelle grinned sheepishly. "What is it I'm supposed to do, exactly?"

"Keep your trousers on until I leave. That's the most important point."

Castelle glared at her. "Thank you, Highness."

"Sit." Redtrue patted the blanket next to her. "And if you wouldn't mind…"

"Wouldn't mind what?" Castelle asked.

"Oh, for spirits' sakes," Katya said. "Hold her, Castelle. She's going to need comfort. This mind communication is more draining than we thought." A little truth, a little lie, but it got the job done. Castelle plunked down at Redtrue's side and put an arm around her shoulders.

Redtrue focused on her pyramid again. When they found Starbride, the first thing she said was, "I'm making my own pyramid so you can't walk off on me."

Redtrue seemed startled. "You can make this pyramid without my direction?"

Katya could almost picture Starbride throwing her hair over her shoulder. "Of course. I have Dekken's to study."

Katya could feel how impressed Redtrue was—and a little alarmed—but she said nothing, and in another moment, Katya felt her presence withdraw slightly, all the privacy Katya and Starbride would get.

"What was it that drew you away?" Starbride asked.

"Nothing of importance, my love." This time, Katya put feeling behind the words.

Starbride sighed as if relaxing into Katya's embrace. They let their love surround them until Katya had to break the mood. They couldn't afford to make love all evening, perfect as that sounded.

"My father wants to talk to Reinholt," Katya said.

"I don't know if I can manage that," Starbride said. "I'm getting better at using this pyramid, but I'm not Redtrue, so I don't think I can enter his mind and let him communicate through Redtrue to you. I *can* relay all the messages you want." A twinge of panic passed through the line. "Are you going to act as relay for your father? I mean, he and I aren't going to connect like this, right? So…intimate?"

Katya hadn't thought of that. After a bit of discussion, they decided that relaying messages would be the best idea, leaving Starbride and Katya in contact. Any relay would have to be brief, though, as having Starbride going in and out of focus and Redtrue serving as conduit was going to be hard on both of them.

When everyone was in place, Da begun with, "My boy, I'm so glad you're safe."

Personally, Katya wanted to throttle Reinholt, and she bet her father did too, at least a little, but he opened with how much he cared. Reinholt would easier listen to happiness about his safety than he would anything else.

"He's glad everyone there is safe, too," Starbride said.

They didn't seem that safe to Katya, not if assassins were going to be coming after them, but she kept that to herself. No sense worrying Starbride with something she had no control over.

Da could have mentioned duty. He could have filled their time with recriminations or threats. He could have wheedled or cajoled, but he spoke mostly of the children, information that seemed inconsequential when compared to the fact that there was a Fiend on the throne. Katya relayed his words dutifully, knowing that Starbride wouldn't pass on any of Katya's wounded feelings that traveled down the line.

Katya tried to be patient as Starbride passed on the message, and Reinholt responded. Finally, Starbride said, "He seems speechless. He just stuttered a few things and said 'well' a lot."

Katya passed this on to her father, who had more stories of the children. He didn't mention if they cried out for their parents in the night or if they asked where their father had gone. It began to sound like a letter any grandparent would write if given temporary custody of his grandchildren.

"He's crying." Starbride's pity mixed with impatience. Katya always felt that way when dealing with the distraught. It seemed a little new to Starbride. Usually, nothing moved her like tears, but this was war.

And it *was* Reinholt.

"He says he's sorry," Starbride said. "He doesn't say for what."

Katya's father sighed deeply and rubbed his temples, reminding Katya of herself. She didn't dare ask him if all his talk of children had been the ploy of a master manipulator. She almost hoped it wasn't, that Da wouldn't play one of his children so. Had he ever played her that way? Could he manipulate so well and still feel the weight of his words?

"Tell him it's all right," Da said. "He'll always be my boy and his mother's. We love him. Nothing will change that."

Katya passed that along, warmed by the words because they also applied to her, but she frowned at the idea that her father seemed to have forgiven Reinholt. When they returned to Marienne, Da might even slap the heir's crown on his head again.

"Careful," Starbride said. "I won't be able to separate the words from your feelings."

"Sorry."

"Don't apologize. I agree with you. But you might want to add a pause between your father's words and your reactions so I can tell them apart." When Starbride returned with Reinholt's response, Katya nearly felt the fatigue traveling down the line. Starbride couldn't keep up with falling in and out of a trance much longer. "He wants your father to tell him what to do."

When Katya came back with, "Whatever his heart tells him to do," Redtrue cut into the conversation.

"I'm tired," she said, "and I can feel that Starbride is, too, so with everyone's permission..."

"If we must," Katya said.

"I hate to say it, but I agree," Starbride said. "Good night, dearheart. Good night, Redtrue. And good night, King Einrich."

"Sleep well, my love," Katya said. "I'm sure my father would say the same if he could hear you."

"Let's hope not exactly the same," Redtrue said. "Sleep well."

Katya felt the connection go dark. She opened her eyes to find that her father had already left. "What a mess."

Redtrue shook her head. "It does not seem so. You wished him to be contrite, yes? You have succeeded."

"I just hope it's enough to make him behave."

"Blackmail with emotions. You once accused me of such."

"Better than using a mind pyramid to get what we want, eh?"

"Eminently better. With blackmail, at least the victim still has a choice."

Katya chuckled as she stood. "Maybe when you start talking degrees of evil, it's already too late."

Redtrue smirked. "There may be hope for you yet."

CHAPTER TWENTY-SIX

STARBRIDE

Starbride faced Reinholt where he sat in her room's lone chair. She had stayed cross-legged on the bed, Dawnmother beside her. And though the door was pulled shut, Starbride knew Pennynail and Hugo waited on the other side. No one trusted Reinholt, not yet.

Now she wondered if such precautions were needed. His shoulders shook in silent sobs. Starbride was moved to pity even as she was pricked by impatience. His life had come down around his ears, but that had happened to all of them. Still, she could pity him a little. After all, Katya would never betray her as Brom had done to Reinholt.

But as Brutal might say, it didn't give him leave to act like an ass.

Dawnmother scooted to the edge of the bed. "Come now. Deep breaths." She pulled a handkerchief from her pocket and pressed it into Reinholt's grasp.

"Thank you," he muttered.

Starbride cleared her throat. "Perhaps you'd like a moment to—"

He leapt from his seat and tottered out the door. Starbride leaned out in his wake. "Keep an eye on him," she said to Pennynail. He followed Reinholt down the hall.

Hugo watched them until they disappeared into another small room. "Is that a good or a bad sign?"

"I have no idea."

"Master Bernard would like to speak with you," Hugo said.

She nodded. They were all on terrible schedules, only sleeping when they were about to drop.

When Master Bernard came in, Dawnmother stood. "Any news of our patients? I was just about to visit them."

"From what I gather, they're both recuperating well. I've come to talk pyramids. We've had a breakthrough."

"With the traps in the monks?" Starbride asked.

He nodded, and Starbride clenched a fist, suppressing a loud whoop just in case anyone nearby was sleeping.

"It's two cancellation pyramids used at the same time," he said. "The first dampens the effect of any trap pyramid, slowing them down for the second pyramid to cancel the trap completely. You need two pyradistés with intense concentration and timing." He smiled proudly. "Ansic and Claudius have gotten it down to an art. They've tested it on several trap pyramids and think they're ready for the monks if we can get a volunteer."

"I have no doubt of that," Starbride said. She had to grin at Master Bernard's still beaming face. "You'll never have to buy your own drinks again if there are strength monks around."

"It was a group effort, and it's not my only news."

She fought not to hold her breath. "Tell me."

"The heads and I have crafted a pyramid that can block mind intrusion."

Starbride let her breath out so quickly, she felt lightheaded. "Master Bernard, that's wonderful!"

"And the quicker we can make them, the faster our friends will be safe. Odd how simple the solution was when Effie finally had her breakthrough. She supposed that pyradistés never tried in the past because they were the ones with the power."

"And why create something that would thwart one of their greatest weapons?" Starbride asked.

"Shortsighted, perhaps," Dawnmother said.

Master Bernard shrugged. "If we had ever conceived of a Fiend-ridden pyradisté taking over the throne and hypnotizing the populace, I suppose so."

Starbride hurried toward the strength chapterhouse, taking Dawnmother, Master Bernard, and Hugo with her but leaving Pennynail to guard Reinholt. Claudius and Ansic had already gone ahead to see what they could do for the monks.

Despite the late hour, there were still a few people out, though most of them hurried as if afraid to be caught on the streets. The only ones who took it slower had the steady tread of the city Watch, and they still seemed wary. Crime had become almost nonexistent, but no one knew what could be declared a crime at any moment.

As they turned closer to the chapterhouse, Starbride's steps slowed. Along the wide avenue, people strolled as if it were the middle of a feast day, and they had no particular destination in mind. Unlike revelers, these didn't look in windows or point out things of interest to one another. A pair of men walked arm in arm but didn't lean on each other's shoulders or share the laughs and smiles of lovers.

Starbride pulled on Hugo's arm. "Wait."

The strolling people didn't seem threatening, but something about them put her off. She reached into her satchel and gripped a flash bomb.

"Perhaps we should find a different way," Master Bernard said.

Starbride turned. Dawnmother did the same only to bump into a Watch officer going the other way.

"I beg your pardon." Dawnmother stepped aside and kept her face low. Starbride ducked hers as well, trying to hide her heritage. Captain Ursula was their friend, but they had no way of knowing if all the Watch felt the same.

"Quite all right," the officer said. To Starbride's surprise, he took his helmet off and bowed. He swayed as if drunk, a dreamy smile on his face. The streetlights winked off the sergeant's stripes on his collar.

"Having a fun night, are we?" Hugo asked.

Starbride nudged him. The starch in his tone could get them all thrown in jail.

But the sergeant brayed a laugh. "Not much to do but drink and be happy, lad. Not since his Majesty cleaned up all the crime." He slipped an arm around Hugo's shoulders. "Enjoy it, lad. Enjoy the peace."

"Peace," the strolling people said in unison. They sighed in blissful contentment.

"He's been at it again," Dawnmother whispered. "Fiend king fever."

Starbride glanced around but saw no obvious pyramids. Could Roland have found a way to mind warp large segments of the populace at once and have the effect be permanent?

The sergeant leaned close. "If you haven't found the peace, my friends, I know just where to take you."

"Take you," the strolling people echoed. Some of them had come very close indeed.

Starbride put on a vague smile. "We were just taking them there," she said.

"Oh…yes." Master Bernard's attempt at dreamy seemed a bit crazy to Starbride's eye, but at least he was trying. "Just taking them."

Starbride looped her arm through Hugo's, and Master Bernard did the same to Dawnmother. They couldn't hurry, though, not if they wanted to fit in. They tried to stroll, but the newly formed crowd followed them.

"That's the wrong way, dear," the sergeant said. He hadn't lost his smile, but in the dimness it turned sinister.

"Temperance." Starbride threw the flash bomb and squeezed her eyes shut, but she didn't hear the normal screams. She ran, keeping the others with her but expecting someone to try to tackle her at any moment. If Roland had found a way to make people immune to flash bombs…

Starbride risked a glance over her shoulder. Most of the crowd had fallen. A few staggered or clung to one another. The pair of lovers had collapsed arm-in-arm.

The sergeant lay on his back, eyes tightly shut and back bowed in pain, but she could still see his tranquil smile.

"Keep running," Hugo said. "We have to get off the street."

It wasn't until they were safe inside the chapterhouse that she relaxed. She told Ruin what they'd seen.

"We've seen them too," he said. "Lucky for us, your pyradistés have been working like mad after we helped them retrieve some hidden crystal from their homes in the city."

"Were they able to remove your pyramids?" she asked.

"They neutralized them, but most of us didn't think surgery worth the risk." Ruin chuckled. "And by that, we mean the risk that we'll be left out of the fighting."

"Are Averie and Maia awake?" Dawnmother asked.

He gestured up the stairs, welcoming them to go and look. Master Bernard went in search of his fellow pyradistés while Hugo followed Dawnmother and Starbride upstairs.

Averie sat on Maia's bed, talking softly to her. They'd only let Maia awake in small doses, or so Starbride had been told. Her neck was healing fine; it was the emotional scars they were concerned with. Her eyes were still a little sunken. Even with the sleeping draughts, she hadn't been resting peacefully. Averie seemed worlds better, though. She bowed as Starbride entered. Starbride waved her back down.

"Feeling better?" she asked both of them.

Averie nodded. "Ready to take to the streets, if you'll have me."

"You're sure?" An archer with Averie's skill would be welcome, though Starbride didn't know how inconspicuous she would be while carrying a longbow. Averie nodded.

"And how are you, Maia?" Starbride asked.

"Ashamed."

"My sweet, there's no need."

"I've told her that," Hugo said as he approached her other side.

"And me," Dawnmother said.

Maia sighed. "And now I'm ashamed of feeling ashamed."

"You will recover from this," Starbride said. "All of it."

"Time is the balm that heals all wounds," Dawnmother said.

Maia managed a tiny smile. "I'll know all of Horsestrong's sayings if I stay here."

"And you'll be the wiser for it," Dawnmother said. "Now, why are you still awake?"

"I'm tired of sleeping. I'm not badly injured. I'm just…" Her eyes grew hazy with tears, lost in the past.

"Maia." Starbride touched her arm. "Stay with us. Did Dawn tell you we've found your elder cousin?"

"Reinholt?" Maia and Averie asked at the same time.

"I mean, Prince Reinholt?" Averie said.

Starbride glanced at her. "You don't have to worry about offending me. My opinion of him as a prince is pretty well known."

"And deserved," Hugo said.

"Is he being a pain?" Maia asked.

"We're having trouble finding a place for him," Starbride said.

Dawnmother cleared her throat. "It's not something you should be worrying about right now, Maia. Focus on recovery."

"To hell with recovery." Maia pushed herself higher on the bed. "Helping you will make me feel a thousand times better than any nap."

Starbride saw her own surprise on the faces around her, but she waited for Maia to settle and continue.

"Reinholt and I weren't incredibly close, not like Katya and me, but I know he has a soft spot for his little cousin. He probably still sees me as a child." Her smile was slight, as if she wouldn't mind being a child again. "If I urge him to go along with you, it might help."

"It might at that," Starbride said. He'd seemed moved by King Einrich's words. Maybe another family nudge was all he needed to go from grudging obedience to eager to help.

Well, maybe not eager. Starbride would settle for compliant.

"I'll make a deal with you," she said. "We'll all nab a few hours' sleep, and then he's all yours."

❖

No more hurrying through the streets; they had to stroll, not daring to look different from anyone else. They hurried whenever they saw anyone as anxious as them, but that sight seemed less common in only one night. If they were going to do something about Roland mind warping the populace, they had to do it soon.

Hugo, Dawnmother, Averie, and Maia carried pyramids that blocked mind tampering. Maia also wore a necklace like Hugo's, designed to keep her Fiend inside, though Starbride didn't think it could present without help. She'd needed to have a pyramid to keep it out, and she'd never Waltzed, but Starbride wasn't taking any chances. Besides, the feel of it seemed to make Maia more confident. She kept touching the spot where it rested under her clothes, as all Umbriels did when they were angry, but their pyramids burned, letting them know their Fiends were close to the surface. Maia seemed to take comfort only in that hers couldn't come bursting forth at any moment.

Starbride had Reinholt brought to her room at their hideout, but only Maia and Dawnmother waited with her inside. If they tried to cram any more people in, it got crowded, and everyone wanted to give Reinholt space.

When he stepped inside the room, he went from frowning to shocked in a moment. "M…Maia? I thought you were—"

"Starbride rescued me." Maia patted beside her, and Reinholt sank down on the corner of the bed. "It's good to see you. We've had a hard time lately."

That was the understatement of the century, but Starbride held her tongue. Maia had some of her uncle Einrich's magic, and Starbride wasn't about to interfere with it.

"Yes." A myriad of expressions flashed across Reinholt's face. He looked at Maia with naked pity. All the troubles he'd gone through must have seemed like nothing compared to what she had suffered, what crimes she'd been forced to commit on Roland's orders.

"Are you well?" he asked.

"No." Her voice cracked slightly. "But I'm mending. We're all mending." She laid her head on Reinholt's shoulder.

Starbride bit her lip. As much as she loved Maia, her feelings couldn't compare to those of Maia's own family. Maia's father had left her long ago, and she'd grown close to her aunt and uncle, to her cousins. With her father returned as a monster and most of her family far away, she clung to the kin she had left.

No matter that he was an ass.

Reinholt wrapped an arm around Maia's shoulders and held her. They closed their eyes as if they'd forgotten the rest of the room existed.

"What are you going to do now?" Reinholt finally asked.

"Help," Maia said. "Your parents are coming and Katya. I'll help Starbride build up strength here and add it to theirs."

He nodded. Maia hadn't included him in her plans, but if his young and obviously injured cousin was going to help with the revolution, what else could he do? "I'll help you," he said.

Starbride held in an exasperated sigh. Help *her*, would he, not the cause? Ah well, if she had to feed her plans through Maia, so be it.

Maia glanced at Starbride, and she took the cue. "We thought the pair of you could work on Dockland, now that you have some knowledge of it." Starbride didn't add that most of that knowledge included being knocked out in an alley and locked in a cellar.

"What did you have in mind?" Maia asked.

"Charm," Starbride said.

Reinholt smiled crookedly. "Bows and compliments? Or should I tell them my collection of naughty chambermaid stories?"

"The chambermaid stories would probably work better," Dawnmother said.

Starbride chuckled. "I was thinking more of you playing on your rogue status."

"Rogue?" He seemed torn between amused and offended. "You think a prince robbed of his throne is going to appeal to the poorest of the poor?"

"They like anyone who defies the law," Maia said.

"The rogue prince, eh? I kind of like it."

Starbride smiled and not simply because Maia swayed him to her thinking. Their plan transformed him from an egomaniacal brat to the misunderstood center of attention. Of course he liked it.

"Wonderful," she said. "I'll leave you two to work out the details."

Chapter Twenty-seven

Katya

Katya stretched in the saddle and shivered. Moving closer to Marienne had brought them more recruits, but it had also brought a drop in temperature. Snow had fallen that morning, though it melted by midday.

Still, better to be out with her scouting party than with the slow-moving army. When she'd awoken to cold air that morning, Katya had wondered how many new recruits wished they'd stayed in their beds, helping their fellows batten down for the winter and preparing for the feast of Dark Night. Katya had thought that a sinister name for what the palace had always called Solstice Night, but she'd learned that the longest night of the year meant something different to those who weren't safe and snug inside castle walls.

Most of the towns Katya visited weren't surprised to see her. Word of the army traveled far faster than it did. She'd grown accustomed to her scouts telling her that the town ahead had already gathered for her arrival, so she wasn't alarmed at first when an Allusian scout rushed toward them from the north.

As the man rode closer, Katya's gut tightened at the panic on his face. They'd had a few misunderstandings with Farradain villagers thinking an Allusian scout meant attack. The last thing they needed was the bad blood that would accompany an accidental death.

The scout spoke quickly to Hawkblade. Katya picked out a few words; her Allusian had gotten better, but she was still lost. Before she had time to frustrate herself, another Allusian said, "Cavalry and troops approaching from the north."

Roland, maybe, but from the north? Why not come straight at them from the west? "Were they flying any colors?"

"Flying…colors?" the scout asked.

"Banners," Brutal said. "Cloth on the end of long poles."

"He says yes."

"What was on the cloth, what colors?" Katya asked.

The scout muttered for a few moments. "He says the largest was green with a yellow…head?" He shrugged. "Something's head."

"Pointed teeth on the head?" Katya asked. "Ruff around its neck?"

The scout nodded. Katya let out a sigh of relief.

"Do you mind sharing?" Brutal asked. "Not all of us are up on our heraldry."

Katya grinned. "A gold hillcat on a field of green, Beaumaris colors, the holding of Countess Nadia Van Hale."

Countess Nadia had been busy. By the amount of troops she'd brought, she had to have laid claim to most of the nobility in the north, their guards, and all the able-bodied villagers. If they were being mind-controlled, Katya and her scouting party were doomed.

Countess Nadia's graying hair had been swept up under a jaunty cap. She wore a dark leather coat and gray suede trousers, all of it covered by a heavy, fur-trimmed cloak. She even had a shortsword strapped to her side, though Katya didn't know if she could use it.

"Your Highness," she called as those around her bowed from the saddle. "I am so happy to see that you're well."

Viscount Lenvis rode at Nadia's side. When Katya hadn't seen him in his holding at Lucienne-by-the-Sea, she'd feared for his life, but it seemed he'd followed the countess into the north, one of the many things a person would do for love.

Or maybe he'd had no other choice.

"We heard King Einrich was on the move," Lenvis said. "We came as soon as we could get everyone together."

"We're more than happy to have you." Katya's glance darted over their party, waiting for one of them to strike, but after a few awkward moments, the two groups fell in together and headed toward the bulk of the army.

Nadia's words seemed her own, but Katya wasn't sure how deep mind tampering could go. She ground her teeth. Roland wouldn't need to keep sending assassins if he could sow distrust amongst his enemies.

"Is the crown princess consort not with you?" Lenvis asked.

"She remains in Marienne, I'm afraid, though we have had word," Katya said.

Nadia sighed. "I'm relieved to hear she lives. I feared she might not the last time I saw her."

"The last time?"

"In Marienne when we escaped. She was being chased by a mob. We led the murderous thugs away, pretending she was with us." Her glance darted sideways. "There was no time for anything else."

"I understand, Countess. Thank you for what you did." Though if Nadia had managed to take Starbride along... Katya told herself to stop dreaming. Starbride would be in her arms soon enough; she swore it by the spirits themselves.

When they returned to camp, Nadia's troops set up amongst the others. Katya sought out her father to give him the news. She was surprised to find him meeting with another new arrival, Mayor Crispin from Pomanse.

A new scar peeked out from Crispin's collar, blotchy, bright pink and red. Katya's stomach dropped at the tale the mark suggested. Before Darren had run off to wreak havoc in the countryside, he'd made good on his threat to Pomanse. Katya winced to see it, even though she knew there was nothing she could have done to stop it.

Crispin bowed low for both Katya and Nadia. They had left the other, lesser-ranking nobles outside. Nadia had suggested it, saving Katya from having to demand it.

"Countess Nadia," Da said as he led her to a seat. "My thanks for your gift of troops."

"We do what we can," Nadia said, "though I'm afraid I bring bad news along with strength of arms."

"As does Mayor Crispin," Da said.

"I didn't bring as many volunteers as the countess," Crispin said, "but I brought what I could, what was left."

Katya's eyes traveled to that pink scar again. "Fire?"

"Nearly half the city gone, and so many people. Mr. Davance..." He coughed, and Katya saw unshed tears in his eyes, the way he clenched his fists. Now she knew why Davance had been so quick to defend Crispin when she'd accused their security of being lax.

"I'm sorry," she said. "We've all lost too much these days."

"We…I should have listened to you, Majesty. I'm sorry."

"The past," Da said, shooing all bad blood away. "And while we're on the subject of bad news, Countess?"

"There's been fighting closer to Marienne," she said. "Not up where we gathered, not yet, but those horrid creatures attacked Duke Robert's estate."

"Does he live?" Katya asked. Duke Robert, Brom's father, had been one of Roland's principal dupes, but he'd seen the error of his ways in the end, before the revolt in Marienne.

"I don't know, Highness. We heard of the attack from the few who escaped, and when we ventured there to help, everyone in the town and the estate was gone."

"Dead?" Da asked.

"Vanished. There was evidence of a fight, broken down doors, smashed windows, and plenty of blood, but not a person, living or dead to be found."

Katya shivered. The bodies had been made into corpse Fiends by now. The living were probably being hypnotized.

"And there are similar reports throughout the countryside," Nadia said, "but Baelyn was the only one I saw with my own eyes."

"And your people, Countess?" Katya asked. "Do you not fear for those who remained behind?"

"Those who cannot fight have gone farther north, to the Roanth Highlands and beyond. Some have kin among the hinters and will seek shelter there."

"Hinters?" Crispin said. "I'm afraid I'm not familiar with that family."

"Being from the coast, I'm not surprised," Da said. "They're not a family, but a group of Farradains who live deep in the northern mountains."

"They're Farradain only in that they look it," Nadia said. "They have no noble; they make no allegiance."

"Only because no one wants to live there." Katya had met some hinters living in Marienne. The strength chapterhouses always sported a few. Some came to town looking for adventure. Those she'd met seemed a good-natured, boisterous bunch, and she could see them welcoming old relatives and new friends into their holds. They'd make good allies, but she couldn't see them going to war for a king they didn't acknowledge or a promise to be part of a government they didn't want.

"My father spoke sometimes of getting rid of them," Da said. "He didn't like the idea of a potential enemy right on our roof, as it were, but there was never enough support among the council."

"Tsk," Countess Nadia said. "They'd have hidden in their holes like ferrets, and we'd never have found them. I doubt this Fiend king could either."

Katya winced. "We call him the usurper."

"Better all around for morale," Da added.

That got a weak chuckle, but their conversation had given Katya a flutter of hope. If they couldn't wrest control of the throne away from Roland, they'd at least have somewhere to hide. The hinters might put them all up for a little while. Of course, more than people lived in the mountains to the north. In the tallest peaks, those so high they tore the clouds to ribbons, wild Fiends still dwelled. She thought for a moment what it would be like to be trapped between Roland and untamed evil and had to draw her coat tighter around her.

That evening, wrapped in the embrace of Starbride's mind, Katya allowed herself to relax a little, to revel in the good news that they had more arms for their company. She told Starbride to watch out for mind-controlled slaves as Roland seemed to be accelerating his plans to warp the population of Farraday into attacking those who were trying to save it.

"I've noticed," Starbride said. "Don't worry for me. We'll counter whatever comes along."

Katya wanted to bathe in her confidence. "I'm so proud of you, Star."

Their love melted together again, and Katya felt Redtrue lean into Castelle's embrace. Katya tried not to succumb to the feelings that had engulfed her before. Even though Redtrue had someone to "comfort" her, Katya didn't want to tow her into some mind-to-mind lovemaking.

"I've been wanting to tell you something," Starbride said. "Well, I didn't want to tell you before because I wasn't sure how it would turn out, but now that things seem to be going so well…"

"You've lost me, Star."

"I thought you might be pained, being so far away and unable to do anything about them."

"And now you're scaring me."

"I'm sorry, love. It's Maia and Averie. I've got them both, Katya. They're alive and well and doing marvelously."

Katya held her breath. Averie and Maia, one dead and one missing, rescued from Roland? "How…oh spirits, Star, you've…you're a miracle!" She couldn't stop her emotions from pouring through the link, love and pride and surprise.

Starbride laughed, nearly giddy, by the sound. She spun a tale of finding Averie in the palace dungeon, of recovering Maia from Roland's grasp and nursing both back to health. "Averie has been coming out with us at night. She's a wonderful tracker, and her marksmanship gives me confidence. And Maia! She's not quite up to skulking yet, but she's taking care of your brother. Seems all he needed to fall in line was his own baby bird to care for."

Katya could say nothing for a few moments. They could all be together again, save Crowe. Well, next thing she knew, Starbride would be parting the veil between life and death and bringing all their loved ones back to them. "I don't know what to say, Star. You've made me so happy. You *make* me so happy. That I met you, that you love me, is proof that every spirit wishes me the best."

She could almost see the delight in Starbride's eyes. "So that's not just Ellias and Elody with us? Or are you saying that loving me requires fortitude as well?"

"When we meet again," Katya said, "by the spirits, I'll show you fortitude." Katya felt heat blossoming within her, and this time, she couldn't stop it. To hell with propriety. What was decorum to love?

"Hold tight to Castelle, Redtrue." Katya summoned every thought, every fantasy she'd entertained when she'd thought of meeting Starbride again. She envisioned tracing Starbride's lips with her thumb, of Starbride biting down gently. Starbride returned the image with one of her slipping her fingers into Katya's belt and pulling the two of them together.

Their thoughts tangled in caresses and kisses. Katya imagined the impatience that would overtake them until they finally ripped the fabric from each other's willing bodies.

"Oh, Katya," Starbride groaned.

"My Star." Images became lost in a swirl of touch and taste, passion growing as they both fed the fantasy. Katya's head snapped back as she moaned, and all the strength left her body. She felt the soft fur underneath her and knew she'd collapsed. Her eyes were shut, but she imagined that if she opened them and looked to the side, she would see Starbride there.

"We have to stop doing this," Starbride said breathlessly. "I've still got work to do tonight."

"I'm going to crawl into bed and dream of you."

"Now I'm jealous."

"You can dream of yourself later."

"Of the going to bed part!" Starbride said. "If you were here, I'd smack you with a pillow."

"If I was there, we'd both be crawling into bed…"

"Enough," Redtrue said. "I must…you must say good night now."

Katya heard the urgency in her voice. Starbride must have, too, for they hurried their good-byes. When Katya opened her eyes, Redtrue was kissing Castelle's neck and guiding Castelle's hand under her shirt.

Castelle opened her eyes long enough to glare. "Get out," she mouthed.

Katya stumbled through the tent flap. Her knees were still weak, and the cold wind felt lovely across her face. New allies, Averie and Maia alive and well, and then a little mind-sex to top off the evening. Things were as well as could be, given the circumstances. There was no guarantee they would stay that way, though. Only a foolish person would expect that. And everyone was still in danger. Crowe would have applauded the dismal thoughts, would have told her that such thinking would keep her from being surprised when the next disaster occurred.

Another part of her, one brought out by Starbride, warned that Katya should revel in the good news while it was there. With nothing in her immediate future but sleep, what harm was there in relaxing just a little?

It must have been the Crowe in her that heard the step in the dark. Years of training, many under his tutelage, made her shift her weight. When someone flew at her, she caught an arm and threw the weight over her shoulder. The attacker huffed as the air left his lungs; not a corpse Fiend then. Katya punched down, catching him square in the chest, doubling him over. Katya flipped him on his stomach and knelt in the middle of his back.

"Brutal!" she cried.

"Katya?"

"Here. Hurry!" The attacker squirmed beneath her. Katya grabbed one of his arms and hauled it up behind him, but a woman's voice cried out in pain.

Brutal was there in a moment. "Hold her," Katya said. As his large body replaced hers, the attacker yelped again. Katya searched her, finding a knife in her boot. If she'd attacked with another weapon, it must have gone flying. "Haul her up."

But where to take her? Katya's tent was too small, and she didn't want to expose her parents to another threat. "The countess's tent is nearby," Brutal said as if reading her mind.

"You," Katya said to a member of the crowd that had gathered. "Tell Countess Nadia's guards we're coming."

He ran to do her bidding. Brutal held the attacking woman's arms behind her back. Someone brought a torch, and Katya gripped the woman's chin and tilted her head up. She was hardly more than a girl; her dark hair was pulled behind her head. Large brown eyes glittered as she smiled.

"Hello, niece," she said. "Do you like the gift I sent you?"

Katya drew back. "What is this?"

"I'm getting very good at this, as you can see"—the girl glanced down as if indicating her own body—"I can be in anyone I want."

"You're not Roland." It wasn't possible. He *couldn't* transfer himself to another body, not wholly, but the thought turned Katya's insides into a hard knot. "You're some kind of puppet." She pointed to another member of the crowd. "Find the pyradisté Rene. Tell him to meet us in the countess's tent."

Katya started that way, not liking the way the girl-puppet grinned as they walked. Except for her plump cheeks, she was as thin as a rail. Had Roland remembered to tell her to eat, or were such things beneath him now that he was a Fiend? Was there anything of the real girl left to save? The would-be assassin from before hadn't remembered what she'd done, but at least her old life was still inside her.

Countess Nadia waved them inside her tent, eyeing the girl-puppet. "I haven't had the pleasure, Highness."

"Neither have I," Katya said.

"Oh, come now, niece," the girl-puppet said as Brutal bound her arms and made her kneel. "You know exactly who I am."

"Niece?" Countess Nadia asked. "Do you propose to be the crown princess's aunt, girl? And who are your parents, hmm?"

"I have a message for you, niece."

"Besides lunging for me in the dark?" Katya asked. "Let's hear it then."

"Wait."

Katya blinked. "Pray, what am I waiting for?"

"Who comes to meet us?" the girl-puppet asked. "Your one pyradisté? Or perhaps an adsnazi? I so look forward to meeting one in my own flesh."

"Is that supposed to frighten me?" Katya asked. "That the usurper has heard who we're traveling with? If he knows about the adsnazi, it should be him who's frightened." Though he might also know that the adsnazi were too afraid of using their devastating anti-Fiend weapon.

"Wait," the girl-puppet said again.

"As I've said to many a thug," Katya said, "I don't need you to talk."

Rene bowed into the tent a moment later. "Someone else for me to read, Highness?"

"As before, anything you get will be useful."

He withdrew a pyramid from his pocket. The girl-puppet gave him a wide smile. He paused and seemed as if he'd draw back. Then he glanced at Katya, shook his head, and pressed the pyramid to the girl-puppet's forehead. She sighed as if under a lover's caress.

"Wait," Katya mumbled. But for what? For this? "Rene…"

The girl-puppet's eyes slipped closed as Rene's brow furrowed. She shuddered, and a bang filled the tent as the girl-puppet burst apart. Blood and gore coated Rene and the carpet around them both, filling the tent with the smell of copper and slaughter.

Katya staggered back, wiping at the blood spattering her face. Brutal yelled for the guards. Countess Nadia pulled Katya farther away, all the while muttering, "Spirits preserve us."

Katya's eyes were fixed on the tableau before her. The girl's chest was gone, as if someone had hollowed her out. Rene dropped to his knees—Katya thought from shock—but through the red veneer of ichor, she spied the shards of crystal embedded in his face. He reached for a shard as long as a finger jutting from his neck.

Brutal yelled, "No," and darted for him.

Rene plucked the shard from his flesh, his expression one of wonder as he stared at the blood that jetted from him. Brutal wrapped his hands around Rene's neck and guided him to the floor, but he was dead within moments.

Katya stepped forward.

"Crown Princess," Countess Nadia said. "I don't think you should—"

Katya waved her back. This was what Roland had wanted her to wait for, to see just how good he'd gotten, not only at mind control but at traps. Especially for her *one* pyradisté, as he'd pointed out. Did he know the Allusians' aversion to mind magic? Did he know how he'd crippled her ability to cleanse his assassins?

"Living bombs," Brutal said as he straightened. "Spirits preserve us, how do we guard against this?"

Katya shook her head. She'd put it to Leafclever. Maybe he'd give up some of his moral high ground then.

First, though, she had to report to her parents, but she couldn't take her eyes off what was left of the girl. Her face seemed tranquil in death. Katya supposed she should look on that as the one blessing here. Roland sent his victims to their deaths happy.

Katya staggered to the tent flap, just making it outside before she retched.

CHAPTER TWENTY-EIGHT

STARBRIDE

Starbride was still sagging against the wall when someone knocked. "Come in."

Dawnmother smiled wryly. "Good chat?"

"Chat doesn't begin to cover it."

"So I heard."

Starbride winced. "How loud was I?"

"Don't worry. I don't think the neighboring warehouse heard you."

Pennynail slipped in the door and closed it behind him before he took off his mask to reveal a wide grin. "I expected to find Ellias and Elody in here with you."

Starbride swatted at him. "Shut up, Freddie."

"Back, lusty wench!" he said. "I just put clean trousers on."

Starbride glared at them. "I thought you were supposed to defend me, both of you."

"I wouldn't defend anyone from what I heard," Freddie said. "In fact, I applaud them." His gloved hands clapped softly.

"Enough," Dawnmother said. "But we are happy for you, Star."

"Yes," Freddie said, "it's just good to know you're also very happy for yourself."

That time, Dawnmother swatted at him. Starbride rolled her eyes. "Is there news or did you just come in here to poke fun?" She pointed at Freddie. "If you make a joke out of that, I will kill you."

He drew himself up. "Then I can only hope my body will fall in such a way as to inconvenience you as much as possible."

"So no news, then?" Dawnmother said.

"No, I've got that too," he said. "Brains and looks and productivity all in one tidy package."

"You *are* in a good mood," Starbride said. "And not just because of what you…overheard."

"The black prince is quite a hit in Dockland, based on what my contacts have to say."

"The black prince?" Starbride said. "Is that the name Reinholt's chosen for himself?"

"If one wishes to do well in Dockland, one does not choose one's own nickname," Freddie said. "Unless one wishes to have the shit kicked out of one."

"You're too pleased with yourself. You started that nickname, didn't you? Did you also find a way to get yourself called Pennynail?"

"That was Owen and my father's idea," Freddie said. "But I might have gotten 'the black prince' off the ground. I also considered his suggestion of 'the rogue prince,' but I was afraid that if written down, he might quickly become the rouge prince, and that's just not the effect we're going for."

Starbride had to laugh. "A good reason to be smug. And the people like the rebel royal persona?"

"Immensely. Of course, it didn't hurt that I started a rumor saying that one of the reasons he was expelled from court was for consorting with commoners, maybe even daring to try and marry one after his upper-crust wife called him too common for her taste."

Even Dawnmother's mouth hung open. "That's all lies!"

"But useful," Starbride said. "I don't know if the truth would win us any allies. What else did he supposedly get thrown out of court for?"

"The usual. Fights, wenching, carousing, all building on the 'commoner' theme." Freddie scratched his chin. "I, uh, might have also put it out there that his sister was a common collaborator in his… misadventures."

Starbride narrowed her eyes. "Oh, did you, now?"

"All over now that she's found true love, of course," he said. "Many people already knew Katya's reputation. I just inflated it a little and stuck Reinholt in. No harm done."

Until Katya and her father retook the city and every barmaid in Dockland tossed her hankie Katya's way. "I'm…I'm just glad things are going well."

"Reinholt's winning them over. He does a pretty speech, and having Maia looking pale and heartbreaking beside him isn't hurting him any."

"It's not too much for her, is it?" Dawnmother asked.

"She's perfectly well," Freddie said, "if sad. My friends are taking good care of them, and having Reinholt's arm to lean on and guide seems to be doing her some good. I always thought she'd turn out to be too fragile for the Order, but she's proven me wrong. She's been through more than we could imagine, but she's persevering, like all of us."

When someone knocked on the door, Freddie pulled his mask on before Starbride called, "Come in." She hoped it wouldn't be someone else come to tease her about her encounter with Katya.

Master Bernard poked his head around the door. "Captain Ursula of the Watch is here," he said softly. "She's asking about mind pyramids, and I don't quite know what to tell her."

"He means," Ursula said from behind him, "that I'm out here raging about what the damned Fiend king is doing to my officers, and he doesn't know how to deal with me."

"By all means," Starbride said, scooting farther back on the bed. "Everyone pile in. Why not?"

Either Ursula didn't detect the sarcasm, or she didn't care. She pushed forward, forcing Master Bernard into the room before following him inside. "You really need a bigger space for meetings," she said.

"This is the best we can do."

"And not for much longer. This waiting for help from the outside was all fine and well a few weeks ago, Princess Consort, but not anymore. You've got too many hiding here. I'm hiding several other groups, and now the Fiend king is seducing not only my people, but members of the general public." She shook her head. "I'm not sure we can wait for the army. They might arrive to find no allies left."

"Do you know how he's getting your people?" Starbride asked.

"They go into the city, they come back with Fiend king fever, if they come back at all. But I don't know if he's got these pyramids set up somewhere or if he's dragging people into alleys and hypnotizing them himself."

"One by one would take too long," Master Bernard said. "He was getting the monks by bringing them into the palace."

"Far as I know, none of my officers have gone anywhere near the palace."

"He must have similar pyramids in the city," Starbride said. "Or maybe he moves them, so we won't figure out where they are."

"But how is he operating them?" Master Bernard asked. "Traps are meant to detonate. Unless the Fiend king is moving himself and using these pyramids."

"Have you had any reports like that?" Starbride asked. "The Fiend king roaming the streets hypnotizing people?"

Ursula shook her head. "But then I wouldn't, would I? Anyone who saw such a thing would find herself hypnotized."

"Some reconnaissance is in order until we've crafted more anti-hypnosis pyramids," Starbride said. "Take a few that we've already made, and send some of your officers scouting. If you encounter the Fiend king's traveling show, be prepared to pretend to be as nutty as everyone else. I'm sure you and Sergeant Rhys can manage."

Ursula looked away. "Rhys is among the missing."

"Oh, I am sorry," Starbride said. She didn't know either of them well, but she'd sensed they were close, at least as colleagues. "We'll find him."

"Needle in a haystack," Master Bernard said. He glanced at Ursula as if just remembering she was in the room. "My apologies. That just popped out."

She smiled sadly. "It's worse than that. Rhys is a needle in a pile of needles. But if I run across him while I'm looking for the Fiend king, I'll knock him over the head and bring him to you, Princess Consort."

"In the meantime," Starbride said, "I think we have some research ahead of us, Master Bernard. If the Fiend king is making pyramids large enough to hypnotize the populace, we have to make some large enough to protect it."

"It's a question of crystal," he said. "We've ransacked our caches in the city."

"Then we either steal one of the Fiend king's," Ursula said, "or it's back into the palace."

Roland would be waiting for them to sneak back into the palace. He'd probably searched it from top to bottom until he'd found Pennynail's old bolt-hole. That or he'd found a way to seal the secret passageways or cover them in traps. "Better to look in the city. Even if we can't repurpose the Fiend king's pyramids, we can destroy them."

"When this erupts into a fight, and it will," Ursula said. "No one is going to be left out of it. Everyone's going to have to choose a side."

"Except for the poor people who've had one chosen for them," Dawnmother said.

"But some of them will be freed," Ursula said, "and if they join the fight rather than trying to hide, we're going to need a way to tell one another apart."

"Like colors?" Master Bernard asked.

"If we were all going about in red," Starbride said, "the Fiend king will have no trouble finding us."

"A sigil, then," Ursula said. "Something we can hide and then show when the time comes."

Pennynail sat at Starbride's desk and began to draw. After a few moments, he held up a sheet of paper. Starbride looked at the hasty drawing for a moment before it dawned on her what it was: the hawk of Farraday, and in its talons—like Katya's rose or Reinholt's crown—it held a pyramid.

"Is that for me?" Starbride asked. When he nodded, she couldn't think of anything to say.

"I like it," Ursula said. "For the Princess Consort's War."

Starbride winced. That wasn't nearly so flattering. "I don't know about the hawk. I'm not Farradain."

"But the Allusians have no…sigils like that," Dawnmother said. "Even if we were to draw Horsestrong, no one would know what he meant."

"I suppose so."

Ursula took the drawing. "I'll show this around. I trust you can draw it again, hooded man?"

He nodded. Starbride watched the two of them carefully. Ursula knew Pennynail's name, though she refused to call him by it. Maybe it was her objection to not knowing who he was.

"I'll be in touch." Ursula left with as little preamble as when she came in. Master Bernard followed her out. When Dawnmother, Starbride, and Pennynail were alone again, he removed his mask.

"She doesn't like Pennynail," Starbride said.

He sighed. "She'd like the fact that Freddie Ballantine's alive much less."

"Are you certain of that?" Dawnmother asked. "She may take joy in the fact that you're alive."

"You're a hopeless romantic, Dawnmother. And I can nearly hear you thinking that the most she could do is scorn me. There you're wrong. The *most* she could do is stab me."

"Well, if you don't trust yourself to best her in a fight…"

Freddie glared at her. "That's not going to work."

"I guess we learn by Ursula's example," Starbride said. "Head into the city tomorrow and look around."

❖

Starbride was confident as they ventured into the city after sundown. They split into two groups: Freddie with Hugo, and Starbride with Dawnmother and Averie. Freddie didn't want to reveal his identity to Averie, but the two groups patrolled near one another, where a commotion would bring the other group running.

When Starbride told Averie why they'd split up, she shrugged. "I don't much care. I've never really been curious about who he is."

Starbride cocked an eyebrow. "Does that mean you don't care to find out his identity, or that you genuinely wouldn't care who he was if you found out?"

"How bad could it be? I mean, he's not likely to be an infamous murderer or anything, right?"

Starbride barked a laugh. When Averie frowned, Dawnmother said, "Of course not. How absurd."

Maybe she wouldn't recognize him if she saw his face. It was the best they could hope for. That, and if she did recognize him, maybe she'd turn out to be equally casual. At the very least, Starbride knew Averie wouldn't give away their identities in order to cause a scene.

Averie pointed off to the side. "That's the third hypnotized person I've seen on this street. I'll scout ahead." She wandered while Starbride and Dawnmother loitered against a storefront.

When Averie ambled back, she said, "There are definitely more of them up there."

"Did you see Roland?"

"No." Averie tapped her chest where the mind-protection pyramid was hidden in a pocket. "Would this let me see through a disguise pyramid?"

"I'm not sure." Starbride slipped into her pocket for her detection pyramid, one of three pyramids she carried outside her satchel. If she used it to detect an active mind pyramid, and if Roland was near, he would know. But if they had a chance to deactivate or break one of the large mind pyramids...

"Put your sunny faces on," Starbride said. Together, they ambled down the street. When they were surrounded by languid faces, she said, "Get ready to run."

She focused, and the world faded to muted grays. There, like a beacon, a golden glow lit up the street, pouring out of a tavern.

Starbride snapped out of her focus. "It's in the tavern ahead."

"Do we go in?" Averie asked.

"We'll meet with Hugo and Pennynail and bring at least one of them in with…" Invisible fingers ran up her neck. She'd never felt it, but she'd read about it. Someone was detecting her pyramids. They would find them active not only on her, but on Averie and Dawnmother as well, mind-protection pyramids for them while hers hid the fact that she was a pyradisté from the corpse Fiends.

"We've been spotted."

"Where?" Dawnmother asked.

Starbride shook her head. They turned down the street, trying not to walk too quickly, still trying to fit in.

"Stop, Starbride!" a voice called.

She looked over her shoulder and stumbled in surprise. It wasn't Roland but another familiar face, though one she'd never actually spoken to. The only time she'd gotten close to him was when she'd spied on him outside Lady Hilda's townhouse and later when she'd taken him to the dungeon.

Hilda's pyradisté, the oldest of the Sleeting brothers, one of the sons of the woman who'd claimed to be the rightful queen of Farraday. He smiled, and she was struck by how much he looked like Einrich and Roland. There had to have been something to Carmen Van Sleeting's claims of being an Umbriel.

"Did you forget about me?" he asked.

Starbride's eyes flicked around. No Roland, no corpse Fiends. He was a pyradisté; if they ran, he could cut them down. Maybe, like Roland, he underestimated her.

"The last I saw, you were in the dungeon."

"Being tormented by your masked man." His hand went into his pocket. "I haven't forgotten."

Starbride went into her own satchel and grabbed a cancellation pyramid. She focused on his pyramids and tried to snuff them like candle lights. She snapped off one and then two. He growled and used his own pyramid, and hers went dark, the feeling of being thrown from it mid-use bringing tears to her eyes.

Damn, she should have gone for his cancellation pyramid first. Averie was already in motion. She hadn't brought her longbow with her, so she darted forward with her long knife. He chucked a pyramid at her feet and danced away. Starbride closed her eyes, keeping out most of the blast from a flash bomb, but she heard Dawnmother grunt and felt her stagger.

Two could play that. "Temperance!" Starbride threw a flash bomb and heard several people in the street drop. That was good. Fewer people to turn against them.

She opened her eyes in time to see another pyramid flying in her direction. She hauled Dawnmother out of its path, but that didn't help several bystanders from bursting into flame.

Even as they burned, they lolled with smiles on their faces. No random mind pyramid could be so strong as to keep them permanently blissful. They had to keep wandering back to recharge that effect. Still, too many of them would be hurt by a pyramid duel in the street. She had to get rid of them somehow.

Starbride dug for her spare cancellation pyramid. Still hauling Dawnmother around while Averie pursued the pyradisté, Starbride fell into the pyramid and set her sights on the tavern. The golden fountain was still there, brighter than the smaller, moving lights dotting the enemy pyradisté.

The large pyramid oozed tendrils of light, leaking its vile fluid into the populace. And where it touched, it left residue behind, but she'd been right, such residue would wear off, and the person would have to come back to this pyramid or another like it for another dose of bliss. If Roland covered the city in these, no one would ever complain about him again.

Anger spurred her as she grabbed hold of the large pyramid with her mind. It felt like plunging her arms into icy water as she reached into its diseased heart to stop its pumping forever. She pushed until it yielded, dwindling until its golden glow became nothing.

"Look out!" Dawnmother shoved her to the side and fell on top of her. A sphere of blackness blossomed behind them. It annihilated all of the people caught within and left a bowl-shaped divot in the street. It had snipped Dawnmother's long hair, leaving it to unravel on her shoulders. Starbride struggled up and saw a leg on the ground, sheared through as if by the sharpest of knives, blood slowly trickling into the bowl in the road.

The street seemed to take a great breath, and then the screams began as people shook off the effects of the mind pyramid. They ran, and Starbride saw the enemy pyradisté again. He caught her eye and bared his teeth. Starbride fell into her cancellation pyramid, finding his just as she felt him tug on hers, but this time, she was faster. She searched for another but didn't find one. She took his pyramids one by one.

He cursed and ran. Starbride followed, Dawnmother beside her. She saw Averie push through the crowd and close on the running pyradisté's back.

He glanced over his shoulder and shouted, "The man I have become is but a sum of the many who came before me."

Starbride had just enough time to wonder before Averie spun and kicked Dawnmother in the face.

"Averie!" Starbride yelled. Dawnmother collapsed beside her. Starbride turned back, but Averie was on her in an instant.

Averie's fist landed in Starbride's stomach, sending pain radiating through her midsection and knocking the breath from her. She reached for her satchel, but Averie tore it off and threw it away. Averie twisted one of Starbride's arms behind her back, forcing her to her knees and sending hot agony through her shoulder. Starbride's head wrenched back as Averie's fingers wound into her hair and pulled sharply.

The pyradisté sauntered toward them, his smile back in place. "He'll be a little angry that I sprang this trap, but I'm sure he'll understand that you forced me, especially when I give you to him."

"Averie?" Starbride gasped.

"No use talking to her. She's merely a tool, like the man said. 'A sum of the many who came before.' She's the epitome of his Majesty's brilliant creations." He glanced at Averie. "Bring her."

Starbride yelped as Averie hauled her to her feet and then marched her along through the very confused townspeople, leaving Dawnmother in the dirt.

Starbride tried to stay on her feet as the taller Averie hurried her along. She could see almost nothing with her head yanked back. Averie's pulls on her hair hurt nearly as much as the arm twisted up behind her. "What did you do to Averie? I would have detected if she'd been tampered with by a pyramid."

"Did you miss it when I said Roland is brilliant? You didn't see any tampering because there isn't any to see. He stripped her memories completely, remade her into the willing tool currently yanking your hair out, and then overlaid her memories, masking the entire process, leaving no seams. Genius."

Starbride's mind whirled. Roland had really tortured Averie, then, to make her injuries real. And she'd endured it as herself before he mind-warped her completely. A mind overlay, undetectable. It was genius, terrifying, awful genius. "I'm so sorry, Averie," Starbride whispered.

Averie made no response.

"He'll kill you one day," Starbride said, "and who you are won't matter."

He leaned into her vision and put a hand on his chest. "Alphonse."

"I don't care what your name is."

"Snarl all you want, little terrier."

"If he broke her, I can fix her."

Alphonse put on a pitying smile. "Nothing left to fix, I'm afraid. Her old memories are gone. He just used them as a coating, see? And when I spoke the code words—an old philosopher's, not mine—the coating was washed away. All that's left is, well…"

Starbride couldn't help a little noise of frustration. Time enough to think on Averie's predicament later. She could barely make out where they were going, yet she was certain that Roland would be waiting.

She had to slow their progress. When they didn't hear from Starbride's group, Hugo or Freddie would come looking. They would find Dawnmother, and then they would be on her trail. All she had to do was stall. If she went limp, she feared that Averie would pull her arm from its socket. She was already on tiptoes; there was no way to drag her feet. When she tried to slow, Averie twisted her arm higher, and Starbride let out a little shriek.

"Come now," Alphonse said, "pick your feet up."

"Did you help with these genius plans?" Starbride asked. He seemed quite willing to talk, and if she could really engage him, perhaps he would slow.

"I'm proud to work under his direction."

"And how long do you think he'll let you keep living?"

"For as long as I'm useful, and I plan on being useful forever."

Starbride had to laugh at that. She patted her pocket, trying to see how many pyramids she had left.

"Something funny?" Alphonse asked.

Starbride tried to give him an incredulous look. With her head pulled back, it wasn't easy. Her cancellation pyramid had fallen. She still had her detector, and there was one other: a flash bomb. She always carried a backup of the pyradisté's best friend. "Once he takes over the city, he won't need you."

"Then I'll move on."

"If he'll let you." And she still had the pyramid around her neck that hid her from Fiends. She couldn't let Roland get a hold of that one.

"Are you not uncomfortable enough already?" Alphonse asked. "Do you want me to make her hurt you more?"

"Whether you do or not," Starbride said, "it won't change reality."

"Oh, just keep walking." He pulled a little ahead.

Starbride grabbed her flash bomb. She closed her eyes and rammed it into her own shoulder, just in front of where Averie's face should be. Bits of crystal dug into her palm. Her eyelids lit up with the glow, and Averie yelped. The pressure on Starbride's arm and hair eased, and she bolted for the alley she'd glimpsed just before she'd acted.

Heat blossomed behind her, but she kept running. She heard the crackle of flames and felt the heat swarm across her back. Starbride dropped to the street and rolled in the dirt.

When she stopped on her back, Averie loomed over her. Starbride kicked, catching her in the stomach, but Averie went with the motion and pushed off the side of a building. She leapt forward again. Her knee landed on Starbride's thigh, spiking pain down Starbride's leg. She cried out and tried to push Averie away, but the shards of crystal dug into her palm.

"Now, what did that get you?" Alphonse called.

Averie grabbed Starbride's wrists. Her face was mostly calm, only a slight frown marring her features, but her eyes were red-rimmed. She couldn't be able to see well.

Starbride brought a knee up into Averie's chest, making her grunt and twist to the side. Starbride sat up and tried to push away, but Averie held on, and now Alphonse was coming. Starbride planted a foot between Averie's breasts and shoved.

Averie lost her hold on one wrist. Starbride tried a backhand, but the blow just grazed Averie's cheek. Starbride didn't want to hurt her. Maybe Alphonse was wrong; maybe she could be saved. Starbride would never know, though, if she let them recapture her.

Alphonse reached for her, but before he could grab hold, a knife punched into his shoulder. He staggered away with a cry.

"Miss Starbride!" Hugo cried.

"Here! Averie's turned against us, but don't kill her!"

When Hugo charged into view, Averie let go of Starbride and leapt to her feet. She whipped her long knife from her belt.

Freddie ran for Alphonse, who reached into the satchel at his side.

"He's a pyradisté," Starbride called. She threw her detection pyramid at him, hoping to distract him.

He ducked out of its path, giving Freddie time to throw another knife. It caught Alphonse in the leg, and he dropped to one knee. Freddie kicked him in the face, and he went down like an empty sack.

"Who are we not killing?" Freddie asked.

They both turned to Hugo, who'd taken a reluctant stance against Averie. She struck at him over and over, and he gave ground, staying ahead of her blows.

"Do you have my satchel?" Starbride asked.

Freddie shook his head. "We put Dawnmother in a safe place." He moved to flank Averie, but she shifted to face both of them.

The satchel couldn't be far down the street. If no one had picked it up, she could grab a mind pyramid, hypnotize Averie… Two steps away she remembered that Averie wore an anti-hypnosis pyramid. "Damn…"

"Knock her out!" she cried to Hugo and Freddie.

More easily said than done. Averie was quick, and Hugo seemed reluctant to harm her. She kicked an empty crate into Freddie's path, and when Hugo came for her, she dipped, grabbed a handful of dirt and flung it in his face.

He staggered back, keeping his rapier on guard.

"Hold it there!" a woman's voice cried from up the street, and Captain Ursula ran closer, shortsword out. "What's this now?"

Averie took to her heels, sprinting across the street and into an alley while Hugo wiped at his face. Freddie tried to fade into the background.

"More hypnotized folk?" Ursula scanned the street and caught Freddie half in shadow. "Just a moment, fellow. I know you, don't I?"

Starbride grabbed her arm. "Captain, wait. We…need your help with this man. He's a pyradisté working for the Fiend king."

That gave Ursula pause, and she glanced at where Alphonse lay bleeding in the street. "I thought the Fiend king wanted to exterminate them."

"We'll never know if we don't question him, and we won't get to if we're caught out here."

Hugo approached, still blinking away grit. Ursula looked again for Freddie, but he was gone. Starbride had no doubt he was still nearby. "Right," Ursula said, frowning. She bent to help them lift Alphonse and bear him away. "But I shall want some answers."

"And you'll have them," Starbride said. Some of them, at least.

CHAPTER TWENTY-NINE

KATYA

Leafclever and Redtrue listened with horrified faces as Katya told them about the newest assassin.

"To abuse the adsna so…" Leafclever and Redtrue paled, as if they were moments from being sick.

"He took her mind away," Redtrue said. "And put his own in its place?"

"And then he put a bomb inside her, one designed to kill the first person who touched it with mind magic."

"And perhaps you if you had been standing closer," Leafclever said.

Redtrue covered her mouth

"I was sick, too," Katya said, "after I saw it."

"I'm sure," Redtrue said. "But we are not only sickened at the death."

"The perversion of the adsna," Katya said. "I know. This is what we're up against. The usurper will turn the adsna however he wishes in order to get what he wants."

Leafclever spread his hands as if gesturing to the entire world. "I sense you are leading to your expression, 'fight fire with fire,' but instead, you are proving our point. We cannot add to the adsna's perversion. If we produce pyramids that can penetrate the minds of others, even to search for these assassins, we add to the evil. And the evil we create will one day be fought by others who will have to defeat it with greater evil and so on."

Katya kept her court face on and looked to Redtrue, who still covered her mouth, staring at nothing.

"What if the pyramid is just a tool?" Katya asked. "And the good or evil comes from the heart of the wielder?"

"The *fana-zi*, the pyramid crystal, is a tool," Leafclever said, "but the adsna is not. It is the spirit of the world, and when someone uses it in a way not in harmony with the world, that is an evil act, despite the intentions of the user."

Katya had to lift her hands, her well of patience already dry. "I think it's far more evil to do nothing while good people die."

Redtrue's gaze snapped to Katya's face, but Leafclever didn't lose his sardonic little smile. "We have been doing more than 'nothing.'" He withdrew a pyramid from his pocket and gave it to her.

The crystalline sides were smooth, but the insides were cloudy, like some poorly made pyramids she'd seen. As Katya peered into it, though, the clouds moved like trapped smoke. "What does it do?"

"It works with the adsna to block mind intrusions."

It sounded like exactly what Starbride was working on. Katya had to wonder if they worked the same, if Farradain and Allusian magic were not so different after all. "What about those that have already had their minds tampered with? Will this free them?"

"Until we are confronted with another such person who survives, I do not know. We are working on larger versions to cover many of our comrades at once."

"Thank you," Katya said. "Do you think you could make a pyramid that stops Farradain magic completely?"

Redtrue spoke up at last. "We cannot stop those that detonate. We can only fight their effects."

"No, I mean something that cancels the pyramids before they can be used." She told them of how Crowe used cancellation pyramids to search for magic and then switch it off, turning enemy pyramids into junk.

Leafclever rubbed his chin. "Interesting. If it were large enough, and we used it constantly…"

Katya nearly rubbed her hands together, excited that they were working together at last. "Could you modify your Fiend pyramids to be less…violent?"

Leafclever sighed. "We have been trying to think of a way, but so far…" He smiled. "But I am glad to see our words of caution affecting you at last, Princess Katyarianna."

"I don't think we'll ever see eye-to-eye on the philosophy, but I'll take what I can get."

"That is why the cycle of evil will continue in Farraday." Without waiting for a response, he wandered off.

Katya couldn't help shaking her head at his departing back.

"You still don't hear his words," Redtrue said, "not really."

"I hear him. I just don't agree. Can you blame me? After all, I've never touched the adsna like you have. And I've had two different groups of people telling me contradictory facts about it. Who am I supposed to believe when I can't really find out for myself?"

Redtrue cocked her head. "I think the evidence is plain enough even for your uninitiated eyes. There are no Fiends in Allusia."

Katya had to wonder what would happen if the adsnazi ever came close to the great pyramid under the palace in Marienne. They might realize that Yanchasa slumbered there, kept asleep by a portion of its own Fiendish Aspect in each of the Umbriels save Katya.

Now that would be a sight to see.

"What are you smiling at?" Redtrue asked.

"Just my dark sense of humor."

"Yes, Castelle often finds things amusing that are not funny in the slightest."

"We that embrace evil have to take humor where we find it," Katya said.

"Tsk. You shouldn't joke about such things. I shall never truly understand your people."

❖

In the distance, light glinted and sparkled, much as it would when striking water. But they'd crossed all the rivers they would need to, and the great Lavine was on the other side of their destination.

"Marienne," Katya whispered. Still not close enough to make out individual buildings, the jewel of Farraday was near enough to catch the light and send it winking back. Soon, everyone Katya cared about would be close enough to embrace: Starbride and Maia and Averie. She imagined shaking Pennynail's hand and clapping Hugo on the back. Spirits, she'd even hug Reinholt. Maybe she'd whisper to him that if he acted like a naughty child, she'd order Vincent to paddle him. That would raise some eyebrows.

Katya urged her horse forward. This close to the capital, her scouting party wasn't the only one out and about, but she veered toward the city while the others ranged over the countryside. They couldn't be too careful.

It was all Katya could do not to ride as hard as she could for Marienne. Without the army, she could probably be there by nightfall, and then she wouldn't have to depend on a surrogate to give Starbride her love.

"You wouldn't make it over the wall," Brutal said.

Katya gave him a look. "You're a pyradisté, aren't you? You've been reading my mind for years."

"Don't need any special powers besides knowing you for those years."

Katya narrowed her eyes. "And you were thinking the same thing."

He winked. "Now you're getting the hang of it."

He and Maia might not have become as close as Katya and Starbride, but they'd been heading in that direction. Before she was taken, Maia had been nursing a crush on Brutal, and Katya knew he cared for her, too. He wanted to make sure she was all right. Even if they couldn't be blessed by Ellias and Elody, they could still be friends.

"I see you two looking wistfully into the distance," Castelle said behind them. "Will I have to tie you to a tree?"

Katya almost remarked on how those were easy words for someone whose current love was within arm's reach, but she bit them back. Castelle had lost friends on this journey, they all had, and she didn't deserve to be mocked for attempting to lighten the mood. Katya would save that for when Castelle did something stupid.

On their right, Count Mathias whistled. Katya craned her neck and spotted a group of riders heading toward them. "Some of ours?"

He stood in his stirrups and shaded his eyes from the sun. "They don't have the look of Allusians, so it's not Hawkblade, and we would have seen any of the others pass us by."

"Form up!" Katya called. It was a small group, and the scouting party of fifteen could fight them off if necessary. Still, they regrouped under a copse of trees where the approaching party couldn't charge. Katya drew her rapier. The newcomers could be coming to join the army or might be coming to stop it. There was no way to know until they got close.

The pack of riders slowed as they neared the trees. A smattering of men and women, maybe twenty. They wore studded leather or mail. All were armed, but they'd not yet drawn. A band of mercenaries, perhaps, but working for Roland or looking to join her side? As one, they slowed to a halt, their movements in sync.

"They must've been working together a long time," Castelle said.

"If you're friends, come ahead," Katya called, "and tell us your names."

They approached slowly. As she looked from face to face, Katya's stomach shrank. They were smiling, *smirking*, a nearly identical look on each face.

Katya frowned. No, not nearly identical, exactly so.

Their heads tilted. "Hello, niece."

"Archers, fire!" Katya yelled.

The two archers raised their bows as the mind-warped attackers kicked their horses into motion. As one, they swung shields up from behind them and ducked under. One of the arrows hit a shield dead center while the other took an attacker in the leg.

That didn't stop or slow him. The attackers wheeled like a flock of birds, splitting into two groups and charging into the trees on either side of Katya's party.

Katya guided her horse to the left and gestured to those nearest her. "All of you, with me. The rest with Brutal to the right." They obeyed, Count Mathias and the Allusians guiding their horses expertly. Katya bit back a curse. She was much better fighting from the ground than from horseback. When the first rider careened into her, she ducked his swing, and then rolled to the ground.

Among the trees, she felt on equal footing with the mounted fighters; they didn't have space to run her down, and she could dip away from their swings and cut at their vulnerable legs. Chaos reigned around her as she darted from tree to tree, making more than a nuisance of herself. Across the way, she saw Brutal on foot as well, tall enough to slam his mace into his foes' backs and knock them from their saddles.

"Focus, niece," a voice behind her said.

Katya ducked and rolled away, coming up facing an older man with a scar across his cheek. He wore the same, familiar smirk. She blocked his thrust and sliced his forearm, making him grimace.

So, they weren't immune to pain.

"Unfortunately for you," Katya said, "my uncle was better at magic than sword play."

His next attack made her rethink that, a series of quick jabs that had her blocking and retreating. So, Roland kept something of the original person after all.

Katya heard a scream from behind her but couldn't place which side it came from. When her opponent swung again, she dodged, came up inside his reach, and bashed him in the nose with her rapier guard. When he staggered back, she pulled a knife from her belt and stabbed him in the gut, up into the heart.

His mouth gaped open, blood pouring from his nose as they stared eye to eye. Katya wondered if this was what Roland would look like when he died for the second time. But then the scarred man blinked, and he was just a tool, not a traitor or an assassin. Katya's stomach turned over, and she had to spin away, cursing Roland while looking for another opponent.

The ride back to the camp was solemn. They had defeated their opponents at a heavy cost, cutting their scouting party down to eight. Katya couldn't get the image of the attackers calling her "niece" out of her mind. She had a sudden picture of an entire army speaking to her so, grinning that obscene smile.

Katya shuddered. None of the attackers had been a match for her or Brutal, Castelle or Count Mathias, but as their losses proved, not everyone was so skilled or so fortunate. And she couldn't know whether the skill of Roland's soldiers was part of them or something he was doing to them. Maybe he was borrowing from different minds and then dropping them into whatever heads he chose. They had to hope that the adsnazi pyramids would help. More than help; they would have to turn the tide.

Katya guided her horse close to Brutal and Castelle. "We need to make a plan tonight to sneak into the city and do something about Roland's pyramids."

"And see a certain someone?" Castelle asked.

"That would be beyond wonderful, but we have to focus on stopping Roland first."

"Well," Brutal said, "maybe not first."

Katya raised an eyebrow.

"We'll have a little time," he said, "to say hello."

"And good-bye?"

He shook his head. "Hello and see you soon."

She couldn't help but be cheered. The thought of actually taking Starbride into her arms washed the whole world away. Afterward, they would ride to war, possibly to their deaths, but Katya would take Starbride's memory to the realm of the spirits or into oblivion. If they perished, perhaps their minds would mix together, entwined for all eternity in the very fabric of time.

It was a lovely idea, and she held it close to her heart.

When the chill first washed over her, she thought it was only the winter wind. But she'd dressed warmly, and the action—not to mention thoughts of Starbride—had warmed her. Still, there was no piece of clothing or thought so warm it couldn't be penetrated. A bitter breeze stung her cheeks and nose.

"Wind's picked up," Brutal said.

Katya breathed out slowly, watching it plume on the air. The back of her neck itched, and knots of worry tightened her shoulders. "We're being watched."

Something familiar pulled at her, and not just the sense of danger. The feeling of eyes on her had a half-remembered quality. Had she been in this exact situation before and just forgotten?

A *thwack* sounded off to the left. Maybe a hundred feet away, the limbs of a tree shook as if something large had leapt from them.

"Right," Brutal whispered.

Katya turned that way and caught a blur of movement disappearing into the coarse bushes that had survived the coming winter. The familiar feeling increased, as if an answer waited on the tip of her tongue, but the answer to what?

"The symbols," she muttered, recalling the Fiend speech that had once led her and Starbride into a trap in Marienne. Then she'd felt as if she'd known them because the Fiend inside her had recognized the writing. Now, there was no speech, and the feelings weren't so strong that she felt compelled. She had no Fiend driving her, so what…

"Oh spirits," Katya whispered.

"What is it?" Brutal asked.

She'd once had a Fiend, and she could almost remember what it was like, the power, the cold…

"Katya?" Brutal asked.

"It's Fiends," Katya said.

"Corpse Fiends?" Castelle asked.

Katya shook her head. She'd been with her family when the Aspect was upon them, but it had never felt like this. Her pulse roared in her ears, and she couldn't keep her mouth closed to breathe. "Not corpses, not people with Aspects. *Fiends*."

"But…how?" Count Mathias said.

"Ride!" Katya kicked her horse into a run, but they'd already ridden far that day. The horses couldn't take much more. But they couldn't fight Fiends, they couldn't. How and why the Fiends were there didn't matter.

As the wind rushed past her ears, she heard the forest come alive with purposeful thumps and crashes. Her horse began to tire, and those around her did the same. If she tried to hurry it, it could collapse underneath her.

"Katya, we have to slow," Brutal called.

She slowed her horse, fighting the rising panic, and the familiar feeling that hung like a weight across her shoulders. She'd been afraid many times in her life, but she'd never fled from a fight like this. She clenched her teeth and told herself that if she didn't stop and find a way to face this, she was a coward.

A deep chuckle echoed around them, followed by a burst of high-pitched titters.

Katya swallowed. "Circle up."

They walked their huffing, snorting horses into a circle and drew weapons. A long sound, like something dragging through the dirt, came from Katya's far left, but she fought the urge to look, keeping her eyes on what was in front of her, trusting those behind.

"Anything?" she asked.

"No," someone said.

"A bush moved, but…there's nothing."

"They're going to be fast," Brutal said.

Probably too fast to see, which meant what she was doing was useless. And what if by not moving, she was letting the Fiends encircle them? "We keep going, slowly."

Her party called softly to one another, a tree limb swaying here, a blur there, but always nothing, nothing, nothing. Katya fought the urge to rub her chest, to try to ease the weight. The space inside her where the Fiend used to be ached for what it'd once had. She wondered if the Fiends could sense it, too. Maybe that's why they weren't attacking.

Wonderful. Now all she had to do was find a way to be with the entire army for the whole attack. The heavy feeling spiked, and Katya grasped her chest. The world seemed to slow and fall away, and she felt compelled to twist around and look back.

There, behind the last rider in their group, something perched.

One of Count Mathias's men blinked at her from his saddle. His mouth moved, but Katya couldn't hear him. Her gaze was fixed on the bright white eyes staring back at her from over the man's shoulder. With no pupil or iris, they seemed to glow inside half of a face mottled blue and white, with horns that arced back over its hairless scalp. She couldn't see its teeth, but she knew it was smiling.

One hand lifted. Claws long as table knives inched toward the man's throat.

"N...no," Katya said, but she couldn't be sure anyone heard or that she actually spoke. The claws came closer. Katya summoned all her will. "No!"

She blinked, and it was gone. The man in the rear clapped his neck and pulled away a dot of blood from a small wound.

"What the..." He stared at Katya. "Highness?"

The world bled back to normal. The crushing feeling lifted, and the sounds from the forest ceased. Brutal leaned close to Katya's side. "What was that?"

She shook her head. Even if she could speak about it, she didn't know what to say.

CHAPTER THIRTY

STARBRIDE

Starbride rubbed her temples. A headache had been building behind her eyes for hours, but she supposed that was only natural. All her sore muscles and bruises, not to mention her cut palm, throbbed and twanged and reminded her that being alive came with its share of pain.

Alphonse's screams didn't help. They'd secured him in a cellar near the edge of Marienne, another of Pennynail's bolt-holes. He'd been unconscious when Ursula and Hugo had tied him up and bound his wounds, but he'd slurred awake when Pennynail joined them. At the sight of the laughing Jack mask, he'd screamed and screamed.

They'd had to gag him, but he still moaned through the rag. Starbride didn't want to pity him after the terrible things he'd helped do to Averie, but she didn't enjoy seeing anyone suffer.

Even Roland? No, she told herself. Would she be sad when Katya finally killed him? No, but she didn't want to watch him writhe.

"If you can't use a pyramid on him, how do we find out the truth?" Hugo asked.

Ursula nodded toward Pennynail. "Seems like your masked man found something out before. Don't know if it was truth, exactly."

Starbride crossed to where Alphonse was tied to a wooden pillar. Pennynail leaned on another pillar, arms crossed. Alphonse didn't take his eyes from the white mask.

"If I take your gag off," Starbride said, "are you going to start screaming again?"

He shook his head, but his gaze never left Pennynail. Starbride slipped the gag off, ready to put it back in an instant.

"Please," Alphonse whispered. He licked his lips. "Please make him stop staring at me."

Starbride glanced over her shoulder. Pennynail slipped around the pillar, mostly out of sight.

Alphonse sagged against his bonds. "Thank you."

Later, she'd have to ask Freddie what he'd done, but she was almost afraid to. The confident man she'd fought in the street seemed far away from this pathetic creature. She wondered what he'd had to do to forget his time in Pennynail's company. "You must be honest with me."

"Or he comes back, I know."

She was just glad she didn't have to say it. "Where are the other mind pyramids in the city?"

"Everywhere."

Starbride heard a foot tapping behind her.

Alphonse shut his eyes so tightly the skin turned white around the creases. "I can't tell you each location because I don't know them all. He does some of them himself, but they are in every district by now."

"Tell me about the ones you placed."

He gave her ten locations, scattered throughout the city, but he added that sometimes Roland moved them without reason, at least as far as Alphonse could tell. Of course, with those words, they could chase their tails all day, and Alphonse would claim that Roland had moved their quarry.

Or he could lead them straight into Roland's arms.

Starbride sent for Master Bernard and the academy heads. They had plenty of questions about how mass-hypnosis pyramids were made and about what Roland had taught Alphonse, including what interested Starbride the most: how to stop the pyramids. Breaking them required getting close. They needed something that worked from a distance.

After hours of questioning, Starbride conferred with the others. After they'd discussed theories, she asked, "Does anyone else have a headache as big as mine?"

"Not me," Ansic said. The others shook their heads. "Perhaps it's stress."

"It hasn't exactly been peaceful," Master Bernard said.

Starbride supposed so. She'd been taxing her brain, thinking of ways to beat Roland, but the pain hammered at her like a pulse.

"I'll meet you back at the warehouse," Starbride said. "Get some rest." She met Captain Ursula waiting near the door.

Ursula nodded at Alphonse. "This is all above my head."

"Trying to knock a Fiend king off the throne should be above everyone's head"

"If there's a job where it's normal, I don't want it. But I suppose none of us really wants it."

"True," Starbride said.

Ursula glanced at her. "Ever wonder just what your masked man did to our prisoner?"

"I'm trying not to."

"I should have taken Alphonse into custody when we nabbed him. I won't condone torture in my city, Princess Consort."

Starbride had to laugh, both at the proclamation and at the formality. "Do you plan to arrest the Fiend king before Katya gets to him?"

"If I can, I will. Something else is eating at me."

"About the Fiend king?"

"About your man in the street today."

Starbride froze but then tried to shrug. "It's nothing."

"He took off when he saw me."

"Lots of people don't like the Watch, I'm given to understand."

Ursula lifted an eyebrow. "Criminals."

"What of it? I'm not going to turn down help. There's more at stake here than the crimes of former thieves."

"So he's a thief."

Darkstrong could have carried Ursula away in that moment, and Starbride would have breathed a sigh of relief. "And you are most definitely a captain of the Watch."

"I didn't hear a no." She rubbed her chin. "A thief that runs at the sight of me. Either he doesn't know how to play it cool, which makes him a terrible ally, or he thought I would recognize him."

"I really don't see how this is helping us."

Ursula pointed a lazy finger in her direction. "Evasion means I'm on the right track."

Starbride lifted her arms and dropped them. "I swear by Horsestrong, I will never try and wheedle a secret out of anyone again."

"Secrets, eh?"

"Please, Captain!" Starbride rubbed her temples again. "I do not have the time or energy for this. So, he's a *former* thief who fears being caught. He's not a thief now, so what does it matter?"

Ursula gave her a flat stare, and even with the pain, the look made her want to squirm.

"No," Ursula said slowly.

"No?"

"I wouldn't waste my time right now on a thief. If he's in your camp, he knows that. Unless he's the greatest thief of all time, laughing Jack come to life." She nodded at Pennynail, and Starbride wanted to laugh and weep at the same time.

"Even then," Ursula said, "I'd get his help chucking the Fiend king out before I tossed his ass in prison. Not a thief, then. Or not *just* a thief."

Starbride wanted to tell Ursula how good a Watch officer she was, but the words wouldn't come. Everything she said gave something away.

Ursula smiled softly. "Nothing to add?"

"I have a headache."

"Anything else?"

"My hand hurts too."

Ursula chuckled. "I see. Well, I'll babysit our prisoner while you go get some rest. Maybe he's seen Rhys."

Starbride let out a breath. The room seemed to open up around her. Pennynail and Hugo came with her back to their hideout, and once the three were alone, Starbride shut the door and leaned against it. "I don't know why Katya called me a ferreter of secrets. Ursula is like a landslide."

Freddie pulled his mask off and sank into a chair. "She's going to figure it out. I can't believe I was so stupid."

"All the brains in the world wouldn't have let you know she was going to come around the corner just then," Hugo said.

"You trying to make me feel better now, Hugo? Your sworn enemy?"

"Just pointing out the facts, and you're not my sworn enemy."

"Thanks," Freddie muttered.

"You're very annoying, though," Hugo said.

"*Thanks.*"

"If you want to fake bicker and grin at each other, I can leave the room," Starbride said.

They both stared at her.

"I'm sorry," she said. "It's been a long day. I need some of Dawnmother's tea."

"The special sleepy mixture," Hugo said.

"I don't have time to sleep."

"But time to wander the streets, distracted, in pain, and blaming yourself for everything that's happening?" Freddie asked.

Starbride gave him a dark look and plonked down on the bed.

"I'll go get Dawnmother," Hugo said.

"What did you do to him?" Starbride asked when she and Freddie were alone.

"Alphonse? You really want to know?"

"Will I still like you after you tell me?"

He shrugged. "My father taught me that torture, the physical kind, only gets you what you want to hear. But there are...other means."

All she could think of was the way Alphonse couldn't seem to take his eyes off the mask. "What? You stared at him until he talked?"

"Mostly."

"You can't be serious."

"When he woke up, I was there with the mask on, staring, not moving. He asked me twice if I was alive. Then the lights would go out, and when they came back on, I was in a different place, staring again. After a while, he just started babbling. If he dozed off, I moved closer, so that soon, he was afraid to close his eyes."

Starbride shivered and didn't know what to say.

"Still like me?" he asked, not looking at her.

"I'm a little more afraid of Pennynail, but I like you just the same, Freddie."

He smiled wider and winked.

❖

Starbride listened to Katya that night with growing horror. "Fiends," she whispered, not quite able to believe it. Dawnmother's tea had worked well, so she'd gotten some rest, but now that she was awake, the headache was back. It had probably followed her into her dreams. And to add to it, wild Fiends were loose in Farraday. "How?"

"I wish I knew." Katya's fear reared between them, the cold wind of terror. "It has to be Roland's doing."

"Something inside the palace, maybe, something we haven't seen before." Or maybe Roland had broken through the cavern door beneath the palace. "He might be using the great capstone."

"I'm going to sneak into the city, into the palace while the army attacks and see if I can put an end to some of these pyramids."

Starbride's heart beat a little faster. "If you take the palace, and I'm attacking in the streets, we're sure to cripple him."

"In the streets? You're coming into the palace with me."

Starbride sighed. "I know these people, Katya, those behind the revolution. I have to be here to lead them."

Katya's disbelief was palpable, but then Starbride felt something else from her: pride. "Oh, Star."

Starbride laughed. "After this is all over, I'm going to kiss you like you've never been kissed before."

"I'll hold you to that. I just can't believe that I'm going to come so close and not see you right away."

"You will," Starbride said, "in passing as we're both running for our lives." She thought for a moment that she could delay telling Katya about Averie, but if Katya was going into the palace…"There's something you have to know." She told the story haltingly, finally able to allow her own tears to come. She hadn't known Averie well, but Katya had, and she could feel the terrible grief.

"Oh, spirits, my poor Averie. I thought…I thought she was alive!"

"She is, Katya. Maybe we can—"

"No. I'm done with false hope."

"Katya—"

"Do you believe it, Star? Really?"

Starbride thought of what Alphonse had said, what he'd continued to swear to under capture. Averie, the real Averie, was lost to them. It would have been better if Starbride had never found her, but at least now they knew. "No."

Katya's grief swelled, but then she brought it under control with the masterfulness that Starbride had come to expect. "If I see her, I'll deal with her."

Starbride squeezed her eyes shut tighter. She had a sudden hope that she would be the one to find Averie, to *deal* with her. As much as the idea turned her stomach, she would save Katya that added grief. "When will you be here?"

"Day after tomorrow. We'll sneak in just before dawn."

"I love you, Katya. Be careful."

"And I love you, Star. Be more careful than me."

"You might find it helpful to meet with Ursula's men stationed outside the wall. They've been feeding us information, and I'm sure they could help you."

Katya was quiet, long enough for Starbride to suspect her mind of racing.

"What are you thinking?" Starbride asked.

"Just that I love how resourceful you are."

"Flattery. What are you *thinking*?"

"Just ahead, dearheart, always thinking ahead," Katya said, and Starbride could almost feel her smile.

Starbride's day was taken up with planning and maneuvering. The sigil for the Princess Consort's War had spread through the city like the plague, though those who carried it kept it hidden. Freddie told her that little old men and women who wanted to do their part had been holed up in their houses for days, sewing their fingers off, making patches as fast as they could.

An army from within the city. It sounded so strange. They'd been their singular, ragtag band for so long. But that wasn't exactly true, was it? They'd freed a number of strength chapterhouses, and Master Bernard and the heads had been busy freeing others when they weren't working on traps. They'd been reaching through the city and countering Roland's mind pyramids. Maia and Reinholt were ready to lead the Docklanders to Marienne and push at Roland's forces from that side. What Reinholt thought of Starbride's colors, she could only guess. Maybe he modified them for the Docklanders to be his own symbol. As long as the two groups didn't forget who the enemy was, Starbride didn't care.

It was after dark when she saw Freddie again. He slipped into her room and pushed his mask on top of his head. "We need you right now."

"What is it?"

"Roland's planted a large pyramid outside the city gates. If we don't take care of it before Katya gets here…"

Starbride grabbed her satchel. Katya would be arriving at dawn, so that didn't leave them much time to slip out of the city, neutralize the pyramid, and get back. Her stomach lurched to the left, almost making her forget her headache. "Do you think we might…see her?"

"No, I'm sorry. With all we have left to do in the city—"

"You're right, of course." She was surprised by the need to blink away tears. She'd already dealt with the fact that she wouldn't see Katya until the fight was done, but just that little bit of hope almost undid her. She tried to put it from her mind and hurried on Pennynail's heels.

They went over the wall that time, on the opposite side of the city as the road to Dockland. Pennynail helped her climb over, and they ran for the forest, using it as cover while they headed for the road that led to the east. When they reached it, Starbride looked toward Marienne's main gate but saw nothing.

"Where is it?"

Pennynail waved her on, down the road. Starbride frowned, her suspicion deepening when they took a small track into the woods. Why station a pyramid so far from the wall?

A cold feeling grew in Starbride's stomach. Maybe Averie wasn't the only one who'd been mind-warped by a pyramid. Pennynail sometimes disappeared for days, long enough for Roland to catch him and treat him. Starbride slipped into her satchel and grabbed a fire pyramid.

But she continued to follow, continued to hope. Horsestrong preserve her, what if she had to kill him? Apart from Katya and Dawnmother, he was her best friend, had been her advisor and confidante. The few times she'd laughed since the troubles began were because of him.

"Pennynail," she whispered.

He waved again, and she saw a glow ahead, torchlight in the gloom. She slowed, letting him get ahead.

In a small clearing, at the end of the dirt trail, sat a farmhouse and barn. She recognized the place from Ursula's description, the farm that the Watch was using as a base. Would they be taking her to the pyramid? Maybe Pennynail didn't know exactly where it was.

A sentry called for them to come forward and be recognized, and Starbride did so, though she kept hold of the pyramid inside her satchel. A few of the Watch officers were standing around, though when they saw her, some turned away as if embarrassed, little smiles on their faces.

"What's going on?" Starbride said.

Pennynail pointed to the farmhouse. Starbride put her fists on her hips. "What's going on?" she said again.

"The captain wants a word," one of the men said.

"Ursula's here?"

"Just inside."

She was still suspicious, but this seemed more like the setup for a practical joke than an ambush. Maybe it was some sort of hazing. Suddenly, she didn't feel bad that she might have to hurt Pennynail after all.

"Honestly," she said as she marched alone toward the farmhouse, "as if we have time for this." She threw open the door, spied Ursula in the gloomy interior, and stepped inside, shutting the door behind her. "Captain, I…"

The words died in her throat as her eyes adjusted. Not Ursula. She knew this particular woman far better, though she couldn't believe her eyes. "Katya?"

"My Star." Katya opened her arms.

Starbride had to pause. There'd been so much deception, so much disappointment. "Are you real?"

Katya smiled softly. If it was a trick, they'd captured every detail, right down to the gray at her temples. "Dearest Princess Consort Meringue, I'm very real."

Starbride leapt into Katya's arms and held on, clutching at her like a drowning woman. Her headache faded to a dull roar. If this was a dream, she didn't want to wake, and no deception could be so pure, so right.

Starbride kissed every bit of flesh that came near her lips. She slipped Katya's clothes away without thinking and felt hers go in turn. It didn't have the immediacy of mind-sex, but the actual physical sensations, the warmth and the feel of Katya's breath on her skin, made up for it. Starbride caught herself saying, "I missed you, I love you," over and over until Katya's mouth silenced her.

The war didn't exist in the one-room farmhouse. Roland was a mere memory. There were only their bodies, standing, kneeling, lying on the bed, entwined and laughing. Starbride couldn't stop touching Katya, over and over. Even after she found sweet release, she had to dive back in again. They couldn't be together enough, couldn't be close enough. Starbride would have been quite content to make love until she died.

CHAPTER THIRTY-ONE

KATYA

Katya caught herself dozing. She shifted and stretched. Beside her, Starbride let out a small noise of protest. Katya grinned so wide her cheeks hurt. She would have liked nothing better than to stay in the narrow bed for the rest of her life, but she had to sneak into the palace in a few short hours. When Starbride's arms went around her neck, though, Katya leaned back against the thin mattress.

"I hoped I hadn't dreamed you," Starbride said.

"You had time to dream in all that?"

"Just now." Her lips pressed to Katya's, and Katya was tempted to forget the war, but the dead would haunt her.

"We have to be going soon."

"I know," Starbride said. "To our separate battles."

Katya caressed her cheek. "And later to meet again. Promise me you'll come through it all unharmed."

"You asked me to promise that once before."

"And?"

"I'll give you the answer you gave me: if you promise me the same."

"Done." As they dressed, a pall settled over Katya's shoulders. When Starbride left her arms, the warmth went, too. They took every chance to gaze at each other, to "accidentally" bump against each other, or cast stray caresses. When they emerged from the cabin, everyone else was waking up from a short rest. Brutal lifted Starbride in a hug, and Katya clapped Pennynail on the back. Starbride laughed at Castelle's courtly bow and greeted Redtrue in Allusian, a trifle coldly to Katya's eye. Starbride had only spoken to her a handful of times and yet had picked up on the fact that Redtrue didn't have the most sparkling of personalities.

Katya joined them just as Redtrue said, "Leafclever and I have modified the pyramids we will use to subdue the Fiends."

"Will it work on the wild Fiends?" Starbride asked. "I can't believe we even have to consider that."

"I cannot think why it wouldn't work. Besides those pyramids, I'm carrying those that will shield us from mind magic."

"Good," Starbride said. "We've developed something similar."

Redtrue frowned. "With Farradain magic?"

Starbride's smile had a brittle edge. "I don't know any other kind."

"A mistake we shall fix."

Starbride turned toward Katya and rolled her eyes.

Katya covered her smile with a cough. When Starbride turned toward the barn, her mouth fell open. She gripped Katya's arm as Katya's mother stepped into the light of the torches. "You brought the queen?"

Katya nodded, though Ma had brought herself. Back in camp, Ma had approached their party as they'd prepared to leave. She'd dressed as simply as Katya had ever seen her: cloth trousers and coat, her hair pulled up behind her. She'd had a long knife strapped to one thigh and a short one at her ankle.

Katya guided Starbride a few steps away, out of earshot of the others. "My parents think that the wild Fiend spared my scout because I told it to, that it recognized I used to contain part of Yanchasa."

"Who knows the mind of a Fiend?" Starbride whispered. "There are any number of reasons—"

"You don't need to convince me. She insisted that there was a *chance*. If it even hesitated because of what I once possessed, there was a *chance* it would obey someone who still carries Yanchasa's Aspect."

"That's a lot depending on chance."

"If we find a wild Fiend, she hopes it will follow her orders."

"Well, it can't be a coincidence that wild Fiends are walking in Farraday. It must be Roland's doing."

"I won't argue on that point," Katya said.

"Then if he's calling them, your chances of meeting one in the palace will be greater." She squeezed Katya's hand. "Now I'm more worried for all of you."

Ma came closer. "Don't worry for me, Starbride. I know I'm not a fighter. I'll stay out of the way."

"You can still stay here with Ursula's officers," Katya said. "There is no 'out of the way' in a fight."

Ma took a deep breath and seemed to grow several feet. "If we encounter wild Fiends, and I cannot control them, I can still tear my necklace off and stand a greater chance at defeating them than you."

Katya didn't know what to say. How could she deny her mother the opportunity to fight and die for their kingdom, the risk they were all taking?

"Careful," Katya said softly. "You might get a taste for this, and then how will you ever be content planning parties again?"

Ma stepped back and seemed to shrink to normal size. "Have no fear on that point."

"Wait," Starbride said. "What if Roland uses wild Fiends in his army instead of in the palace?"

"Einrich will be with the army," Ma said.

Katya raised an eyebrow. "Da's going to take his necklace off in front of all those people?"

"Better that than watching them all die, don't you think?"

Katya returned the pressure on Starbride's hand. Come tomorrow they could all be dead, like so many already.

She had to close her eyes at the thought of Averie, a world-class lady-in-waiting, and one of her dearest friends. Alive, then dead, alive, and now killed again.

Starbride led her farther away. "What is it?"

"I was just thinking of Averie, the jewel of my heart. I can't remember when I gave her that nickname."

"Katya, I'm so sorry. I—"

Katya bent and kissed her. "Nothing done to Averie is your fault, dearheart. You tried to save her, and for that I love you even more."

"And I love you, and I won't have an easy moment until I see you again."

"Focus on the plan," Katya said. Anything else would get them killed, but Starbride knew that.

They went over a few last minute details. Starbride would start a distraction in the city just before dawn, and Katya would use the commotion to sneak into the palace. All they had to do now was part. After a long kiss, Katya nearly vaulted into her saddle. "Hold my reins, Brutal."

She passed them over so she could look back, knowing that one gaze could be her undoing. Starbride stood in the gloom of the clearing, watching Katya ride away. Their eyes locked until Starbride was lost to the night.

❖

Katya and her party paused outside the wall as close to the palace as they could get.

"Looks clear," Brutal said in Katya's ear.

It had been a long time since Marienne had to repel raiders. They didn't normally bother to put sentries on the walls. She thought Roland might have brought back the practice, but so far, they'd been lucky—a fact which couldn't hold.

But they couldn't sit outside the walls all day, waiting. They threw their hooks and ropes. Castelle and Brutal climbed first and then hauled Katya's mother up. Katya was surprised when Redtrue climbed on her own. Most pyradistés weren't known for physical activity. She'd always thought of Crowe and Starbride as unique.

Of course, that was in Farraday. Just being so close to home made her forget that Redtrue was adsnazi, not a pyradisté. How many problems would such thinking cost them after the fighting was done?

Instead of traveling along the wall, they dropped into the streets in a middle class neighborhood, the only place in town near the wall that didn't house the poorer residents of Marienne. Being near the palace carried some prestige, even if the residents never felt any breeze and had to deal with water sheeting off the wall when it rained.

"Ready?" Brutal whispered. Their trip to the palace would be a dash. Katya stuck close to her mother's side.

"If I lag behind," Ma said, "leave me."

Katya snorted.

"It's the right thing to do," Ma said.

"Not even Crowe would have said that. If you need a practical reason, we can't let Roland have you."

When Brutal said, "Go!" they ran. Halfway there, they slowed to catch their breath. It wouldn't do to arrive at the palace and have to sag against the walls and heave. Katya listened to the blood pound in her ears. Her stomach shifted as if she'd eaten something sour. A chill gust of wind passed through her sweaty clothes and made her shiver.

When Katya's mother grabbed her arm, she froze. The pounding blood, the tightening in her gut, and the chill. They could all be...

She felt eyes on her back. "They're here," Ma said.

If Katya had only vague feelings of unease, her mother must have been shaking. But her face had a reluctant smile.

"Ma?"

Her mother gripped her harder. "I can feel it…there." She pointed to a nearby alley.

Katya saw nothing. "Then why are you smiling?"

Ma reached up and touched her lips. "Was I? It's like…like…" Her smiled widened, but then she shook her head and closed her eyes hard. "You are not!" she spat.

Brutal moved closer and lifted a fist to his chest. His eyes locked with Katya's, and she nodded. If they had been wrong, if the Fiend was able to control Ma and not the other way around, they'd have to knock her out quickly.

"Ma?" Katya asked again.

After a deep breath, she let go of Katya's arm. "It was strange, Katya, a feeling that…mimicked seeing my children again after a long absence, but that thing," she pointed ahead, "is no child of mine!"

"Was it communicating with you?"

She shook her head. "It was just this sense that it…missed me."

Katya still felt eyes upon her, not as intense as in the woods, but enough to make her chest tighten. "Is it just going to watch us?"

"I don't know."

"We should move," Brutal said.

Katya hated to proceed without knowing whether they'd have to deal with a wild Fiend, but they had a job to do. "Let's go." As soon as they started to run, she felt it again, that crushing sense of being hunted. Her heart hammered, but she heard her mother's gasp. The Fiend leapt above them, a streak out of the corner of Katya's eye.

Ma tugged Katya's head down until they could look at each other. Ma's eyes flickered, turning all blue for a moment, and when she opened her mouth, her breath was bitterly cold.

"Keep moving." The voice was deeper, tainted by the Fiend, but it got Katya's legs going again. Heavy weights seemed to press on her shoulders. Ma's grip tightened again, her fingernails pricking like claws.

Ahead of them, Redtrue drew a pyramid from her pack. It flared yellow-white, and the light of it washed over Katya like summer rain. She sighed, engulfed in a scent that harkened to mind a sun-warmed meadow.

Ma muttered something in her own voice. The crushing feeling dissipated, and the watching eyes vanished. Katya captured her mother's arm this time as they ran faster. When they slid to a stop near the palace, Katya stepped to Redtrue's side.

"What was that?"

Redtrue threw her single braid over her shoulder. "I told you I had modified the Fiend pyramid. I turned the power down in order to drive the Fiends away."

"That was turned down?" Ma asked.

"No one exploded," Redtrue said. She bent to Katya's ear. "Including your mother."

Katya's belly went cold. "So…"

"Did you think I would not sense it given enough time?"

"I hoped," Katya said. "And what does this mean for us?" In her mind she pictured Leafclever packing up the Allusians and taking them home, not willing to ally with monsters.

"It means your family needs our help more than we ever imagined." She tapped Katya's chest where her pyramid necklace would have lain had she still had a Fiend. "There is hope for *you*."

"You don't understand," Katya said, "and I don't have time to explain it. There's a reason—"

"There is always a reason."

"What's happening?" Ma asked, looking between their faces.

"We need to get into position," Castelle said.

"As you wish," Redtrue said, "but I don't need to look into your future to see all the lengthy conversations ahead of you."

"Wonderful," Ma said. "I excel at conversation. Now, shall we?"

Chapter Thirty-two

Starbride

Starbride could still feel Katya's warmth. It kept her from shivering and tempered her headache as she and Pennynail crept through the city in the pre-dawn chill. When she returned to their hideout, she had to face three knowing looks, Freddie's as well as Hugo's and Dawnmother's.

"So, this was all of you from the start?" she asked.

"The princess's idea," Dawnmother said, "but then again, who else?"

"She just needed our help putting it together," Freddie said.

"And Captain Ursula's help," Hugo added. "She had to get in contact with her men so they knew the princess's party was coming."

"Fabulous," Starbride said, feeling her cheeks warm. "Now everyone knows exactly what I was doing out in the woods this evening."

"Well, there are probably a few people who don't, but we could tell them," Freddie said.

Starbride grabbed her satchel. "Katya's getting into position; I suggest we do the same." She rounded on Freddie. "And if you make that into a joke, you'll wake up in the well."

His grin disappeared under his mask as he pulled it in place. The four of them left the warehouse together, gathering Master Bernard as they went. Runners had returned from Reinholt and Maia saying they were ready. Everyone was waiting for Starbride to light the match.

A voice inside her kept insisting it should have been Katya starting the fight. It was her kingdom, her people. They would trust her more than they ever would Starbride, and no matter what might happen, Katya could handle it.

Starbride squared her shoulders. She could handle it too. Hadn't she proved herself enough already, hadn't the people surrounding her proved they could weather any storm?

Instead of sapping her confidence, she let memories of Katya build it. They were both strong, both capable, intelligent, and willing to do whatever it took to take Farraday back from the monster that had stolen it.

Now, if only her damn head would stop hurting.

Starbride climbed with her four companions to the roof of Marienne's main beauty chapterhouse. It hosted one of the tallest spires in the city, shorter only than those of the palace. A small walkway curled around the outside, normally reserved for the beauty monks who sought enlightenment through the wonders of the night sky. Once Master Bernard had freed them, they opened it to the rebellion. Starbride wondered how they'd feel about that once they saw the ugliness to come.

"Everyone ready?" she asked.

They each pinned a swatch of fabric the size of her palm to their chests. It showed the hawk and pyramid, the princess consort's sign. The sight brought tears to Starbride's eyes, but she swallowed them down and faced the city.

"Show your colors!" she cried as loudly as she could. Beside her, Master Bernard held up a pyramid that flashed white and red.

For a moment, silence reigned, and Starbride feared that Roland had found a way to destroy all their carefully made plans. Then, from a rooftop, she heard the cry repeated from multiple mouths, spreading so far across the city that it grew faint, but it still seemed to echo around her.

"Let's go," Starbride said. All across the city, citizens would be wearing her sigil, a sign to others that the fight was on. Ursula would dash through the streets with anti-hypnosis pyramids, hitting sections of the city Alphonse had told them about. Ruin and the strength monks would lead the charge on corpse Fiends and the hypnotized, seeking to kill the first and capture the latter. Any un-hypnotized servants or courtiers who remained in the palace would lock themselves in their rooms or seek to ambush Roland's guards. Once Maia and Reinholt heard the cry, they would lead the Docklanders over the wall.

And Katya would sneak inside the palace with Horsestrong himself watching over her.

Starbride had her own section of the city to cover, ready to destroy any pyramids or fight Roland's creations. After what Katya had told her of the hypnotized people in the countryside, Starbride bet Roland had sizeable forces outside the city as well. If the army could get through, Starbride hoped to have most of Marienne ready for them to take. And if Katya didn't show up at the rendezvous, Starbride was going in after her.

As they ran into the streets, Starbride's headache ripped through her temples. She did her best to ignore it as they approached the first of their targets, a shop Alphonse had claimed held a pyramid. They found nothing and moved on. Again nothing.

"The swine fed us bad information," Hugo said.

Starbride pressed her lips together hard. Alphonse had also said that Roland moved his pyramids, but if the other pyramid hunters were having similar luck...

"Go get him," Starbride said to Master Bernard. Even if his information continued to be bad, maybe they could find some other way to use him.

"What are you thinking?" Hugo asked.

"I don't know."

The ring of steel on steel echoed ahead of them. Starbride hurried to see a group of townspeople fighting a pack of corpse Fiends. Roland must have been holding them in reserve; she hadn't seen any lately. She dipped into her satchel and ran forward. When one corpse Fiend leapt from the fray, Starbride nailed it with a fire pyramid. It lurched toward them, but the flames slowed it down enough for Pennynail to launch a dagger into its pyramid.

Pennynail and Hugo raced in to help the others fight while Dawnmother helped the wounded to safety. Starbride lifted her cancellation pyramid, ready to try to dispatch the corpse Fiends by deactivating their pyramids, when one turned toward her. She tried to focus on it, but it sprang away. She refocused on another in the pack when the first one let out a long, blood-curdling howl.

The others took up the cry as they fought, and Starbride heard the howl roll across the city much as her own call had done. They couldn't sense the fact that she was a pyradisté anymore, so it must have been something else that set them off.

Dawnmother hurried over. "They're calling something. We have to leave."

Hugo and Pennynail were holding back the corpse Fiends. Though the townspeople were fighting, few appeared seasoned. They might die without help.

"Star," Dawnmother said, "what if they're calling something because *you're* here?"

Starbride focused on her pyramid again. In her augmented sight, dark golden tendrils flowed from the corpses' pyramids down into their bodies like tainted roots. It was a powerful pyramid, a mixture of Fiend and mind magic. She lamented the fact that she'd never really gotten to study one.

When she tried to darken it, the corpse Fiend cut down the man it was fighting and charged her. Hugo barreled into it. He landed on his side, but the corpse Fiend kept its feet under it as it slid across the lane. Before it could launch itself again, a knife shattered its pyramid.

"That one!" Starbride cried, pointing at another. Like before, it came at her, and she didn't have time to darken its pyramid before Hugo engaged it and ended its un-life. Again she tried to darken the pyramids, but they resisted her, giving their wielders time to attack. It worked in saving the townspeople, however. As soon as she focused on a corpse Fiend, it turned its attention to her, and the others had a chance to kill it. Even the townspeople proved effective with the Fiends' attentions elsewhere.

When the last lay dead, Dawnmother tugged on Starbride's arm again. "We have to go."

"Why?" Hugo asked.

"One of them got a call out," Starbride said. "Dawn thinks something's headed this way."

"It's Horsestrong guiding my thoughts," Dawnmother said.

Hugo lifted his chin. "Whatever it is, we shall defeat it."

Dawnmother snorted. "Put your big head in its path."

Master Bernard dragged Alphonse into the street behind them. "None of the pyramids have been where you said," Starbride called.

"I told you—"

Starbride slashed a hand through the air. "Tell me something else, or I give you to him." She jerked her thumb over her shoulder at Pennynail, not even caring anymore about Alphonse's terror.

An explosion boomed several streets over, followed by a series of screams. Starbride and the others ducked to the ground as flaming bits of wood rained down around them.

"It's getting closer," Dawnmother said.

Alphonse sighed. "At last." He hadn't ducked, no longer even looked worried.

"You knew he'd come for you," Starbride said.

Alphonse laughed. "I don't care about him."

"You don't care about the man who's coming to save you?" She took one of his arms and led him down another street, the others with her.

"I don't need anyone to save me."

She tugged on his arms, but they were securely bound, and he didn't have a pyramid on him. "Is that so?"

"Talking of big heads," Dawnmother said.

Alphonse leaned close to Starbride's ear. "I'm coming for you, Starbride."

She pushed him into Pennynail's arms. "What are you talking about?"

"Rebuilding Averie's mind from scratch was difficult, time-consuming. It gave me an idea."

Starbride's belly grew cold. "What?"

"Did you know before you tortured Alphonse what three of his biggest fears were? Mummer's masks, starving to death, and being buried alive; that was about all I could get out of him. He never made much sense."

"Mummer's masks?" Starbride asked. "What in Darkstrong's name—"

"Yes, if you can believe it!" Alphonse said. "Street performers with painted masks, what's there to be scared of? But your masked man fit the part." He nodded over his shoulder at Pennynail. "And you left him in the dungeon in the dark, playing into the buried alive part, and he was quite...hungry when I finally found him and nearly insane."

"You're not Alphonse," Starbride whispered.

"What's going on?" Hugo asked.

Pennynail tugged sharply on not-Alphonse's arms, but he only laughed. "Averie was easier. I erased what she had and wrote over it, but this one... Tsk. As a pyradisté, his mind was closed to me, but I didn't really need his thoughts." As much as he could, not-Alphonse leaned forward, ignoring the fact that Pennynail twisted his arms nearly out of their sockets. "I stuck a bit of metal above his eye, through the bone and into the brain, and then I just sort of...messed about. The knowledge monks helped me with the research. Fascinating stuff."

Starbride felt her gorge rise, and her headache spiked. She swallowed three times before she asked, "Roland?"

Everyone but Pennynail took a step back. "How?" Master Bernard said.

"Fool, I just told you. I scraped out what I needed and put myself in its place. Once we'd scratched him out, the rest was...cake."

They heard screams again, closer.

"Ah, that'll be me," not-Alphonse said. "I'm so glad I'll get to see it."

Starbride had been right from the very beginning. Roland never trusted anyone he couldn't control. She should have known that, should have gotten rid of Alphonse when she had the chance. He was already dead!

Starbride's head pounded so hard she saw purple spots at the edges of her vision. "Whatever you've done, it won't matter. You won't win."

He snorted. "Spare me the heartfelt speeches. I'll take that army apart."

Hugo touched Starbride's shoulder. "Maybe we should do something with him."

"Like introduce him to his grave," Dawnmother said.

Freddie nodded, but Master Bernard frowned. "I don't really think cold-blooded—"

"Everyone, please shut up." Starbride pressed her thumb against her forehead and tried to think.

"Headache?" not-Alphonse asked cheerfully.

Dawnmother glared at him. "Be quiet. Are you all right, Star?"

"Of course she's not," not-Alphonse said. "She's too busy thinking of me ripping her new family limb from limb." He smiled, a look that was all Roland. "How do you want Katya? Burnt and blackened? Blood and bones scattered like seeds?"

He sounded more and more like Roland all the time. "Shut up." Her head pounded so hard she could hear it, and she felt her grimace become a snarl.

"Or maybe…" He shut his eyes tightly and gave a delighted little laugh. "Maybe I'll scoop out what's in her head and take up residence." His eyes opened to slits. "I'll let you get close, take you in my arms, wait until you whisper in my ear—"

Starbride moved. The pounding in her head seemed to pull her along. Before anyone could ask, she pulled a knife from one of Pennynail's many sheathes, and as the others cried out, she rammed it into not-Alphonse's chest.

When her headache momentarily muted, she knew she'd made the right decision.

Not-Alphonse sagged, and Starbride helped lower him to the ground. He still smiled but now with blood-stained teeth. "See you soon," he whispered.

Chapter Thirty-three

Katya

When they heard the cry to show their colors, Katya couldn't help but grin. Starbride was a woman who hadn't come from royalty, wasn't used to leading, and had even expressed the desire to never be put in that position. How she'd taken to it and refused to abandon those that looked to her for leadership took Katya's breath away even more than the wild Fiends did.

As they watched the palace, Redtrue concentrated on a pyramid, her brow furrowed.

"Anything?" Katya asked.

"It's…difficult. I've had this large headache ever since we came near this place. It must be the Fiend magic in the air."

"Or the fact that we're sneaking into a viper's nest headed by an insane pyradisté who also happens to be a monster," Castelle said.

"Look." Brutal pointed toward the palace. A group of corpse Fiends barreled out of the doors and streamed into the street.

"Well, that's one less problem to worry about," Katya said. After she spoke, she saw what she'd been waiting for: Roland, with a host of people surrounding him, left the palace and ventured into the city.

Where Starbride was.

Katya's mother clutched her arm. "If we cripple him in there, Starbride will have far less to worry about."

They hurried around the palace to the royal stables. A quick peek through the gate showed it abandoned, empty of horses and grooms. They scaled the gate and hurried into the barn nearest the palace walls. When Katya had lived there, the secret door into the palace had been guarded by a pyramid tuned to open for anyone in the Order. She was certain Roland hadn't left it that way.

"Make some room," Katya said. "Redtrue, you're up."

They gathered in one of the stalls and crouched in the hay, out of the way of any exploding shards of brick and wood. "Do it, Redtrue."

"There is a pyramid on the door. I knew that already."

"I didn't see you scan it," Katya said.

"I don't need a pyramid to sense other pyramids, not from close by. Your pyradistés do?"

"Never mind that now. Can you cancel this pyramid?"

"Shame that there exist pyramids that need to be cancelled," she muttered. "It's done."

"Fast," Castelle said.

Far faster than anything Katya had ever seen. "Are you sure?"

Redtrue gave her a sour look. She strode forward and pushed on the door, and it swung open under her light touch.

Katya stepped inside. "Are there any more?"

"Nearby? No."

Katya glanced at the locking pyramid. Instead of the darkened state she was used to seeing with cancelled pyramids, this one glowed a soft, milky white. "What did you do?"

"Cleansed it. The adsna flows open and without limits. Locking, trapping, killing, these are not its usual states. It wants to be cleansed."

"An interesting discussion for another time," Ma said as she stepped inside. "Right now, we need to be moving and cleansing all we can."

Redtrue made a light pyramid glow, one of the things both adsnazi and pyradistés had in common, and they hurried into the secret passageways. Starbride had heard of a large mind-control pyramid in one of the ballrooms, so that would be their first stop. Redtrue kept rubbing her head and grimacing, and Katya had to wonder if it was the capstone under the palace that was giving her fits. If she thought a door lock needed to be cleansed, Katya couldn't imagine what she'd think of the pyramid that housed Yanchasa.

But maybe she could get rid of him entirely. The thought nearly gave Katya pause.

As they approached the door that led into the back of the ballroom, Katya couldn't help but become lost in memory. She'd crept down a similar tunnel months before, hoping to save her father from a mob.

She'd fought Roland in that ballroom, seen Earl Lamont and Magistrate Anthony die there. She'd lost Averie there.

Katya forced a snarl instead of letting sadness overtake her.

Redtrue cleansed the pyramid that guarded this door, but it took her longer than last time. She'd leaned on Castelle's arm, her face drawn in pain. "There's something here," she said.

"The mind control pyramid?" Katya asked.

"It's all around us." Redtrue patted the smaller bag she carried. "Stay near me, and the mind control should not affect you."

Katya eased the door open a crack. This one had no curtained antechamber, but did have a small dais and large chair reserved for royalty. Roland hadn't removed it. He'd need somewhere to sit, after all.

Beyond that, Katya glimpsed the glinting edge of the pyramid. A guard crossed into her vision and then out again. There had to be quite a few in the room, and they'd all be under the influence of the pyramid. If she dashed in, she might get the upper hand before they realized what was happening.

"Redtrue," Katya whispered, "can you cleanse the pyramid that's out there from in here?"

Redtrue focused. Her chest fell up and down heavily, and she couldn't seem to breathe without opening her mouth. "I need to be closer."

If the pyramid was sapping Redtrue's strength, Katya didn't see how being closer would do any better. "Can you walk?"

"Of course I can."

"Give me the pyramid that's protecting us from mind control," Katya said.

Redtrue frowned but handed it over. Katya slung it around herself. "We stay together, move toward the pyramid, and break it the old-fashioned way. We'll keep the guards busy, Ma. You hack at the pyramid."

Her mother nodded and clutched her long knife.

"Am I to stay here and weave your shrouds?" Redtrue asked as she sagged against the wall.

"You come in after everyone is distracted and focus on any corpse Fiends. If there aren't any, try to cancel that pyramid. We'll get it one way or another. Ready?"

When they all nodded, Katya barreled through the door. A man standing just inside turned in surprise and fumbled for his weapon.

Katya ran him through. Wounding was a luxury they didn't have, not when there were at least fifteen guards in the room.

They struck down a handful in the first few seconds. As a strength monk charged them, the real fight began. Brutal caught the monk's mace on his own, and the two traded blows. Katya slowed; they all had to stay together. She went back to back with Castelle, keeping Ma and Brutal as close as the fight allowed. Katya heard the ring of steel behind her and knew Castelle had engaged an opponent.

Another monk closed with Katya. She was a large woman, heavily muscled, but strong didn't always mean fast. She launched a haymaker that would have taken Katya's head off, but Katya ducked and sliced at the monk's unprotected knees. She fell with a shriek. Katya rammed her pommel into the monk's forehead with an audible crack. She collapsed, and even with everything, Katya hoped she wasn't dead. She couldn't have been more than an initiate.

"Katya," Ma said, "the door."

A pair of corpse Fiends slinked inside, but Katya had to turn her attention to another opponent, a leather-wearing swordswoman who was far from an initiate. "Keep an eye on them, Ma."

Katya blocked the swordswoman's thrust and launched her own attacks, which were blocked with quick precision.

"They're down," Ma said.

Katya almost jerked in surprise. She locked her rapier with the swordswoman's blade and pushed, getting enough room to see Redtrue grasping a glowing pyramid and leaning on the room's only chair. The corpse Fiends lay on the dais in front of her like cut marionettes. Katya felt new strength flow through her limbs. She blocked the swordswoman's next thrust and stepped close to punch. The swordswoman grunted as Katya struck her chest, but she didn't double over. She pushed Katya away.

Ma darted in from the side and stabbed the swordswoman's arm with her long knife.

When the swordswoman glanced that way, Katya stabbed her in the neck. "Stay behind me, Ma."

Brutal and Castelle were still fighting and appeared unwounded. Katya's spirits lifted further. They could defeat any pack of fighters Roland had mind-warped, and the Fiends were no match for Redtrue.

Brutal dispatched his newest opponent and turned. "Katya—"

An arrow punched into his chest, and he staggered back. "Brutal!" Katya yelled. She turned, searching for the archer. Averie stood in the doorway, expressionless as she nocked another arrow. "Take cover!"

Castelle and Ma hooked their arms under Brutal and sought to drag him behind the pyramid. Katya kept the remaining attackers at bay with wide swings of her rapier. The pyramid shielded them, but not for long. All Averie had to do was step to the side.

"Averie!" Katya called. "Don't do this!"

An arrow hummed through the room and sank into the chair just after Redtrue half-collapsed behind it. Katya drew her knife from her belt. She could lean around the pyramid and throw it, sink it into Averie's heart.

She clutched the grip and squeezed her eyes shut. It wasn't Averie, wasn't Averie, not anymore. Katya leaned around the pyramid, staying low. An arrow hummed over her head, and she threw.

The knife sliced into Averie's leg and clattered to the carpet. Katya cursed. She'd never had Pennynail's aim with a knife. Still, Averie stumbled and grimaced. She reached for another arrow. Katya leapt forward and landed in a sprint. Averie backpedaled. She drew another arrow, but Katya swung and knocked the bow from Averie's grip, not slowing. They hit each other so hard, it drove the breath from Katya's lungs.

They crashed to the floor together. Averie grunted but grabbed Katya's rapier guard and tried to shove the blade at Katya's neck. Katya leaned up, grinding her knee into Averie's thigh. She used her weight to push the blade back down, and it sank toward Averie's pain-filled face.

Averie's arms shuddered. One quick punch with the guard and Katya could knock her unconscious. Maybe Starbride had been right after all. Maybe there was a chance.

"Katya!" Ma screamed.

Fire punched into Katya's back, and she knew she'd been stabbed. Averie shoved the blade upward again. Katya used the momentum to roll away, but every movement sent tearing agony through her muscles, and she felt warm wetness spread across her skin. A man with a bloody short sword pulled Averie to her feet. She bent to grab her bow and then staggered back as a blur launched itself at the swordsman. He flew through the air as if thrown by a catapult, his chest such a ruined mess that when he hit the ground he did so in several parts.

Averie ran for the door. What had been Katya's mother turned to face her. All blue eyes regarded Katya with nothing but malice. Her four crow's wings had torn through her shirt in the back, and her fangs pressed down from her upper jaw against her lower lip in a snarl.

Two more corpse Fiends came through the door. Ma threw herself at them with wild abandon and tore them apart within seconds. Katya dashed for the pyramid again as fast as she could. Castelle was still fighting, but she shoved her opponent closer to Katya's mother, who sank her fangs into his arm and bit down in a gush of blood.

Castelle and Katya crouched by Brutal. He still breathed, the arrow rising up and down, but his skin was pale and bathed in sweat. His eyes fluttered open. "Katya."

Castelle covered his mouth, and they listened to the sounds of Katya's mother clawing and biting her way through the room. At last, there was no one left, and they heard her footsteps coming closer. Katya gripped her rapier and tried not to think of the hole in her back, the blood. She'd have to stab quickly, as soon as Ma showed her Fiendish face.

Yellow-white light surrounded them, and Katya heard her mother's gasp. She stood, her wound making her grunt with the sudden motion. Ma's look was one of wonder as her eyes faded to normal, and her wings and fangs receded, leaving bloody trails on her face. Her eyes rolled back, and she collapsed. Behind her, Redtrue held a pyramid aloft in one trembling fist.

Katya sagged. "Castelle, bar the door."

"You're wounded," Redtrue said, sagging to the floor beside Katya.

"We all are."

"Let me see."

"Brutal first."

"I've got him," Castelle said as she returned. "Your former lady-in-waiting's not out there with the rest of the corpses."

Katya nodded. She'd be bringing more guards. As Redtrue tended her back wound, Castelle sliced open Brutal's shirt to examine the arrow. "It's not in his heart, or he'd be dead. We need to get him to a healer, or we might still lose him."

Katya spied a glint from near the pyramid's base. She picked up her mother's pyramid necklace, intact on its long chain. She'd taken it off to save Katya's life.

Freshly bandaged, Katya carried her mother into the secret passageway, her back aching like fire. She laid her mother on the stone and left the necklace with her.

Redtrue held one palm against the mind-control pyramid and clutched her pyramid in the other. "This one is cleansed."

Together, they dragged Brutal into the passageway just as someone began pounding on the barred wooden door. Once they were all inside, Katya stuck a knife in the locking mechanism. It wouldn't keep their pursuers out forever, but it would slow them down.

Katya leaned close to Brutal's face. "How are you?"

"Hard to breathe," he said. His eyes slipped shut again.

"Hold on, Brutal."

"We need to move," Castelle said.

It would be slow-going dragging two unconscious people while wounded, but Castelle was right. The light from Redtrue's pyramid bounced along the walls like flickering candle flame. Katya turned to her ashen face before reaching out and touching her trembling hands. "Are you going to be all right, Redtrue?"

"The corrupted adsna…it's…" She pressed the heel of her palm to her forehead. "The call of the Fiends…" Blood trickled from her nose and dripped from her top lip.

"Red!" Castelle reached for her.

Redtrue crumpled. The light from her pyramid winked out.

"Oh spirits," Katya whispered in the dark. She heard the muted sound of snapping wood and knew her enemies had broken down the door to the ballroom, Averie leading their charge.

About the Author

Barbara Ann Wright writes fantasy and science fiction novels and short stories when not adding to her enormous pen collection or ranting on her blog. Her short fiction has appeared twice in *Crossed Genres Magazine* and once made *Tangent Online's* recommended reading list. Her first novel, *The Pyramid Waltz*, was one of *Tor.com's* Reviewer's Choice books of 2012, was a Foreword Review Book of the Year Award Finalist, a Goldie finalist, and won the 2013 Rainbow Award for Best Lesbian Fantasy.

Books Available from Bold Strokes Books

Timeless by Rachel Spangler. When Stevie Geller returns to her hometown, will she do things differently the second time around or will she be in such a hurry to leave her past that she misses out on a better future? (978-1-62639-050-8)

Second to None by L.T. Marie. Can a physical therapist and a custom motorcycle designer conquer their pasts and build a future with one another? (978-1-62639-051-5)

Seneca Falls by Jesse Thoma. Together, two women discover love truly can conquer all evil. (978-1-62639-052-2)

A Kingdom Lost by Barbara Ann Wright. Without knowing each other's fate, Princess Katya and her consort Starbride seek to reclaim their kingdom from the magic-wielding madman who seized the throne and is murdering their people. (978-1-62639-053-9)

Uncommon Romance by Jove Belle. Sometimes sex is just sex, and sometimes it's the only way to say "I love you." (978-1-62639-057-7)

The Heat of Angels by Lisa Girolami. Fires burn in more than one place in Los Angeles. (978-1-62639-042-3)

Season of the Wolf by Robin Summers. Two women running from their pasts are thrust together by an unimaginable evil. Can they overcome the horrors that haunt them in time to save each other? (978-1-62639-043-0)

Desperate Measures by P. J. Trebelhorn. Homicide detective Kay Griffith and contractor Brenda Jansen meet amidst turmoil neither of them is aware of until murder suspect Tommy Rayne makes his move to exact revenge on Kay. (978-1-62639-044-7)

The Magic Hunt by L.L. Raand. With her Pack being hunted by human extremists and beset by enemies masquerading as friends, can Sylvan protect them and her mate, or will she succumb to the feral rage that threatens to turn her rogue, destroying them all? A Midnight Hunters novel. (978-1-62639-045-4)

Waiting for the Violins by Justine Saracen. After surviving Dunkirk, a scarred and embittered British nurse returns to Nazi-occupied Brussels to join the Resistance, and finds that nothing is fair in love and war. (978-1-62639-046-1)

Because of Her by KE Payne. When Tabby Morton is forced to move to London, she's convinced her life will never be the same again. But the beautiful and intriguing Eden Palmer is about to show her that this time, change is most definitely for the better. (978-1-62639-049-2)

Wingspan by Karis Walsh. Wildlife biologist Bailey Chase is content to live at the wild bird sanctuary she has created on Washington's Olympic Peninsula until she is lured beyond the safety of isolation by architect Kendall Pearson. (978-1-60282-983-1)

Tumbledown by Cari Hunter. After surviving their ordeal in the North Cascades, Alex and Sarah have new identities and a new home, but a chance occurrence threatens everything: their freedom and their lives. (978-1-62639-085-0)

Night Bound by Winter Pennington. Kass struggles to keep her head, her heart, and her relationships in order. She's still having a difficult time accepting being an Alpha female. But her wolf is certain of what she wants and she's intent on securing her power. (978-1-60282-984-8)

Slash and Burn by Valerie Bronwen. The murder of a roundly despised author at an LGBT writer's conference in New Orleans turns Winter Lovelace's relaxing weekend hobnobbing with her peers into a nightmare of suspense—especially when her ex turns up. (978-1-60282-986-2)

The Blush Factor by Gun Brooke. Ice-cold business tycoon Eleanor Ashcroft only cares about the three P's—Power, Profit, and Prosperity—until young Addison Garr makes her doubt both that and the state of her frostbitten heart. (978-1-60282-985-5)

The Quickening: A Sisters of Spirits Novel by Yvonne Heidt. Ghosts, visions, and demons are all in a day's work for Tiffany. But when Kat asks for help on a serial killer case, life takes on another dimension altogether. (978-1-60282-975-6)

Windigo Thrall by Cate Culpepper. Six women trapped in a mountain cabin by a blizzard, stalked by an ancient cannibal demon bent on stealing their sanity—and their lives. (978-1-60282-950-3)

Smoke and Fire by Julie Cannon. Oil and water, passion and desire, a combustible combination. Can two women fight the fire that draws them together and threatens to keep them apart? (978-1-60282-977-0)

Asher's Fault by Elizabeth Wheeler. Fourteen-year-old Asher Price sees the world in black and white, much like the photos he takes, but when his little brother drowns at the same moment Asher experiences his first same-sex kiss, he can no longer hide behind the lens of his camera and eventually discovers he isn't the only one with a secret. (978-1-60282-982-4)

Love and Devotion by Jove Belle. KC Hall trips her way through life, stumbling into an affair with a married bombshell twice her age. Thankfully, her best friend, Emma Reynolds, is there to show her the true meaning of Love and Devotion. (978-1-60282-965-7)

Rush by Carsen Taite. Murder, secrets, and romance combine to create the ultimate rush. (978-1-60282-966-4)

The Shoal of Time by J.M. Redmann. It sounded too easy. Micky Knight is reluctant to take the case because the easy ones often turn into the hard ones, and the hard ones turn into the dangerous ones. In this one, easy turns hard without warning. (978-1-60282-967-1)

In Between by Jane Hoppen. At the age of 14, Sophie Schmidt discovers that she was born an intersexual baby and sets off on a journey to find her place in a world that denies her true existence. (978-1-60282-968-8)

Secret Lies by Amy Dunne. While fleeing from her abuser, Nicola Jackson bumps into Jenny O'Connor, and their unlikely friendship quickly develops into a blossoming romance—but when it comes down to a matter of life or death, are they both willing to face their fears? (978-1-60282-970-1)

Under Her Spell by Maggie Morton. The magic of love brought Terra and Athene together, but now a magical quest stands between them—a quest for Athene's hand in marriage. Will their passion keep them together, or will stronger magic tear them apart? (978-1-60282-973-2)

Homestead by Radclyffe. R. Clayton Sutter figures getting NorthAm Fuel's newest refinery operational on a rolling tract of land in Upstate New York should take a month or two, but then, she hadn't counted on local resistance in the form of vandalism, petitions, and one furious farmer named Tess Rogers. (978-1-60282-956-5)

Battle of Forces: Sera Toujours by Ali Vali. Kendal and Piper return to New Orleans to start the rest of eternity together, but the return of an old enemy makes their peaceful reunion short-lived, especially when they join forces with the new queen of the vampires. (978-1-60282-957-2)

How Sweet It Is by Melissa Brayden. Some things are better than chocolate. Molly O'Brien enjoys her quiet life running the bakeshop in a small town. When the beautiful Jordan Tuscana returns home, Molly can't deny the attraction—or the stirrings of something more. (978-1-60282-958-9)

The Missing Juliet: A Fisher Key Adventure by Sam Cameron. A teenage detective and her friends search for a kidnapped Hollywood star in the Florida Keys. (978-1-60282-959-6)

Amor and More: Love Everafter edited by Radclyffe and Stacia Seaman. Rediscover favorite couples as Bold Strokes Books authors reveal glimpses of life and love beyond the honeymoon in short stories featuring main characters from favorite BSB novels. (978-1-60282-963-3)

First Love by CJ Harte. Finding true love is hard enough, but for Jordan Thompson, daughter of a conservative president, it's challenging, especially when that love is a female rodeo cowgirl. (978-1-60282-949-7)

Pale Wings Protecting by Lesley Davis. Posing as a couple to investigate the abduction of infants, Special Agent Blythe Kent and Detective Daryl Chandler find themselves drawn into a battle over the innocents, with demons on one side and the unlikeliest of protectors on the other. (978-1-60282-964-0)

Mounting Danger by Karis Walsh. Sergeant Rachel Bryce, an outcast on the police force, is put in charge of the department's newly formed mounted division. Can she and polo champion Callan Lanford resist their growing attraction as they struggle to safeguard the disaster-prone unit? (978-1-60282-951-0)

Meeting Chance by Jennifer Lavoie. When man's best friend turns on Aaron Cassidy, the teen keeps his distance until fate puts Chance in his hands. (978-1-60282-952-7)

At Her Feet by Rebekah Weatherspoon. Digital marketing producer Suzanne Kim knows she has found the perfect love in her new mistress Pilar, but before they can make the ultimate commitment, Suzanne's professional life threatens to disrupt their perfectly balanced bliss. (978-1-60282-948-0)

Show of Force by AJ Quinn. A chance meeting between navy pilot Evan Kane and correspondent Tate McKenna takes them on a roller-coaster ride where the stakes are high, but the reward is higher: a chance at love. (978-1-60282-942-8)

Clean Slate by Andrea Bramhall. Can Erin and Morgan work through their individual demons to rediscover their love for each other, or are the unexplainable wounds too deep to heal? (978-1-60282-943-5)

Hold Me Forever by D. Jackson Leigh. An investigation into illegal cloning in the quarter horse racing industry threatens to destroy the growing attraction between Georgia debutante Mae St. John and Louisiana horse trainer Whit Casey. (978-1-60282-944-2)

Trusting Tomorrow by PJ Trebelhorn. Funeral director Logan Swift thinks she's perfectly happy with her solitary life devoted to helping others cope with loss until Brooke Collier moves in next door to care for her elderly grandparents. (978-1-60282-891-9)

Forsaking All Others by Kathleen Knowles. What if what you think you want is the opposite of what makes you happy? (978-1-60282-892-6)

Exit Wounds by VK Powell. When Officer Loane Landry falls in love with ATF informant Abigail Mancuso, she realizes that nothing is as it seems—not the case, not her lover, not even the dead. (978-1-60282-893-3)